Praise for

DEVILS WITHIN

✧

William C. Morris Award Finalist
Alabama Library Association 2019 Young Adult Award Winner
Kirkus Best Book of 2017
2018 Best Fiction for Young Adults, YALSA
2019 Sequoia Master List
2018-2019 Green Mountain Book Award Master List
2019-2020 Volunteer State Book Award Nominee
2020 Georgia Peach Book Award Nominee

✧

(*) "Henson's debut novel sheds a light on white supremacy and other cloaked forms of racism. While the events of Henson's novel may seem too extreme to be true, they are based in reality. . . . A timely and informative book."

—*Kirkus Reviews*, starred review

"This story is a truly revealing and all-too-relevant examination of the psychological underpinnings of a complicated, young former neo-Nazi desperate to change his life for the better."

—*Booklist*

"Henson is unflinching in her portrayal of the racism and bigotry that is still pervasive in our society. While at times this book is a thrilling adventure, it is also a fever dream that I know is far too real for many Americans. As the novel approached an impending and climactic confrontation, I wanted desperately to stop reading and yet could not put the book down. In my mind, that is as high praise as I can give."

—*The Herald*

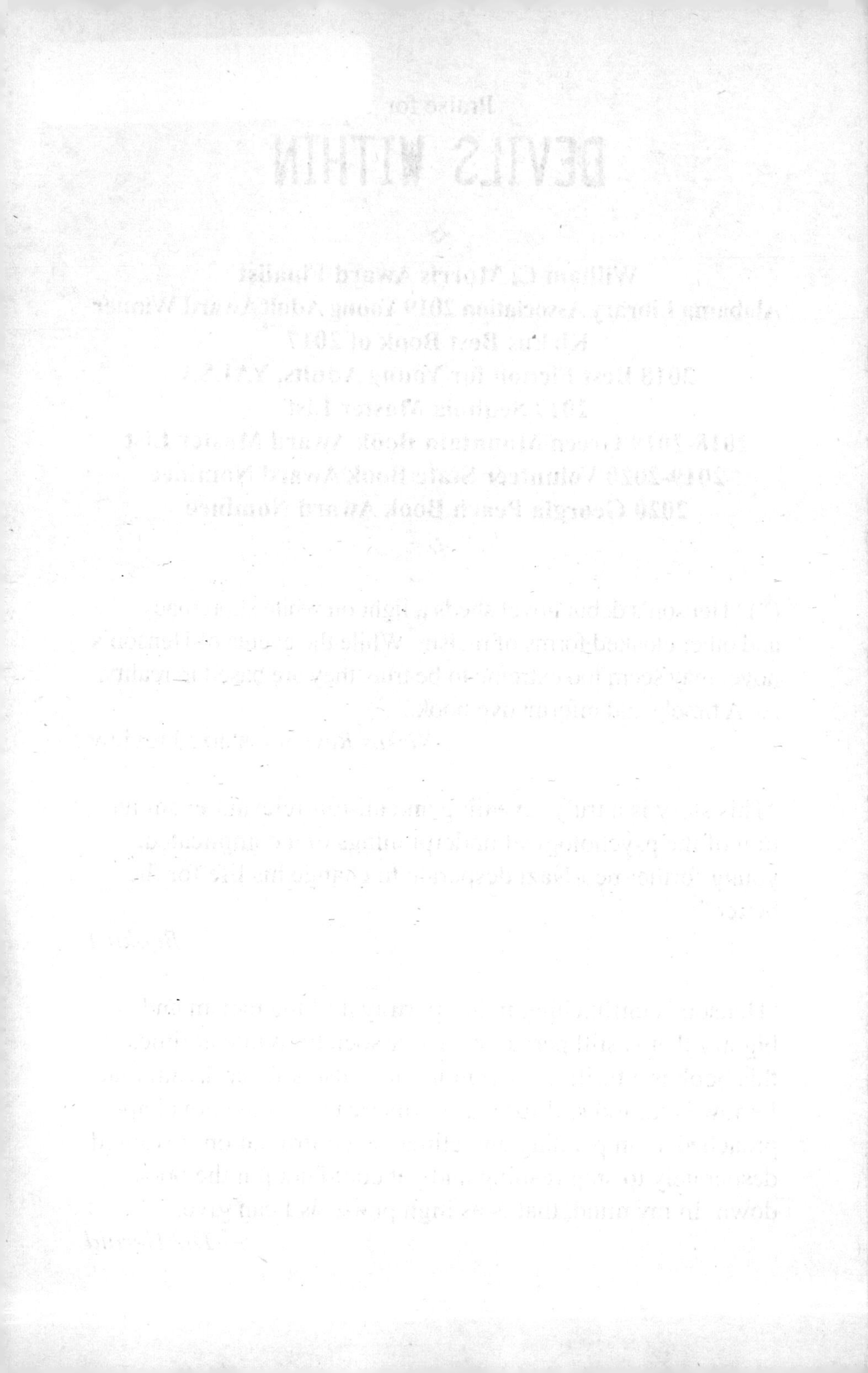

DEVILS
WITHIN

S.F. HENSON

Sky Pony Press
New York

First Skyhorse paperback edition 2020.

Sky Pony Press books may be purchased in bulk at special discounts for sales promotion, corporate gifts, fund-raising, or educational purposes. Special editions can also be created to specifications. For details, contact the Special Sales Department, Sky Pony Press, 307 West 36th Street, 11th Floor, New York, NY 10018 or info@skyhorsepublishing.com.

Visit our website at www.skyponypress.com

10 9 8 7 6 5 4 3 2 1

Library of Congress Control Number: 2017950091

Cover image by iStock
Cover design by Sammy Yuen

Paperback ISBN: 978-1-5107-5183-5
Ebook ISBN: 978-1-5107-1458-8

Printed in the United States of America

For my daddy, Andrew Frederick (1965–2009),
and for Phillip, *always*

This novel is inspired by true events.

587

If *he* catches me I'm dead.

Literally dead. Like the trees I'm racing past. Like Mom. Like no longer part of this evil freaking world.

So I run. I'm tempted to stop, to give up and let *him* kill me. Because when it comes down to it, death might be a relief, since it's the only way I'll ever be free.

"Nathaniel!" *His* scream echoes through the dark woods, seeming to come from everywhere at once. It rattles my bones, chilling me to the core, shaking my instinct for self-preservation loose.

I'm not ready to die yet. Not by *his* hand. Not while *he*'s still alive.

I kick it into another gear. Spindly brush scratches my arms like sharp fingernails. My lungs burn with the cold. Snowflakes sting my cheeks. The snow falls so fast and thick, *he*'s nothing but a blur when I glance over my shoulder. Then I'm on the ground. Wet snow seeping through the knees of my jeans.

My boot is tangled in a tree root. The red laces are streaks of blood against the snow.

"Nathaniel!" *he* bellows again. Closer. Much closer.

I struggle against the root, clawing at my laces. I have to get the boot off. Have to get free.

I didn't mean it earlier! I want to live! *I want to live!*

My boot slides off. I scramble up the embankment, trying to ignore the freezing water creeping up my sock. A crushing weight tackles me from behind and I'm buried in the snow again. *He*'s on top of me. *He* rolls me onto my back, pinning my arms at my sides with *his* knees. *His* fist slams into my windburned cheek and bombs explode in my skull.

His gun is in *his* hand. The butt sails through the air toward my temple.

This is it. This is where I die.

I squeeze my eyes shut.

No.

I can't die like this. I have to do something. Stop *him* from—

"Nate?"

My eyes fly open. I raise my fists, ready to fight *him* off.

Long brown hair grazes my shoulder, tickling my neck. "Nate, are you okay?"

I blink a couple of times, forcing myself to focus. Ms. Erica, my social worker, leans over me, brows furrowed, eyes scrunched in concern.

I'm not in the woods. My fingers curl around the navy button hanging from the string around my neck. I'm in the office of the West Kentucky Psychiatric Center.

I repeat it over and over in my head.

He's not after me. Not anymore.

Not ever again.

"Do I need to get Dr. Sterling?" Ms. Erica asks.

"I'm fine," I say.

"You sure?"

I nod once.

"Did you take your meds this morning?"

Of course not. The little oblong pills make me feel fuzzy. Like my brain is lined with cotton that's been teased apart. I haven't decided which is better. Always fuzzy, or so sharp a crack or shout or blast of cold air rockets me back to that night in the woods.

My free fingers trace 587 on the arm of the chair in an endless loop.

"You have to take the meds if you're ever going to have a normal life," Ms. Erica says.

I snort. "There aren't enough drugs in the world for that to happen."

"Fine. A *chance* at a normal life."

I'm not certain what normal even looks like. It sure as hell isn't anything I've ever known, and it's not like the stuff they show on sitcoms at night in the common area. No one is that happy. Real problems aren't comical. They're deadly.

Ms. Erica straightens out her short green skirt, then smooths a hand over it. "I'll call Stanley and have him bring your meds."

"No!" I catch her slim wrist before she can leave. "I can't be fuzzy today. I'll take them when I'm out. Promise. Just . . . not today."

Her glance shifts to the window and her brows furrow. "All right." She sighs. "But only for today. No breaks when you're out."

"Deal."

She pats my hand and I realize I'm still clinging to her wrist. Life is going to be weird without her. Ms. Erica and I have worked together since the beginning. She was my first social worker, and I was her first client.

What an introduction to social work. A demented fifteen-year-old with fresh blood on his hands.

"Are you ready to go?" she asks.

I can't possibly be ready. I've been in the Psych Center since it happened. Except for the weeks in the Farmer jail and a month stint in juvie before my lawyer sprang me. A year and a half since I've been part of the outside world. Although, I guess I've never *really* been part of it.

Not the one Ms. Erica knows anyway. I've only known two versions of the world and they both sucked.

I don't remember my first few years, other than flashes here and there. A wood-paneled room, Mom in a blue dress, *his* arm around her. Tufts of grass dotting a big backyard. A white dog with brown spots rolling in the dirt. Rusty red splotches streaked down the white porcelain sink in the tiny bathroom. Bruises on my arms. Angry welts on my legs.

The first clear memory I have—the first actual *moment*—is so tainted with fear I can't be sure I recall it accurately. I was five. Mom and I were on the run and had stopped at a grocery store for bread. Her hand tightened around mine and the loaf slipped to the floor with a soft thump and a crinkle of plastic. A big, bald man in a green jacket stood in front of us. A tattoo etched into his neck in hard, angry lines. I'd seen that mark before, back at The Fort, but I didn't know what it was. I do now. All too well.

Mom hurried down the aisle and around the corner, looking back every few steps. As soon as we reached the sliding glass doors, she scooped me up and broke into a run. Her nails dug into my skin and I cried out, which only made her squeeze harder.

We raced down the street to the motel, to our room at the back. The one with the busted lock. Mom shoved me in the closet. Someone pounded on the outside door and a hot trickle worked down my leg. A sour smell followed, but I didn't move. I stayed crouched in the hot, stuffy closet for I don't know how long. Hours probably. Just like every other time it happened. Every time she'd see someone with that tattoo or one of the white and black patches on their jackets. The ones that said, "Skinhead—*weiss & stolz*."

That was my world for four years. Flitting from town to town, not telling anyone our real names. Then she died—not from one of them, but in a random gas station robbery.

Wrong place, wrong time. She died, and my worlds smashed together like lumps of old Play-Doh, all cracked and crumbly and ugly.

The judge sent me back to The Fort. To *him*.

To daily mantras and Indoctrinations. Combat boots in my ribs and fists in my face until the day it happened.

The Psych Center is the only safety I've ever known. What I really want is to stay here and be different forever—not to leave with some stranger.

Ms. Erica sits on the hard plastic chair beside me, grounding me in the present as much as my button.

"You can do this, Nate. You have this under control. As long as you take the meds."

That's the problem. If I were insane, it would be easy. They'd keep me here. Safe. Unable to hurt anyone else. I should've pretended to be worse than I am.

"What if it happens again?" I whisper, running my button along its string. "What if I snap?"

I got off on self-defense once. *Mentally unstable*, my lawyer said. Once they release me, once I'm declared officially sane, that's it. I lose myself and it's jail.

"You'll be fine," Ms. Erica says.

"I still don't see why I can't stay."

She covers my hand with hers. "The judge required nine months. That's up today. Dr. Sterling says you're cleared, so it's time to move into the next phase of treatment. Besides, you don't want to spend your life cooped up in this place, do you?"

I give her my most pleading look.

She smiles. "You'll have a brand-new social worker to torment now."

"I don't want a new social worker. I want you."

Ms. Erica knows me—who I am down deep inside—and she doesn't judge me for it. Only three people in my life have truly cared about me: Mom, Kelsey—my only friend at The Fort—and Ms. Erica. And all three have been torn away from me.

"Trust me, Nate, if I could stay on with you, I would. But I can't follow you across the country."

"It's only two states."

"You know it doesn't work like that. I'm sure you and your new caseworker will get along fine. Give her a chance, okay? Don't forget how far you've come. Keep moving forward."

I stifle the scoff working up my throat. I'm a snake eating its tail. Every time I try to move "forward," I end up worse than when I started.

"You won't be alone again," she says, as though she already knows the comeback ready on my tongue. "You'll have your uncle."

Right. The uncle I didn't know existed until a few weeks ago. I have vague memories of Mom making tear-filled phone calls from those motel rooms, pleading for an answer, then slamming the receivers in their cradles, crying "the stinking traitor was no help to anyone." She never talked about a brother—never talked about anyone—but that must've been who she meant. I know she wouldn't have been calling The Fort.

And now I know there *was* someone out there, an uncle who could've helped us. One who never came forward. Not when she died. Not when *he* told the judge Mom had kidnapped me. Not when the judge sent me back to The Fort.

Not until my social worker tracked him down and somehow convinced him to take me in.

Ms. Erica tucks her hair behind one ear. "Are you sure you don't want to tell your unc—"

"I'm sure." I'm not about to let her blab the details of my life to some man I've never met. If he cared enough to want to know about me, he would've picked up the phone years ago. Dr. Sterling and Ms. Erica are the only ones who know the things I've done. And I didn't actually *tell* them. I wrote it down during our sessions. It's all too horrible to say out loud.

"Okay," Ms. Erica says. "Your choice. But I hope you'll change your mind."

The heavy wooden office door creaks open. A short, slim man pokes his head in and glances around. His eyes slide past me like butter on hot toast and settle on Ms. Erica.

They're Mom's eyes. Dark and deep set. He has her nose, too. Thin and narrow. Same high cheekbones. All I have of Mom is the navy button around my neck from her one good shirt, and the images in my mind. Blurry memories, wearing at the edges like battered photographs.

This man throws them back in sharp contrast. This man who abandoned us.

How dare he look like her?

A darkness crawls through my veins that I've been trying to figure out how to destroy since I arrived here. Before then, really. It's always there. A low heat in my gut that has to be smothered before it morphs into a full-on geyser.

That's when I hurt people.

Truth is, sometimes you have to hurt people to survive. Look weak, and you might as well be dead. You'll sure wish you were.

I wasn't always this way. Or maybe I was and the beatings drew it out. This dark beast dwelling under my skin. And the more I let it out, the harder it became to keep it caged. The beast prowls in my blood—*his* blood—restless, waiting for a reason to show itself.

Like now.

I see myself getting up. Running at the man. Slamming his head into the thick door. I hear the sound it makes. A squelchy *thunk*, as if I'd hit a watermelon with a mallet.

Instead, I close my eyes, breathe deep, and picture a clear night sky. Focus on a point far away. A single dot of light. A needle prick in black paper. I usually picture it getting closer and closer until it becomes a planet, until it swallows me and the darkness and there's nothing but light.

Sometimes it doesn't work, though. Sometimes the dark is too great. It nibbles at the edge of the pool of light, refusing to allow it any closer. Sometimes I'm afraid the darkness will swallow me instead.

"Mr. Clemons," Ms. Erica says. "I'm Erica Tufts. Follow me. There's some final paperwork to fill out."

I don't open my eyes. My fingers find one another and weave together. Not touching anything that might ground me.

I search for the light, begging it to come closer, the way a kid might charm a kitten out of a tree.

Eventually, the curtain parts, a sliver of light pokes through, way off in the distance. My breaths deepen. My body relaxes. The shimmer glides closer. Closer.

Closer.

"Nate?"

Ms. Erica slides in front of me, replacing the light. Her hands are clasped the same way as mine. Does she ever have to find the light? I don't think so. I think her life is all light, with pieces of darkness like me slinking along the border.

"We're all set," she says. "Do you have your things?"

I pick up the rectangular tote bag with West Kentucky Psychiatric Center printed on both sides.

She smiles wide. It looks genuine, but sometimes I can't tell. "Your new social worker will check on you next week. If you need anything before then, don't hesitate to give me a call." She hands me a bright white business card.

I drop it in the bag with the stuff I'm taking with me. The only things I own in the world. Three moleskin notebooks—spiral-bound isn't allowed because the metal could be used as a weapon—four pencils, a deck of playing cards, a toothbrush, a tube of toothpaste, and a comb.

First time I can remember owning a comb. First time I've needed one.

It was easier to fit in at The Fort if you went full skinhead. I've got two cowlicks and hair like a hard-bristled brush, so I didn't mind getting rid of it. Not at first. Not until I figured out what it meant.

The Fort does that to you. It didn't seem like such a horrible place in the beginning. It was easy to shelve all the things Mom had told me. The people seemed nice. They welcomed me. I was their *bruder.* Brother.

They use occasional German words to make themselves feel connected to the shit they believe. Words like *weiss* and *stolz—white* and *proud.* Words I saw on the backs of green flight jackets once it started getting cold.

If the Indoctrinations weren't enough to make me stop swallowing the crap they tried to shove down my throat, those words would've sealed it. Every time I saw them, I was that little kid hiding in the closet all over again.

I'm that kid now. The Psych Center is my closet and the rest of the world is the big bald man with the swastika tattoo.

My uncle stands beside the tall, wood-paneled reception desk, staring at his hands, at the lines of dirt under his slightly too long fingernails. Calling him "uncle" feels weird. He's a stranger. A traitor.

Ms. Erica says something I can't hear and gives him a business card, too. "Okay, you two. Call me if you need anything," she repeats.

We don't budge.

"Don't you need to change or something?" my uncle—jackass, traitor—asks, addressing me for the first time.

I glance down at my bright yellow scrubs and tan slippers. "This is all I have."

The cops took the clothes from that night for evidence. Not that I want them back. They're covered with *his* blood. And if I never wear another pair of black combat boots it'll be too soon.

"Great," he says. "I've gotta buy you clothes, too."

Ms. Erica plasters a big smile on her face. "That should be fun. Something you can do together."

I don't think the Traitor finds the idea any more fun than I do. Ms. Erica holds the door open for us. I stand and follow Traitor into the wide hall.

"Remember to keep your head down when you go out there," Ms. Erica says. "Don't acknowledge them. Stanley will lead you around to the back lot." She lowers her voice, as if she doesn't want Traitor to hear. "This is a great chance for you, Nate. Start over fresh."

Start over. What does that even mean?

Ms. Erica doesn't follow us. I watch her until we reach the front doors, then she disappears inside the office. Maybe she's having as hard of a time with this as I am.

Four orderlies wait by the entrance. Stanley, who is as close to a friend as I have in here besides Ms. Erica, hands me a white doctor's coat. "Cover your face, son. So they can't get no pictures."

I muster a smile, even though I'm shaking a little. Then I cover my head like I did during my trial. Traitor pushes open one of the double doors and watery sunlight washes over the floor.

"There he is!"

I peek out from under the coat at the mass of people by the iron fence out front. Cameras—digital and video—aim at me and fire. Microphones and voice recorders are pushed through the bars, as if a few extra inches will allow the reporters to catch something they couldn't otherwise.

The orderlies surround me and Traitor. Reporters surge against the fence, lions smelling blood.

"Nathaniel! Nathaniel!"

"Are you sure you're ready to be released?"

"Do you regret what you did?"

Stanley leads the way down the chipped concrete steps to the narrow path around the building. The reporters try to follow, but tall, boxy hedges block their way. So they shout instead.

"Nathaniel, are you still a member of the Nazi Socialist Party?"

"Are you moving back to The Fort?"

Traitor unclips a big, round ring from his belt. It's dripping with more keys than one person could possibly need. We stalk to the back lot, toward a gray truck, older model. Dingy silver toolboxes line the sides. A rusty ladder rack clings to the bed walls. Faded bungee cords loop through the holes where ladders should be.

"Nathaniel! Talk to us!"

"Do you have any remorse at all for killing your father?"

The question hits me like a rock. I stand, frozen, wanting to bolt back into the safety of the Psych Center, but unable to move.

It's a question I've been asked before. After my arrest. During my trial.

Problem is, I still don't know the answer.

Gentle hands push me forward. Stanley helps me into the truck cab. "Pay them no mind, son. Take care of yourself, all right?"

I can only nod.

I slide onto the gray, sun-bleached seat. Empty burger wrappers and Skoal cans litter the cab. Stale chewing tobacco spit taints the air. As Traitor backs out of his spot, I crack the window and watch Stanley and the other orderlies until they round the corner and vanish from sight.

The reporters are still hollering. They've pounced on other prey, attacking the orderlies with questions about my stay in the Psych Center.

Except one. A tall lady with straight, blonde hair emerges from the hedges as we drive through the hidden back gate. She scribbles something on a notepad. I sink lower in the seat.

Tearing my eyes from the lone reporter, I steal a look at Traitor. He obviously doesn't want me, so why is he taking me in? Part of me wants to tell him to turn around, to give me back. The Psych Center can't turn me out on the street, can they?

I don't have anywhere else to go. Foster families won't touch me. Five were lined up before Ms. Erica found Traitor, and all five backed out. Once the freaking media got on their trails, they didn't last long. That leaves a group home, which is definitely out of the question.

I stayed in one once while the judge tried to locate *him*. It wasn't as bad as The Fort, but close.

I keep quiet and ride away with the only family I have left to a state I've never seen.

The Farmer Gazette

MURDERED!

Community in Mourning After Death of Prominent Local Figure

By Sam Lawson
Staff Writer

Jefferson Fuller, leader of a local political organization, was murdered at 1 a.m. on Dec. 3.

Neighbors Jason Connor and Al Bolton said Fuller was involved in an altercation with his 14-year-old son.

They witnessed the boy, Nathaniel Fuller, attacking his father. Before they could intervene, Nathaniel Fuller fled to the woods, followed by Jefferson, who told Connor and Bolton to stay behind and call the police. Several minutes later Connor and Bolton heard multiple gunshots.

"At least four or five," said Bolton. "Nathaniel always did have it in for his father."

Connor was noticeably shaken at the scene.

"Me and Al found Jefferson's body. Or what was left of it," Connor said. "I've never seen such a thing in my life."

Sheriff Charles Michaels confirms the murder was the result of a domestic scuffle, but officials aren't releasing any details at this time. Farmer city police located Nathaniel Fuller in a dumpster behind Home Grown Books.

The police have neither confirmed nor denied Fuller's involvement in the murder. However, Ella Pritchett of Pritchett's Platters, a favorite restaurant of Jefferson's, thinks Nathaniel is "guilty as sin."

"I was there when they found him," said Pritchett. "That white T-shirt of his was covered in blood. You don't get that much blood on you if you ain't guilty."

Sheriff Michaels did state that

while no arrests have been made, the full force of the County Sheriff's Department is investigating this brutal murder.

"Jefferson Fuller did a lot for Farmer," said Michaels. "The whole area loved him. He was committed to his community, so his community is going to do everything it can to ensure his killer is brought to justice."

Continued B6.

588

Killing isn't supposed to be easy.

But it is.

Squeezing a trigger is the easiest thing in the world. One firm press and *BOOM*, a life isn't in this world anymore.

It's the *after* that's hard to deal with. After you take the step that can never be taken back. After a single pull of the lever rips a person from his soul.

Although, to be honest, I'm not sure *he* ever had a soul. If *he* did, it left a long time ago.

It doesn't matter that the person I murdered was the most miserable excuse for a human being ever to walk this earth, shy of Hitler. It's knowing *he* didn't have a chance to find some humanity, that I took it from him. It's knowing *he* was the bad guy, but I'm the one who has to suffer for the rest of my life.

Even remembering the things *he* did—to me, to Mom, to anyone who looked different or talked different or *acted* different—even then, I can't escape the guilt. Every time I look at my hands, that cold pistol drags them down like an anchor in thick creek mud. When I see my reflection, *his* face stares back, the face of a murderer.

Even if the jury said I'm not. Not according to the law. The law says self-defense doesn't count as murder.

But it does to me.

Because—and this is the hardest part—it felt *good*. Killing him was a relief. Finally, after years of abuse, of hearing *his* voice crack mid-scream, of the snap of the belt, the slam of *his* fists, finally I had quiet.

Not that it lasted long.

Every day since—all 588 of them—*his* deep voice fills my head with hate-filled words. I don't share *his* hate. I really don't. But that doesn't stop the thoughts from creeping into my mind.

Maybe *his* words got to Mom, too, and no matter how far we ran, she couldn't escape them. Maybe, regardless of what I do, I'm beyond hope.

Traitor thinks so.

He gave me the room on the second floor as far from the stairs as possible. I have to pass his room to leave the house. It's like he thinks that if he gives me the chance I'll sneak away to hurt someone else. Maybe he sees the darkness swirling inside me like ribbons of chocolate syrup in milk. Maybe he thinks I'm as damned as my father.

Not that anyone could sneak anywhere in this house. There's no carpet, only bare floorboards that groan like I'm hurting them when I take a step.

I don't think Traitor knows what to do with me. We drove for pretty much a solid day, all the way from West Kentucky to Northwest Alabama, stopping only for food and to buy me clothes at a thrift store.

When we got to Traitor's cabin last night, he fed me a fried bologna sandwich and chips and sent me to bed without saying more than ten words to me. Not that I got much sleep. I never really sleep anyway. Or maybe I've never really woken up. I live in that blurry space between awake and asleep. Every night, I just lie there, reliving that night. The woods, the gun, the wet slap of brain slop hitting bark. All of it.

This morning, my second day outside the Psych Center, isn't any different, except the dream—memory, flashback, whatever the hell it is—was more intense. Brighter. Colder.

I stay in bed until I can't stand it anymore. It's still dark out. I pull on a pair of ripped jeans and pace the room, making myself feel the cool boards beneath my feet, the scratch of denim on my legs, the smooth plastic of my button. Real things. Not the woods, not the snow, not the gun.

My lungs crave real air, too. Not the canned shit pouring through the vent in the floor. I flick the lock and shove open the window that overlooks the front yard. The windows at the Psych Center were sealed shut. So no one could jump, I guess. Or try to escape.

I didn't realize how much I missed fresh air.

Misty morning fog creeps through the screen, curling its wispy fingers around the mesh like it wants to hold hands for a minute before it melts into droplets on the sill. I sit in the blue velvet armchair beside the window and peer at the trees around the house, tracing 588 in the damp dust on the window ledge.

The scent of earth and pine needles creeps in with the fog. It's something I haven't smelled in a long time. More than just a smell. Memories. I take a deep breath and think of me and Kelsey lying in the woods, reading our secret books, the ones we wrapped in plastic bags and hid in the hole under the holly bush.

The books were her idea. We were around nine and on a supply run in town. Kelsey dragged me in the bookstore when her mom wasn't looking. She'd never seen that many books in one place. I had, thanks to Mom. Libraries are great places to spend a summer day when you have no air-conditioning. I still remembered the tall stacks and bright spines, but all Kelsey had was the handful of propaganda that passed for The Fort's library.

She'd raced from aisle to aisle, unable to stand still long enough to do more than read the titles. Not until we heard her mother calling. Then she grabbed one randomly and shoved it under her shirt while I stood there, terrified.

We'd sprinted into the woods as soon as we got back to The Fort and read until the sun set and the words got lost in the shadows. That book would become her favorite. *Bridge to Terabithia.*

I wonder what happened to our books. They're the one thing I wish I had from The Fort. I guess I could start a new collection. There don't seem to be any books here. At least not in my room. The whole place is like the window ledge, dirty and worn, as if it hasn't been touched in years. Like it's been here this whole time, waiting on me to come and claim it. I lean back in the chair and take a good look at what I'm stuck with for now.

A thinning quilt covers a twin bed in the center of the room. It was enough to keep me warm last night, but I'm screwed when winter comes. There's no headboard. Hell, I'm surprised there's even a bed frame and not just a box spring and a mattress sitting directly on the floor. The mattress, itself, is hard as bone, but I've slept on worse. A nightstand wobbles to the left of the bed. At least the lamp and alarm clock are metal so they're not liable to break when I knock them off—which I'm bound to do.

The chair where I'm sitting is catty-corner to the window. The nap is smooth from what must be decades of wear, and shallow grooves etch the arms like someone interrupted a cat in the middle of sharpening its claws. A small wooden desk is jammed like an afterthought in the far corner in a nook between the closet and the wall.

Across from the bed is a black, dinged-up dresser with one handle missing on the second drawer. I suppose I could put the few clothes Traitor bought me in there.

I cross the room and yank open the drawers. They're all empty except for a bar of lavender soap in the top one.

Mom used to do that. She liked the way it made her clothes smell. Said it made her feel fancy, even in her ratty jeans and moth-eaten sweaters. This bar's scent has all but abandoned it—only the slightest hint of lavender remains—but it's still enough to make me see Mom, dark hair brushing the shoulders of her navy shirt, asking me if she looked pretty. I can't answer, though, because her features are all blurred together by time and distance.

I snatch the soap out of the drawer and toss it in the small wire trash can beside the desk. The breeze catches the lacy curtains that hang on either side of the window. They waft like ghosts. Dingy, yellowy ghosts. The color of dirty dishwater.

A flash of memory hits. Me on the floor of our house at The Fort, sticky with blood. Curtains near my head, with half a red handprint at the bottom.

I shiver and rub my hands down my pants legs, feeling the rough fabric. It takes less than a minute to yank the curtains down. I wad them up and smash them down in the trash can with the soap.

The clang of metal on metal makes me jump. My eyes snap to the yard below, to a pop of red in the fog. Another truck is parked beside Traitor's, also with a bed full of tools but no ladder rack. A slim figure in a tight tank top and baggy jeans bends over the tailgate and drags a bucket from among the various toolboxes.

Even though the person's hair is shorter than mine, there's something distinctly feminine about the way the shape moves, the slight swing of the hips as she hauls the bucket from her truck to Traitor's. It's hard to see in the dim sunlight, but I'm certain it's a *her.*

She slams the tailgate shut and wipes her hands on her jeans, before crossing the yard and banging on the screen door. "Dell! Get a move on!" Her voice is deep for a girl.

The toilet flushes down the hall and the floor creaks. "Gimme a minute," Traitor yells.

The front door opens followed by quick footsteps on the stairs. I crack open my bedroom door. The second floor is kind of a loft area that overlooks the living room. Traitor's room is on one side, bathroom in the middle, then my room.

The girl's short, spiky hair doesn't move as she bounds up the steps, two at a time. It's black as motor oil except for a deep red streak down the center.

She's short and built like a boy, with narrow hips and slightly wider shoulders.

Holy crap, she's Oriental!

I stare openly. I've never seen an Oriental in real life. Only on TV and in pictures in the history books Kelsey and I stole. I can't take my eyes off her. She's beautiful in the way the oleander growing along the highway is beautiful, in a dangerous sort of way. Pretty, but poisonous.

She leans against the railing, precariously close to the edge.

Years of brainwashing trigger and the sudden urge to shove her rushes over me like a tornado tearing across a cloudy spring sky. Only thin wood rails separate her from the living room floor below.

His words flood through me. Angry words that I don't even want to think, and could never actually say. But there they are, pooling in my brain. I stare at the Oriental girl in the hallway, fighting against my Indoctrinations, against the voice in my head commanding me to hurt her.

Traitor comes out of the bathroom, tucking his blue T-shirt into his tan work pants. The thunk of his boots on the wood snaps me back. I press the heels of my hands to my eyes, searching for that prick of light in the darkness, trying to force *his* thoughts out of my head.

"We're not even late yet," Traitor says.

Find the light. Watch it blossom. Grow bigger. Closer. Come on, come on, come on.

"*Yet*. We will be if you don't hurry." Her deep southern accent throws me for a minute. Shouldn't she sound Oriental? What do real Orientals even sound like?

"I had things to take care of," Traitor says.

"I bet," she answers in her husky twang. "Things like sleep, right? Or were you—Dell, who is that?"

I drop my hands from my eyes. My bedroom door inched open more than I meant it to. Without thinking, I slam the door and lean against it, breathing hard.

"Nate, what the hell are you doing?" Traitor snaps.

I don't answer. What am I supposed to say? Trying not to kill your girlfriend? That'll go over great. My ass will be on the street in a flash.

"Nate!"

I reach up to flick the lock, but there isn't one. Just like in *his* house.

Coming here was a mistake.

I have to get out of here. The window?

"Wait a minute," the girl says. "Is that . . . is that Nathaniel Fuller?" Her voice is edged with steel. If that tone had hands, it would slice through the door and cut me to shreds.

Traitor doesn't respond.

"Do you have a death wish?" she screams. At first, I'm not sure if it's directed at me or at Traitor. "We talked about this. You let him in your *house*?"

"I had to, Bev."

"Like hell you did."

"He's Mae's son. What was I supposed to do?"

"Leave him to rot for all I care," she growls. "Think about yourself. This isn't good for you, Dell."

I squeeze my eyes shut, expecting the darkness. Her tone, Traitor's shouting, my unwanted thoughts—they should be making me angry enough to tear the door off its hinges. But the darkness isn't there. The light isn't, either. All that's behind my eyes, in my head, is a deep blue . . . sadness.

She wants me dead. I've never even met her and she wants me dead.

Not that I'm much different—seeing as how my first inclination was to kill her, too. But I didn't *want* to do it. My reaction was instinct, hers is . . . judgment.

I haven't experienced judgment like this since my trial. Is this what it's going to be like on the outside? Most people only know the sensationalized story the media showed. Since I'm a minor, the judge barred reporters from the courtroom, so they made up whatever they wanted. Whatever would sell papers and draw viewers.

The only people talking were from The Fort and the town of Farmer, which was really just an extension of The Fort, seeing as how most of them—cops included—came to the rallies every Saturday night. The Fort trains its members on how to handle the media and how to paint themselves as victims, regardless of the situation. They claimed I was trying to overthrow *him* and take over leadership. No one got to hear my side. No one knows what really happened.

Is everyone like Traitor's girlfriend? Do they all hate me?

Traitor's boots echo on the bare boards as he crosses to my room. This is it. He's going to throw the door open and beat me senseless. I'll have to fight back. Let the beast out.

I'm going back to juvie.

A piece of notebook paper slides under the door.

"If you're gonna live here, you're gonna pull your weight," he says. "I expect these chores to be done before I get home at five."

I don't move.

"Dell, you can't—"

Traitor clears his throat, cutting her off. "There's bread in the pantry and meat in the fridge. Help yourself, but don't go wild. And don't leave the property. Or use the computer. One slip, and you're goin' back."

His heavy footsteps retreat, followed by her lighter ones. She's yelling at him again, but I can't make out the words. The stairs creak, then the front door slams shut. The roar of an engine slices through the fog.

I'm alone.

I could run.

And go where? Hop between towns again, hoping no one recognizes me? I had enough of that with Mom.

No. This is my chance. My shot to leave all that behind. The running, the anger, the fear. This is it.

And I guess it starts with chores.

✧

The list is long. Sweep the entire house, clean the kitchen and bathroom counters, mow the grass, organize the pantry. I'm surprised Traitor doesn't want me to scrub the floors with a toothbrush. The list should be titled "Things to Keep Nate Occupied So He Doesn't Murder Someone Else."

Traitor doesn't keep much in the house. There's very little furniture, nothing on the walls, no photographs on the tables. I'd hoped he'd have a picture of Mom, or something of hers around here, but there's nothing. It's almost as if she never existed.

The house is unnervingly quiet.

The Fort was never quiet. Someone was always barking commands or fighting or listening to Nazi Socialist black metal so loud it made your organs vibrate.

The Psych Center was better, but at least a few times a day, George, the schizophrenic down the hall, would scream at the creatures crawling up his walls or an argument would erupt in the common room over the remote. Nurses were always in and out dispensing meds. There were group therapy sessions.

Now, the only sounds are my footsteps and the occasional tweet of the birds at the metal feeder outside the kitchen window.

And my own terrifying thoughts.

This is the first time I've been alone, truly alone, since right before it happened. Since the last time I waited for Kelsey by our holly bush.

I'd been lying on my back in the snow watching the shadows of the bare branches dance across my jeans when boots crashed through the underbrush. *His* thugs jerked me to my feet and pinned my arms behind my back.

Then Thomas Mayes and the Connor brothers pushed into the clearing, holding Kelsey between them. Jeremy Connor shoved her forward so hard she almost fell. She shivered like a scared dog. Blood streamed down her cheek from a gash over one eye, which was already swelling shut. Fresh bruises splotched her face, reminding me of when she had chicken pox when we were ten. Mud clung to her wild hair and her thin sweater.

They hadn't even let her put on a jacket after they beat her, which for some reason struck me as the worst part. Like everything would be better if she were only warm.

She wouldn't—or couldn't—meet my eyes as she pointed to our holly bush.

When they found the secret books, Thomas Mayes punched me until he knocked me out. He was grinning the entire time. They didn't let me out of their sight after that.

So I take advantage of the situation now. I could use a talk with Ms. Erica, her calm, low voice soothing my nerves, but there's no phone. I don't feel like starting my chores yet, so I snoop through Traitor's things, starting with his bedroom. There has to be at least a fragment of my mother *somewhere.* A picture, clothing, a letter. Anything besides the button around my neck.

It had come loose from her interview shirt the morning she died. She pressed the button in my palm and told me not to let go of it while she ran to the gas station for a needle and thread. If I lost it, her shirt wouldn't close and she wouldn't get the job we so desperately needed.

I may have forgotten other things she told me, but I never lost her button. I hold it now in one hand while I rummage through Traitor's room.

It's a lot like mine. The bed is bigger, the quilt's not quite as worn. There's a desk against one wall and a dresser on the other—both are practically empty. The closet is crammed with clothes and several pairs of boots. No black ones. None with laces. Nothing that even resembles a combat boot. One pair's camouflage, one has rubber around the bottoms, and one pair are brown leather pull-on work boots.

I push the clothes back and find a brand-new gun safe in the corner, the orange price tag still hanging from the handle. A chill rocks through me. In spite of myself, I give the handle a quick turn to be certain it's locked up tight, that I'm safe from the guns.

Or maybe that they're safe from me.

The handle holds firm. I let some camo coveralls swing back in front of the safe and start to leave when light glints off something on the floor.

Behind the boots, under a blanket, is a black trunk. Silver brackets cover the corners. I pull the blanket back and try to lift the lid. It doesn't move. A hinged latch holds the trunk shut. Locked.

Is this where he keeps her, hidden away so he doesn't have to see? Traitor doesn't seem like the kind of guy who has a lot of valuables. He and Mom obviously had some kind of falling-out—one so bad she never breathed a word about him to me. If he's kept anything, it has to be in there.

The keyhole is about the size of a dime, so the key should be small and, unfortunately, easy to hide. I rifle through all the desk drawers again, even feeling underneath in case he taped it to the bottom. No key. Nothing in the dresser but underwear, which I feel weird touching.

I run downstairs and go through all the kitchen drawers, the end table by the couch, the coffee table compartment.

Nothing.

It's probably on that giant key ring of his. Of course that's where he'd keep a *key*. But how the hell am I going to get it?

589

Traitor—and his keys—left bright and early, but not before giving me a fresh list of chores. My main task is cleaning up the flower beds.

The day is so humid even the grass is limp, like it's trying to snake under the dirt where it's cooler. Pulling weeds is a nightmare, and not just because I have to stop and rub sweat out of my eyes every few minutes. The weeds keep slipping out of my grasp. I eventually chuck the leather work gloves on the porch and use my hands to get a better grip, even though the dirt stains them a brownish-red and leaves dark crescents of gunk under my nails.

Anything would be better than this. Although, at least the cabin is nothing like the houses at The Fort.

Kelsey called it Auschwitz because it reminded her of the bunk buildings in pictures of the concentration camp.

Pictures we weren't supposed to see of a camp The Fort denied existed. The sameness and uniformity made me sick. It made Kelsey long to be different, to do something totally distinct, like dye her hair blue.

I guess she never got the chance.

I force The Fort from my thoughts and climb to my feet and push the wheelbarrow of weeds and dirt—although clay is a better word for the thick red mud that passes for dirt in Alabama—to the edge of the woods and dump it in a deep hole I found while mowing yesterday. I'd almost gotten the mower stuck in it when I was trying to avoid the woods. I haven't stepped foot in a forest since that night, and I'm not about to start now.

I can't tell how far down the hole goes, but it's deep enough that only a weak trickle of sunlight reaches the bottom. And in that trickle, is a small tree. It's a scraggly, thin thing. Hasn't even reached the edge yet, and Lord knows how it started growing, but it's there: a flash of pale green leaves in the dark struggling to rise above the muck it started in and stretch toward the full stream of sun on the surface.

I pause at the hole and think about yanking the tree free and putting it out of its misery. The roots can't be too deep yet. Its weak trunk would be easy to rip from the dirt. But I'm curious to see if the seedling will ever make its way above the hole, so I carefully dump the dirt around it rather than on top of it, then I right the wheelbarrow and angle back toward the house. Traitor pulls into the yard before I start pushing. The Oriental girl hops out and crosses to her truck without so much as a glance my direction. The sun sets fire to the red streak across her head, like a wrongly colored skunk.

Skunky. That's what I should call her. It sounds better than the Oriental. Calling her that makes me feel like I'm labeling her by her race, which is too much like what *he* would do.

Does she know what's in that trunk in Traitor's closet? She apparently knows Mom existed, but does she know what happened between Mom and Traitor?

I guess it doesn't matter. It's not like she'd ever tell me.

Traitor takes his time getting out of the truck. I already have the wheelbarrow back at the porch for the next load when his boots crunch on the gravel walkway. A forest green backpack with thick black straps thumps to the ground beside me.

"School starts Monday," he says.

I twist my head around, wishing the house faced the other direction so the sun would be in my eyes. Then I wouldn't have to actually look at him.

He can't be serious. There's no way he can expect me to go to school with regular kids. "I don't need school," I say.

He snorts. "'Cause you got such a great education at The Fort."

"I'm sixteen. I don't have to go."

"The State says otherwise."

"I'm not living with the State anymore. They don't get a say."

Traitor nudges the backpack toward me with his toe. "Take it up with Mrs. Hayes tomorrow afternoon." He turns and clomps up the steps, his keys jangling against his thigh.

This is bullshit. And that's exactly what I'll say to this new case manager when I see her.

The backpack is as limp as the grass. I should leave it there. Ignore it. Or toss it in the hole with the tree. Make Traitor bitch about the money he spent.

Instead, I pick it up. Someone colored in the logo on the front with black marker. The straps are torn at the edges and the threads along the top are fraying. It's heavier than I thought it would be. I peek inside. The front pocket has two black BICs and two mechanical pencils. The big section holds three brand-new notebooks, spiral-bound.

Guess Traitor doesn't care if I kill myself or not.

591

"I'd be better off at the Psych Center. Send me back to Kentucky." I cross my arms and stare the social worker down. Ms. Erica's business card burns a hole in my pocket. She's the one I should be talking to, not this old holier-than-thou bitch. I have to find some way to get a phone.

The new social worker leans forward, balancing her elbows on her khaki-clad knees. She's older than Ms. Erica, and not near as pretty. "I know you're scared, Nate."

"I'm not scared," I snap. This lady has no clue. If she did, she'd understand that *I'm* not the one who should be afraid. All she knows is whatever that thick blue file in her bag says, and since I decided to keep my past private, there's no telling what that is.

"Okay, good. Because there's no reason to worry." She smiles. "I've spoken to the principal and the guidance counselor. They think you were in a juvenile facility for behavioral issues before the Psych Center. They're going to watch out for you."

I slump against the lumpy couch cushions. Great. They think I'm some out-of-control delinquent. Okay, maybe I am, but it might've taken them a while to figure that out.

"What about reporters?" I ask.

Traitor comes out of the kitchen carrying a glass of ice water. He hands it to the social worker, but she doesn't drink. Just passes it from hand to hand.

"You're enrolled as Nate Clemons so—"

"No," I bark. "I won't take *that* name."

Traitor stiffens. "It's a hell of a lot better than the one that jackass gave you."

"What would you know about it?" I glare at him. From where I'm standing he and "that jackass" have a lot in common.

Traitor pushes off the doorway and takes a step toward me. "Enough."

"Stories from biased reporters don't count for shit." I cross my arms.

Traitor looks like he wants to say something, but the social worker cuts in before he can.

"It's for your safety, Nate. It's not only the media we want to keep away from you."

I swallow hard. It's suddenly a million degrees inside this house. My palms are sweating like leaky faucets. My knee bounces up and down. "Do you . . . do you think they'll find me?"

I'm not scared of some bitch-ass kids, but anyone with sense would be afraid of The Nazi Socialist Party. I don't care how far I am from The Fort. There are white supremacist groups in forty-eight states. If they find me, it's game over. They made no secret of the fact they think a stint in the Psych Center isn't enough punishment for taking out their dear old leader, and they aim to fix what the jury got wrong.

The social worker puts her cool palm on my arm, but it's not comforting. Not like Ms. Erica's hand. "You're safe here," the woman says.

I slide away from her. "They knew Mom. Nate Clemons will be almost as obvious as Nate Fuller."

Despite the heat, Traitor gives me a look that could freeze Hell. "You don't even know your own mother's name?"

I clench my jaw to keep my mouth from dropping open. It wasn't Clemons before she got married? *He* never called her anything but Mae or Bitch, and she was a dozen different people when we were running, but she was always Mom to me.

The social worker shoots Traitor a warning glance. "Your mother's last name was Reese, Nate. Your uncle changed his name to Clemons a long time ago. That's why it took Ms. Erica so long to locate him."

Is that why Mom didn't find him? Did he change his name to hide from us? What happened between them? I want to ask all these questions, but I know he won't answer. He wouldn't help me then, and he won't now. The State must be paying him to keep me. That's the only reason I can come up with for why he'd let me live here.

"If Ms. Erica found him, The Fort can, too."

Traitor scowls. "I've been off their radar for a long time. Ms. Erica had access to records they can't possibly get ahold of."

Why was he on their radar in the first place? Unless The Fort thought they could get to Mom through him. I bet that's why he didn't help us. To protect his own ass.

"As long as you go by Clemons, you'll be safe," the social worker says. "Your records are sealed. You're at least four hundred miles from The Fort. No one who isn't associated with your case knows where you are. Not even the school administrators know your past since you've refused to release details."

She says the last part like I'm a horrible person for holding back information. Dr. Sterling said it's my choice who I disclose my medical history to, and I chose not to disclose to anyone but her and Ms. Erica. I told them to only release what they absolutely have to, which isn't much. Even to this lady.

The social worker sighs. "Keep a low profile and The Fort won't bother you."

Traitor crosses his arms. "Don't do anything that will land your ass back in the news."

I glare at him. "Skunk—that lady knows. She knows exactly who I am." And she'd love to see me dead.

The social worker raises an eyebrow.

"I had to talk it through with someone," Traitor says. "Bev won't tell. She doesn't want them after me, either."

"See?" I say.

The social worker sets her full water glass on the coffee table. "I wouldn't get involved in sports or clubs that might post your picture somewhere, but otherwise you'll be fine. This will be good for you, Nate. It's time to reintegrate into society."

*Re*integrate. As if I was ever integrated to begin with.

"And what happens if I don't go?"

Her smile falters a little. "This is the next step of your court-ordered therapy. The State will compel you to attend school."

"How?"

"Just go and we won't have to worry about that." She stands and slings her bag over her shoulder as if that closes the matter. She could at least *pretend* to care about what I want.

I'm not letting this go without a fight. "What about home-school? Can't I—"

"Who's gonna teach you?" Traitor snaps. "Sure as hell ain't gonna be me. It's public school or a job."

It's an empty threat. From the number of "looking for work" flyers I saw stapled to phone poles on the way into town, no one is hiring.

"Nate, give it a chance," the social worker says. "What's the worst that could happen?"

594

I stabbed someone for the first time in school. It was in the second grade.

Thomas Mayes.

He was a few years older, and a hell of a lot bigger, than me. I stabbed him in the gut with my pocketknife. Only once. Our classmates pulled me off after that. But I wish I'd gotten more jabs in. I wish I'd stuck that knife in him again and again and again until he didn't have a breath left in his body.

I wish *I'd* gotten the last laugh.

My first day of school at The Fort—homeschool really—went fine. Everyone loved me. Who wouldn't love the leader's son? I sat at the front of the meeting hall, riding high on their smiles and friendly words. The teacher handed me a slip of paper and told me to memorize it.

The mantra.

A racially pure people which is conscious of its blood can never be enslaved by the antiracists. In this world, we must fortify the future of the White people and the White people alone.

I recited it that first day without knowing what I was saying—just read the words off the page along with everyone else in the hall.

But I thought about it that night. And the more I thought about it, the more I remembered Mom's warnings.

The next day, I refused to say it.

That led to my first Indoctrination.

Because *he* was afraid *he*'d kill me if *he* got *his* hands on me, *he* had my classmates do the Indoctrination. Guys I'd been throwing a baseball with the day before—Thomas Mayes and the Connor brothers.

They cornered me during free time. Thomas Mayes punched me in the face, then threw me to the dirt. The Connor brothers stretched me out and held me down, so I couldn't protect myself. Then Thomas Mayes kicked me in the stomach with his steel-toed combat boots, saying he'd keep doing it until I said the mantra and believed it.

I was eight.

I said the words. I hate myself for it, but I said them.

But they could never make me believe them.

I lay there in the dirt, curled in a tight ball, tears mixing with sweat and blood to make tiny mud puddles, when a small hand reached toward me, palm up, the way you approach an unfamiliar dog. And like a dog, I sniffed first. Oranges. That's the first memory I have of Kelsey. She sat there, orange slice extended toward me, and waited until I sat up and took it. Then she offered me another. I thanked her and she just shrugged one shoulder.

"You looked like you needed it," she'd said.

I never knew if she meant the orange, or the kindness.

She helped me up with her sticky hands. "Don't let them get away with it. Otherwise, they'll keep coming for you. That's what *he* always says, anyway." She nodded to the edge of the field where my father stood, watching.

I waited a few months until the right time, until I found Thomas Mayes alone in a corner of the field during free time. I flicked open the blade of my pocketknife and pulled my sleeves over my hands to hide it.

He was only twelve, but had already been lifting weights. It felt like cutting a thick steak when I plunged the knife in, but it made a sucking, deflating balloon noise as I pulled it out. A satisfying, soul-draining sound.

Thomas Mayes might have acted tough before, but all that toughness spurted out of him with the blood from his belly.

He didn't bother me again.

Not until that day in the woods.

✧

Monday morning comes too quickly. The truck is silent as Traitor drives me across town to the high school, me gripping the worn handle on top of the backpack until my knuckles turn white, him doing the same with the steering wheel. Lewiston looks to be more worthless than Farmer, the blink-and-you-miss-it town near The Fort. At least Farmer had a Walmart. Almost every store in downtown Lewiston is closed. I spot one restaurant, but it's in a trailer behind some lady's house, so I don't think that counts. Skunky didn't show this morning, so it's the two of us and the cloud of quiet, interrupted only by the rumble of the engine and the jingle of his keys—which I still haven't been able to get my hands on. Every time they knock against one another, I think about the trunk in the closet.

It's barely seven when Traitor pulls up to a red tin awning in front of the ugly gray cinder block school. I half-expect media to rush through the glass doors, assaulting me with questions, but the sidewalk remains empty.

Traitor catches my arm. "Don't cause no trouble."

I grab my pack and jump out. As he drives off, it occurs to me that the building may not even be unlocked this early. I cross my fingers. All I want is to figure out where I'm supposed to go and be tucked away in the back corner of a classroom when everyone else gets here.

The door swings open easily. A blast of cold air and a stale, musty odor hit me as I step through it. Chill bumps prickle my arms, making the hairs stand at attention. There's a glass window to the right—like the kind at the Psych Center where they distributed meds—that says OFFICE. I sidle up to it and shift on my feet.

The office is dark, but someone has to be here if the place is open, right? Do I holler? Stand here like a loser until someone sees me? I look around the corner. Empty. But a bar of light peeks out from under a door a little ways down the hall. A sign on the wall beside it reads TEACHER'S LOUNGE. Below it, someone has taped a piece of white paper with "No Students Allowed" in bold. I put my ear to the door and listen, but the wood is too thick to hear through.

I'll just open it really fast, peek inside, and see if someone can tell me where to go. They can't be mad about that, right? I turn the handle and push the door in one fluid motion.

It hits something solid. There's a loud crunch, followed by a scream.

Oh, shit.

My heart pounds. I hurt someone. Not just someone. A teacher. My first day, without even trying. What is *wrong* with me?

I could run. They haven't seen me yet. I can get the hell out of here. Rewind. Start over. Start fresh. That's what Ms. Erica said, although I don't think she meant this. I even take a step. Then the door slams open.

A blonde girl glares at me over the blood spurting from her nose. Bright red flecks of it dot her white shirt like the Queen Anne's lace I used to pick for Kelsey on her birthday. A bluish bruise is already starting to form along the bridge of the girl's nose. She holds one hand to her face, trying to catch the stream flowing down her chin.

"What the hell?" she yells when she sees me. "Look what you did!"

"I . . . I'm—"

Her eyes dart to my feet and back up to my face. "Oh my God, were you *leaving*? You weren't even going to see if I was okay? You were just going to leave me like this?"

"No, I—"

"Who even are you? What are you doing here?"

The blood in my own veins starts to boil. I didn't mean to hurt her, and she's acting like I did it on purpose. I open my mouth to answer, but she starts in again before I can get a word out.

"Don't just stand there. Get me a paper towel or something. What's wrong with you?"

That's what does it. Hearing my thoughts echoed through her lips. The beast rises up inside me. "Will you shut up already?" I yell. "I didn't mean to."

Her jaw flops open. Blood drips onto the creamy tile. I clench my fist and turn on my heel. Staying here will only make it worse. I told Traitor this was a bad idea. At least now maybe he'll scrap the whole school thing.

"Hey!" the girl yells.

I ignore her and keep walking. I only make it a few steps before a short, round white woman blocks my path. Her tan pantsuit is too tight to be comfortable and her red hair is too bright to be natural. She looks from me to the blonde girl, who's still bleeding all over the floor.

"What's going on here?"

"He did it," the girl says.

Aw, shit.

The woman clucks her tongue. "It's okay, Maddie. Nose injuries always look worse than they are. Let's get you cleaned up." She starts toward the girl, then looks back at me. "You. Wait right there."

Son of a bitch. Staying in school may not even be an option. Not if I get expelled on my first day. That will look great on my record. I stand beside the dark office like I should've done to begin with. The woman returns a few minutes later.

"Mrs. Roger is taking care of Maddie." She sorts through a key ring big enough to rival Traitor's. "Here we go." She separates one of the keys and unlocks the door. Fluorescent lights buzz awake. A wood grain sign on the wall says MARY RAWLS, PRINCIPAL.

I look from the sign to the woman.

"Yep, that's me. If you'd get a move on, we can have a proper introduction."

I follow her into my first principal's office. We enter a reception-type area with a tall counter and a couple of plastic chairs, then skirt the counter and enter another room. The principal sits behind a wide oak desk and motions to the two faded red chairs across from her. I perch on the edge of the closest one as she places her elbows on the desktop.

"Now, then. You must be Nate. Not exactly the best start at Lewiston High." She plucks a thin manila folder out of a drawer. "Ms. Tufts and Mrs. Hayes made me aware of your situation." She pauses. "You're taller than I expected."

I don't really know what to say, so I don't say anything. A slice of dark yellow glides by the window. Brakes squeal as the bus stops, then voices float through the open window of the outer office. Students are already starting to arrive and I'm cooped in here instead of holed up somewhere safe.

The principal opens the file. "Fighting, threatening teachers, destroying property, lack of respect for authority. And now assaulting another student."

"I didn't—"

She holds up a finger. "I believe today was an accident, but you have an admittedly bad pattern of behavior. I want to be clear here. We're giving you a chance, and we want this to work out, but we'll be watching you closely. I have to look out for my students."

Good Lord. First the incident with Nose Girl, and now this bullshit file on me. They couldn't construct a better story than that? I mean, it's not that far from the truth, but still, not exactly the "fresh start" I thought everyone wanted for me. Must be the new social worker's doing.

"Do you understand, Mr. Clemons?"

I bristle at the name. Another bus pulls up. More students flood through the front doors. Loud students. I just want out of here, so I bite my tongue. "Yes, ma'am."

"Good." She pushes a gray folder toward me. "There's a map inside. Not that this place is hard to figure out. There are only two hallways. Your prior homeschooling and the independent study in the Institution was good enough for the State to consider you a sophomore, but we'll be monitoring your grades closely. If you can't keep up, we'll drop you to a freshman."

Better than I expected. I'll be seventeen in a few months and should be a junior, but honestly, I'm surprised the education I've gotten so far was enough to be in high school at all.

I take the folder and open to my class schedule. Behind it is the code of conduct, the map she mentioned, and a bunch of other papers I don't feel like reading. I flip to the map. Besides the front entrance, there are exits at each end of the T-shaped halls. Not ideal, but at least I have options if things get messy. Mess*ier* anyway.

Heavy footsteps stomp on the tile in the main office behind me. "Mrs. Roger," a girl says, hard and clipped. It sounds like Nose Girl. "I can't take these classes. I *can't*. You have to change my schedule!"

It's a tone I'm familiar with. Kelsey sounded just like that when she was mad at me, which was usually any time I disagreed with her. Over small things like what we thought a poem meant, or big ones like when we should leave The Fort. She'd get so pissed she wouldn't talk to me for days, or even weeks. There was no compromise with Kelsey.

This girl isn't Kelsey, but she *is* talking loud enough to draw a crowd. And I don't want to be part of that. I keep my eyes forward, silently begging the principal to hurry so I can get out of here and get to class before more people show up.

She seems oblivious. "Your first class is homeroom. Mrs. McAvoy, second door on the right. Your locker is number two-nineteen, near the lunchroom. That's down to the left. The combination is in your folder. Don't give it to anyone. You'll pass the first number once, pass the second, then directly to the third." She stands and puts both hands on the desk. "If you have any questions, ask Mrs. Roger at the window."

Questions? I have a ton. Like what the hell did she say? I close the folder, grateful she's finally letting me leave, and start to stand. But she's not finished yet.

"First bell is at seven forty-five. Homeroom starts at eight sharp. Lunch is two dollars, or you can bring your own. Do you have money for today?"

I shake my head. She beckons for me to follow her to the main office. Nose Girl stands at the counter, a red towel pressed to her nose.

"You don't understand," the girl says to the skinny older white woman behind the desk. "This won't work!" She slams a piece of paper on the counter. Her eyes narrow when she spots me. Her face glows like the fires of Hell dwell in her skull.

My body tenses. I glare back, not willing to be the first to look away. I've already shown enough weakness. Especially for the first day. The girl's frown deepens. She seems like she wants to say something, then the principal pushes around me. Nose Girl turns back to the woman but gives me the side-eye. My muscles relax in triumph, but it's only momentary.

The day hasn't even officially started and I've already had two confrontations with her.

"Mrs. Roger," the principal says. "This is Nate Clemons. Give him a lunch pass. Only for today, though." She drops my file on the counter. "Oh, and Nate? Make sure you read the code of conduct. Carefully." She sweeps into her office and closes her door behind her.

Nose Girl glowers at the old woman. "I was here first."

"Just a moment, Maddie," the lady says, pawing through a gray plastic cup.

I keep my head down until she hands me a piece of yellow construction paper with LUNCH PASS stamped on it. Fancy. "Here you go, dear," she says. "Give that to the lunch lady when you get your food."

I slip it in my pocket and head to the hall. The floodgates have definitely opened. The place is packed. There are way too many teenagers for a town this size.

Mostly white people, with a few other races peppered throughout the crowd. My whole body is on edge. Not wanting another run-in, I stare at my shoes and weave toward the lockers. People knock against me with their elbows and backpacks as they push past. Lockers slam and people shout and the air blows at arctic levels and it's been 594 days since it happened. 594 days and it's August, not December, but it's so cold and crowded and too much, too much, too much.

And I didn't take my meds. I wanted to be sharp for my first day.

But nothing is sharp except the dead branches scratching my arms.

The faces in the hall blur together into a featureless mass and stretch to the ceiling. Except it's not the ceiling. It's dark, open sky. Fingers stretch and claw and scratch. I close my eyes and try to focus. This can't happen. Not now. I struggle to get my button out of my shirt collar, but the string is pinned by my backpack.

A guy yells. Something heavy crashes to the tile, loud as a gun blast. The sounds echo around me, growing into a roar until it's white noise.

And it's so cold. *So freaking cold.*

Snow brushes my eyelashes. It sticks in my arm hair.

He's behind me.

It's not real. It's been 594 days since it was real. But, *oh my God* he's *coming.*

Crashing through the brush.

My pulse pounds out a drumbeat in my ears.

He's got a gun.

And I'm standing still.

I want to live.

I break into a run, shoving branches out of the way. I trip over a root and crash to the ground.

The snow is heavy and wet. I didn't have time to grab a jacket, or even a long-sleeved shirt. My white undershirt isn't much protection. I'm struggling to get free, to get away.

Then *he*'s on top of me. Punching.

The gun butt swings at my head, smashes into my temple, and I see fireworks.

I'm going to die.

I can't. Not yet.

I free an arm and knock the gun out of *his* hand. It thumps to the snow and we're both scrabbling for it. My elbow catches him in the eye. *He* roars and smacks me hard enough to see stars. *He*'s pulling me back, but my fingertips graze the gun handle. I've almost got it. But *his* hand gets there first.

Fire spreads through my limbs. My arms are suddenly heavy. The snow turns to gunpowder, swirling around my head, so dark and dense I can't see.

Then I'm at *his* mercy.

✧

The first thing I feel when I come to is red-hot humiliation. It spreads through me, thawing the last traces of cold fear the flashback left behind.

Oh God, I had a flashback. On my first day.

Freaking principal. If she hadn't kept me so long, I could have found a quiet corner to wait out the storm. I would've been fine. Now I'm waking up on a cot in the corner of a small room. The back of my head throbs when I move, but I still turn to see where they've stuck me.

To my right, a balding man sits behind a beat-up wooden desk with a green plant on one end. Behind him, a short bookshelf spits books, like it ate so many it made itself sick. They're three deep on the shelves and piled on the floor, almost up to the broken, wood fiber ceiling tiles. The fluorescent lights make everything look artificial, as if I'm peering in on a wax scene in a museum.

The cot's stiff fabric creaks as I push myself upright. The man's head snaps up.

"I see you've decided to rejoin us."

Decided isn't the word I'd use.

The man slides over to me, propelling himself forward on his chair's squeaky wheels. He extends his hand. "I'm Mr. Paulsen, the counselor here at Lewiston High. I'd hoped we'd meet under better circumstances."

And I'd hoped we wouldn't meet at all. Still, I shake his hand.

"Your uncle is on his way with your medication. How are you feeling?".

We'd be here all day if I tried to unpack that one, so I simplify. "Dizzy."

His head bobs up and down. "I bet. It's barely"—he checks his watch—"eight thirty and you've already had quite a day. First the incident with Maddie, then this episode. Combined with the stress of a new school."

I slump back on the cot. Shit. Does everyone know about Nose Girl by now? I close my eyes.

"Nate? You okay? Feel like you're going to pass out again?"

My eyes flutter open. The counselor frowns.

"You know, it may be a good idea for you to go home for the rest of the day."

I straighten. "Seriously? I can go home?" And never, ever come back.

"Dr. Sterling warned me these episodes take a lot out of you. Besides," he leans closer, conspiratorially, "it won't hurt to get a do-over of your first day."

Irritation buzzes through me. I don't want a do-over. I don't want this at all. "You talked with Dr. Sterling?"

The counselor absently pokes at a tuft of yellow stuffing coming out of one of the chair arms. "I spoke with both her and Ms. Tufts before we allowed you to enroll. They told me about your PTSD. We're all on your team, Nate."

I've never been on a team, but this—whatever *this* is—doesn't strike me as one. From what I can tell, a team is a bunch of people with a common goal. This is no team. This is me, standing alone in the middle of a field watching everyone try to push me in a certain direction.

"What was the trigger?" the counselor asks.

I swing my legs over the side of the cot, stretching them in front of me, and lean against the wall. I don't want to talk to this guy, but he seems like the sort who won't stop pushing until I give him something. There were a few like him in the Psych Center. They'd usually feel proud of themselves for getting me to talk and leave me alone.

"Everything. The cold, the yelling, the doors slamming. All of it. Maybe I can't go to a regular school."

The counselor rubs his hand over his chin. "Or, and hear me out, maybe you need to take your meds and receive a little extra accommodation?"

I already hate this guy.

The speaker by the door crackles. "Mr. Paulsen," a voice says. It sounds a bit like the old lady in the office, but it's hard to tell. "There's a woman here to see you. She says she's here for Nate."

The counselor stands and pushes a button beside the speaker. "Thanks, Mrs. Roger. Is it his social worker?" He releases the button and looks at me. "I can't imagine she got here so quickly. She was on the other side of the county when I called."

"You called my social worker?" A tiny bit of excitement stirs inside me. Maybe this won't be so bad after all. If she sees what one morning at school did to me, she can't force me to come back.

"No, it's not Mrs. Hayes," the voice says and my chests swells with hope. Ms. Erica. I don't know how she got here so fast, but she'll listen to me. She'll understand. Maybe even take me back.

The speaker crackles again. "This woman says Nate's uncle sent her."

I flop my head against the wall, deflated. Traitor wouldn't call Ms. Erica.

"Okay, send her in." The counselor crosses the room in two steps and looks out the long, narrow window in the door. "I thought your uncle was coming himself. I'd hoped to talk to him. Do you know who he'd send?"

"Is she Oriental?"

The counselor looks back at me, his eyes wide. "Nate! You can't say that."

"What, Oriental? Why?"

He does a literal double take. "What do you mean, *why*? It's . . . it's offensive."

I stiffen. Is *Oriental* a slur? "How?" I ask. "I mean, there are a lot of worse words—"

"Just because it isn't the worst doesn't mean it isn't harmful." He glances out the window again and puts his hand on the knob. "You've never said that to your uncle's friend, have you?"

My face feels hot. "No."

"Good. Promise me you'll never say it again. If you don't know where someone is from, use *Asian*. Okay?"

"Okay," I mumble. A prickle of shame works down my throat, like swallowing a pinecone. I don't like Skunky, but now I feel guilty just thinking that word about her.

The counselor opens the door and Skunky breezes in.

"I'm Bev Liu. Dell sent me with Nate's meds." She says my name like she's hawking up venom.

"Thank you, Ms. Liu." The counselor takes the two white bottles she's holding out and hands them to me. One is my regular medicine and one is a sedative. Just like they used to give me at the Psych Center when I had a flashback. "There's a water fountain down the hall, Nate. Think you can manage, or do I need to bring you a cup?"

"I've got it." I shake a tablet out of each bottle and squeeze past them. There's barely room for two people in here, let alone three. The counselor closes the door behind me, muffling his voice so I can't make out whatever he says to Skunky next.

Traitor couldn't even spare the time to bring me my meds. It's like he wants me to fail. It hits me all of a sudden.

If I fail, then he'll have an excuse to tell the social worker I'm a lost cause. Then the Psych Center may never take me back.

I can't let that happen. Things here may suck, but at least it's not a group home or the street.

The hall is still freezing, but at least it's quiet now. The closest water fountain is almost at the complete opposite end from the counselor's office. I dip my head and drink for a long time, only straightening up again when I become aware of a persistent tapping behind me.

A short girl with hair so black it's practically blue scowls at me. She's tapping her foot impatiently. "Do you mind?"

I wipe my mouth with the back of my hand. "What?"

She crosses her arms, still *tap, tap, tapping* her toe against the tile. "The water, Newbie. Mind getting out of the way, or are you going to block it all day?"

The girls at this school are all so aggressive. I almost feel like I'm back at The Fort. "Newbie?" I ask. What the hell does that mean?

She sighs. "You're the new kid, right? The one who passed out."

Great. I'll be forever known as the guy who fainted on his first day of school.

"Watch it, Newbie," she says. "I heard about you."

She knows? I freeze like I did outside the Psych Center. They said no one knew. The social worker said I'm safe. I knew I couldn't trust her!

My face must register my shock because the girl grins and steps closer. Her short, dark hair frames her face.

"Don't look so surprised. It's a small school. Word travels fast." She takes another step, completely invading my personal space. "We don't tolerate that kind of crap here. Got it?"

The beast inside me perks up. Anger wells in my blood. I picture my hands around her skinny throat, squeezing until her face turns purple.

Light. Think of light.

All I see is her dark little head.

I clench my hands into fists and straighten, towering my full six feet two inches over the girl.

Her smirk fades.

"If you know so much, then you should know better than to poke a bear. I might bite." I snap my jaws and she jumps.

I whirl away before I do anything reckless, stalking back to the counselor's office.

Fan-*tas*-tic. This day is going absolutely fantastic.

Clenching and unclenching my fists, I focus on taking slow, deep breaths. I can't lose my cool. Especially not on some know-it-all girl. The counselor's door opens and Skunky appears, holding my backpack.

"Get some rest," the counselor says. "We'll see you tomorrow."

I jerk my bag away from Skunky. She lets go before I get a good grip, like she doesn't want to even touch me, and walks to the front door without a word.

"Remember what we talked about," the counselor calls before I can follow Skunky.

How could I forget? Despite all my efforts to not be like *him* there's still so much I don't know. Thank God I never said the word aloud. If Oriental is as bad as the counselor says, it might have caused Skunky to completely lose it. Which might have caused me to lose it right back.

And I don't want to hurt anyone else.

I hitch up my backpack and follow Skunky to her truck. It's old and dinged, but cleaner than Traitor's. The cab smells of pine and lavender. I try not to like it.

We don't speak, which is perfectly fine with me. My meds are starting to kick in. The fuzzy, floating feeling works its way through my body, like my head is a balloon and my neck is the string.

Before I know it we're at Traitor's house. My feet barely hit the grass before Skunky is squealing away. Whatever. I'm too tired to care. I fumble up the stairs and collapse into bed, ready to forget the entire damn day.

The Farmer Gazette

Murder Suspect Has a History of Violence

By Sam Lawson
Staff Writer

Is Nathaniel Fuller the victim he claims, or is something more sinister lurking beneath his skin? The now 15-year-old, arrested on suspicion of murdering his father, community leader Jefferson Fuller, has quite the history of violence and aggression.

Neighbors say when he was just 8 years old, Nathaniel attacked his best friend with a knife. The friend, who was 12 at the time, had to receive emergency care and almost 100 stitches for the deep gash Nathaniel left in his stomach.

It doesn't stop there. The Sheriff's Department claims there are at least a dozen similar attacks across the county that they attribute to Fuller. Who knows how many have gone unreported?

Who is this boy really? Damaged victim? Or menacing murderer?

Continued A5.

595

On my second day of school, the halls are silent, but the place is electric with hostility. It buzzes in the spaces where conversation should be—a lamp with faulty wiring. The counselor must've said something to everyone. The other kids whisper and point and stare. I can't hear what they're saying, but I can guess. Their narrowed eyes and tight-lipped frowns say enough.

The girl from the water fountain catches my eye and immediately whispers something to the large guy beside her.

Please don't let this be another Thomas Mayes incident. I don't want to have to walk around with a knife on me all the time—if I can even find one. Traitor's are all locked up along with his guns.

I find my locker without confrontation, but can't figure out how to get the damn thing open. I turn the dial a million times, but nothing works and no one offers to help.

The hall starts to empty as people head to homeroom. I'm aware of someone standing beside me, closer than anyone has gotten. Is he going to help? I turn my head and my breath catches.

A n— NO! I stop *his* voice before it can go any further. My brain sifts through all the words I know, searching for one that isn't a slur. *Black* is all I come up with, but after talking with the counselor, I don't know if that's okay or not.

Something deep in my gut wonders if it's okay to use color as an identifier at all, but I describe everything with color. Green leaves, brown desks, white refrigerators, blue sky. It's one of those things that feels like it shouldn't matter, but at the same time, it should.

Is this something I picked up from The Fort, or does everyone think this way? How am I supposed to find out if no one will talk to me?

The black guy glances over, and I realize I'm staring. I jerk back to my combination dial. He opens his locker, blocking his face, and unloads his backpack.

This is as close as I've been to someone with his skin color without attacking them.

That sounds horrible.

It *is* horrible.

I never wanted to. But it's one of those things. If I didn't attack the people *he* commanded me to go after, *he* would hurt me instead.

The instinct still rears its head, just like it did with Skunky. *His* voice rings in my ears, ordering me to slam the guy's locker door on his head. I can hear the crunch of metal on brittle bone and the snap of breaking cartilage.

I close my eyes and find the light. It isn't far this time. I beckon it close and bathe in it. The hate washes out of me. When I open my eyes again, the black guy is gone.

The bell rings and the few people left in the hall rush into classrooms. Doors close softly. I look at the map again and find my homeroom. All conversation stops the moment I poke my head through the door. Dozens of eyes sear my skin as I make my way to one of the only empty desks. In the front row.

All those eyes are behind me. All those people doing God-knows-what, talking about me, quietly taunting me, getting ready to throw things. I miss my name when the teacher calls roll. She says it three times before I remember that I'm Clemons now, not Fuller. She makes a few announcements I don't hear. Everything sounds far away. That's probably the meds Traitor made sure I took.

This morning he'd threatened to hide my pill in a piece of cheese like he would for a dog. It made me wonder why he doesn't have one. He seems like a dog guy. Although, any pet Traitor owned would probably be as mean as he is. Instead of cheese, he'd stood over me, watched as I put the pill in my mouth, and made me open up to prove I'd swallowed it.

I swallow hard now, almost as though I can feel the phantom pill haunting my throat. I fiddle with one of my pencils as a distraction, flipping it between my fingers. It slips and flies through the air, landing under a desk in the next row.

The guy beside me leans over and stares at it, then looks at me with wide eyes.

Instead of picking it up and giving it back, he pushes it my direction with his toe. It rolls in front of my desk. I have to slide out of my seat to retrieve it. Thanks, asshole.

Traitor either picked the nastiest school he could find, or most people in the "normal" world are almost as cold and mean as The Fort.

I let the meds float me from class to class. Each one is exactly the same. Full of wide, gaping stares and harsh whispers. This must be how zoo animals feel. I'm surrounded by an invisible cage, separated from everyone. I can live with that. As long as the cage stays between us, as long as nothing shatters it and lets the beast out of its enclosure, I'll be all right.

And so will they.

At The Fort, we were all animals, free to roam and destroy each other if necessary. The world is safer if I'm in a cage.

I spend each class period with my head down, scrawling 595 in my notebook and making lists of everything that could possibly be in Traitor's trunk. Anything to avoid all the eyes boring into my skull.

Each teacher gives me a textbook and a stack of handouts. By lunch, my backpack is so heavy I'm afraid the straps will break.

The long rectangular lunch tables in the center of the room are packed. Only the one on the far wall is mostly empty. I sit alone at the end and eat the turkey sandwich

I made this morning. The meat is warm from being in my backpack all day and the bread is squished and stale.

I choke down the disgusting sandwich and scan the room. Real school isn't like anything I've ever known.

And it's not like on TV, either. Everyone isn't separated into neat categories. Guys with thick, geeky-looking glasses laugh with guys in "Lewiston High Football" T-shirts. The pretty girls sit with the not-so-pretty ones. The kids dressed all in black are mixed in with the ones in tight jeans and cowboy boots.

Whites and blacks and Mexicans and Or—Asians. Everyone here seems to get along with everyone else.

Except me.

No one even looks at me. They all laugh and talk easily. Clapping each other on the back and pushing each other playfully.

It's shocking how carefree they are. Everything at The Fort was tense and strained. I bet these kids have never been afraid their teasing would turn violent. Never had to worry about getting, literally, stabbed in the back. Never wondered what evil missions their parents would have waiting when they got home. If they'd have to punch someone until their face was bloody, or curb-stomp them until their face completely collapsed in on itself like a crumpled paper bag.

Suddenly, I can't watch anymore.

I shove the last bite of sandwich in my mouth and go back to my locker to try to unload some of these books. My combination is supposed to be 31–17–4, but as I run through the numbers over and over again, it feels like a cruel joke.

"Pass the first number," I mumble. "Pass the second, to the third." I lift the handle but it doesn't slide. "Ugh!" I hit the door with the side of my fist.

"That only helps on the freshman lockers," a deep voice says.

Startled, I turn. The black guy is beside me again. He's slightly taller than me, and a little more muscular, with a fuzz of hair on his head. I want to touch it, to see if it's as hard and brittle as it looks—like steel wool—or if it's coarse and springy like a sheep. I realize I'm staring like a weirdo and drop my gaze to his nice clothes. His bright green polo fits well and his dark jeans aren't the slightest bit baggy. Shit. That was probably racist. Honestly, though, his clothes are better than most people in this place. It makes me self-conscious about my thrift-store jeans and faded T-shirt.

He smoothly turns his own combination dial and tosses a book into his locker. I start to twist my dial again, but he swats my hand away.

"Dude. I can't take it anymore. Look, start at zero, then turn right. What's your first number?"

"Thirty-one."

"Okay, you're gonna pass it the first time around, then go straight to it." The dial stops at thirty-one. "Next?"

"Seventeen."

"Turn left and do the same thing. Last one?"

"Four."

"Go right again, but stop soon as you get to the number." He pulls the handle and the locker door swings open. He immediately shuts it again. "You try."

It takes two attempts, but it finally opens for me. "Thanks."

"I could only watch you struggle for so long, man." He shrugs. "You look familiar. Did you transfer from Holly Bluff?"

I can feel my blood pumping. He recognizes me. Oh God. "No," I say as calmly as I can manage. "From out-of-state."

His eyebrows furrow. "I swear I've seen you somewhere."

"I just have one of those faces."

He closes his locker. "Ah, I thought I might've played ball against you. Anyway, see you around."

That was close. As I watch him lope away, it dawns on me: I had my first actual conversation with a black person. There were a handful at the Psych Center, but I rarely saw them and we never spoke. I don't know if the orderlies intentionally kept me away from them, or if it was a coincidence.

For half a second, I wish *he* was still alive. Because this moment would kill *him* all over again.

609

One day bleeds into the next. Fresh ink on damp paper. No one speaks to me. Not teachers, not students, not the black guy at the next locker, although he did smile my way a couple times. Not even Traitor talks, other than a few grunts. I'm invisible to everyone except my stinking social worker, who I *wish* would shut the hell up. All she does is babble about how good school is for me.

So I'm shocked to hear someone call my name on the Tuesday morning of my second week of school. I'm almost to the glass double doors when heels click on the pavement behind me.

"Nathaniel?" a woman says.

My blood turns to ice. Only people at The Fort and the media call me that. I told the social worker I wasn't safe. Now it's too late. I've been found.

Where can I run? Not the parking lot. Others could be waiting there. Inside? To the office to call for help?

"Nathaniel," the woman repeats. It isn't a voice I recognize. I turn my head slightly and catch a glimpse of blonde hair. "I'm Shaw Holt. Can we talk?"

Shaw Holt. I know that name, but I can't remember from where. The Fort? Is she one of the Skynbyrds? They're the women who paper areas with racist flyers. That's how it starts. The Fort picks a town—one that's too diverse, or where political tensions have been rising, or just where they think they can get a foothold for some reason. If the flyers don't get enough attention, the men step in and make sure the message can't be ignored. Graffiti, meetings, marches, even bloodshed. Whatever gets them noticed and spreads word of the cause.

I teeter on the edge of standing my ground or bolting inside. If she's small, I can overpower her before anyone else shows up. I turn and face her. Instead of the fatigues and white- or red-laced combat boots I expect, she's wearing crisply creased khakis and tan high heels.

She sweeps her long blonde hair over one shoulder and flashes a bright white smile that takes up half her face, kind of like a clown. Or a shark. The gears in my brain click into place.

Shaw Holt.

Reporter.

I remember seeing her name on articles about me. She's the woman who watched me and Traitor leave the Psych Center.

My heart rate slows slightly. She's not a physical threat, but a threat all the same. I turn and reach for the door.

She darts in front of me. "It'll just take a minute."

"How did you find me?" Somehow, my voice stays even while my insides are flipping all over. They said no one could find me.

They lied.

If this chick can, The Fort can. I have to leave. My hand slips into my pocket where I put Ms. Erica's card every day when I get dressed. I'll use the office phone. Ms. Erica will believe me. She'll insist they take me back to the Psych Center where I'll be safe.

"Finding people is what I do," the reporter says, flashing her fake smile again.

I glare at her.

The smile fades. "Fine. I hid behind the mental institution and wrote down your uncle's tag number as you drove away. From there, it was pretty easy."

"Who have you told?"

"No one. Not a soul, I swear. I'm one hundred percent alone on this."

Like her promise means anything. Reporters lie and twist and manipulate. It's their job. Not that different from The Fort when you think about it. Both feed on people's fear.

"Why would I tell anyone?" she asks. "I don't want to get scooped. I want—" A diesel engine rumbles by, bringing the first load of students. The reporter glances toward the bus. A flicker of irritation passes over her face, but it's gone so quick,

I wonder if I imagined it. "Is there somewhere else we can talk?" she asks.

"No." I go for the door again, this time yanking it open. Cold air rushes over me.

The reporter's heels tap on the tile. "I want to hear your side."

"Leave me alone," I say, a little too loudly. It echoes through the empty hallway. I face her again and lower my voice. "Go back to wherever you came from and forget where I am. *Please.*"

Not that it will matter, because soon as I call Ms. Erica, I'm out of here. But I don't want this lady hounding me at the Psych Center, either. The first few months there were miserable. Reporters camped outside, trying to sneak in, bothering other patients' families.

The reporter drops the fake smile completely. "Don't you want to get your side out there? To let people know the real Nathaniel? I want to tell *your* story. All the articles and reports about you have been unbalanced. No one has ever gotten your perspective. I don't know about you, but I don't think that's fair."

Her eyes are steady. I shift my weight. Of course I want my side out there, but on my own terms. Not from the perspective of some shady reporter who tracked me across two states.

"No thanks." I turn.

Her hand jets out and latches onto my backpack. "Just hear me out."

I jerk away and the strap rips. The bag slips off my shoulder and hits the floor with a *thunk*. "Shit! Thanks, lady."

Her eyes go wide. "I'm sorry. I didn't mean—"

"Hey!" a voice booms. "What's going on?"

I whip around. The black guy stands near the office, dressed nicer than most of the teachers dress.

"Just talking," the reporter says, smiling again.

The locker guy folds his arms. "I don't think you're supposed to be here. Let me get Principal Rawls and check."

"Actually, I was leaving." She takes a couple steps, then looks back over her shoulder. "I meant what I said. Think it over."

She walks away as the first wave of students enter the building. Her blonde head bobs through the crowd and disappears behind the bus.

I kneel and scoop up my torn bag. It wasn't much, but it was mine.

"Hey, man, you okay?" The black guy appears beside me, eyes narrowed.

"Yeah, fine."

"Who was that?"

I sling the intact strap over one shoulder. "No one. Thanks for—"

"No problem," he says. "They don't call me the Bodyguard for nothing."

"Who calls you the Bodyguard?"

He laughs. "The basketball team. I hold the record for taking the most charges in a season, although I'm looking to break that this year. You like basketball?"

"Yeah. It's kind of a big deal in K—" My face flushes. "Um, where I come from."

"And where's that?" The Bodyguard walks toward our lockers.

I start to follow, then stop short, glancing back at the office. I can call Ms. Erica about the reporter or continue talking to the only person who's been nice to me since I moved here. I trot to catch up to the Bodyguard. I can call Ms. Erica later.

"It's nowhere important."

He raises an eyebrow. "Can't be all bad if they like basketball."

I hitch up my lopsided backpack. "Guess not." Geez, I suck at conversation. We reach our lockers and toss our stuff inside.

He starts to walk away, but turns back at the last second. "Hey, what are you doing after school?"

"Huh?"

"Want to hang out?"

I rock back on my heels. He can't be serious. I don't think anyone has ever asked me that. Kelsey never asked. She told. I can picture her clearly, plopping down in the desk beside me, scooting it so close to mine that her hair brushed my arm. *"You're coming over today."* No choice. I never had a choice with Kelsey.

"What . . . what do you want to do?" I ask.

He grins. "I'll meet you after the last bell. Okay?"

Traitor's usually waiting out front as soon as the bell rings. He'll be pissed if I'm late. "Okay."

The Bodyguard sticks his hand out. "My real name's Brandon, by the way."

I shake. His hand is warm. "Nate. Why are you being nice to me?" I ask as he pulls his hand away.

"Because I don't think you're like everyone says, Nate."

"What does everyone say?"

The bell rings. "We'll talk after school," the Bodyguard—Brandon—says, before he's swept up in the flow of students heading to homeroom.

✧

I wait by my locker after the last bell, but Brandon doesn't show. This is a setup. He and his basketball friends are going to dump pig's blood on me, or something. Right when I'm about to give up, he walks briskly down the hall, out of breath, tucking his white polo into his creased khaki shorts with one hand.

"Sorry. Coach held us long because Fletcher couldn't finish his sprints without complaining the whole time. I swear if he keeps this up, I'm gonna hide my sweaty socks in his car."

"Oh, it's cool." But I'm looking around for strings and buckets and other signs of the prank.

Brandon stuffs some books in his bag and shoulders it. "Ready?"

"Where are we going?"

"You'll see." He leads the way out the front doors, almost colliding with Traitor. "Excuse me, sir," Brandon says.

Traitor's eyes settle on me. "Nate, where the hell have you been?"

"Waiting on Brandon. We're going, well I don't know yet, but somewhere."

Brandon sticks out his hand. "Brandon Kingsley."

Traitor's eyes widen. "Whose idea was this?" he demands.

Brandon drops his outstretched hand back to his side. "Mine, sir."

"He asked if I wanted to hang out this afternoon," I say. "Is that a problem?" The beast is waking up in my gut. Someone is finally nice to me, and Traitor comes along to ruin it. I clench and unclench my fists and close my eyes. I can't lose control here. Not now.

"No," Traitor says. "It's not a . . . I mean . . . Nate, can I speak to you alone a minute?"

My eyes fly open. The darkness closes in.

"I'll wait over here," Brandon says. He retreats to the sidewalk near Traitor's truck.

"What in the hell do you think you're doing?" Traitor spits.

"Hanging out with a guy from school," I growl. "What's wrong with that?"

Traitor presses me against the door and I drop my broken bag. "If you plan to hurt that boy, I swear to God, I'll—"

My breaths come in fast, shallow bursts. "*Hurt* him? That's what you think I'll do? So what, I convinced him to ask me to do something this afternoon so I could lure him away and kill him? Another notch in my belt?" I shove Traitor away.

He stumbles, but recovers quickly and pushes me back. I'm several inches taller than my uncle, but his burst of strength catches me off guard. "Look here, you little nazi shit. That black boy gets one scratch on him, and I'm calling the cops, you hear me?"

The beast is roaring now, screaming for me to rip Traitor's head off. My flimsy thrift-store shoes aren't heavy boots, but I bet I could still do damage. I catch sight of Brandon by Traitor's truck. His brows are furrowed. His cell phone is out, like he's ready to call the police, himself.

I think about the light. Breathe. *Breathe.* Traitor has one thing right. I let the beast loose and it's jail for me. No more Psych Center.

I can't do juvie again. That place only fed the beast. Too much longer and there wouldn't have been any light left. Thankfully, my attorney saw what was happening and got me moved.

I won't be so lucky a second time.

I leer at Traitor. "His name isn't 'black boy,' it's Brandon. And if your first thought is hurting him, then maybe you're the nazi shit, not me."

All the color drains from Traitor's face. I push past him and hitch up my backpack. "Let's go," I call to Brandon.

"You all right?" he asks me for the second time today.

"Yeah. Let's get out of here."

✧

The river. That's where Brandon's taking me. We stopped at a large brick house long enough for him to drop off his books and grab a couple fishing poles. I craned my neck to see inside, but couldn't catch more than a hint of the dark entryway. What is a black family's house like? Especially a family like Brandon's?

Is *that* racist? I hate that I don't know these things, and I don't have anyone to ask.

Poles in hand, Brandon leads me down a path through the woods.

I haven't entered the woods since that day. The closest I've come is the hole with the tree where I dump everything during yard work.

I keep telling myself this isn't my forest of blood and shame and fear. It's similar to my woods in Kentucky, but . . . warmer, more alive. Dense underbrush, thick oak trees, elms, and maples, and tall pines towering over them all. And it's quiet, but not *bad* quiet. Not silent. Cicadas sing, frogs croak, and mosquitoes the size of quarters buzz around my head. By the time we reach the water, I already have at least five angry red welts rising on my arms. I'd have more if I'd worn shorts like Brandon. He doesn't seem to have a bite on him. Is that a black thing? Do they not bite dark skin?

Not that I can be too thankful for my jeans. I only have one pair that isn't ripped, and I'm wearing them today of all days. The denim sticks to my sweaty legs, making it hard to walk after a while. At least when we hit the river, the woods clear enough to let a little breeze through.

Brandon rests the rods against a tree. "So, what do you think?"

I glance around, trying to figure out what he's talking about. All I see is woods and brown water and a muddy riverbank. "About what?"

"This." He spreads his arms wide. "I figured, being new and all, you should see a place in town that doesn't suck. Lewiston doesn't exactly have a lot going for it." He laughs. "This is the best spot in the whole damn town."

It doesn't look like much more than a mudhole to me. Brandon follows my gaze to the water's edge.

"It's kind of low right now, but trust me, there's good fishing here in the summer. I caught a ten-pound bass right over there a couple years ago."

"Wow," I say, and I mean it. I can't fish for shit.

He smiles as he talks. Little creases form at the sides of his eyes, like the pictures of Santa Claus on the Christmas cards in the Psych Center in December.

"The guys and I use this spot more for drinking beer than for fishing, so I can't say if there are any fish here right now or not. I thought we could give it a shot, though."

"Sure. Okay." I can't remember the last time I went fishing. Probably with Kelsey in the pond at the edge of The Fort. She always caught a bunch while I got nothing but mud and sticks.

Brandon flicks his wrist and the line sails out to the middle of the water. He makes it look easy.

"There's something about this place," he says. "You just sort of forget the rest of the world exists. That's probably not too impressive." He laughs and reels in the empty lure. "What about where you're from? Please tell me it's more exciting than this."

My body tenses. There's only one place where I'm from where the world could fall away: the holly bush in the woods with Kelsey. And even then, it never completely disappeared—not like Brandon's describing—it only faded a little. No matter how much I tried to shut it out, a part of me was always aware that the shadows lurking in the trees were attached to real monsters. That's not something I can talk about, though. Not that the holly bush really counts anymore, anyway.

I shrug. "There's not much where I'm from. I don't like talking about it. It . . . wasn't a good place."

Brandon's mouth turns down slightly.

He casts again. "I hope we're different then."

I stare at my fishing pole.

Brandon teases the line across the water. "The people here aren't that bad," he says. "If you give them a chance."

"They haven't really given me a chance."

Brandon arches an eyebrow. He looks like he wants to say something else, but focuses on the dancing lure.

"Brandon . . ." I hesitate. He's been nice so far, but I don't know if we're to the point where he'd be honest with me. I decide to risk it. "What have you heard about me?"

"Doesn't matter, man," he says. "Don't listen to that shit."

I twirl the fishhook. "Could you tell me anyway?"

He keeps his eyes on the water. "You're fresh out of juvie. That's not a secret."

I get hot all over. "How do you know?"

"I mean, everyone knows about you hitting Maddie on the first day. There's a debate about whether it was intentional, but come on. You didn't even know her. Why would you do that on purpose? Unless you're Superman, I'm pretty sure you couldn't see her on the other side of that door. Anyway, I know Maddie, and she tends to exaggerate."

He reels in and casts again. "It only made things worse that Maddie peeked in your file."

My hook catches on the dead skin at the end of my thumb. "What? How?"

"Mrs. Rawls left it on the counter the first day. Maddie didn't read much. Just enough to cause trouble, if you ask me. Then Caitlyn Somers said you threatened her at the water fountain." He starts to reel in again, but stops. "It's cyclic. You have a bad first day, folks learn you had a rough past, they spread rumors, you hear them and withdraw even more, which reinforces the rumors that you're scary and mean, so everyone stays away from you."

Yeah, if only they weren't rumors. I guess I did kind of threaten Water Fountain Girl. I'm not exactly a small guy, and I know how frightening I can look. I've seen all my expressions on *his* face more times than I can count.

At least one person at school is willing to give me a chance. But I can't help but wonder how Brandon would react if he knew my actual past.

"You're not scary and mean, though," Brandon says. "You seem like a nice guy to me."

But I'm not a nice guy. Not deep down. I can pretend to be nice, but underneath the sheep's skin, I'm still a wolf. I still have *his* blood in me, and nothing will ever change that.

Brandon claps me on the back. "Don't worry about it. You'll prove them wrong. Let's move downstream aways and see if we can't get one of these suckers to bite."

The Farmer Gazette

The Secret Life of a Killer

By Sam Lawson
Staff Writer

Most teenage boys obsess about the girl they like, sports, or getting laid. Not Nathaniel Fuller.

His obsessions are blood and hate. A known violent Skinhead Neo-Nazi, Nathaniel has a well-documented history of brutal attacks on innocent victims, mostly minorities and homosexuals. Of the unsolved attacks on African Americans, Jews, and Muslims, witnesses put Fuller at the scene of almost all of them.

It should be noted that not all Skinheads are violent, and not all share Nathaniel's hate. Al Bolton, a friend of Fuller's father, said The Fort, where he lives, is a peaceable place.

"We're united with a common purpose, to stop the genocide of the White People, but we do it quietly," said Bolton. "We've chosen to live separately from society. Occasionally, we distribute flyers to alert others to this growing issue and invite them to join our cause. We don't condone violent acts like Nate's."

How did Nathaniel stray so far from the peaceable path? It wasn't without help. Bolton says there is a small subsect who strayed from Jefferson Fuller's teachings. This group has all but disappeared in the wake of Jefferson's murder and Nathaniel's incarceration.

Then there's the mystery of his mother. Sources say Mae Fuller kidnapped Nathaniel when he was four. The pair drifted across the country, leaving a trail of fake names and unpaid bills behind them, until Mae was shot in a gas station robbery.

Why was she alone that day? Where was Nathaniel? Was the death of Mae Fuller actually random, or did her son kill both his parents?

Only one thing is certain: the devil is behind bars. We can only hope the court decides to try him as an adult, so he'll stay imprisoned, and away from society, for a long, long time.

610

The bed is as hard and cold as a cave floor. Every time I roll over, a spring stabs me with its angry fingers. *"You're nothing,"* the springs squeak. *"You have nothing. You don't matter."*

I was actually good with nothing. Then Brandon came along and was friendly. He thinks he has me pegged, that I'm a "nice guy." He doesn't know shit. I've rocked from grateful that he looked closer at me than the others to pissed that he made me question the cage I've constructed around myself. I was doing fine on my own. I didn't need a friend. Not until I realized how good it feels for someone to talk to me like I'm a human instead of a monster.

Now I just have one more person to lose.

I shove my pillow over the poky spring and roll over again.

Brandon and his mom dropped me off at Traitor's place around dark. He was waiting on the porch. When the car pulled into the yard, Traitor watched me get out, then went in the house and locked himself in his room.

No dinner. No list of chores. Nothing but a slammed door.

I fixed a bologna sandwich, did my homework, and went to bed.

Instead of falling into my normal, hazy half sleep, I watched the dented metal clock on the nightstand. The hands methodically knocked me into a new day, calling out the time that has passed since that night—*610, 610, 610.*

I stay on the crappy bed, listening to the stubborn clock until I can't take it anymore, and get up, stuffing it under the curtains in the trash can, before pacing the room.

"You'll prove them wrong." Brandon's words rattle in my head like loose dice in a board game box.

How can he be so sure? He barely knows me. Hell, *I* barely know me. I know the person my mother started to build in me, and I know the person The Fort twisted me into. I don't know what I am now.

A murderer?

A victim?

What does *his* blood make me?

Certainly not a nice guy, but I can't see where I fall on the scale, or where I fit in this screwed-up world.

One thing The Fort did well was give people a place. They took your weaknesses and made them strengths. Most members had spent their entire lives being told they weren't good enough, that they were dumb and worthless. The Fort turned that on its head. They'd tell recruits the problem was that they were *too* good, so good others had to hold them down. But The Fort, well, it would lift them up, make them what they were meant to be.

Kids who'd been bullied transformed into the aggressors. People who felt like they didn't belong suddenly had a group where they felt like they fit in. A safe place. A warped clubhouse.

Only a handful of members were actually born in The Fort—people like me and Kelsey and the Connor brothers. Most, like Thomas Mayes, found their way there. They were runaways, kids whose parents were abusive or neglectful, or ones who didn't have families at all. People who were young and hurting, who just wanted to belong somewhere.

It seems kind of sad until you see what they became. Until you witness the damage they leave in their wakes.

Not that it's only kids. Lots of adults look for a home with the demented family at The Fort, too. Adults who had been those bullied, neglected kids once, or who had shared a cell with a *bruder*, or who'd joined the *bruderhood* for protection, either in prison or on the street.

The recruiters are good. They don't start off hocking hate like street-corner preachers. They spot the beaten and broken and gradually lead them along the path to Hell, dressing up hate as pride and rights.

He forced me on a few recruiting trips, but *he* quickly learned I hurt the cause more than helped it, so *he* gave me other duties.

The pitch always started the same.

They'd spot some poor asshole and ask about his heritage. Irish or German or French or Swedish or whatever. If the potential recruit didn't know, they'd prompt them. "You look like a good Irishman. Strong jaw and quick wit." Made them proud of who they were, probably for the first time in their lives.

Then they'd feed on the recruit's weaknesses, searching for an old wound so they could dig their fingers into it, squeezing and scraping until it was fresh, oozing with all those feelings of worthlessness that drove him to whatever dump they happened to be sitting in. All leading to the source of all their problems.

Jews, gays, blacks, Mexicans, Asians.

If they stayed around other good Irishmen or Germans or Swedes, people who were the same species, they wouldn't have those problems.

The recruiters always slipped that last bit under the radar. According to the neo-nazis, anyone who wasn't "White" was a completely different, and inferior, species, as valuable as mangy, stray dogs. And, of course they knew just the place where recruits could be around other strong "Whites." Where they could matter and would be important. Where they would never have to feel weak again. Where they could help destroy those that led to all their problems in the first place.

Except it's all a lie. The people don't matter. Only the cause does.

I gradually learned that I was nothing.

My mother had taught me I was smart and worthy of love and respect. That only I could dictate what I did with my body and mind. But I only got four years of her kindness. Important years, but short ones.

And that power they preached at The Fort was intoxicating.

Because I *didn't* have control over my body there. Other people dictated what I had to do and when. Enough of that over enough time starts to eat away at your mind. In the end, I wasn't any better than anyone else—same low self-esteem and loss of control, same fear, acted out in the same ways.

I bundled all those feelings inside, and since I couldn't unleash them on the person who caused them, I let them out on strangers.

"You'll prove them wrong."

Will I? Or will I prove them right?

I'm afraid if I dig too deep, that nice guy my mother started creating will be gone, and all I'll find will be the beast.

Brandon has the luxury of living entirely on the outside, without fear of showing his true self to anyone.

There was a guy at the Psych Center who loved old cartoons. He had a movie with a ton of them that he'd watch over and over in the common room. One was about this kid who swung over the swing-set bar and turned inside out. That's Brandon. He's Inside-Out Boy. In one afternoon, I learned his favorite smell is fresh baked bread and his favorite color is blue. I know he has a scar on his thumb where a fishhook got stuck when he was nine, and another at the base of his skull from when he fell off a slide on his fifth birthday.

He knows I live with an uncle I can't stand, pass out occasionally, and have a reporter hounding me, though he doesn't know why. Surface things.

A breeze comes through the open window, brushing my face with inviting pine scent and suddenly I can't stay in this house anymore. I slip into the closest T-shirt and jeans and pick up my beat-up tennis shoes.

I'm learning where the creakiest floorboards are. I step over them, shifting my weight to move as quietly as possible, and open my door. Traitor's light is off and he's snoring softly. I haven't figured out how sound of a sleeper he is, so I walk carefully to the stairs.

The top board groans and I stop, balanced on my toes. I have to grab the bannister to keep from tipping over. My pulse thumps so hard I can feel the veins in my wrist working.

He was such a light sleeper that a loud thought would wake *him*. And *he* didn't appreciate being woken up. *He*'d fly out of bed so fast I sometimes wondered if *he* ever slept at all. I was certain *he* stayed behind *his* bedroom door, waiting for me to make a sound so *he* could beat me with *his* wide belt.

The last time I'd gotten up in the middle of the night was to sneak canned food into the woods. Not the hole under the holly, but a different spot closer to the perimeter fence where Kelsey and I could collect them quickly when we ran. We'd been hiding food and cash out there for over a year, waiting until we were both sixteen so we could legally drive and work.

I was lucky *he* caught me before I picked up the food. No way could I have explained carrying four cans of Spam outside in the middle of the night. *Lucky* is a relative term, I guess. *He* whipped me so hard, I had to throw out the pants I was wearing because I bled through them.

Traitor doesn't seem to have that particular trait, though. He doesn't run out of his room, belt looped in his fist.

Still, I take my time going down the stairs, placing each step like it'll crumble beneath me. When I hit the front porch, I shove my feet into my shoes without untying them and break into a run, careful to skirt the hole at the tree line. The woods aren't so intimidating after my afternoon with Brandon. The trees reach their leafy arms toward me, welcoming back their old friend. I rush into their grasp without giving myself time to reconsider, ducking under branches and swatting brush aside. Brambles stick to my jeans and damp cobwebs cling to my hands.

It's glorious.

I run until I reach a clearing barely big enough for two people to stand. The full moon peeks through the trees, watching me. I slump against a pine, breathing heavily, then sink to the dewy ground. Beads of cool sweat dot my forehead and under my arms.

Most people at The Fort, as bad and scary as they were, were afraid of the woods at night, but I always felt more comfortable there than anywhere else. Until that night.

Now I'm back home again.

Night is the best time to be among the trees. When it's most quiet and calm. When bats swoop and owls hunt and spiders spin webs, all hoping to catch a late-night snack. When I don't have to worry about what I say or what people think or if my lies are consistent. It's only me, and the other dark creatures, and the spying moon.

The night woods are my river.

It's been tainted for long enough. It's time for me to take it back.

My fingers close around my button.

I love the forest. Not just the one back home, or the place with Kelsey. All of it.

And I like the color green. Vibrant green, like leaves after a heavy rain.

I close my eyes and inhale the sweet earth, excited to tell Brandon something real about myself.

✧

The ceiling has a leak. Water drips on my face lightly at first, then heavier. I hate this old-ass cabin. Guess I can add "fix the roof" to my list of chores for today.

I stretch and open my eyes to an awning of leaves reaching toward a halo of watered-down gray sky. Adrenaline bursts through my body, jolting me completely awake. I'm on the wet ground in the woods. Is *he* coming?

I'm on my feet, quick as a snake strike, ears pricked for *his* angry scream.

But there's no snow beneath me, only fat raindrops from above.

The air is muggy and heavy, not cold and thin. The branches are thick with leaves that are just starting to turn.

This isn't a flashback.

Holy shit, it's real. I fell asleep in the woods. It's raining too hard to figure out where the sun is, but knowing how little I sleep, there's basically no chance I slept through the day. It must be morning. Traitor might not be awake yet.

I turn toward the cabin and run as fast as possible through the underbrush, so fast, I almost forget about the hole. I leap over it at the last second. The toe of my shoe slips on the soft dirt at the edge. I catch myself before I fall in, scrabble back upright, and take off again.

When I get to the porch, I stop and listen. There's no clatter of dishes or clomp of boots. I tug off my wet socks and shoes and ease the door open. Water rattles through the old plumbing.

Traitor's in the shower.

I take the stairs two at a time, no longer caring if the boards creak. The water cuts off right as I'm closing my bedroom door. I strip off my wet clothes, shove them under the bed, and jump under the covers in case he decides to poke his head in.

A few minutes later, Traitor pounds on my door. "Nate, get a move on. We're late."

"I'm up." I stay a little longer, though, catching my breath. That was way too close. I can't do that again.

As I slowly get up again, I try to forget that I feel more rested after my nap in the woods than I have in years.

✧

I linger at my locker longer than necessary, hoping to catch Brandon before class. I feel ridiculous just standing here, so I slowly open my broken backpack and unload my books, then arrange them in my locker.

He's usually here by now. I twist around and glance at the giant clock mounted on the wall. Five minutes until the bell. I rearrange my books again. Maybe he's avoiding me. I don't think I did anything to offend him. God, I hope not. But I didn't think *Oriental* was offensive either, so who knows? The bell rings and I slam my locker. He's probably late. People can be late. It happens all the time.

Cutting through the crowd, I duck into homeroom. The morning slips by like rain sheeting off a tin roof. At lunch, I sit at my corner table, casting a sideways glance at the group Brandon always sits with. He's not there. Worse, his friends are quieter. They're usually the rowdy guys, cutting loud jokes and throwing food. Not today. Today they're mellow.

Oh my God. Did something happen to Brandon? A wreck or some other accident?

I twist, ears pricked for a hint of conversation. A guilty feeling gnaws at me, even though it couldn't have been my fault, because usually when people disappear after I've been around them, it *is* my fault.

The intercom buzzes. "Nate Clemons, come to the principal's office."

Dozens of faces swivel toward me. My muscles tense, ready for a fight. Or flight.

This is it. Something terrible happened to Brandon and his mom. I was the last person seen with them. There will be cops in the hallway or waiting at the office.

Run.

I stand slowly and throw my lunch away. I can't look guilty. I did nothing wrong. Traitor saw them alive and well last night. Surely, he'd vouch for me. Wouldn't he?

As I make my way down the hall, I rehearse what I'll say: *They were fine when I left them. My uncle is a witness. They were fine.*

The principal waits by the front desk, alone. When I enter the office, she holds out a brown box. "We are not a post office, Nate. Next time, have your packages delivered somewhere else."

I rock back on my heels, caught off guard. "My packages?"

She sighs and thrusts the box in my hands. "Don't play dumb with me. Your name is right there. And don't do it again. We have the authority to search these things, you know."

I stare at the box, stunned. "Um, yeah. Sorry." I stumble into the hall and tear it open. An envelope rests on top of a mound of tissue paper.

> *Nathaniel,*
>
> *Sorry about the backpack. I hope this is a suitable replacement. I'm serious about wanting to help you. Here's my card. Call when you're ready to talk.*
>
> *Shaw Holt*

A sleek black business card is stapled to the note. *Shaw Holt, Senior Correspondent, News First Network.* She's awfully pushy. A random gift isn't going to loosen my lips. I crumple the note in my fist. Inside the box is a new backpack, all black with red ribbing.

I don't want to use it, but it's better than the crappy thing I'm lugging around. I dump the box in one of the big trash cans in the hall and reluctantly keep the bag. I'm about to throw away the letter and the business card, but shove them in my pocket at the last minute. I may need proof a reporter is hounding me, especially if Brandon doesn't turn up soon. I don't know if she'd do anything to him to get me to talk, but I don't know that she wouldn't, either. A little extra precaution never hurt anyone.

611

I walk into school wearing the new backpack, and feel like everyone is staring at it—at me—but it's probably all in my head. Traitor grilled me about it when I got home yesterday. I told him my old one completely gave out so the school found one in the lost and found. He seemed to buy it. It's not like he's too eager to get me a new one himself.

Brandon isn't at his locker again this morning.

I tell myself not to freak out, but this is what happens whenever I let someone in. They disappear. I shut my locker, trying to ignore the ball of worry knotting itself in my gut.

"Nate!"

I startle at the sound of my name, cursing the meds for making me jumpy. Brandon walks down the hall, waving something. The knot unwinds inside me. It takes all of my willpower not to sigh in relief. He's okay. A grin spreads across my face. It feels strange.

Brandon shifts his pace to a fast walk and catches up with me. "Check it out!" he says, brandishing a small rectangle of paper. "My parents finally caved. I got my license!" He smiles so wide I can count all thirty-two teeth. "My brother took me yesterday, then we drove around all day."

"That's awesome," I say. His enthusiasm is like a virus, spreading to me whether I like it or not.

"Isn't it? I turned sixteen *months* ago. Think of all that sweet freedom." He looks at the card, still beaming. "We have to celebrate. Let's go cruisin' this afternoon."

"Cruisin'?"

"Driving around because we can. How about it?"

I want to say no. I'm afraid of how glad I am to see him. I should end this right now, but Brandon's excitement is contagious. I don't know which would be worse: being the loner everyone is afraid of, or letting someone know the real me. Well, the version of me I'm pretending to be.

"Sure," I hear myself say. "We'll go cruisin'."

"Awesome," he says.

"So, uh, who all is going?" I ask, suddenly terrified of what I just agreed to do.

He claps me on the back. "Not sure yet. You're the first person I've asked. It'll be fun, though." He beams. The bell rings and he turns toward his homeroom, waving his license like a flag. "Hey, Fletch, check it out, man. I can drive! Rainey! Look! Freeeedom!"

Why does he want to hang out with me again? He has all these other friends. The whole school seems to love him. He weaves through the crowd, handing out high fives the way the Skynbyrds distributed flyers.

I'm not ready for this. I barely got through an afternoon with just us. No way in hell am I going to make it in a car full of guys. I'm not a cannonball kind of person. Back on the run with Mom, I always eased into the motel pools, letting my body adjust a little at a time. This feels too much like jumping in.

I watch Brandon before heading to my own class. His joy infects the whole school. Everyone who passes him ends up with a smile on their face.

I want that.

I want to be able to cannonball, like Brandon.

It smacks me like a leather belt. I don't want people to fear me. I want them to smile when they see me. But I don't know how to get there. It's like everyone else is standing on some tall-ass platform and I'm at the bottom with no way up.

Especially not with *his* shadow holding me down. It trails behind me, a dark stain of hatred and fear and paranoia that I can't shake loose.

Everyone disappears into their classrooms, leaving me in the cold hallway. Just me and my shadow.

✧

Brandon is at the lockers when I get there after the last bell.

He grins and jangles his keys.

Traitor's giant key ring flashes across my mind. If I could convince him to let me get my license and drive, then I could get my hands on those keys and at least look through them. That's about as likely as the sky turning green and raining candy, though.

"So, who else is coming?" I ask, impressed that my voice doesn't betray my nerves. That's probably the meds.

"Just us. Fletcher has to run some errands for his mom, and Rainey is going down to Florence for new basketball shoes."

Relief washes over me. This is easier. The river was me putting a foot in. Today, I'm moving a step deeper.

We head through a door I've never used and angle toward the student parking lot, matching strides.

I wonder what *he* would do if *he* saw me right now?

What would *I* do?

The thought throws me out of step with Brandon. Would I react on instinct if *he* told me to hurt Brandon once we're alone on some back road? Or could I fight it? I'd like to think I could. I hope so. I haven't thought about hurting Brandon since I met him. I feel like I'm in control for the first time, but the beast has a way of taking over sometimes. In my head, I repeat Ms. Erica's words to me before I left the Psych Center. I'm in control. As long as I take my meds. And I've taken them every day since the last flashback. I think of those signs at construction sites: NO RACISM RELATED ACCIDENTS IN 611 DAYS.

I can ignore *his* shadow.

I can do this.

I follow Brandon through the student lot. It's mostly full of white people. Do they only integrate during school hours? Is hanging out with a black guy after school weird? Is this not okay? Several folks lean against their cars talking. Water Fountain Girl sits on a tailgate between the legs of the big dude she whispered to on my second day. She shoots me a glare that could make stone explode.

Because of our run-in or because I'm with Brandon?

Brandon unlocks the doors to an old green Camry and throws his bag on the backseat.

"How dare you?" someone shrieks.

Guilty heat blasts my cheeks, reminding me of the first time I got caught stealing from Home Grown Books back in Farmer. I feel like all my evil thoughts are tattooed on my forehead. My head jerks toward the yell. Nose Girl stands by a beat-up Camaro a row over. A guy grabs her wrist. Nose Girl shoves the guy.

I slump against Brandon's Camry. It's not about me. No one seems to care who I'm with.

They would if they were in my head. I'm certain of it.

"Let *go* of me!" Nose Girl screams.

"Baby, I—" the guy pleads.

"Seriously? Did you seriously call me that?" She gets in his face and jabs her finger in his chest. "Go use your pet names somewhere else."

The guy dips his head. "Ba—Maddie, I'm sorry. Alyssa was a mistake. It meant nothing."

"That's what you said the *first* time," she yells.

Brandon shoots me a look over the roof of his car. "This is about to get good." He nods to the sidewalk behind us. A girl I recognize from my history class grins wickedly.

Pretty much everyone in the parking lot is staring at Nose Girl and the guy. My muscles tense instinctively, like a dog getting ready for a fight. Last time I saw this many people silently focused on an argument . . .

I shiver and turn back to the girl from history. She's smearing some kind of shiny, pink gunk on her lips.

"I slipped up," the guy says. "It won't happen again."

Nose Girl flaps her hand like a mouth. "Blah, blah, blah. I'm so over this. I can't even look at you. I'm changing my schedule tomorrow. And this time, I'm going through with it!"

The douchebag must've cheated on her before and she got stuck taking all her classes with him. That's why she was so upset that first day. I just made things worse.

History Chick drops her books on the car trunk beside me and strolls across the parking lot. The guy opens his mouth to say something else to Nose Girl, but History Chick reaches him before a word comes out. She slips an arm around his waist.

"Finally," she says loud enough for everyone to hear. "I don't have to share you anymore."

"Arrrrgh!" Nose Girl lunges forward and swings at the guy. He scrambles away and she falls into History Chick, who pushes Nose Girl back against the car. That sets her off.

The girls are a mass of tangled arms and flying hair. I've never seen such a thing in my life. At The Fort, girls fought no different from guys. We all learned how to throw a solid punch before most kids could string sentences together.

Everyone gapes at the screaming, scratching girls. Water Fountain tears herself out from between big dude's thighs and rushes to Nose Girl. A couple other people do the same. They try to pull the girls apart, but it's like separating two pit bulls.

The guy all but vanishes. He's exactly the kind of asshole The Fort recruits.

Brandon starts for the girls, but big dude and another couple mini-giants reach the fight first. Brandon shrugs and comes back to the car. "*Whew,*" he says. "I wanted to get in the middle of that like I want to run suicides after practice."

They manage to separate the girls and take them to opposite ends of the parking lot.

"Looks like the show's over," Brandon says. "I hope Maddie's okay. Her nose was just starting to heal. She'll be pissed if Alyssa messed it up again."

Guilty heat flames up my cheeks. "I thought everyone got along here."

He laughs. "Oh, there's drama. You just have to wait for it to bubble to the surface."

We slide into the car and back out of the lot. Seems I was wrong about this place. They don't all like each other. They've just been good about hiding their problems until now.

"That was . . . What was that?"

Brandon throws an elbow out the open window and settles into his seat. "Everyone knows Alyssa and Chris have been bumping uglies since last spring. Everyone but Maddie. They had a big fight at Fletcher's field party right before school started and called things off for the millionth time, but Maddie always goes back. Maybe she'll finally move on to someone who deserves her now."

I raise an eyebrow. Seems to me like she and the douchebag were made for each other.

Brandon glances over and catches my look. "You've only seen her bad side. She's really thoughtful and sweet when you get to know her. Like last year, she made study packs for everyone in her chem class before finals because she knew they all were stressed out. Chris kind of smothers that side of her, though."

"Holy crap. You like her."

He shrugs, not taking his eyes off the road.

I try to imagine her without the grimace, talking rather than yelling, but all I see is her twisted, angry face.

Is that what people see when they look at me? Maybe everyone has a hidden dark side waiting for the right person to bring it out. *He* brought out mine. Douchebag brings out Maddie's. I never thought to look for any brightness in her.

I realize with a start that The Fort didn't just teach me to make snap judgments of minorities, but of everyone. Although, I guess the folks in Lewiston aren't much better. Like Skunky, they all made up their minds about me before I even got to homeroom. Is this just what people do? Judge others because of how we see them, without even trying to get to know them?

Maybe there are others like Brandon, too. People with x-ray eyes that see below the surface, to the real person beneath the layers of darkness.

A smile tugs at Brandon's lips. Of all the chicks in this school, she's the last one I imagined someone like him would have a crush on. There's still so much I don't know about him. So much I don't know about all these people.

Apparently, everyone has secrets. And secrets have a way of coming out.

What's going to happen if someone finds out my secrets?

"What about you?" he asks. "Any girls on your radar?"

Only one, but she's a million miles away. I shake my head, but I wait a beat too long and Brandon catches it. "Yeah, there is! Who?"

My instinct is to clam up, but something tugs at me. This could be my chance. Get out some snippets of truth and see how it goes. "There's a girl. Back home. There was, anyway."

Brandon nods knowingly. "Ah, had to leave her behind."

My blood runs cold. That's exactly what I did. I left her. An image of Kelsey's swelling eye and bloodied nose pops into my head so suddenly tears spring to my eyes. I blink them away before Brandon notices. "Something like that," I say.

"Wish I could say you'll find someone here to help you move on, but the pool is pretty small."

I shrug. "I'm not looking anyway."

Brandon turns onto a road that's more gravel than asphalt. The tiny rocks rattle in the wheel wells. "Sounds like this chick was serious. What's she like?"

I close my eyes and see Kelsey's long hair pooling under her head on the forest floor, her deep brown eyes drinking in every word of our stolen history books. *Beautiful* is the first word that comes to me. "Strong," I say instead. "She had more strength than anyone I've ever met."

Even though Kelsey gave up our secret, even with her mistakes, the fact that she held on for as long as she did—it took them hours to break her—shows that she had serious guts.

"Like this one time. She found a kitten, but the thing was covered in mange. Her parents told her to get rid of it." I don't tell Brandon that they wanted Kelsey to kill it. The first innocent blood they wanted her to spill. "Of course, she didn't. She hid it in the crawl space under her house—which she was terrified of because we were like ten and there were spiders down there—but every day before and after school she'd army crawl under there to feed and pet it."

It was a pitiful thing, with these scabby spots where fur should be. Kelsey didn't care. She used to bring it to the woods with her, bundled in her coat, its tiny gray head poking through a gap in the buttons. She'd loved that damn cat. Right up until the day her mom found it.

Kelsey cried for a month after. But only in front of me. At home, she'd raise her chin and defiantly looked her parents dead in the eyes as they whipped her for disobeying them.

"And she loved pictures of horses."

Brandon raises an eyebrow. "Pictures?"

"Yeah. She thought they were gorgeous creatures, but she hated to see them in real life, trapped behind fences. She always said they were meant to run free, so that's how she liked to see them. In pictures with the wind in their manes, being wild."

"What's her name?"

I pause. Her name might jar a memory of my trial loose. But not telling him would be weird. "Kelsey."

The name feels funny in my mouth. It's been so long since I've said it out loud.

"Sorry you had to move, man," Brandon says. "She sounds pretty awesome."

"She was my best friend. I miss her more than I miss my mother."

It's a tiny fraction of fact, but it's the most honest thing I could ever tell him.

We turn onto an abandoned county road and Brandon opens the sunroof. The wind is hot, but not uncomfortable. Kind of refreshing. Freeing.

Or maybe it's telling a truth that's freeing.

"You know, I think I have a place like your river," I say.

"Yeah?"

"Yeah. The woods at night. That's my place."

Brandon glances at me. "See? I told you Lewiston isn't all bad." We hit a straightaway. "Now, how fast do you think this old bag will go?" He rams down on the accelerator.

I let my arm hang out the window and watch the pavement. We're moving so fast the asphalt is a blur. I can't make out any distinct shapes.

Not even a shadow.

613

I almost fell asleep in my own bed last night. I closed my eyes, starting to drift, and then the shadows came alive and choked me awake. After the third try, I finally welcomed the shadows and took to the woods.

The sun barely tints the sky when I wake up and head back inside. Traitor is at the kitchen counter sipping coffee. He's never been up this early on a Saturday. I freeze in the doorway.

His eyes narrow over the top of his cup. "Where the hell have you been?"

Shit, shit, shit. I keep calm, but brace myself, just in case. "Walking. I got up early and couldn't fall back to sleep."

He watches me carefully.

"What do you think I did, rob a bank? Kill some old lady in her sleep? Geez, can't I even walk around without you thinking I've committed a crime?"

He takes a final gulp and plonks his mug down on the counter. "Since you're already up and apparently so restless, you're comin' to work with me."

He waits for a reaction, but I don't even know what the hell he does all day. "Okay. What do I need to wear?"

"Something grubby."

"So, my regular clothes, then."

He glares. "Cut the sass."

"I'm just saying, last time I checked all my clothes were worn-out hand-me-downs, but if that's too fancy for where we're going, I'm seriously intrigued."

Traitor takes a deep breath, then turns his back on me and rinses his coffee cup. My teeth feel like they grew moss while I was outside, so I climb the stairs to brush my teeth before we leave for this mystery job.

"You'll need boots, too."

My heart thumps against my sternum, sounding so much like goose step in my ears that I want to rip it out and silence it forever.

"What size are you?" Traitor asks.

I swallow hard and keep the shake out of my voice. "Twelve, I think."

"I'm an eleven." He pushes past me on the stairs. "Try a pair of mine."

I follow him to his closet. My eyes immediately fall on the space at the back where I know the chest sits, full as a tick and waiting to burst with secrets. A single silver bracket gleams, rocketing my pulse again. My fingers itch to reach for it. To throw back the blanket and demand to know what's inside. I jam my hands in my pockets and make myself look away. A direct approach won't work on Traitor. I'll be better off relieving him of a few keys. He slides some coveralls aside and removes a pair of brown leather ranch boots. I sit on the edge of his bed and tug them on. They're a little snug, but manageable. Not any worse than my tennis shoes, honestly.

"That work?" Traitor asks.

"They'll do."

"Good. Ass in the truck in fifteen."

Wearing boots again feels weird, but not horrible. Nothing like combat boots. The leather is softer, the soles are squishier and quieter, and, of course, there are no laces. I'm not trading in my tennis shoes, but the experience isn't as bad as I'd worried it would be.

Traitor already has the truck cranked by the time I get downstairs. We turn onto the main road and drive through downtown. What's left of it anyway. Half the buildings are boarded up—a diner, a furniture store, a movie rental place. Main Street curves around a statue of some guy in the center, then turns to the stores that are actually open.

Two blocks from Main Street, Traitor pulls into a broken concrete driveway beside a small house with dark green vinyl siding. The porch sags in the middle. Paint peels off the white shutters like dried-out frosting. Four white posts hold up the rotting porch roof. Each one sits off center of its stone base. The wind could topple them without even taking a deep breath. The front door is the only decent thing on the place. It's bright white with a wreath of fall flowers hanging around the peephole. That wreath is the only sign that someone actually lives here.

Traitor knocks on the door. I hang back at the truck, not sure what we're even doing at this junk heap.

After a few minutes, the door swings open and the little old lady from the school office appears.

"Dell!" she says. "I wasn't expecting you today."

Traitor tips his faded ball cap back on his head. "We're gonna fix your porch up, Mrs. Roger." His voice is completely different from when he speaks to me. Softer and twangier.

"Y'all don't have to do that. It'll do."

"No, ma'am. Every time we get a storm I'm terrified your roof is gonna cave in. So me and Nate here will make sure that don't happen."

Mrs. Roger peers around Traitor. "Where's Bev?"

"She ran up to Tennessee to get stone for another project. Don't worry. I'll make sure she gets your cookies."

Mrs. Roger's mouth quirks to one side. "You better. My lemon cookies are her favorite."

I can't picture Skunky eating lemon cookies. It seems too . . . dainty for her. Of course, I couldn't imagine Traitor sounding this pleasant, either, so Skunky could sip tea with her pinky in the air for all I know.

Traitor lopes back to the truck and opens one of the toolboxes on the side. "Grab the big ladder."

I fumble at the bungee cords and maneuver the tallest ladder to the side of the house. Traitor shows me how to extend it, then starts pulling posts out of the truck bed. "Check the bases first," he says. "Make sure the rocks are all secure and there's nothing we need to putty."

"Is this what you do all day?"

He drops a post at my feet. "What, fix porches?"

I nod.

"I do all sorts of things. Carpentry work, plumbing, minor roof repair, and electrical work. Whatever's needed."

"Is there a lot of that in Lewiston?" A town this size can't possibly have that much work.

He adds another post to the pile. "Enough. These old houses need a lot of upkeep. Why? You wanna be a handyman one day?" He sounds genuinely interested for the first time since we met. In fact, everything about him is different—his voice, the way he stands, the glimmer in his eyes—almost as if the chance to work woke up a side of him I've never seen. I don't exactly know what to do with it.

"Maybe," I say. "I don't think about the future much. I mean, I never thought I'd have one, so . . ." That's not exactly true. I had a future all planned out for myself. I just didn't want it. Now I have no idea what I'll do once I'm eighteen and Traitor turns me out.

He cocks his head to the side and looks me over. Not wanting to be studied like some fancy fruit at the grocery store, I turn and start examining the first stone column. His boots thump on the grass beside me.

"Grab the tub of grout from the toolbox," he says. "I already see a few places we need to patch."

He shows me how to squish grout in the seams and smooth it out with a plastic paint scraper. When the holes are filled in and the stones are secure, we start replacing the tilting beams, knocking out the old ones with a sledgehammer and wedging the new ones in place.

After a while, Mrs. Roger comes outside and sits on a bench under a big oak tree in the yard, knitting from a pattern that looks like it's written in a foreign language. The clack of her needles is strangely soothing. By the time we finish, the sun hangs low. I'm drenched with sweat, coated in sawdust, and starving. My feet ache from the too-small shoes, but I'm in a surprisingly good mood. It felt good to work. It channeled the fire in my gut into something productive. Maybe this place really is calming the beast.

I'm loading the tools when Mrs. Roger appears with a tin of cookies. "Be sure to give these to Bev, dear. You can have a few, but don't let Dell near them or he'll eat them all."

"I heard that," Traitor says. He closes the toolbox and locks it. "I'll make sure Bev gets at least a couple."

He and Mrs. Roger laugh like this is some old joke. She tries to hand him cash but he pushes her hand away. "We've talked about this, Mrs. Roger. No money until the job is done."

"This old house will never be done. You know that. Now take the money."

He dusts his hands off on his jeans and climbs on the truck seat. "No, ma'am. I'll be back tomorrow after the wood glue dries to paint the columns. And don't give Nate money, neither."

Mrs. Roger drops her wallet back into her giant purse. "Dell Clemons, you're the biggest spoilsport I ever did meet."

Traitor laughs again and cranks the engine. I hop in the passenger seat and watch Mrs. Roger toddle across her now straight porch and back inside. We did a pretty good job. Blisters bubble across the top of my palms. I'm strangely proud of them. This is the first time I've ever done something good with these hands. Something besides break bones.

I reach for a cookie, but Traitor knocks my hand away. "Those aren't for you."

"But—"

"I don't care what she said. Those weren't baked for you. They're Bev's."

"She wasn't even here. I did the work and I can't eat one lousy cookie?"

"Nope."

Gone is the soft-spoken, nice guy who fixed an old lady's porch for free. The hard-ass, I-hate-this-kid uncle is back. Why don't I get any of that softness? Does he use it all up on other people? I don't understand why this man despises me so much. So much that he automatically believes what everyone else says about me and has never even asked my side. Not that I would tell him, but still, it would be nice if he asked.

We turn into a gas station and Traitor hands me a ten. "Grab a couple bottles of water. And I want my change."

The beast growls down deep inside, reminding me that a few nice moments can't cleanse my blood. I resist the urge to slam the door. I thought we'd had a good day. Guess I was wrong. I worked my ass off, and I get nothing. It's not like I asked for money, just a damn cookie. I snag a cold bottle of water from the cooler and a hot one from an endcap.

Screw him. If I can't have a cookie, I'm getting a candy bar. Maybe a Kit Kat. Those were Kelsey's favorite. She'd sneak one in her pocket whenever the Skynbyrds hung flyers in a grocery store. She always brought it to our spot in the woods. We'd each grab half and make a wish as we snapped it in two, like it was a turkey's wishbone.

I pick up the candy and can almost feel her fingers holding the other side. Brushing against those fingers was the only way I ever got up the nerve to hold her hand. It amazes me how something as simple as a touch can be so exciting, and it hurts me to know I'll never get the chance to feel that thrill again. Not with Kelsey.

Longing rushes through me like sudden blast of freezing air.

On second thought, a 3 Musketeers would be better. I drop the Kit Kat and reach for the candy bar at the same time as someone else. "My bad," I say.

"You go ahead," a familiar voice says. "Oh, Nathaniel!"

I stiffen and face the reporter. "What are you doing here?" I demand. "Are you following me?"

She smiles. "I rent a room around the corner. Running into you is a total serendipity."

Too coincidental if you ask me. "Why are you still here?"

"I told you I'd be around in case you change your mind. Did you get the backpack?"

"You know gifts aren't going to win me over, right?"

She picks up a candy bar. "It wasn't a gift. I was replacing something I broke. Anyone would do that."

I guess. I grab the candy bar and head to the counter, eager to get away from this woman. She's right on my heels. I glare at her.

"What?" she asks. "I have to pay, don't I?"

I roll my eyes and plunk everything down. "What do you get out of this?"

"Out of writing your story?"

"Yeah."

"Four seventy-two," the clerk says.

I hand him Traitor's ten and pocket the candy and coins the clerk hands back.

"An interview with you would obviously help my career," the reporter says. "You're the impossible get. The story everyone wants. But, then again, there are tons of those stories. Like the serial killer they caught in Maine last year."

"So why not interview him?"

She turns to me with a gleam in her eye. "He doesn't need my help." She drops her change in the cup beside the register. "I meant what I said. I think there's more to you than everyone says. I really do want to help you, Nathaniel."

My eyes dart to the clerk, but he's vanished into the room behind the counter. "Say that a little louder, would you?"

The reporter waves me off. "People around here won't connect the dots unless you do it for them."

A horn beeps in the parking lot. Traitor flashes the truck's headlights several times.

I tuck the water bottles under my arm and start for the door.

"I'm sticking around town for a while," she calls. "Just in case. Call me if you change your mind and need to talk."

Déjà vu washes over me. The last person to say that was Ms. Erica.

But unlike this lady, I think Ms. Erica really meant it.

624

I'm at my usual corner table, lost in trying to figure out how to break into Traitor's trunk, when a tray smacks the table beside me.

"This seat taken?" Brandon asks.

I swallow my bite of sandwich before I've finished chewing. He always sits with his friends. They're the loudest group in the lunchroom. Did something happen? Are they mad that Brandon's been hanging out with me?

I scoot over to make room. "What's up?"

"I just can't deal with them today. Do you mind?"

I actually don't. Are people staring at us, though? Wondering if the scary new kid is being a bad influence on the clean-cut popular guy? I gaze around the lunchroom, but the only person who seems to be staring is Brandon. His eyes are fixed on his group of friends. His shoulders are slumped.

The crinkle is missing from the corner of his eyes. I'm afraid to ask—he could be private, like me—but it feels weird not to.

"Everything all right?"

"Yeah, it's just . . ." Brandon's brows furrow. "Ever feel like there are some things no one else will understand?"

"All the time," I blurt before I can stop myself. If only he knew how much I get that feeling.

He twirls some spaghetti around his fork and slurps up the noodles. I'm not sure what to do with this new, gloomy Brandon. I'm supposed to be the quiet one. A burst of laughter erupts from his friends and Brandon scowls.

"I was going to ask her out tomorrow," he says. "Maddie. Football game, and then dinner in Fletch's field under the stars. Cheesy, huh?"

Better than any date I could've come up with. The best I ever planned for Kelsey was stealing the beer she liked from the meeting hall fridge and drinking it together in the woods.

I crumple my sandwich bag into a ball. "So, ask her."

"Can't." He points across the room. "Scott Ryman got to her first."

I follow his fork and spot a tall blonde guy with his arm around Maddie. She giggles and presses her mouth to his cheek.

Brandon sighs. "That could've been me."

"Dude, hate to be harsh, but you sound pathetic."

He stabs his fork into the stale bread stick. "I know. I know! I've had a crush on her for three years. I finally get the balls to ask her out and Scott beats me to the punch."

Maddie flips her blonde hair over her shoulder and leans into the guy.

"They look more like brother and sister than boyfriend and girlfriend," I say.

"I know, right! Super creepy."

"Definitely." I roll my sandwich bag back and forth between my hands. A question simmers under my skin that I've been afraid to ask since I found out Brandon liked her. "Would she have even said yes?"

He twists the fork in the bread stick, flinging dry crumbs across the table. "What do you mean?"

I summon my courage. "I mean—and don't take this the wrong way—but she's . . . white, and you're . . . black." God, I hope that was the right word. I watch Brandon closely for a reaction. He stopped twirling the fork and is staring at me. "Would that be a problem here? Because it *never* would've happened in The . . . where I'm from." I clamp my mouth shut. I screwed up. Not only have I offended him, but I almost told him about The Fort. This is what I get for talking.

Brandon considers for a minute, then puts his fork down and looks back at Maddie. "I think she would've. Not sure if her parents would've approved, but . . . we grew up together. I hope it wouldn't be an issue and they'd just see the kind of guy I am. That's all anyone ever wants, right?"

Not me. That's what terrifies me more than anything.

"Besides, I think Lewiston has come a long way."

"What do you mean?"

"It was never as bad here as it was other places. My grandfather integrated in 1963 pretty easily. That's why there's a statue of him in the center of town. Well, for that and for the civil rights work he did in the late fifties and early sixties. But there are assholes everywhere. I don't think the Lyons family are assholes, though. At least I hope they aren't."

I hope so, too, for Brandon's sake, but Maddie and Blondie could be on an Aryan Youth poster.

All of a sudden, Brandon laughs. "Maddie's family moved here from Vermont when we were five. I don't think she'd ever seen a black person before then. She came to class that first day and couldn't stop staring at me. At recess, she tapped my shoulder and whispered, 'Are you that color all over?' I was so surprised that I got hit in the head with a kick ball and fell down. I caught her peeking up my shorts before I could stand back up."

"I caught Kelsey watching me pee in the woods one day when we were kids. She went crying to her mother, afraid that her body parts were falling off because she didn't have the same pee tube that I did."

Brandon laughs so hard he snorts, which sets me off. Now people really are staring at us, but I don't care. The lunch bell rings and we dump our trash, still laughing. We manage to go quiet for a minute, then Brandon says, "Pee tube," and we lose it again.

I haven't laughed like this in years. On one hand, it feels amazing, but on the other, it depresses the hell out of me. It shows what I could have if things were different, and I know that deep down, this happiness isn't real.

It can't be real. Because Brandon doesn't actually know the real me.

✧

The laughter carries me through the rest of the day, right up until I find the envelope sticking out of the slats in my locker. *Nathaniel* is written on the outside in slanted script. My pulse spikes like thorns in my veins. I yank the envelope free and check the hallway for signs of whoever left it. And here I thought that happy feeling would last a little longer.

When I'm sure the coast is clear, I tear open the envelope, certain I'll find some kind of warning note from The Fort.

Four folded pages are crammed inside. The first is a letter from the reporter.

> *Nathaniel,*
>
> *Okay, so this may be a bit stalkerish, but I thought it was better than showing up at your house. These are articles I wrote about you during your trial, that* News First *never ran. A new assignment is going to pull me away soon. I hope these will show you that I really am on your side.*
>
> *I hope to hear from you before I leave, but if I don't, you have my number.*
>
> *Shaw Holt*

Unbelievable. At least she's leaving soon. So she claims.

I skim the articles. They have headlines like "Wrongly Accused" and "Teenager Stands Trial for Self-Defense." They do seem more slanted toward my side of things, even if the facts aren't exactly right. The last paragraph of the last article sums it up pretty well:

> *We know that a man is dead, and a fourteen-year-old has blood on his hands. We know the deceased was the leader of a white supremacist group, and the kid was likely brainwashed by him. What we don't know is exactly what happened in the woods. Only one person can tell us, and he's not talking.*

I stuff the articles in my backpack and dart into the library. The librarian is sorting books at the counter.

"I'll be here for another half hour, then I'm locking up," she says.

I flash her a thumbs-up and sit at the first computer. When I search "Shaw Holt," a long list of links appears. Articles she's written, pictures, achievements. I read through a few of the articles. Every one of them has a ton of comments at the bottom.

Most people love her. She has a lot of regular readers and commenters. One guy says he only reads her articles. Another link takes me to a poll of "America's most trusted newsperson." Her name is near the top.

Maybe this chick is on the up-and-up. That doesn't mean I trust her. She definitely has her own agenda. But maybe I should give her more credit than I have been.

632

I unhook the bag from the lawnmower and dump the clippings down the hole. The tree is taller now. While the leaves on all the trees aboveground are changing, this puny thing doesn't seem to have gotten the memo. I grab the hose and shoot some water down there, figuring it can't hurt.

"Nate!" Traitor calls.

I kink the hose with one hand and push the mower back to the house with the other. Thank God this is the last time I'll have to cut the damn grass until spring. If I'm still around by then.

"Get washed up. Bev's bringing supper."

The hose pops out of my hand and sprays the porch. Traitor jumps out of the way, but not before his jeans get splashed.

"Damnit! Watch it with that thing. What the hell were you even watering?"

I bend the hose again and turn off the spigot, ignoring his last question. For some reason, I feel like I have to protect the tree, like if he knew about it he'd think it was a problem and get rid of it.

I take my time putting the lawnmower back in the shed. Skunky has been over plenty, but she's never eaten with us. I have this nagging feeling that something's up.

She's already inside by the time I go in. She cleared off the kitchen table and is setting out real plates and silverware. I pull a clean T-shirt out of the laundry hamper and wash my hands. The smells coming from the kitchen make my stomach growl.

Skunky has laid out fried chicken, green beans, macaroni and cheese, and corn bread.

"What's the occasion?" I ask.

Traitor plops down in one of the high-backed chairs. "I figured it's high time we had a decent meal around here."

I agree, but I can't relax. Traitor and Skunky pile food on their plates, but I watch, waiting for the catch.

"Eat." Traitor tears into a chicken thigh.

Catch or no catch, I'm not about to waste my chance at something besides bologna, and if I eat, I don't have to talk.

Skunky and Traitor keep swapping glances over their forks, like they're both waiting for the other to speak. Finally, Skunky makes eye contact with me. It's the first time she's looked me in the eye. Her irises are a muddy brown, not that different from Kelsey's. Her expression, however, is. She doesn't look angry, exactly, but she's not pleased, either.

"What's the deal with you and the Kingsley kid?" She crosses her arms, her gaze boring into me, like she can see through me, see my soul, see the beast. "And don't give me some bullshit about being friends. I want to know the truth. What's in it for you?"

There's the catch. *His* voice rattles in my skull. *Don't let this chink talk to you like that.* My muscles automatically tense. *Teach her a lesson, boy. You know what to do.*

Shut up, shut up, shut up! It takes a shit-ton of willpower not to press my hands to my ears to block *him* out.

I slowly lower my chicken thigh to the plate and push my palms against the cool, sanded wooden table, forcing my lungs to take deep breaths. "You think I have some master plan? To what? Destroy this town one minority at a time?" If I did, wouldn't I start with you?

"Of course not," she says. "That would be ridiculous. But it does seem strange. The first 'friend' you make is black." She uses air quotes. "Why him?"

"We just think it's odd," Traitor says. "With your history."

The beast growls. "My history?"

"You have to admit it's weird," Skunky says.

I stare at her like she's speaking a foreign language. Does she speak another language? Where's she from, anyway? I know even less about her than she pretends to know about me. I turn to Traitor. "Why her? Of all the people you could date, why'd you pick her?"

"We're not talking about me," he snaps.

"I am. Where did you find her? Why can't you date someone your own race?"

Shock smacks both of them across the face.

"I mean, that's what you're asking me, isn't it?"

"That's not—" Skunky starts.

"Yeah, it is. Why do I have to hang out with a black guy? Why can't I have made a white friend?" I wipe my greasy fingers on a paper towel, ball it up, and fling it on the table. "Would we be talking about this if Brandon was white? Or if I was anyone else? Would you care?" My chair legs scrape the floor as I stand. Good. I hope I gouged tracks in the wood. "What do I have to do to prove to you people that I'm not a murderous freak?"

Skunky leans across the table. "We just don't want him to get hurt."

"And I just want a friend." I regret it as soon as it's out of my mouth. They don't deserve to know that, but it's out now. "He's nice to me. In fact, he's the only person in this Godforsaken town who is." The beast takes control of my legs. I kick the chair into the wall, knocking one of the bottom slats out.

"Nate," Traitor says, but that's all I hear. I'm already on the front porch by the time he finishes his sentence. It feels good to let the beast out a little. Like stretching a tight muscle. I want to let go so badly, but if I do, that's it. I'll never come back.

Night has fallen and everything is dark, dark, dark. I breathe it in and feel the darkness expand inside, like a brain freeze that hits my entire body. I want—no, *need*—to destroy something. The beast has been pent up too long.

Crisp air snakes around me. I stalk into the woods, intentionally avoiding glancing at the tree in the hole. If I see its hopeful branches right now, I might shred them out of spite.

There's one good thing in my life and they want to strip it away. They want to leave me empty, alone, dark, and cold.

Can't they see I'm not *him*? I've been here a couple of months without a single episode. Do they honestly think it's some kind of trick? That my friendship with Brandon is a cover to ease everyone into a false sense of security before I strike? Can't they see that I'm *trying*?

Why can't a single damn person see the real me?

I push through the brush less carefully than normal, breaking any sticks or branches in my way. I'm hot all over. I trip over a fallen branch and barely catch myself before I go sprawling.

"Asshole branch." I heft it off the ground and swing it at the closest tree like a baseball bat. An animal scream escapes my mouth as the branch connects with the tree. I swing it again and again and again until the branch is toothpicks and my throat is hoarse.

My knees give and I sink to the cold dirt. I cling to the button around my neck, running it back and forth along its string but, surprisingly, I don't need to be grounded right now. The beast curls up inside me and sleeps, satisfied with its time out of its cage.

I know this isn't healthy. It isn't how Dr. Sterling or Ms. Erica would want me to cope, but losing control, even for a minute, felt good. Too good. But that may not be such a bad thing. Maybe it's okay to lose control once in a while, when I know I can't hurt anyone.

Despite the argument, I fall asleep in my clearing peacefully as a bear that's gorged itself before hibernation.

636

I belong in the woods. I could stay there forever, away from people, living in the trees and shadows, safe from myself, the world safe from me. Because when it gets down to it, I'm a snake. Cold-blooded and venomous. Lowest of the low. At night, the outer skin slides off, and I'm bare and open, the real Nate.

That's when the beast can show itself. I keep it hidden under that dead shell all day, but once I'm in the woods, I let it out of its cage. It snaps and destroys, opening the pressure valve a little at a time. That's why I've been going to the woods every night. That release helps me keep the shell on during the day. It helps me live with the pretend Nate that Brandon thinks he's friends with. Helps me live with the guilt.

And I've really been feeling the guilt lately. Brandon and I have been hanging out more and more. Pretty much every day that he doesn't have basketball practice. Usually at the river. Thanks to him, my fishing skills have improved. I actually caught one the other day. A tiny bass, but it's something. Brandon acted excited, but something was off. Like the light had dimmed in his smile. I worry that I'm rubbing off on him. Or maybe his friends aren't happy he's been hanging around with me. He's sat with me every day at lunch this week instead of splitting time between me and his friends like normal. And today, we've been fishing for almost an hour and he's hardly said a word. I keep starting to ask, but I don't want to seem like I'm forcing him to talk. Sometimes, you just need someone to *not* talk to. I can't do much, but I can be that person for Brandon.

Another twenty or so minutes pass that way, then Brandon catches a fish. Almost catches it. I hear him scuffling up the bank beside me. He lets the fish run, then jerks and reels, but the line messes up. It doubles back around the reel getting knotted and tangled. The piece of line still in the water goes slack as the fish slips the hook. "Argh, I can't with this shit today!" Brandon throws his rod to the grass and scrubs his hand over his hair—which I've learned has different textures depending on how it's treated, and that black folks *don't* like people touching it.

I reel in my own line. "What's wrong?"

"I'm so over this place," he says as I get close. His jaw is set and the happy crinkles have vanished from the corners of his eyes.

"The river?"

"All of it. This town. These people. They're impossible to talk to. Unless it's about the way Kara McElroy's boobs bounce in a sports bra." He picks up his rod. "You ready to go?"

"Yeah, sure," I say, feeling like an ass for not asking earlier. I follow him back to his car and throw my rod in the backseat with his. Technically, they're both his, but he's been letting me use the same one for a while now. Brandon cranks the engine, but doesn't move.

"You want to talk about it?" I ask.

"No. Yes. I don't know. You don't want to hear it." He puts the car in drive and flings gravel as we pull onto the road.

The speedometer needle creeps up to sixty-five, fast for a country road, but Brandon keeps accelerating.

"Dude, you've been awesome to me. Least I can do is listen."

He glances over. The speedometer drops back to sixty. "You know my brother, Henry?"

"Yeah."

"He's dropping out of college to be a fly-fishing guide in Tennessee. My parents are pissed."

Brandon's still holding the wheel like he wants to snap it off, but we've slowed to a reasonable fifty miles per hour.

"I'm not supposed to discuss it because my folks are trying to talk Henry out of it, and they don't want anyone to know. Not a lot of people around here go to college. Henry is, like, the poster boy for good life decisions. Everyone tells their kids to be like Henry Kingsley. Not to mention, my dad's a professor at West Alabama University. It's really stressful at home and none of my friends care about anything besides Kara McElroy's jugs."

"I care," I say. "About this, I mean. Not Kara's boobs. They're not even that great." This is me being a friend, I guess. Kara's boobs are *amazing*. Especially in that tight sports bra she wears in PE. I may not have grown up like them, but I'm still a guy.

Brandon laughs, but quickly goes quiet. "Fletch and Rainey don't get it. Neither of them want to go to college anyway. Fletch's dad will probably get him a job at the lumberyard and Rainey wants to work for the power company. Which is great, but they wouldn't get it. They'd shrug this off like it's no big deal. But it is in my family. It's so awkward at home. And they keep dragging me into it."

My hand rubs the fake leather console, my fingers automatically drawing 636. "If there's one thing I totally get, it's not wanting the same thing as your friends. Or family." Holy shit, do I get that.

Brandon gives me a curious glance. If there was ever a time to say more . . . My truth is right there, balanced between us. But I can't get the words out. Not to Brandon, and definitely not now. He needs to talk about his problem, not hear me whine about mine.

"How do you feel about it?" I ask to keep the focus on him. "About Henry leaving to teach fishing."

Brandon sighs. "I don't know. He's really smart. He wants—wanted—to be an accountant. But if he doesn't love it"—he shrugs—"I guess I think he should be happy, even if that means dropping out of school. It's not like he can never go back."

"Yeah," I say, even though I know nothing about college. "Maybe he needs to do this for a while. Get it out of his system. I mean, it sounds kind of fun."

Brandon smiles and the crinkles return around his eyes. "It does, right? The rush of the water, the thrill of the catch. I don't blame him. Maybe that's what my folks are so worried about."

"Eh, they'll get over it. I'm sure it will blow over soon."

"You think?"

I have no idea. My family never let anything go. But the Kingsleys aren't anything like my family. "Yeah. I do."

"Thanks, man."

"For what?"

"For listening when no one else would."

"Any time," I say, and I mean it.

Brandon's way of dealing with things is way better than mine. Every night when I let the beast out, it's harder and harder to put the walls back up. Like trying to squeeze toothpaste back into the tube. I wish I could open up to Brandon the way he just opened up to me, but it's not fair for me to weigh him down with everything. It kind of makes me miss the Psych Center again. At least I knew I could be honest there. It wasn't exactly trust, but that's probably too much to ask.

The last person I truly trusted was Kelsey. No matter what, we were completely honest with each other. No judgment. Not when she admitted she enjoyed hurting someone who wronged her, like the checkout girl who made a smart-ass comment about the amount of snack food she was buying. Not when I admitted I enjoyed it sometimes, too. Because every time I hurt someone, I pretended it was *his* blood splattered across me.

You only get that kind of understanding from someone who has shared your experiences.

I'll never have a bond with anyone else the way I did with Kelsey, but that doesn't mean I can't listen. Keep my mouth shut and be Brandon's ears. I want him to have someone he can talk to, even if I can't.

I swallow hard and stare out the window. This time we're driving north, the sun beating down on Brandon's side of the car, all the shadows over on mine like they never really left.

640

I lean back on Traitor's springy couch and toss up a green stress ball I found during one of my trips to the river with Brandon. The ball bounces off the ceiling, and a shower of that gross popcorn stuff rains down, sprinkling the couch and floor like dandruff. Sweeping and mopping is on my list of weekend chores anyway, so I throw the ball again.

"Nate, are you listening?" asks the social worker. She's perched on Traitor's scuffed leather chair.

The ball arcs to the ceiling. *Thunk.*

She raises her voice. "I hear you're making friends."

Traitor snorts. He's at his normal post in the kitchen doorway, like he's ready to intervene if I suddenly attack the social worker.

"Tell me about them," the social worker says.

The ball drops into my hand. I roll it between my palms, feeling its pitted surface where a dog, or something, took several bites out of the foam. "There's nothing to tell."

"Your uncle said you've been fishing almost every day for the last few weeks."

I scowl at Traitor. What'd he do? Go run to her as soon as he met Brandon?

"This will be easier if you talk to me, Nate." The social worker balances her tablet computer on the chair arm and leans forward. "Tell me about Brandon."

I throw the ball. "He's nice to me. I'm nice to him."

The social worker picks the tablet back up and types something. She looks smug. I'd love to smack her in the forehead with the stress ball, but I hit the ceiling again instead.

Traitor grumbles something under his breath. I ignore him and throw the ball harder.

The social worker looks up from her computer. "What do you and your friend talk about?"

More ceiling breaks off and tumbles to the floor. I'm not telling this lady shit.

"Nate?" The social worker crosses her legs and bobs her foot like the red and white floaters Brandon uses to fish.

"Not much." I bounce the ball again and again and again. I've already worn a circle on the ceiling.

The social worker plasters a fake smile across her face. She's showing her teeth, but the corners angle down, like she had a stroke. Her patience must be wearing thin. This lady is never going to last as my caseworker.

I almost jerk that damn tablet out of her hands and type the shit that's missing from my file. If she knew all the things I've done, she'd hightail it out of here so fast, all we'd see is a cartoon puff left behind.

Hell, just a snippet would make her head for the hills. Like the Jewish kid we attacked outside a synagogue in Louisville. And I barely touched him—that was all the Connor brothers, with me doing just enough to keep them from tattling.

All I'd have to do is write how his feeble hand latched onto my pants leg as I half-heartedly kicked him, or the pleading look in his eyes right before Jacob Connor bashed his face in.

Even Ms. Erica had a hard time reading that story.

The social worker shifts her tablet again, moving it out of reach. "Tell me something you *do* talk about."

I catch the ball and glare at her. "Why? You think I filled him in on my plot to burn down the town?"

She blinks several times. The pretend smile is all down-turned corners now. Traitor looks like he's about to snap at me, but doesn't. He deepens his frown until he resembles a ventriloquist dummy.

A ventriloquist came to the Pysch Center once as a "treat." As soon as that wooden puppet started "talking," I faked a flashback so I could get out of there. Wonder if that would work now?

"We talk about fish," I say. "And school, and he asks about where I'm from."

Traitor and the social worker both take sharp breaths. "You haven't told him anything about your past, have you?" the social worker asks.

Traitor pushes off the door frame and steps closer to us. "He better not have. Or I'll—"

"I haven't," I snap. "But I can't keep this secret forever." Lately, the words have been burning inside me. My time in woods, letting out the beast, has made me crave a greater release and hearing Brandon spill his secret makes holding mine in seem like an even bigger sin.

The social worker's eyes widen. "Nate, you can't. You—"

"Over my dead body," Traitor growls. "I've built too much in this community for you to—"

"What if he tells someone?" the social worker cuts in. "It's too much of a risk. You could be found! If The Fort learned where you are—"

I throw the ball and block her out. Geez, how would they react if they knew I've already been found? The reporter's crumpled business card is in my pocket beside Ms. Erica's. I thought about telling them—and came really close to calling Ms. Erica about her—but it never seemed like the right time. Besides, they probably won't believe me. Not too long ago, the social worker, herself, said no one could possibly know where I am.

I slip my hand in my pocket and run my finger along the thick edges of both cards. Traitor and the social worker pepper me with more questions. I close my eyes, breathe deeply, and look for the light, trying to block the frigid gusts of anger swelling from their storm of panic.

Boots clomp on the wooden floor. Voices shriek. Light. I need the light. Traitor's jeans brush against mine. Breathe. The social worker's heels follow. I spot the light. It's faint, but it's there. A distant lighthouse at the edge of a black ocean.

She's trying to calm Traitor down, but he won't stop yelling. Waves swell, pushing the light further out of reach. The social worker raises her voice to match Traitor's. The light slips away, sand between my fingers, and all that exists is the penetrating darkness within me.

"Enough!" My bellow vibrates my throat and chest, startling even me.

I open my eyes. Traitor and the social worker stand in front of me, slack-jawed.

"Enough," I say. Calmly this time. The stress ball falls from my hand to the floor. Or what's left of it. Seems I tore it in two. "You want me to be normal, to rejoin society, to make friends, start over. But how can I do that if my life is built on lies?"

The social worker blinks. Traitor crosses his arms. I've been thinking about this a lot since Brandon opened up to me. He seemed so much lighter afterward. More like his real self. Things with his other friends went back to normal, too. He still hasn't told them what was going on with Henry, but he said he didn't need to since he'd gotten the weight off his chest.

My secrets are iron ships compared to Brandon's, but if it worked for him, maybe it could work for me, too. If I can clear my conscience somehow, maybe that'll be enough.

Maybe with a clean conscience, I can start over.

If they'd only let me.

The social worker sits beside me. I scoot away.

"Opening up about your past is too dangerous, Nate. You could put both your uncle and you in jeopardy." Her hand juts out like she wants to pat me, or something, but I stand and move out of range. "Think about it. Carefully. You'll realize we're right."

"There's nothing to think about," Traitor says. "He's not going to say a damn word. Don't you mess this up, boy."

I meet his eyes and the darkness swirls and swirls and swirls, blocking him and the social worker and the entire cabin. It's been 640 days since I hurt someone, but I'm so freaking close right now that I can practically smell the rusty tang of blood. And I don't care. I'm sick of other people controlling my life. Where I go and what I do and who I like and don't like and what I say and don't say.

My fist rises.

I clutch my button the way a drowning person clings to a life preserver.

I can't do this.

The real me is going to come pouring out one way or another, by my actions or by my words.

I have to take control now. Before it's too late.

I brush past Traitor, bumping my shoulder into his, and retreat to my bedroom. I lean against the closed door, my button in one closed fist and the business cards from my pocket in the other.

The thick card stock bites my palm. The possibilities within the cards slice me open. I unclench my fist and smooth the cards' creases, running my fingers over the raised print. Ms. Erica's soothing voice breezes through my memory and I'm back in Dr. Sterling's office. *"It's okay, Nate. Write it out. Whatever you can manage right now. We're not going anywhere."* And they didn't. Not after they read those first pages. Not after the next set, or the next. They were always there.

Because they had to be. It was their job.

I stare at the letters on the business cards until they blur and my eyes ache. When I blink, I finally see everything clearly.

I tear open my backpack and flip to a clean notebook page, uncap a pen, and write.

Ink flows like blood from a freshly cut vein. My soul bleeds onto the paper. Bleeds and bleeds and bleeds until there's nothing left. Not a single word.

Only when I'm empty do I see how to fill myself again, how to start being a whole person for once.

643

The pages are hot pokers in my pocket. The words sear my skin with every step. I was too paranoid to leave them at Traitor's. Afraid he'd do a random room search and find them stuffed in my pillowcase or between the mattress and box spring. Besides, that's not where they go. These pages don't belong tucked away somewhere like the beast. They belong in someone's hand.

Traitor is obviously out. He'd have me locked up before he got through the first page. The new social worker, too. There's only one person I can think of who might be willing to keep an open mind.

Which is why I'm pacing outside the school counselor's office. The final bell rings. My resolve leaks away with the fading sound. All day, I tried to talk myself into doing this, and all day I backed out. This is my last chance. My best chance.

The school will be empty. No one to interrupt, no principal for the counselor to run to if my words freak him out.

The door opens and I will my jelly spine to become steel. A tall brown girl in a volleyball uniform comes out.

"Just keep working on that spike, Camila," the counselor says from behind her.

The girl smiles. "Thanks for your help, Mr. Paulsen. That scout is coming to the game tonight because of you."

He waves her off. "It's my job. Now go warm up and kill those Cats!" He turns to go back in his office and notices me for the first time. "Oh, Nate. I didn't see you there. You need something?"

I hesitate. The halls are filling up with students pouring out of their last classes. I can join the current and let them sweep me out to the asphalt sea. But that won't stop the paper in my pocket from burning through me. The counselor said he was on my team. It's time to find out if he meant it. "I, uh, I was wondering if we could talk?"

The counselor checks his watch. "School is over. Sure you don't want to get out of here? I'm free in the morning."

I swallow hard. The temptation to run is stronger than ever. "No. It needs to be now."

He opens his door wider. "Then let's talk."

The cot from my first day is gone, so instead I sink into the one chair in front of his desk. Although "sink" isn't the right word. The stiff fabric doesn't give much, like the chair doesn't want anyone to get too comfortable and stay too long. The counselor plops down in his wheeled chair and scoots up to the desk.

"So, what can I help you with?"

Where do I start? I've never had to have this conversation. Everyone else has already known something about me going in. Do I tell him my real name first, or where I'm from? My tongue swells at the thought. Fills my entire mouth.

No. I can't *tell* him anything. The words are glued to my soul. To say them would rip me apart worse than the stress ball.

I could give him what I wrote. The letter to no one.

My hand goes to my pocket. My fingers rub the edges of the folded pages. It would be so easy to pull them out. Lay them on the desk. No different from turning in homework. One quick motion and that would be it.

That would be *it*.

The gravity of it hits me. Presses my hand tight against my leg. We learned about g-force last week in science, and I suddenly get it. A million Gs are bearing down on me right now. My body feels like it's about to collapse in on itself.

"Nate?"

"I'm sorry." My voice sounds like it's light-years away. "I . . ." *I can't tell you,* I want to say.

The counselor stands. "Are you okay? Are you having another episode?"

He seems genuinely concerned, I'll give him that. But he's used to helping volleyball players who need scholarships, not weirdos like me who are haunted by their pasts. He can't read my words. They would break him as much as my fists could. Not to mention that he might tell someone else and my cover would be blown.

No, telling one person, in Lewiston, won't work. Especially not if it's Nate *Clemons* doing the telling. This has to come from Nathaniel Fuller. And if it's going to make a difference, then it needs to go wider. Not to the people here who know me as a juvenile delinquent. To the people who got the wrong story in the first place. Telling one person isn't going to matter. It didn't with Dr. Sterling and Ms. Erica. That was just using a Band-Aid to treat cancer.

I have to dig the cancer out. Lay my insides bare. It has to hurt. In the right way. The counselor is all wrong.

"Can I use the phone?" I manage around my hundred-pound tongue.

The counselor's eyebrows furrow. "Do you need help? Medical help? Medicine?"

I shake my head. "I need to go home."

"Are you sure? I can help you."

"Just the phone." I start to stand but the counselor springs to his feet.

"You probably shouldn't move." He fumbles in his pocket. "Here, use my cell."

My hands shake as I take the phone from him. An invisible vise squeezes my chest.

I've memorized the number by now. My fingers dial it automatically.

"Hello?"

"It's Nate," I say. "I'm ready."

652

"I'm glad you called." The reporter sips her coffee, then flashes her hundred-watt smile at me.

She may be glad, but I'm not so sure. All my inner strength spilled out with the words I scrawled last week. And the resolve I'd had after dialing the reporter's number has gradually seeped away in the days since.

Dim afternoon light filters through the old, yellowed newspaper covering the windows of the abandoned diner where we'd arranged to meet, casting shadows over the reporter. I hadn't thought about that during the hours I'd spent arranging and rearranging the dusty table and broken chairs, searching for the spot I felt safest. I settled on the middle of the room, with the table at a slight angle so I can see both doors but also have the freedom to bolt if necessary.

Now I'm questioning if I should've chosen the other side, so *my* face would be the unreadable one.

"What made you change your mind?" she asks.

I swirl my fingers through the dust, wiping away 652 before she can read it. "I thought about what you said, and you're right. The story isn't balanced, and I'm not either." Shit. That didn't come out right. "Not that I'm unbalanced, but . . ."

Her forehead crinkles. I'm losing her. This is why I don't talk about these things. I take a deep breath.

"It's like a seesaw and all this shit against me is piled on one side." I tilt my hand to show her. "And I'm all alone on the other."

The reporter places her hand over mine and flattens it. Her hand is warm from her coffee cup, and not entirely unpleasant, not like the social worker's. "I know exactly what you mean," she says softly.

I slide away from her and pick at a seam on the table where the particleboard split. "I think telling my side will even things out."

"I'm glad you chose to give your story to me." Even though she's shadowy, I hear the smile in her voice. I hate the satisfaction this is giving her.

I narrow my eyes, hoping she can see me clearly. "Don't get it twisted. You weren't my first choice. But you already know some of my past."

"And that makes it easier," she says.

"You're also the only one who's shown any interest in *me*."

"So, you trust me?"

"No. But your readers do. I read the articles you gave me, and looked up some others. People read what you write, and they believe you. I can't get that on my own. I could post my story online, but who would see it, and why would they think it's true? That's why I called. To give you this." I remove the crumpled pages from my pocket and smooth them out on the table.

"What is that?" The reporter leans in, but I pull the papers back.

"My story. It's yours, but first I have a few conditions."

She rocks back and folds her arms. "If you don't trust me, what makes you think I'll follow your conditions?"

"Because if you don't, I'll go to one of your competitors and deny the whole thing."

She sighs. "Okay, so what are your terms?"

"One, you can't advertise this until the story prints. I find out you've even thought about telling folks you met with me, and I swear I'll make you regret it."

She presses her lips together, but I can't see her expression. I hope she's scared. I can't—won't—actually hurt her, but I want her to think I might.

"Two, you can't reveal my location. Not even generally. And no pictures."

"I have to use a picture."

"No."

"But—"

I stand. I'm telling my story. Nathaniel Fuller's. Nate Clemons has to stay out of it if I want to stay safe. People in Lewiston can't know who I really am if I'm going to have any sort of life here. If she prints a picture, then she might as well print my zip code or call The Fort and tell them where to find me.

"This is my way to clear my name—and my conscience—not get myself killed."

"Fine," she says. "No pictures."

Uneasiness stirs in my gut, but I can't tell if it's because my past is about to come out to this stranger, and then the world, or if she's hiding something.

The truth is a blister on my soul. It's going to burst if I don't get it out soon. Besides, she's a reporter—of course she's hiding something. No reporter is going to show all their cards—they never do—but I don't see another option. If I want to tell my side, she's all I've got. I sit back down. "Final rule. This is my story. My words. Not yours, not theirs. Mine. Print it exactly as it's written here."

I could've emailed it to her, but I don't trust email. Too many things can go wrong. This way I put it directly in her hands.

She cocks her head to the side. "It's your story, but it is *my* article. My readers will expect my authorial voice in the piece. You said yourself, they trust me. I can't just print random pages without context."

My eyes narrow. "Direct quotes from me, or you get nothing."

Her hand jabs toward me so suddenly I think she's about to slap me. "Deal."

Shaking her hand feels like bargaining with the Devil, except I've dealt with the Devil before; *his* blood runs through my veins.

Everything will be fine, though. As long as she upholds her end of the deal.

The reporter removes her navy blazer and hangs it on the back of the tattered camp chair I'd dragged into the diner. She pulls a notepad and pen out of her bag. "Okay, Nathaniel—"

"Nate."

She smiles. Not the super bright one, but still forced. "Nate, let me see the letter."

I take a deep breath. The pages look like a serial killer wrote them. Lines are jotted then crossed out and rewritten so that it flows logically, from the beginning up to that night.

I push the papers toward her, but I only release them once she tugs. She rifles through the pages. "There's a lot here."

"I have a lot tell."

"Then why don't you *tell* me?"

Goose bumps break out down my arms. I fold them over my chest and hope she didn't see. "Because I already wrote it all." The uneasiness shifts into full-on nerves. I did my part. I wrote it down and delivered it. Now it's up to her to print the painful words that have been tattooed inside me for so long. I sling my backpack over my shoulder and start for the door.

"You're not going to stay while I read them? I thought this was an interview."

"This is me giving you a story. My story. Do you want it or not?"

She jumps up and darts in front of me. "Of course I want it, but you can't just dump it in my lap and walk away. Why don't you stay while I read it? To make sure I understand everything. Isn't that what you want?"

I don't get why she can't just print the whole damn thing in the paper or put it on the Internet and let that be that. Nerves rake their jagged fingers down my stomach at the thought of watching her read my words. I never had to watch Dr. Sterling or Ms. Erica. They always read after I left, then talked to me about it during the next session.

"Some of this handwriting is awfully cramped," she says. "There are parts I can't quite figure out. You don't want me to make assumptions, do you? They're your words, not mine. That's what you said."

I drop my bag to the dusty floor. "Fine." But I switch sides of the table. I want to be in the shadows now, so she can't look me in the eye when she discovers my real past.

The reporter sits in my old seat and unfolds the pages. "He broke my leg when I was four," she says aloud.

I wince, grateful she can't see my face. "To yourself." The words in that letter taste like battery acid in my mouth. I can't imagine what they'll sound like coming out of hers. Worse than nails on a chalkboard.

She smiles gently. "Of course." Then she drops her eyes to the letter again. I read upside down, so I'll know which part she's at.

> *That's the first time I remember* him *touching me, but I don't recall the whole thing. Everything is spotty, like a radio station that's just out of range. Mom said I blacked out. She filled in the gaps later when we were running. She said I'd left the dog in while we attended a gathering and it peed on* his *bed.* He *whipped off his belt and beat me. Each crack of the leather was fire. I remember how it split my back open the way a seam bursts in clothes that are too small. The blood got on my hands. It could've been spilled paint, if I'd been* allowed *to paint. I tried to get away and crawled through it.*

Mom's curtains pop into my mind. With that half a bloody handprint on the bottom where I'd tried to pull myself upright.

> *I was almost up when* his *boot came down on the side of my shinbone. Snapped it in two. There was blinding white heat, and then nothing. For days.*
>
> *Mom must've taken me to a hospital because I remember being unable to move*

my leg, and seeing the white cast. We found another hospital a couple months later and they cut the cast off.

The reporter points to the paragraph. "Is this when Jefferson claimed your mother kidnapped you?"

My eyes snap to hers. The beast stirs in my blood at the thought of all the lies *he* told about Mom. The lies people believe. I grip the edge of the table so hard bits of particleboard fleck off. "Yes," I say through gritted teeth. "She rescued me from Hell and *he* turned it on her. It's bullshit. The abuser made *her* out to be the bad guy."

A piece of table breaks off in my fist. The reporter jumps a little, but recovers quickly.

"What a monster," she whispers.

For a second, I'm not sure if she means *him* or me. I release the table, but hang on to the chunk in my hand. "We would've been fine if she hadn't . . ." I take another breath. "She died, and no one spoke for me. Except *him*."

"You didn't speak for yourself?"

"Like they're going to believe an eight-year-old kid? And I was terrified of *him*. I was always terrified." I jab a finger at the letter. "It's all in there."

Thomas Mayes, the mantra, the fights, the hate, the ignorance. Kelsey and our stolen, secret books. How *he* quoted *Mein Kampf* while *he* beat me. How *he* made me salute. Taught me to goose step. And punished me when I didn't do it right.

All before I was old enough to figure out girls don't actually carry cooties.

The reporter flips through page after page, scribbling notes in her pad as she goes.

She stops scribbling and looks at me suddenly. "What are red laces?"

The goose bumps return. This was one of the hardest parts to write.

"A prize," I say. "A reward for spilling blood for the cause. See, until then, you wear white laces in your combat boots. That shows you're a member of the Nazi Socialist Party. White for White Power. But red, that means you've fought. Most kids get theirs when they're fourteen or older. But I was *eleven*."

I pause and let it sink in. Her hand goes to her mouth. "That's horrible," she says through her fingers. I drink in her reaction, soak it up while I can. She'll feel differently after she reads what *he* made me do. Her eyes drift back to the paper and I read along to judge her reaction.

> *It was early spring, warm, but not hot. The kind of day that makes you want to play outside forever. But I couldn't. I had to go into the city for fencing supplies with* him *and two of his buddies. We got what we needed and headed back late that afternoon, when it's not dark enough for businesses to turn on their lights, but too dark to see well.*

As we passed an ice cream shop, a Middle Eastern boy came out. He looked like a normal kid, wearing shorts and a band T-shirt. Nothing strange or threatening about him. He tied a plastic bag to the handlebars of a bike in front of the shop. I remember being jealous of this kid who could go and get ice cream and ride his bike and be normal.

It pleased me that I could be jealous of a minority. It meant The Fort hadn't completely infected me.

I wasn't jealous for long.

He *parked the truck at the curb and told me to get out.*

His voice rattles in my ears.

"This is your time, Son. Make that terrorist regret infecting our country."

The words didn't register until he *dragged me out of the truck bed. I'd been too busy craning my neck to see the different flavors inside the ice cream parlor. When* he *shoved me toward the boy, though, I realized what* he *wanted me to do.*

The kid straddled his bike and I hesitated, thinking if I waited long enough they'd give up and take me home. At first, I thought it worked. The kid started pedaling and he *made me get back in the truck. We pulled away and I thought it was over.*

But we followed the kid.

He didn't seem to notice at first. Not until we'd stuck with him for a couple blocks without passing. He kept glancing over his shoulder, then pedaled faster. The truck sped up to match. They herded him onto a dead-end street and down an alley.

The kid was like a cornered animal. He cowered behind his bicycle, trying to make himself small, as though the thin, metal tubes could actually protect him. I hid, too. Curled up in the truck bed, afraid to watch. Then my shirt collar pulled tight and he *yanked me out of the truck.*

"Take care of that towelhead," he *said.*

I stood there, numb as the boy. We were both afraid to move. The men were jeering and shouting. It was full dark by this point. The truck's headlights were spotlights on the kid, illuminating the puddle at his feet where he'd wet himself.

The reporter isn't writing anymore. She's staring at the letter with her mouth slightly open.

I hate myself all over again. I want to bury it. Dump it down in the hole with the tree and throw thick, claylike dirt on top of it. It will all be over soon, though. Once the reporter's article comes out, I can leave the past in the past where it belongs.

Once the article is out.

These stories are going to be out there for everyone to see.

I can barely stomach the reporter reading my letter. Will I really be able to handle other people reading it? Other people.

That means The Fort.

The reporter turns the page. "Oh my God."

I know which part she's at without looking. The memory of *his* voice shakes my skull, almost as loud as it was that night in the woods: *"Do I need to show you how it's done?"*

> He *grabbed one of the metal fence poles we'd just bought, stalked up to the boy, and slammed the pipe into his kneecap. The kid howled and dropped to the asphalt.* He *threw the pipe at me and got in my face. "Don't embarrass me, boy. Pick it up and show that sand n—"*

I couldn't write the word. There's an ugly slash in the paper where I marked out what I'd started and rewrote it.

> *"—which race is supreme. Or I'm coming after you next." The sound of the pipe crushing the boy's knee rang in my ears. I didn't want to*

hear it breaking my own bones. So I did it. I hit the boy until the pipe was slick with his blood.

The bike fell over at some point. The plastic bag thumped to the ground, reminding me of the loaf of bread Mom dropped in that grocery store when I was four. Not long after I'd gotten the cast off. Except, this time, I was the bald guy with the swastika, doing the Devil's work to an innocent kid.

They threw a party for me when we got back to The Fort. *He* awarded me my red laces himself. All I could think about was hiding in the bathroom to scrub the boy's blood off my shoes.

That was only the first time. There were other boys, other blood splatters on my black boots, other nights of scrubbing until my hands blistered.

He broke me. Groomed me.

Because *he* wanted me to take over for *him*. *"Otherwise, what's the point in having a son?"*

But I didn't want it.

I wanted out.

Just like now. I want out of here. I don't want to do this anymore. I start to say so, when the reporter looks up suddenly. "What about the police? Did they find the boy you attacked? They definitely press charges for something like that."

I laugh dryly. "They're just as racist as The Fort. Hell, a lot of them are members, and almost all of them are paid off.

These cases either go unsolved or The Fort puts up one of their fall guys."

Her eyebrows crease. "You can't tell me these men are sacrificial enough to take the fall for crimes they didn't commit."

"Of course they are. The fall guys are respected for putting the cause above themselves. A lot of them served so much time they don't function well in society. They'd probably do something to go back anyway. They recruit in there. Jail is what they're good at."

"If you wanted out so badly, why didn't you become a fall guy?"

"*He* never would've allowed that. Besides, prison is a nightmare. As bad as The Fort. At least, at The Fort I had Kelsey."

The reporter flips through her notes and taps a line with her pen. "Yes, Kelsey Sawyer. Let's talk about her."

Let's not. My throat closes up, making it hard to swallow. Let's forget I called the reporter, let's go on about our lives.

The reporter is already flipping through the pages. "Ah, here we go."

I want to rip the paper from her hands and disappear. She picks up her coffee and leans back, out of reach.

> *Kelsey and I were going to run. Anywhere but Kentucky. As far as possible. Soon as we turned sixteen, so we could get jobs. We'd grab our supplies from the woods, steal a truck in town, and be miles away by morning.*

> *We didn't make it to our sixteenth birthdays.*

The reporter turns the page and reads about that night in the forest. I shred the piece of particleboard and think of my woods. Of Kelsey's battered body.

After Thomas Mayes knocked me out, they dragged me back to the meeting hall. *He* had called a freaking gathering to determine how to deal with us.

> He *pulled us on stage. Kelsey on one side of* him, *and me on the other. Then* he *delivered our sentences. I had to Indoctrinate Kelsey.*

The reporter stops again. "What does 'Indoctrinate' mean?"

I stare at the pile of shredded wood on the table to keep from looking at her. "It's a beating that happens until the guilty person repents of straying from the beliefs of the Nazi Socialist Party, swears to never stray again, and gives a heart-felt recitation of the mantra. The beating continues until the leader is satisfied the person means it."

The reporter's face turns green, but it could just be the light. "And Jefferson Fuller wanted you to do it? To attack your girlfriend."

I can't sit any longer. I shove off the table and pace in front of the windows, feeling like the crumbly edged news-papers that are taped to the glass. If this woman picks at me much more I'm going to fall apart. "If I Indoctrinated her, *he* would forgive me of my sin and let me off with a boot party. That's when a bunch of them gather around and kick you with their steel-toed boots. It sounds bad, but it's better than Indoctrination. With a boot party, you can curl into a ball and protect your face and organs. During Indoctrination, they stretch you out and tie you down. You're completely exposed. Completely vulnerable." My voice hitches and I avoid her gaze. "It's all in the letter."

I know this part by heart—it's seared there for eternity.

> *Kelsey begged me to do it. She knew what* he *would do to me if I refused* him *in front of the entire Fort. I approached her with the rope, squeezed her hand, and whispered for her to run. As we bolted, I hurled the swastika flagpole at* him, *hoping the huge metal nazi eagle on top would hit* him *and distract* him *long enough.*
>
> *It didn't.*
>
> *I thought Kelsey was behind me. She was fast and strong. I'd never had to worry about her holding her own before. I didn't realize how badly she was hurt. I'd gotten ahead of her and when I turned around, they had her. She screamed for me to go.*

I'd hung, frozen, on a tightrope of time. I could've gone for her and fought them, knowing I was outnumbered and she was injured and slow. Or I could run and come back for her later, slip back in and rescue her.

Her face floats in my memory, hair stuck to her bruised cheeks, the Connor brothers and two of his thugs pinning her arms behind her back, Kelsey kicking and thrashing.

Then one of them hit her over the head with the butt of his gun. Her scream cut off and she slumped to the snow, and my choice was made. There was no way I could get us both out. She was thin, but muscular, and deadweight. The tightrope snapped and I did the only thing I could.

"You left her?" the reporter asks. Her tone is so even she could be asking my favorite color, but disgust is written across her face as plainly as the horrible confession on the page. It twists a knife inside me. All the guilt rushes to the surface, surging so violently that, for a horrible second, I'm afraid I'm going to vomit on her.

"There were too many of them. I planned to go back. I wanted to save her, but I . . ."

The reporter takes a deep breath and regains her composure, wiping the emotion off her face. "You couldn't save her," she says.

"I was in jail!" I crush the remaining chip of particleboard in my fist and something inside me snaps with it. "I couldn't help her if I was dead! *He* would've *killed me*!"

I'm standing over her, and now there's real fear on her face. She grips the arms of her chair. All the color washes out of her like chalk in the rain.

"O-okay," she whispers. "I get it. I get it."

I shove the table and the pages scatter. This is the wrong person to lose control with. If I hurt her . . . I take deep breaths, searching for the light that seems to have turned its back on me now that my crimes are out in the open.

"I did what I had to do," I say. The reporter shirks away from me as I grab my backpack. This is too much. All the unease I've been feeling since I called her erupts from me. My secrets are a land mine and my foot is on the trigger—one step away and they'll explode. And take me with them.

Once The Fort finds out about the article—once they're incriminated—they'll come after me, and they won't hold back. They'll kill me.

"This was a mistake." I scramble for my pages. "No story. No article. I take it back. All of it."

"Nate, wait!" the reporter cries. "Your story needs to be told. It—"

I whirl on her. "You can't run this. The Fort . . . they'll go batshit. Promise you won't run the article."

"But, think of all—"

I slam my fist into the table, breaking it along the seam. Her coffee cup falls to the floor, splattering its contents across the dirty tile. "Promise!"

She throws up her arms, part in surrender, part in protection. "Okay! Okay, I promise. But you have to promise me something, too."

I'm breathing heavy, sweating, emotionally raw. What more does this woman want from me?

"I'm the one you come to when you're ready. You owe me that."

I'll never be ready, so I say, "Okay, fine. You're the one I call." I crumple the letter and shoulder my backpack. My shoes kick up dust as I cross the room and slam the door behind me.

Memories I'd long buried scramble to the surface, like fast-moving zombies piling up as I stalk away from the abandoned restaurant. Split lips and broken noses and sliced guts and gashed foreheads. Image after image of things I've done, people I've hurt. Pressing down on me until I can't breathe.

I'm pissed and overwhelmed and disgusted with myself. I cling to my button so tight I'm afraid I'll snap the string. The desire to punch something spurts up with the zombie memories.

Not something. Punch some*one*.

To feel *his* bones crack beneath my fist until *his* face feels like a bag of broken chips.

But I can't. Because the person I want to hurt is already dead. I killed him.

Why did I let *him* off the hook? *He* should be the one talking to reporters. The one being overrun with ghosts of all the evil *he* committed. The one on trial, the one in jail, the one who can never have a freaking normal life.

My lungs burn and my legs ache. I don't know when I started running, but when I look up, the lights from Traitor's cabin wink across the darkening sky. Sweat pastes my T-shirt to my skin and the notebook paper in my fist is damp. I peel off my backpack, drop the letter, and place my hands on my knees to catch my breath.

I killed *him* because I had to.

Because it was *him* or me.

If I hadn't, *he*'d be walking around free right now, terrorizing the world while I rotted in an unmarked grave in the woods behind The Fort. With all the others. In the same makeshift cemetery where *he*'d started making me drag bodies back when I was ten. All the people *he* made me bury . . . all the battered corpses . . .

Gravel digs in my knees and I notice I'm on the side of the road. Guilt and grief stab my gut and I'm retching. The remnants of the stale bologna sandwich I had for lunch splatter into the long grass beside me.

I'd blocked out that damn body farm out in the hills. Not even Ms. Erica or Dr. Sterling know about it. No one on the right side of the law knows. But almost everyone at The Fort is aware of what goes on in those hills. They don't discuss it, but they know. And no one has ever done a damn thing to stop it.

Not even me.

I focus on the blotch of yellow light on Traitor's porch until my eyes glaze over. The light pulls me away from the darkness of the body farm and all the things I did in my past. My anger fades, replaced by the steady light ahead. I take slow breaths, calming myself down.

When I'm breathing normally again, I wipe my mouth with my shirttail. The pages I'd dropped flutter across the road, each word on them a piece of me I want to rip apart and leave behind. Since I can't, I do the next best thing. I shred each page until the entire thing is nothing more than gruesome confetti. Then I pick up my backpack and start walking toward the house, leaving those purged memories on the side of the road with my lunch.

653

When I open my eyes, I'm shocked to see my bedroom. I slept so well, I thought I was back in the woods. I can't remember the last time I slept like that, inside or out.

So maybe meeting with the reporter wasn't as terrible an idea as I thought. Even if she's not going to print the letter to the world, letting one person read it, one stranger who doesn't owe me anything, might have been enough to ease my burden.

Not that the shadow is completely gone. It's still there, but faded. Like a cheap black shirt that's been washed a gazillion times.

I stretch and throw on some clothes, expecting Traitor to thump on my door any minute. I usually barely make it out of bed before his fist woodpeckers on the other side. Today, though, I get completely dressed—shoes, packed bag, and everything—and no Traitor.

He knows where I was yesterday. He found out about the reporter and the letter and has some terrible punishment waiting.

Nervous, I poke my head into the hall. The house is still and quiet as death. The deer head-shaped clock over the bathroom mirror says it's seven forty-five. I'm supposed to be at school . . . now.

I rush through brushing my teeth and am darting down the stairs when the front door bangs open. Skunky hurries in so fast we almost slam into each other.

She pulls back just in time. "Oh. Um, you're late."

Thanks, Captain Obvious.

"Well, let's go," she says.

My instinct is to take an involuntary step backward, but I hold my ground. "Go? Go where?" What is Traitor going to do to me for violating his gag order?

Skunky rolls her eyes. "School. Get a move on."

Traitor's truck is in the yard, so why is she here? "Where's . . . my uncle?" I'm not sure what to call him out loud.

"Dell had to fix a leak for Mrs. Roger. His truck wouldn't start, so I had to pick him up and come back for you since you can't be trusted to operate a vehicle on your own. This is what I get for knowing jack shit about plumbing."

So, he doesn't know? This isn't some elaborate plan to dump me on the street?

Skunky snaps her fingers in front of my face. "Earth to nazi. Are you ready to go?"

I glare at her. Part of me wishes I'd pushed her over the banister that first day and gotten it over with. I shake the evil thoughts away. "Yeah, except food."

She glances at her phone and groans. "Hurry up, will ya?"

I dart into the kitchen and grab a Pop-Tart and a loaf of bread to make a sandwich.

"I've got places to be, too, you know," she calls.

"Give me a sec." I rifle through the stack of junk mail on the counter, looking for a baggie. My hand hits something heavy. I move the papers and there it is: Traitor's key ring.

"I'll give you some freaking lunch money. Let's just go!" Skunky yells.

This could be my only chance. Traitor's keys are like a third arm. I can't believe he left them behind, dead truck or not. I swing my backpack around and sweep the keys into the big pocket.

"Okay, okay!" I pick up my Pop-Tart and trot back into the living room. "I'm ready."

Skunky marches to her truck. I follow, slower, conscious of the key ring with every step, paranoid she'll hear it jangle and demand to know what I'm doing with it.

We don't say anything else on the way to school. The air isn't as hostile as it was last time we were alone, but her body is still taut as a power line, like she's ready to snap if I say or do the wrong thing.

It's eight thirty when we pull into the school lot. I scoop my backpack up off the floorboard. There's a metallic clank as I slip my arm through the strap.

"Hey," Skunky says.

Panic tightens my chest. What's my story? I grabbed them by accident? That'll never fly. I should've tossed in some of the junk mail to make it look like I knocked a bunch of shit from the counter into my bag in my rush.

Skunky's hand plunges into the center console, and for one horrible second I'm certain she's grabbing a pistol.

But it's a phone.

A small, black, low-tech thing.

I relax a little.

She holds the phone out to me. "If you're going to be running off places after school, Dell needs to be able to get in touch with you. Our numbers are already programmed. Leave it on at all times."

My hand grazes hers as I take it. She flinches slightly, but not as bad as I thought she would.

"Thanks."

"Don't thank me. I think you need a police tracking bracelet. Just don't use it during school. Get it taken away and I'll kill you."

She'd love that, wouldn't she? I guess it's an improvement, though. After our last argument, I'm pretty sure she would've killed me for breathing too loud.

"Oh, and here." She hands me a five-dollar bill. "For lunch."

I take the money and slip out of the truck, impressed with my ability to have an almost civil conversation with her.

I'm halfway to my locker before I realize I've never been late before. Can I just walk into class, or do I need some sort of special permission? I'd rather be even later than get called out in front of the entire class, so I turn around and head for the office.

Mrs. Roger has always been nice—she'll tell me what to do. I tap on the glass and play with my new phone while I wait. Okay, so "new" is kind of a stretch. Several of the numbers are half worn off, and lines of dirt live in the grooves. It still works, though, and there are even a few games.

I shove it in my pocket before the games tempt me too much. There are a couple teachers who are definite phone collectors.

Mrs. Roger should've come by now. I tap again, this time leaning through the window. I'm about to call out when I remember that Traitor's working on her house this morning, so she's probably not here.

Not sure who else I can ask. The counselor's door is partly open. I take two steps and stop. I've avoided the counselor since I almost told him the truth about me—thank God I changed my mind. He would've been even less understanding than the reporter.

"You don't have that kind of authority," a girl growls.

I know that growl. Water Fountain Girl.

"I certainly do, Caitlyn. If you pose a threat to other students, I can have you removed."

"I'm barely five feet tall. What sort of danger can I possibly pose?"

Her? A danger? I choke back a laugh. She's got a stare that can freeze water, but she's right. The only dangerous thing on her is her mouth.

"Several students have complained about your behavior."

She scoffs. "Who?"

"And your teachers tell me your grades are slipping. You're unfocused, aggressive. You have to take your ADHD medicine."

I lean closer to the gap. Water Fountain's on meds, too?

"You can't force me to take medicine against my will."

"No, but your parents can. You're still a minor."

Water Fountain laughs. "Go ahead and call, see what good it does. If you can even find them."

Seen as dangerous, on meds, missing parents. If she weren't so troll-y, me and Water Fountain might actually get along.

Feet shuffle on the tile and I jump back, but not quick enough. The door swings open the rest of the way.

Water Fountain glares at me. "Were you eavesdropping?"

"What? No."

She darts into the hall, closing the counselor's door behind her. "It was you, wasn't it? Who said I'm aggressive. I thought you were all bad and scary, and you freakin' *tattle*?"

My natural instinct is to show her how bad and scary I can be, but I notice the glisten in her eyes. She's on the verge of tears.

"It wasn't me," I say.

She brushes her hair out of her eyes and starts down the hall with a *humph*.

I don't want to follow her, but she's headed the same direction as my first class. "I'm on meds, too."

Water Fountain pauses. "You're just saying that."

"Do I look like the kind of guy who'd invent something to make someone like me?"

She tilts her head and scans me up and down. "You want me to like you?"

"Not what I said."

She shrugs. "That's what it sounded like."

This girl is impossible. "All I'm saying is, it's not just you. I hate that I have to take meds, but they do work. Something to think about." I hitch up my backpack and stalk past her.

"Thanks," she says, low.

For both our sakes, I pretend like I didn't hear her and keep walking.

✧

Turns out the teachers here only give tardies for being late, which is just some tick mark beside my name. Way better than the laps we had to run at The Fort. I do get stuck in a front desk, though, so I have to ignore the weight of the keys in my bag and pay attention.

As soon as the bell rings, I beeline for second period and slip into a back-row seat. I keep my head down and quietly sift through Traitor's keys. Most of them are out right off the bat. Nothing looks small enough to fit the lock on the trunk. By lunch, I've narrowed it down to eleven possibilities. I snag some Post-its off my history teacher's desk on the way out, and mark the remaining keys with the sticky side.

I've never bought lunch before, so I'm not sure where to go. I follow the line winding around the edge of the lunchroom, hoping I'm in the right place.

"Nate?"

My head jerks toward the sound. Brandon cuts the line and slides in behind me.

"This is new," he says.

"Woke up late."

He nods knowingly. "You're lucky. It's chicken sandwich and tot day. Also known as the best day ever."

I follow the lead of the girl in front of me and grab a bottle of water from the cooler by the wall.

"Some people live for pizza day," Brandon continues. "But they always overcook it and the cheese gets hard."

The girl stops at a salad bar full of wilted lettuce and too-yellow cheese. Brandon taps my shoulder and hands me a tray. "Skip the salad, man. The ag kids have first lunch and they don't all wash their hands after messing with the animals." He points to the hot bar. "Chicken sandwich gold."

It doesn't much look like gold to me until I compare it to the salad bar. I put a sandwich and tots on my tray and start checking for an empty corner table on my way to pay the lunch lady.

"Sit with us today," Brandon calls.

I stop mid-stride. "Us" is Brandon and his basketball buddies, guys I've nodded at in the halls, but never talked to. One of them is the dude who kicked my pencil the second day.

"I don't—" I begin, then I think of Water Fountain Girl—Caitlyn's—conversation with the counselor. It couldn't hurt to start giving people here the benefit of the doubt. "Okay."

"Sweet." Brandon heaps more tots on his tray.

I hand my money to the lady and scan the tables for Brandon's friends. They're sitting in the middle of the freaking room, farthest away from the exits.

It's all right. Just lunch. No brawls have broken out yet this year. It'll be fine.

I hope.

The guys are laughing at something as I approach, but quickly go silent.

"Um, hey," I say.

"Hey," Pencil Guy replies.

I stand there awkwardly, not sure where to sit.

"Dude, move over," Brandon says from behind me. "Make room for Nate."

Pencil Guy shifts down a seat, leaving me a spot right in the center. It's like there's a neon sign pointing at my head commanding everyone to make me feel as awkward as possible.

"Nate," Brandon says, "tell the guys about that bass you caught the other day."

I pause with my chicken sandwich halfway to my mouth. "It was pretty big."

Please don't make me do this, Brandon. Come on. Can't you see how uncomfortable I am?

Brandon tosses a tater tot in the air and catches it in his mouth. "Mine was bigger."

"Yeah, sure," Pencil Guy says.

Brandon hits him in the forehead with a tot. "Like you've got room to talk, Fletch. Yours is smaller than that tater tot."

"Ooo," several of the guys say at once.

Pencil Guy throws a tot back at Brandon. "At least I know how to use it, Bodyguard. Yours is gonna fall off before Maddie even realizes you exist."

Brandon shrugs. "Nah, not with Kara's boobs to think about."

They go back and forth like that for the rest of lunch. I have to admit, some of them are kind of funny. I'm a rock, and the rest of them are a river. Until now, I've been a big eyesore out in the middle of the water. But the dam broke today and raised the tide so now it flows right over me. I'm not exactly part of their group, but I'm not entirely on my own, either. I think I could live with this.

"Hey," Pencil Guy says as we're dropping our trays on the conveyer belt to the kitchen. "We're playing a pickup game after school. You in?"

Part of me wants to go. I almost say yes; then I remember the key ring covered in stickies. "I can't today."

Brandon raises an eyebrow.

"Chores," I say. "Maybe another time."

Surprisingly, I actually mean it.

✧

I rush home after school. It seems even more secluded now that I realize how far I'm running. It's almost four by the time I see the cabin.

Traitor's truck stops me mid-stride before I remember he left it this morning. That doesn't mean he's not here, though. Skunky could've already dropped him off. I slam the front door.

No yelling.

I don't know how long I have, so I run up the stairs two at a time, tearing my backpack open as I go. Miraculously, all the Post-its stayed on the keys.

I burst into Traitor's room. Every cell of my body is tense, ready for Skunky's truck to come roaring into the yard, but the only sound is my jackhammering pulse.

The trunk is exactly how it was last time I saw it. I drop to my knees and plug the first key into the lock. It doesn't go farther than the first tumbler. I tear off the yellow tab and flip to the next. It doesn't even make it that far. Another key, then another, then another, until I'm down to four.

How long have I been up here? Feels like five minutes, but it could've been an hour for all I know. The next key is smaller than the others. This could be it.

I push it in the lock. The first tumbler gives, then the second, then the third.

The key is in! It fits!

With a shaking hand, I twist the key clockwise. It doesn't move. I try the other way. Nothing. Back and forth, back and forth. Applying more pressure, then less, then lifting as I turn, then pushing down. Doesn't matter. This isn't the key.

None of the next three even come close.

I slump against the closet wall. I've searched every inch of this house. Every nook, every drawer, every loose floorboard. The key ring was my last hope.

"Where is it?" I kick the trunk. It slides toward the gun safe.

The gun safe! One of these keys has to open it. Could the trunk key be hidden in there? The safe is obviously new, so I find the shiniest key on the ring. With shaking hands, I slide the key in the lock. The tumblers fall into place. The key turns.

I'm quivering like a wet dog as I turn the handle. Three rifles and two shotguns gleam at me. I recoil to the other side of the closet.

I blink and see blood on the snow, bits of gray brain matter stuck to the tree trunks like old Silly Putty.

I'm shivering, wishing I'd brought a jacket.

I stand suddenly and burst into Traitor's room, breathing heavy, holding my button. "I'm in a house. A house. Not woods. A house." I mutter it over and over again, holding my button firmly.

These guns aren't *that* gun. They aren't pistols. They aren't murder weapons.

I have to see if the key is there. I can do that without actually touching the guns. I force myself back in the closet and peer into the safe. No nooks or crannies. No hiding spots. I manage to run my hands along the inside edge in case Traitor taped the key there. No luck.

If I could hold a gun, I could shoot the trunk open. Blast the damn lock to bits.

But there'd be no hiding that. Even though we're in the middle of the woods, these aren't Kentucky woods. Town isn't that far away. Neighbors would hear the gun blast and call Traitor. He'd see the trunk blown to pieces and confirm his suspicion that I'm nothing but a gun-shooting criminal.

Besides, I could damage whatever is inside.

Not that it matters. Just the thought of picking up a gun again makes me break out in a cold sweat. I swing the safe door closed and lock it tight. It's no use. The key isn't anywhere.

I throw the blanket back over the trunk and slide the clothes in front of it. When I'm positive the room is how I found it, I go downstairs and cover the key ring back up with the junk mail on the counter.

What if Traitor threw the key away? Tossed it down the hole out by the woods?

The thought almost sends me back to the gun safe.

Mom is closer than she's been in years, but still so far out of reach. I can't give up yet. If the key doesn't exist, then by God I'll find a way in that trunk somehow.

654

The social worker brought candy. Like I'm a freaking four-year-old. She looked so pleased with herself as she dumped the bag of miniatures on the coffee table. Ms. Erica would've never pulled that shit. Of course, she never needed to, since she actually cared.

The social worker perches on the edge of the chair and looks at me hopefully. I cross my arms. She's been here ten minutes and hasn't said a word beyond "hello." In fact, we haven't moved beyond that since our screamfest.

That sounds like the name of a NSBM band. I shudder and slump further in my seat. I wish I had that damn stress ball back.

Traitor's leaning against the kitchen door frame like always. After a while, he throws up his arms. "Oh, for God's sake, someone say something. This is getting ridiculous."

The social worker just stares. This must be one of the tactics they're taught to get clients to open up. Good luck, lady. I want to talk to her about as bad as I want to scratch a swastika into my skin and go back to The Fort. Traitor clears his throat and holds up a piece of paper behind the social worker.

"Talk and she'll leave."

He flips it over.

"Longer she's here, the longer your chore list gets."

I give him an exaggerated eye roll. Whatever. He has a point. If I say something, this lady will at least get the hell out of here. "So . . . Snickers." I nod at the table.

Her face brightens. "You like?"

"Oh, yeah. You found my one weakness. I go wild for Snickers." It's hard not to smirk. Traitor shoots me a warning scowl.

"I found them at an early Halloween sale. I could bring more next time."

Good Lord, she's trying so hard. I pick up a candy bar and shove the whole thing in my mouth. Okay, so maybe an offering of candy wasn't a terrible idea.

"How's school?" she asks.

A nervous current runs through me. She talked to my teachers. She knows I spent all day yesterday looking at keys. Traitor knows I took them.

That's ridiculous. No way she knows. I play it cool and shrug. She pushes the pile of candy closer.

"Fine," I say.

"Your uncle tells me you and your friend have been hanging out a lot."

"Yep."

"That's good! Sounds like you're making real progress."

I eat another Snickers. I mean, if it's right in front of me, I might as well. The social worker smooths her skirt. Geez, even the first time she came wasn't this awkward. The tension from that damn argument smothers us like a house full of smoke. My chewing is obnoxiously loud with no one talking, but I'll be damned if I encourage this woman.

"You should get a dog," I say to Traitor.

He shoots me a hard look. "Too much work."

"I'd take care of it." I'd said it just to say *something*, but now that I think about it, I could handle a dog. Something big and floppy that's all ears and skin. Like a bloodhound. The only dog I ever had was the stray when I was a kid, back before we ran. He was gone by the time I returned to The Fort.

Traitor frowns. "I don't give you enough to do?"

"Look at how much y'all sound like a family," the social worker says brightly.

We both glare at her. She pops a Snickers in her mouth and this time *her* chewing is obnoxious.

After a few minutes, I can't take it anymore. "I'm just saying, you seem like a dog guy."

"We're not getting a dog!" Traitor snatches a candy bar off the table and stomps into the kitchen.

The social worker scribbles on her tablet. "Well, I think everything is going just great. I told you not telling your friend about your past was a good idea. See how great you are?"

She and I have different definitions of great. Although things really aren't so bad, when you get right down to it.

"Great progress," she says. "Just great."

Is that the only word this woman knows? I'd buy her a damn thesaurus if it wouldn't be a waste of money. Or if I *had* money.

She packs up her stuff, except for the candy. "I'll see you in a couple weeks, then."

Traitor reappears once the front door closes. We watch her haul her crap to her ugly Ford sedan. "I can't stand that woman."

"Me, neither."

"I liked that other one better," he says.

"Ms. Erica?"

"Yeah. She seemed nice. Reminded me of . . . never mind."

We make brief eye contact, then turn away before this becomes some bonding moment. Questions gurgle up my throat. I clamp my mouth shut before any come spilling out. Who was he about to say? Mom?

I can see some similarities. They were both kind, they listened, they gave me a chance. I want to know more. Traitor knew Mom longer. Were there other traits of Mom's he saw in Ms. Erica?

If I asked, would he tell me? What if I came out and asked about the trunk?

I glance at him out of the corner of my eye. He looks so much like Mom. The resemblance stops there, though.

He won't answer my questions. And he'll just be pissed if he finds out I was in his room.

I choke my questions down and leave him to sweep the remaining Snickers into a bowl. I go upstairs to my chair by the window, running my fingers along Ms. Erica's battered card, thinking about her and Mom. A knife of longing stabs me in the chest.

Skunky's cell phone is open and in my hand. I punch Ms. Erica's number in before I can stop myself. I haven't made a call yet. The first one should be her.

It rings once. Twice. Three times. This is probably her office number and it's Friday afternoon. She's not going to—

"Hello?"

Her voice is so soft and familiar it catches me off guard. A sudden pang of homesickness rolls through me. That one word warms me like a bonfire—hot with comfort and cold with loneliness. I should tell her about the reporter, and the crappy social worker, and everything that has happened in the months since we last spoke. I should tell her to take me back to the Psych Center. Back home.

"Hello?" she repeats, more firmly. "Hell—"

"Hi. Um . . . It's Nate. Fuller."

There's a pause on the other end. Did the call drop? Did she hang up? A surge of fear rises like bile in my throat.

"Nate?" Her voice is higher. "Is something wrong?" She sounds almost nervous.

"No! I'm okay. That's why I'm calling, actually." I don't realize it until it's out of my mouth. "I'm not doing terrible," I say. Not a complete lie. "I made a friend, and it doesn't totally suck here."

I can't tell her the truth. A few months ago, I was certain she would've come to get me, would've made everything better. Now, I'm not so sure. Am I remembering her wrong, or has our relationship changed that much?

She hesitates. "That's amazing, Nate."

Amazing. Not great. Ms. Erica knows more than a single word.

"But you can't call like this," she says.

My mouth hangs open. "You said I could call if I needed anything."

"I know, but I'm not your social worker anymore. You're supposed to go to someone else now. Have you talked to her about how you're doing?"

"She's horrible."

"How so?"

This isn't right. The flow of conversation is off. Is there a lag with the phones, or are we different? Either way, I don't like it. I also don't know how to phrase all the problems with the social worker. The biggest one being, she isn't Ms. Erica.

"Has she acted inappropriately?" Ms. Erica asks.

"No, nothing like that. She just . . . doesn't care enough. Not like you."

"Nate." Ms. Erica sighs into the receiver. "I wish I could do something. Really. But I'm not even supposed to be talking to you. You should contact the office there and let them know if it's not working."

"But that's not—"

"I'm sorry, Nate."

To her credit, she sounds genuine.

"I just wanted to let you know I'm okay," I say.

She pauses. "I'm really happy for you."

"Yeah."

"I have to go. Keep it up, okay?"

"Okay."

She hangs up, taking her warmth with her, leaving me cold and hollow. I shouldn't have called. It makes me miss her and the way we used to talk. And the Psych Center. What kind of person misses a mental hospital?

But I do. The security and the schedule and the ease. I thought I was moving past this, but a piece of me is still back in Kentucky. And I'm afraid it always will be.

655

Boots stomp me awake. Rhythmic. Practiced. Goose stepping. In a few minutes, *he*'ll jerk me out of bed and demand to know why I'm not out there. Then *he*'ll whip me until I want to die, and force me to march even though I can barely stand.

I'm terrified to open my eyes, but I have to be ready. It's worse when I'm caught off guard. I crack my eyelids and see the rough wooden walls of my room in Traitor's cabin. Not The Fort. The only things goose stepping outside are the geese migrating south for the winter. I slump against my wafer of a pillow and check the time on my cell phone. Five thirty in the morning. There's a chance I can get a little more sleep before Traitor wakes me up for chores.

But the thump of boots doesn't stop. It vibrates the floor, almost like it *is* real, like—

My bedroom door flies open. I rocket out of bed, ready for a fight. Traitor's on me in an instant, slamming something into my chest.

"What the hell did you do?"

The beast shakes itself awake. I shove Traitor off. "What's your problem?"

"This is my problem." He shakes a crumpled newspaper. "*You're* my problem. I explicitly told you to keep your trap shut, and you immediately defied me. Do you have a death wish?"

I rip the paper away from him, tearing it, but not enough to block the headline: NEO-NAZI COMES CLEAN.

The words weigh a thousand pounds. My knees can't handle the extra load. They buckle and I collapse onto the bed. Under the headline is a name I know all too well. Shaw Holt. She still wrote the article.

No.

No, no, *no*! How could she do this? After she read all the shit that *he* put me through. After she looked me in the eye and acted like she understood. After I told her not to write it. I told her what could happen if she did. She promised.

That lying, manipulative bitch.

My eyes skate down the page taking in snippets of what she wrote, including a picture of my back and shots of the letter.

She stole some of the pages. The worst ones. My story about getting my red laces.

It's out there for everyone to see. In my words. Which is what I thought I wanted, but seeing them here, set apart, it's so much worse. Especially this part on its own. Without context.

"How could you be so monumentally stupid?" Traitor barks. "Does your brain not work? What were you thinking?"

I ignore him and read the article. Each word pisses me off more and more. She always intended to write it. She always meant to twist my words to fit the story she wanted to tell. Same as all reporters.

"Hey!" Traitor shouts. He flings his arm in front of me, stopping my fist in midair. There's an indentation in the wall where I've apparently been punching it. The skin across my knuckles has torn open and blood drips around my fingers. "You don't get to take this out on my house," Traitor snaps.

The beast roars, begging to be unleashed. I need to get into the woods, need to destroy something before the beast bursts through me.

"When?" Traitor demands.

"When what?"

"When did you talk to a reporter?"

I wipe my bleeding knuckles on my boxers. "Wednesday."

"When you were supposed to be with Brandon?"

I nod.

Traitor swipes his ball cap off and settles it on his head again. "You lied to me. You're on house arrest."

I glare at him. "What does that mean?"

"You can't leave your room. You're . . ."—his mouth screws to one side—"grounded. Yeah. No Brandon and no whatever the hell it is you do in the woods. You eat, do your work, and sleep. That's it."

My hand throbs. Each pulse of pain is Morse code from the beast, begging to be set free. Brandon is how I get through my days. The woods are how I make it through the nights. What am I supposed to do without them? How do I go back to the way I was now that I've tasted the air on the other side?

"Grounded? Seriously? For shit I did in the past?"

"No, for directly disobeying me. You know good and damn well I told you not to talk to anyone." His angry face looks so much like Mom's that I have to look away. "I'm going to town to do damage control."

"Like what, hijack the paper trucks?"

"If that's what it takes." He brandishes the torn newspaper. "This can't get out. And it sure as hell can't get back to me."

"How is anyone going to know? It doesn't say 'Nate Clemons' anywhere."

Traitor holds up the front page. "It has your damn picture!"

"The back of my head, and barely that." It's a crappy shot with a camera phone as I'm walking away, toward the sun. Just a shadow. "You'll make things worse. Raise a fuss and everyone will know something's up. Then they *will* look closer."

Traitor crumples the paper. "Don't leave the house."

"What about school? Are you going to keep me from that, too?"

"School? You'll be lucky if your ass isn't in jail for assault by this afternoon. Hell, I may send you there myself."

My hands ball into fists. I won't go back there. I'll run first.

He slams the door and clomps downstairs.

I stare at the door, unsure of what to do. He can't force me to stay, but it will only make things worse if I leave. The need to destroy something rages within me, but my hand is killing me. So instead of breaking anything, I fix it. A half-empty bottle of rubbing alcohol sits in the bathroom cabinet. I pour it over my knuckles, appreciating the burn before mopping it up and wrapping my hand in gauze.

Could I really go back to jail? The cops would have to connect "Nate Clemons" to "Nathaniel Fuller." Even if they make the connection, I don't know what they can do about it. Can they really indict me for anything I admitted in my letter? Can they even prove I wrote the damn thing or met with the reporter in the first place? If the Internet worked in this Godforsaken cabin, I could look up the statute of limitations on assault and battery.

I piece together the torn newspaper and read it again, and then again. Each time stings worse than the rubbing alcohol.

Does what I did even qualify as assault? Or would it be attempted murder?

There are no fall guys to save me this time, no insanity plea, no self-defense claim. Nothing to protect me.

Just like the kid I helped attack.

The Birmingham Post

NEO-NAZI COMES CLEAN!

By Shaw Holt
News First Network Senior Correspondent

Death is too good for some people. Nathaniel Fuller is one of them. Although he was found not guilty by reason of self-defense in the murder of his father almost two years ago, Fuller is far from innocent.

I had the privilege of a one-on-one exclusive interview with Fuller. During the interview, Fuller was nervous, erratic, and threatening. He claimed he wanted to clear his name; however, he refused to speak a word regarding his past.

The best he could do was write a letter confessing to his crimes—several pages of which are included with this article so everyone can see—in his own handwriting—how dangerous he truly is.

Fuller is a monster, and it's something I have personally known for years.

Almost four years ago, a then 13-year-old Fuller brutally attacked my nephew, Samuel Hirsch, outside a synagogue in Louisville, Kentucky. Hirsch, who did nothing to antagonize Fuller or his skinhead posse, suffered multiple head contusions, broken ribs, a punctured lung, and underwent three plastic surgeries to reshape his face.

Fuller did not face charges for the assault. I spent two years attempting to bring Fuller to justice for the attack, only to learn someone had already confessed—someone not meeting Hirsch's description of the perpetrator.

During our recent interview, Fuller admitted his Neo-Nazi organization, known as The Fort, had several "fall guys" on its payroll.

"The fall guys are pretty well respected for putting the cause above their own needs," Fuller said. "They recruit in there [prison]. Jail is what they're good at."

Jail is not what Nathaniel Fuller is good at, however. Of the many incidents he is accused of having participated in, he only served time for one: his father's murder. The same father who wouldn't permit Fuller to pay for his own crimes. In Fuller's own words: "He never would've allowed that. Besides, prison is a nightmare."

Fuller would know. He spent a little over a month in the West Kentucky Penitentiary before his attorney petitioned for removal to a psychiatric facility due to Fuller's extreme mental anguish.

Why would a teenager have such extreme mental anguish? Here it is in his own words. This excerpt comes from a letter given directly to me by Fuller.

Continued C19

656

That damn kid.

That's the wrong reaction, I know it, but all I can think about is that damn kid.

Of all the faces for him to latch onto, it had to be mine. I had to be the one to get caught in his fearful stare. Not the Connor brothers, who did all the damage. Me, who never wanted to be there in the first place.

Of all the people to be related to a freaking reporter.

When I close my eyes, all I see are those black pools of his dilated pupils staring back and that dirty footprint marring his bright hat. A yarmulke, according to the article. I'm glad Traitor's Internet is about as good as a hole in a bucket, because I have this desire to see that kid again, to see if what the article said about his face is true. To see how the Connor brothers—how *we*—ruined his life.

Not that I can touch a computer. Or anything really.

Traitor's rant has continued all weekend. Every time he sees me, he lays into me again, screaming and hollering until his words aren't words anymore, just a series of sounds. That must be how animals hear humans: grunts and shrieks.

He was too late to stop the papers. He's spent the weekend on the phone with Dr. Sterling and my attorney in Kentucky, trying to figure out what to do about the article.

And what to do about me.

Even though the reporter has made appearances on all the twenty-four-hour news channels, who have dug their Nathaniel Fuller and neo-nazi montages out of the archives for the occasion, she hasn't disclosed anything more than what she said in the article. Not the name I'm using or my location or when she interviewed me. She may hate me, but at least it doesn't seem like she wants me dead. Yet, anyway. Part of me thinks it would be better if she'd put it out there already. Each interview and article drops the pendulum lower and lower. It's like she's waiting until the right moment to level that final swing and chop my head off.

So far, no one has put it all together. Traitor and my attorney seem to think I'm safe. The news channels will talk about it for a couple days, then forget about me when the next big scandal hits. Dr. Sterling thinks it's best for me to carry on like normal and wait for it all to blow over.

But I don't know how to do that. My nerves are frayed wires. My emotions are their own shorted circuit. I go from being pissed about the article to disgusted with myself to terrified of what will happen if I'm found to being pissed at Traitor. The feeling that keeps twisting back to the top, though, is anger at myself.

I'm such an idiot. I knew better than to trust a reporter. I let my damn emotions get in the way. My ridiculous freaking *need* to be normal.

I feel scooped out. Raw. I'm angriest with myself for being outside that synagogue in the first place.

I drop to the edge of the bed and pull at the ends of my too-long hair. How do I keep screwing up so badly? How do I keep missing the right thing to do?

I shouldn't have talked to the reporter.

But really, I shouldn't have gone after that kid.

That poor, scrawny kid.

Reading about what happened to him after the attack hurts. It was easier when I closed myself off. When I could think of my victims not as real people, but as tasks to be checked off a list so that I wouldn't be punished.

Now they're real. This kid is real. His pain, his fear, his internal scars that he may be able to keep hidden but will never shed.

I did that.

The hell of it is if the reporter had asked about him, I could've let her know what really happened. It probably wouldn't have mattered. I might not have caused the worst of his injuries, but I didn't stop them either.

I never stopped any of it.

660

Dr. Sterling convinced Traitor that I need to stay in school. I'm more grateful for that than I thought I would be. School gives me a chance to get away from Traitor and it gives me something to focus on besides all of my sins.

Traitor stopped driving me, though. I figured he wouldn't let me out of his sight, but he's taken a different approach, punishing me by making me get up at an ungodly hour to walk. I'm exhausted by the time I reach school, but I'm actually glad for that, too. I think less when I'm tired.

This morning, Brandon is already waiting by our lockers by the time I drag in. "Whatcha doin' next Friday night?" He bounces on the balls of his feet nervously.

I shove my textbooks in my locker. "Probably a shit-ton of chores."

Brandon waves me off. "You can do those anytime."

"Why? What's up?"

Brandon glances around, then lowers his voice. "My brother is coming home. I could use a buffer. Come eat dinner with us."

He wants *me* there to ease a stressful situation. Wrong guy. I'm dirty fingers in a gash. I'll only make things worse. "Why me?"

"You're the only one who knows." Brandon fiddles with his backpack straps. "I'll owe you."

The idea of favors doesn't sit well with me, but I feel like I owe him for being so nice to me so this would put us square, and it would get me away from Traitor. He said "no Brandon" but he can't mean this, right? "Okay, yeah."

"Awesome!" His grin takes up half his face. "Oh, and basketball. Today."

"I'm—"

"Nope. The other day you said another time. This is another time."

I grab my math book and notebook. "I don't have any gym clothes with me."

"I gotcha covered." Brandon smirks. "Meet me in the gym after school."

"But—"

He holds up his hands, then turns away, singing some song about basketball. Every few feet, he leaps up and bumps the ceiling tiles with his fingertips. I should've said no the first time the guys asked.

We played a lot of basketball at The Fort. Kentucky is basketball country after all. But games rarely ended well. We played prison rules: a thrown elbow, an overeager rebound, a sneaky screen, and the game suddenly wasn't so much about who scored the most points as which team could beat the ever-loving shit out of the other one. The free-throw line was a head-shaped blood splatter where this guy called Heavyweight knocked out his own brother for fouling him.

All day, I picture that rust-colored spot, marking not just the line, but also what happens when dangerous people play dangerous games. Basketball is a beacon for the beast. A giant flashing "unleash here" sign. If I could go home first and wreak havoc in the woods, it might be different, but there's no time. Not like Traitor would let me anyway, since the woods are off-limits since my grounding. So is Brandon, technically, but since Traitor isn't picking me up anymore, he won't know if I don't go straight home.

When the final bell rings, I wait in the hallway until it clears out, debating what to do. Left takes me out the front doors and home to safety. Right takes me to the gym and to risk.

Maybe I should give myself the benefit of the doubt.

I turn right.

Brandon's waiting by the gym door. His baggy basketball shorts and T-shirt with the sleeves cut off catch me off guard. It's the first time I've seen him in something that wasn't neat and pressed and tucked. "For a minute, I thought I was going to have to come get you." He tosses me red shorts and a gray T-shirt with PROPERTY OF THE BULLS printed on the front in blocky red letters. "Snatched these from Coach's office. Get changed. You're on my team."

The locker room is an all-red horror that doesn't ease my worries. The walls already seem smeared with blood. I find an empty locker and shove my stuff inside. The gym clothes are baggy. Every few steps I have to stop and pull the shorts up.

"Well, don't you look like you've got spirit," Brandon says when I come out of the locker room.

I'm tempted to say screw it, change back, and head home, when Pencil Guy throws a basketball at me. "Let's see what you've got, Juvie."

I dribble a couple times then shoot a jumper. It bounces off the rim and shoots off to the side. "I haven't played in a while."

"No shit," another guy says. He's the other one Brandon is always running around with. "He better not be on our team, Bodyguard."

"Better you than me," Pencil Guy says, shooting a three-pointer that swishes through the net.

Eight of us showed up. I'm with Brandon, his other friend, and a Mexican dude from math class. Pencil Guy, a thin, dorky-looking black kid with glasses, a ginger from my homeroom, and a buff blonde guy are on the other. I recognize Blondie as the guy Maddie has been all up on since the parking lot fight.

It quickly becomes clear that these guys don't mess around. They weave between one another, running plays as complex as Mrs. Roger's knitting pattern. I try to keep up, half-heartedly shuffling up and down the court with them, but I'm more in the way than anything.

They're a fluid unit. A team. Watching them makes the counselor's team comment on my first day seem even more ridiculous. The only teamwork I've been a part of has been hunting minorities with a pack of racist lions, which hardly counts.

I should walk off the court now. How could Brandon ever think I'd fit in with these guys?

The Mexican kid throws up a brick. It ricochets off the backboard, almost smacking me in the face. My hands fly up on instinct and catch the ball before it takes my head off. I shoot without thinking. The basketball bounces off the white square on the backboard and drops through the hoop.

"Atta way, Juvie." The Mexican claps me on the back as he runs to the other end to set up on defense.

A smile breaks out across my face before I can stop it, and an electric thrill thrums through my fingertips.

It couldn't hurt to stick it out a little longer.

I have to figure out something else to call that guy, though. I can feel *his* shadow smiling when I think of my teammate as the "Mexican." I can't let the grease of *his* thoughts stain the only good feeling I've had all day.

Blondie dribbles down court. The Mex—the math class guy—darts in front of him, steals the ball, and lays it up in our basket.

"Nice one, Mateo!" Brandon slaps his ass as he runs by.

"Yeah, good job, Mateo," I say, smiling again. The shadow shrivels inside me like a raisin. I jump for a rebound and pass it to Other Friend. I still don't understand the plays they're running, but at least I'm adding to the team.

This isn't so bad. I'm not sure what I was worried about.

I sink another couple layups and a mid-range jumper and hit a stride. I'm not terrible. Especially for not having played since The Fort.

Brandon shoots from outside, and my body naturally swings into position, boxing out the ginger. He juts his bony hip into my side and chops my arm, cracking his hand against my funny bone. Jagged barbs of pain shoot through me and the beast springs to life.

I shove him hard. "What the hell, man? Foul!"

The ginger sprawls under the net. The ball swooshes through and bounces off his head.

I tense.

He's going to come up swinging. The adrenaline starts to pump. The ginger rolls over, a red spot on his knee. I move into a fighting stance. *Shit.* This is what I was afraid of. This is where it all goes to Hell.

The guys all stop and stare at me. "Whoa, Juvie," Pencil Guy says. "Take it easy."

Brandon lays a hand on my arm. I shrug him off. He's the last person I want to hurt if the ginger comes at me.

Other Friend extends a hand to the ginger. "You all right, Griff?"

His knee is skinned, but he seems fine otherwise. He stands and backs away with his hands up in surrender. "Yeah, Rainey, I'm good. Sorry about the foul," he says sheepishly.

"No," Pencil Guy snaps, glaring at me. "It's basketball. Fouls happen. Fights don't."

I stand there, stunned. My body isn't sure what to do now, hanging on the edge of fight or flight, now quickly tipping toward flight.

"My bad," I say. "That's . . . that's how we always played. I thought . . ." Embarrassed heat burns my cheeks. I screwed up. No way they'll want to keep playing with me.

Blondie squeezes the ball between his palms. "Damn, Juvie, you did have it rough."

All their expressions soften. Ginger—Griff—extends his hand. "No hard feelings, man. Just, tone it down in the future, okay?"

I shake his hand and he grins.

"So, are we gonna play or what?" Griff says.

Blondie inbounds the ball to the Dorky Guy and everyone else takes off down the court.

"Come on, Nate," Brandon calls. "Don't tell me you're already winded."

I shake off my daze and trot after them. Pencil Guy throws an air ball and the Dorky guy and I lunge for it. His sharp elbow catches me in the ribs. He jets in front of me, grabs the ball, and thunks it off the glass and through the hoop.

"Nice hustle," he says. "You've got good reflexes for a tall guy."

My ribs sting, but the urge to fight swirls away like blood down a drain. I would've cut someone for doing that at The Fort. Then again, the people at The Fort meant to hurt you when they played. These guys don't. They just want to have fun.

I inbound the ball to Mateo and follow him down the court.

We play to twenty-one and my team loses four of the five games, even after we mix up teams. By the time we're done, I'm dripping with sweat and exhausted, but energized. The hollowness I've felt since talking to Ms. Erica is replaced with . . . warmth. Happiness, almost.

I'm standing on the side with my hands over my head when a towel hits me in the face. "Not too bad, Nate," Fletcher says. By the end of the games, I figured out that Pencil Guy is Fletcher, the other black guy is Ellis, and Blondie is Scott. It feels weird to think of these guys by their names after so long. Until now they've just been "Brandon's friends" in one big lump.

"Thanks." I wipe my face with the towel and drape it around my neck.

"Yeah, man." Scott stops beside me. "You need to work on that jumper, but you've gotta nice layup."

"And pretty good rebounding," Griff says, smiling. "You'd make a good forward."

Rainey tosses the ball in a canvas bin. "You should think about joining the team. Practice doesn't start for another few weeks."

Joining the team. The warmth expands through my chest. Then I snap back to reality. "I don't know. My uncle probably won't let me."

"He seems like a nice guy," Ellis, says. "He and Bev fixed our roof last spring after that big tornado. They didn't even charge us full price. Said they were helping out neighbors affected by the storm."

Sounds about right. Traitor helps everyone except me. He'd only let me play if he thought it would hurt me and help someone else.

I drop my towel in the basket by the locker room door. "I don't exactly have the most freedom."

"Oh, yeah, I forgot about the whole juvie thing." Fletch shoots his own towel like a basketball. It lands beside the clothes basket with a wet thump. "Just tell him it will be good for your rehabilitation."

Rainey glances at his phone and his face goes pale. "Shit, man. I gotta go. Ma's gonna have my hide if I forget to pick up Beth from cheerleading again."

"Drop me off on your way home?" Fletcher asks.

"Only if you promise not to hit on my sister again," Rainey says, scowling.

Fletcher picks up his towel and dunks it in the basket, then trails after Rainey. "I can't help it if she's hot."

Everyone else follows them until it's just me and Brandon. "That went well," he says.

I shrug.

"You really should think about joining the team. We could use another forward."

"You've met my uncle. You really think he'd let me?" Not to mention it goes against the whole stay out of the public eye thing.

"Maybe you don't know him as well as you think." Brandon pushes the dirty clothes basket into the locker room. "Talk to him. He might surprise you."

✧

"Absolutely not." Traitor scowls at me. I see Skunky raise an eyebrow over the screen of the laptop that's balanced on the edge of the kitchen island.

"Hear me out," I say.

"Nope. You do know what grounded means, right? It means you can't do the things you want."

"It's not like I'll even play much. I'll probably just sit the bench."

"Then what does it matter?" He swigs his beer. "Tell you what, keep your ass in line and maybe I'll let you go to a game. You'll get the same experience on the bleachers as the bench."

"No, I won't." It's not the same at all. I'm already a bystander in my own life. I want to do something, to be part of something. And as much as I hate to admit it, a long buried part of me wants to belong somewhere. Here. With normal guys—guys who aren't deeply screwed up. "I want . . ." I struggle to put it into words Traitor can understand without giving him too much of myself. "I want to be part of a team."

I didn't even realize how badly I wanted this until he said no.

Traitor's deep-set eyes are shadowed by the awnings of his eyebrows. One is open wider than the other. Mom used to do the same thing when she lectured me. I hate that he's wearing her expression.

He gulps down the last of his beer and plunks the empty bottle on the counter. "The answer would be no, even if you weren't grounded. I swear, it's like you *want* The Fort to find you."

"How? How is wearing matching clothes and sitting on a chair going to lead The Fort to me?"

"Team pictures, newspaper write-ups, TV coverage if the team does well." He counts off each thing on his fingers like they're charges against me. "This is the exact opposite of what I told you to do."

"I'll be sick on picture day. And there's just as much chance of me landing on TV on the bench as there is in the crowd."

"Okay, then you can't go to the games, either," he says.

Now I'm getting pissed. This is ridiculous. "You wanted me to fit in."

"Not like this."

"But if I'm careful—"

"I said *no*!" he yells.

"Dell," Skunky warns, closing her laptop.

Traitor throws the empty beer bottle away. "I'm your guardian, Nate. And I say you can't play. End of discussion." He jerks the fridge door open, knocking the glass jars in the door together like poor man's wind chimes. He never drinks more than one beer a night, but he grabs a second and snaps the cap across the room. It hits the wall and clatters to the floor. He turns the bottle up and guzzles it down.

"Seriously?" Skunky slides off her stool and throws the abandoned bottle cap in the trash. "Take it easy, Dell."

"I'm a grown man. I can have two beers if I want," he snaps.

She crosses her arms. "Not what I meant."

Traitor lowers the bottle and wipes his mouth with the back of his hand. "The boy has to listen to me, Bev. The rules are in place for a reason."

Skunky shoots him a pointed look. "I know, but do you really think this is the way to enforce them? Besides, it's just basketball. It might be good for him to channel his energy."

I start to respond and end up gaping at her. Is she on my side?

"Channel his energy?" Traitor says. "Yeah, he'll channel it right into someone's face."

"He hasn't hurt anyone yet, Dell."

Traitor tips his beer to his lips. "Yet," he says before taking another gulp.

The beast perks up inside me. "Why do you hate me so much?"

Traitor turns his head to me so fast I'm certain he gave himself whiplash. "Sure you want to talk about hate?"

My jaw clenches. "Oh, so it's back to that," I say through gritted teeth. He has to be kidding. I can't live a normal life because I had the bad luck of being born in Hell? The darkness swirls in my blood like creamer in coffee. I choke it down, leaving a bitter taste on the back of my tongue.

"It *always* comes back to that."

The hollowness inside gnaws at me. It's a black hole in my stomach, chewing up everything good and swallowing it in an eternal vacuum, leaving only darkness. Only beast.

I move closer to Traitor on instinct, my hands curled into fists. "How can you expect me to move on if you won't let it go?"

"Let it go?" he scoffs. "It's that easy for you, huh?"

Skunky hops between us. "Guys, chill."

Traitor talks over her. "It's that simple to forget all the evil you've done? All the people you've hurt? Lives you've ruined?"

"You don't know anything about it!" I yell. The beast claws me, scraping its way out. I shove Skunky aside. I can't unleash on her—I don't want to. I want it to be him. "You have no idea what I've done, what I have to live with."

We're nose to nose. As close as we can be with our height difference, anyway. My fists beg to be unleashed on Traitor's face.

A few hours ago I was fine. Almost normal. Running and playing like a regular guy. Now, here I am. Feeding Traitor's opinion of me the way kids feed ducks bread at the park. He's baiting me. He wants me to lose control. Then he'll have an excuse to get rid of me.

Just when I was starting to think I don't want to go.

"Think carefully about what you say next, boy."

I sneer down at him. "Take a trip to The Fort. See that hellhole for yourself. See how long you last there, you self-righteous, know-nothing prick."

Traitor throws his beer against the wall. Glass shatters. Skunky screams and covers her head. "Get out of my house," Traitor yells.

I hold my ground.

"Dell," Skunky says. Frothy beer puddles on the floor at her feet.

"Now!"

Spit flies out of his mouth as he screams. The veins in his forehead bulge. This is it. We're about to throw down. I picture my fist connecting with his nose, shoving him over the island, smashing his head into the counter, blood spurting from his face. I even take a step.

Then I stalk past him and outside, slamming the front door behind me.

The night air carries a chill that raises goose bumps on my skin. I expect it to bring a flashback with it—arguing with a family member and storming into the woods should be enough—but the medicine does its job. The flashback is a timid cat, lurking on the fringe of my brain, refusing to come any closer. I don't know if I'm relieved or not.

I storm to my clearing in the woods and smash branches until my fingers are sore and blisters start to rise on my palms.

I thought I was done with this. Letting the reporter in on my past was supposed to calm the beast—to help me get on with my life—but I'm still stuck. Rooted in it like that damn tree in the hole. Every time I try to grow, my roots hold me down.

Or maybe it's me. Maybe *I* hold me down.

Should I have done things differently? Told *him* no when *he* commanded me to unleash holy terror on innocent people? Taken whatever punishment *he* handed out? Run away sooner? Talked to reporters? Tried to expose all the shit that happened at The Fort?

No one would've listened to me. I was just a kid. How much power does one kid have? Besides, as soon as I opened my mouth, The Fort would've weaseled out of it like they always did. They would've destroyed me instead. It wouldn't have been a boot party, or even an Indoctrination. It would've been so much worse. I might have even ended up in the body farm. And my scumbag father would have been alive to ruin more lives.

Should I have at least tried?

I busy my hands with the tiny twigs, repeating 660 over and over until a weird vibration comes from my left front pocket. Oh, right, the phone. I reach my dirty, blistering hand into my pocket and pull it out. A message scrolls across the screen:

BEV: COME BACK, NATE.

She used my name. Not nazi or the probably worse things they call me when I'm not around. Whatever. I'll live here in the woods before I go back to that asshole's house.

The phone buzzes again.

BEV: DON'T MAKE ME DRAG YOU BACK. IF I HAVE TO COME AFTER YOU, I'LL BE SERIOUSLY PISSED.

Like she could drag me anywhere. I don't want her trying, though. These woods are the only thing I have that's all mine. Even the button is technically Mom's.

Skunky is waiting at the tree line when I emerge. "Five more minutes and I was coming after you."

"What's the point? He kicked me out. Where else am I going to go?"

"Nate," she starts, then takes a deep breath.

Fear whips across my chest. This is it. She's taking me away. A group home or some other place where I won't have a choice but to let the beast live on the surface to protect myself.

"He's not kicking you out."

I narrow my eyes. "Why not?"

"Does it matter?" she snaps. "Just be grateful for a place to live."

She starts for the house, pausing long enough to make sure I'm following.

"Why are you here?" I ask.

"Believe it or not, I'm on your side this time."

I stop suddenly. "Are you high?"

Skunky whirls. I wish I could see her face better, but the porch light barely licks the edge of the yard where we're standing. After several seconds of silence, she sighs. "You're trying. I see that."

"He doesn't."

Skunky looks over her shoulder toward the cabin. "Dell has . . . he's . . . he'll come around. Just don't stop trying."

She turns her back to me and walks to her truck.

"Why are you being nice to me? You hate me."

"You use 'hate' too much," she says. "I don't hate you."

"You don't want me here."

She pauses, one hand on the truck handle. "I'm coming around, too."

I shouldn't push this. I should accept her answer and let it be enough for now. "But why?" I want to understand her sudden shift—how she can change her opinion so easily. Though, now that I think about it, it's not really that sudden. The dinner, the phone. She's been softening like butter left out of the fridge.

"Let's just say I have a soft spot for reforming assholes."

The porch light flips off. The truck door creaks open and headlights wash the yard before my eyes can adjust to the dark.

"Get in there and finish your chores before you piss him off more," *Bev* says. Then she's gone, leaving me standing in the yard alone.

Of all nights to sleep in the woods, this is the one. I'm torn between going back out there and going inside. Bev stuck her neck out for me tonight. She's making an effort. Maybe I should, too. If she, of all people, can believe in me, then maybe I'm not a lost cause.

I want to prove her right this time. Prove that there is some good in me. Prove that Traitor's wrong.

I turn and climb the rickety porch steps. Least I can do is try to make this work. Try harder. For her.

664

When I first see the red flyers on my way to school, I think they're for the fall yard sale and don't give them a second look. Then the wind tears one free from a light pole. It tumbles down the sidewalk before getting caught against a trash can long enough for me to glimpse the bold, white words.

STOP WHITE EXTINC—

I catch the red paper before it blows away and glance up and down the quiet street. Someone could see me with this. They could think I hung it up. Main Street seems to be abandoned, but the few remaining stores will open soon.

When I'm certain I'm alone, I pick up the piece of paper, even though I already know its message by heart.

STOP WHITE EXTINCTION! DID YOU KNOW THE ANTIRACISTS ARE TRYING TO ELIMINATE THE WHITE PEOPLE?

It's one of the messages the Skynbyrds plaster all over a target area. Standard message. Standard link to their "white extinction" website.

This is Step One. Try to recruit more people to the cause.

The paper slips through my fingers like fresh blood. Its meaning slowly seeps in as the page drifts to the pavement.

They found me. The Fort has finally found me.

I don't know how, but they did. That's the only possible reason for this flyer. Another hate group randomly targeting Lewiston is too coincidental. This is a warning.

Are the Skynbyrds still here? Lurking? Waiting? They usually work in packs, hitting a targeted area without the men first, but they rarely travel this far from home. If this is a message—intimidation or worse—they could have backup.

My heart's suddenly a hummingbird thrumming inside my chest, beating its wings against my rib cage. The bird migrates up my throat to my head, twitching it from side to side. My instinct is to press myself against the bricks of the closest building. Protect my back. Keep someone from sneaking up on me.

But red and white pages flutter on every pole in town. I catch the one I dropped and shove it in my backpack. I can't stand seeing those messages everywhere I turn. I run from pole to pole, ripping down the signs until I have them all.

All the ones I find, anyway. A man arrives at the grocery store as I'm pulling down the last flyer. He gives me a curious look. I ignore him and shove the papers in my backpack. He couldn't have seen anything. And even if he did, even if someone else saw the flyers before me, I have them all. I stopped the Skynbyrds from spreading their message.

Now what? I can't go to school with a backpack of hate, and I can't throw these away here where anyone could find them. I can't throw them away *anywhere*. My hands shake as I pull out my cell phone. I'm scared to go home. Afraid I'm being watched.

Did the reporter finally drop the blade and give up my location? Does The Fort already know about the cabin?

I can't go back there alone. Safety in numbers, that's what they always taught us. I linger near the store and autodial the number Bev programmed for Traitor.

"This better be an emergency," he growls. "I'm elbows deep in pipe slud—"

"They're here. The . . . The Fort. They found me."

He doesn't respond. Did he not hear me? Did he pass out?

"Hello?"

"Where are you?" Traitor asks.

"The grocery store."

The phone goes dead. The nervous bird in my head flaps harder. Veins throb in my forehead. I struggle to keep my face calm, my hands still. If they're watching, I won't let them see me react. Won't let them think they scared me. I wish I hadn't taken my meds this morning. I need to be sharp now, not hazy and slow.

An unfamiliar truck putters down the road. I stiffen, clenching my jaw, steeling my gaze. The driver passes without looking my way. Seconds stretch like a rubber band. I constantly press the phone's power button to check the time. Where is Traitor? Is he even coming? Or did they find him first?

After what feels like an hour—but is only five minutes—the rubber band of time snaps back. Traitor's truck rounds the corner. He slows enough for me to jump in the passenger seat then roars away from the curb.

"How do you know?" he asks.

I unzip my bag and pass him a flyer. He sucks in a sharp breath and turns down an unfamiliar road.

"Did they see you?"

"I don't think so. I kept a lookout as I tore them down."

His hands tighten on the wheel. "That's just going to piss them off."

"I killed their leader and got away with it. They're already more than pissed off." They're murderous. Hungry for blood. Fear breaks through the dam that I've built and crashes over me. I can't stop my hands from shaking now. Wave after wave of memories roll through my head. Those bodies in the woods. That'll be me.

I can't breathe.

I roll down the window and suck in cool air.

We fly down back roads turning so suddenly I'm afraid the truck will flip. I cling to the oh-shit handle for dear life.

"How the hell did they find me?" I say, the panic rising like acid up my throat.

"I think we both know the answer to that," Traitor replies through clenched teeth.

I hug my backpack to my chest. "But . . . but the reporter didn't say where I am."

"As far as we know. Either way, they figured it out. The how doesn't matter." He glances over, and I see my fear mirrored on his face. I've never seen him look afraid. "The question now is are they still here and, if they are, what are they going to do next?"

The truck bursts through the trees and into a field. We're at the back of Traitor's property. It looks different from this view. Bigger. He slams on the brakes and idles at the edge of the field, his gaze sweeping the yard like radar, taking in every corner, before he guns it, tearing across the field until we reach the back door.

"Get your ass in that house, lock the doors, and don't come out until I call you."

"Why? What are you going to do?"

He yanks the backpack out of my arms. "Clean up your mess, *again*. Someone has to make sure there isn't any more of this shit in town. This is it, Nate. Threatening me is one thing, but threatening the safety of my town, of the innocent people here? I'm done. Get inside and pack your shit."

My hands automatically ball into fists. "You can't be serious."

Traitor reaches over me and throws open the truck door. His face is inches from mine and the beast is going wild. Resisting the urge to head-butt him takes everything I've got.

"Where am I going to go?"

"I don't care." He shoves me and I fall sideways into the mud. He slams the door and roars away back over the field, leaving me in his dust.

Traitor thinks he's so much better than me. Like he doesn't have a past? He obviously did something so bad Mom forgot he existed. So bad he can't even think about her.

My fear gives way to searing anger. Screw him. Screw walking the line. Screw being worried about what he thinks. Screw trying to make this work. It's too late for that. If he's kicking me out, I'm getting some damn answers first.

I storm to the shed. An ax hangs from a hook. I tear it off the wall, knocking a box of nails off a shelf, scattering them across the floor. If any pierce my thin shoe soles, I don't feel them.

In fact, I feel nothing but anger. I'm a ghost hovering outside my body, not in control of my own hands.

I watch myself march upstairs. Watch as I fling open Traitor's closet door and swing the ax at the trunk. It buries itself deep in the wood. I heave it out and the beast swings again and again and again. Splinters fly. The lock thuds to the closet floor. I hack and hack until there's no lid left.

I'm raising the ax again when I see it. The boxy, black scar that's plagued me all my life. My legs vanish from under me, and I'm on the floor, not feeling the chips of wood that must be digging into my skin. Not aware of anything except that symbol.

Why am I seeing that symbol?

Why am I four hundred miles from The Fort staring at a swastika?

I'm repulsed by it, but I have to touch it. Have to be certain it's real. My hands push the fragments of trunk lid away and remove the red and black flag. Why does Traitor have this? This can't be Mom's.

It can't be.

The fabric burns worse than my anger. I fling the flag away as though it's a venomous snake, watching it warily, as if it will bite me at any moment. Then I turn back to the trunk, unsure if I even want to know what else is in there.

My ghost hands move on their own, tearing through the contents of the trunk: a metal nazi eagle, a swastika armband, black combat boots, a green flight jacket.

No. This can't be her stuff. This can't be all she left.

No, no, no, no, no!

I tear through it all, digging, hoping.

My fingers hit something flat and cold. For a second, I'm afraid it's a gun. But when I look down, I realize it's a metal picture frame. Three people stand beside a jacked-up black truck that has a swastika flag hanging off the antenna. I know that truck. That's *his* truck. More importantly, that's *him.*

I haven't seen *his* face in 664 days. Not outside the memory in my mind—but that image is tainted with fear and blood. This one is clear and sharp and steals my breath. I almost drop the frame. There's something off about *him.* I see the same cold eyes, the same closed-off stance, the same hard, thin nose.

But *his* mouth is different. *He's smiling.* A real smile. Not the one I always saw—the one as laced with danger as *his* combat boots. *His* arm is around a girl, one with deep-set eyes and long brown hair that's blowing in an invisible breeze.

Mom.

My finger trails down her tiny, frozen cheek. One side of her mouth is lifted in a half smile. She's leaning into *him*. One hand is behind *his* back, the other's on her swollen belly.

Holding me.

Water plops on the glass over the picture, making her image waver. Is there a leak? I glance up, but the ceiling's clear.

It's me. I'm leaking.

I've missed her face. Until this moment, I didn't realize that I could barely remember her smile. I hate that I'm seeing it now with *him*.

I wipe the tear away with the tail of my black T-shirt.

My eyes fall on the guy on the other side of Mom. He could almost be her twin. He's the only one not smiling. I know that scowl pretty damn well by now. But that's not what makes me hurl the picture against the wall.

No, it's the giant swastika tattoo on Traitor's bare chest that allows the beast to take control.

✧

I don't know how long I've been in the closet, surrounded by splintered wood and shattered glass and smashed memories, trying to figure out what to do now.

Boots thunk beside me. "What in God's name—"

I'm on my feet in a flash, slamming Traitor into the gun safe, holding him by his throat. He claws at my hands. I squeeze tighter.

"Nate," he squeaks. His face is bloodred. His toes scrape the floor.

I let go with one hand and rip open his shirt, popping the first few buttons. Instead of the boxy tattoo I expect, I'm met with gnarled gray skin. My grip on his throat loosens.

Traitor roars and buries his shoulder in my stomach, tackling me into the busted trunk. Clothes fall around us. A metal hanger scratches my forehead, and the jagged lip of the trunk digs into my back. I bring up a knee, aiming for Traitor's crotch, but he swivels at the last minute and my knee glances off his thigh.

I'm at an awkward angle, half-in, half-out of the trunk. I punch him across the jaw. There isn't much behind it, but enough to knock him off balance so I can scramble upright. He moves to attack me again, but suddenly stops.

All the color drains from his face as he takes in the closet, matching the weird scar on his chest. Before I can go after him again, he sinks to the floor, completely unaware of the glass beneath him.

"So you know," he whispers.

I want to hit him again. Actually, I never wanted to stop. "All this time, you've been judging *me*. Making me feel small and dirty and evil. While you had that." I point at his chest.

He picks up the broken picture frame, his finger sweeping over Mom just like mine did.

"I . . . I'm sorry."

"Sorry?" I jerk the picture away. "That's all you've got? *Sorry?*"

"Oh my God."

Both our heads jerk up. Bev stands in the doorway, hands over her mouth.

"What the—" She moves for us and steps on the swastika flag. "Oh."

She looks from me to Traitor and back again. "Well, it had to come out eventually." She pushes past me and takes Traitor's arm. "I think it's time to talk."

Traitor knocks glass and wood from his pants and nods.

"Come on, Nate." Bev guides Traitor to the stairs, one arm supporting him. Traitor looks strangely small beside her. He's taller than she is, but right now he's crumpled paper in her arms.

Wait, *she* knows? She's seen all this shit and is still with him? Why did she want to kill me then and not him? What the hell is going on?

I follow them more out of curiosity than anything else. I finally have some answers, but all they gave me is more questions.

Bev eases Traitor down into the social worker's usual chair. She sits on the chair's arm and points at the couch. "Sit."

I hold my ground.

She cradles Traitor's hand in hers. "First of all, Nate—I tried to stay out of it before and let Dell handle it—but you're foolish for talking to a reporter."

"That's already been established, thanks."

She holds up her free hand. "But, you're not the only foolish one here. We all do reckless things. Some more reckless than others." She gives me a pointed look. "None of us are perfect."

I rub my temples. The left side of my head is tacky with dried blood from the hanger. "I'm aware of that," I growl. "But that doesn't explain the trunk of hate up there."

"It does, though," she says.

"Why are you defending him? He's no better than me. Worse probably."

"I didn't kill her," Traitor manages to say. His eyes glisten with tears.

"Kill who?" I ask.

"Mae." His voice is thick with emotion. "I've done some terrible things, but I didn't kill her. You did."

I'd be on him already if the damn coffee table wasn't in my way. I drop the picture and start to climb over the table.

Bev leaps up and spreads her arms wide, blocking Traitor. "Whoa. Hey, easy," she says.

"That's right, let your girlfriend protect you." I snarl. "What are you going to do, stay here all the time? Because I'm *going* to beat his ass for that."

"For what? The truth?" Traitor barks.

"Because I killed one parent, you think I did in the other? That I go around murdering parents all the time?" I knock my shins against the coffee table. Bev scoots in front of me again. "Why would I kill the only person keeping me away from *him*? The one person who gave a single shit about me."

"She was dead the moment you were conceived." Traitor picks up the broken fame. "We were going to leave. I had . . . Jefferson pushed me too far. If I stayed at The Fort, I knew I'd end up crossing a line that I couldn't come back from. I'd convinced Mae to run. The abuse had gone on too long. She agreed to go, and then . . ."

His finger rests on Mom's stomach. On me.

"She found out she was pregnant. She thought it would maybe change Jefferson, soften him. I tried to talk some sense into her, but she wouldn't have it. I told her if I left, that was it. I'd have to cut ties completely or they'd find me. Nothing I said mattered. She loved him. In spite of everything, she loved him. So I ran without her and never looked back."

I sink to the couch. A million bricks have fallen on my chest. I can't breathe and I don't want to. He's right. I killed her, just like I killed Kelsey. If it wasn't for me, Mom would be here, living a new life alongside her brother.

"I didn't know she was dead until your trial," Traitor says. "Then, a few months ago, Ms. Tufts showed me the court records from when Jefferson regained custody. The lies . . ." He grips the frame so hard I'm surprised he doesn't bend the metal. I killed her. Not directly, sure, but . . . I killed both of them.

I deserve jail. Worse. I deserve every shitty hand I've been dealt.

Bev moves to the couch and, for a moment, I'm afraid she's going to hug me. But she pats my shoulder, instead, and motions for Traitor. He drops his head in his hands. The frame clatters to the cold floor.

"It wasn't your fault, Nate," he says. "I do know that. I'm just . . . angry." He lifts his head. "You know that feeling, don't you? Anger at your shitty life, your shitty choices? I'm angry at Mae for staying and you for existing and myself for not carrying her, kicking and screaming, away from that asshole."

"If you know that, that Mom's choices weren't my fault, then why? Why have you been such a dick? Ever since I came here. Before then."

He meets my eyes. "Because every time I look at you, I see Jefferson, and I see myself—the things I had to do at The Fort. I hated you for bringing my past to life."

"I can't help the way I look," I say. I wish I looked like Mom instead. I wish I could go back in time an undo everything. "I wish I'd never been born."

Traitor's jaw goes slack. He scrubs a hand down his face. "I *am* a dick. Nate, being born, *existing,* that is not your fault. I'm sorry for holding all of this against you. For not letting myself actually see you. I came into this thinking Jefferson got to you, and that the self-defense angle was exactly that—an angle to keep you out of jail. Being around that shit, it does things to you. It's hard to come back from it."

I wipe my face with the back of my hand. I'm leaking again. He actually gets it. He had to do terrible things, too. He ran and left someone he loved behind. I couldn't have taken in someone from The Fort. I already have enough reminders of the horrors I've committed. Choosing to live with someone else with that same past every day would've been too much. "So why did you come for me at all? Why not leave me at the Psych Center or let the State figure out what to do with me?"

Traitor picks up the picture. "Because I thought about how much Mae loved you. She loved you more than him, and more than me. She loved you enough to finally run."

665

I removed the picture from what was left of the frame and folded it so I could only see Mom and Traitor. Dell. His name rolled around in my head all night while I sat in the chair by my window staring at the photo, tracing 665 in the curlicues built into the frame. Around dawn, I got up and dug Mom's curtains out of the overflowing trash can that I haven't dumped since my first day here. Fortunately, I'd only thrown away balls of paper and a couple empty drink cans, so they were only a little wrinkled.

She did make them. Dell told me so last night. The curtains and the picture were the only things he took with him when he left. It turned out it hurt too much to see the curtains every day, so he hung them in the spare room where they could waft like her ghost at the other end of the house.

And the only picture he'd been able to grab had *him* in it, so it went in the trunk with his neo-nazi stuff.

He said he kept it all for two reasons: as a reminder of The Fort, so that he'd never forget what clothing himself with hate looked like, and in case he ever gave up and decided to go back for Mom. So he could blend in.

I hang the curtains again just as the first morning rays slant through the window, filtering through the thin cotton. I close my eyes and try to remember Mom's hands, try to picture them sewing these strips of fabric together. My brain is a TV with poor reception.

I push the curtains back and prop the photograph on the sill so I can see Mom next to her work. Beyond the picture, a flash of red catches my eye.

Bev's truck is still in the yard. She's never stayed over before. Is this going to become a regular thing now? Everything already feels shifted. An earthquake rocked us, tearing down the walls we'd all built around ourselves.

It's weird. All this time, I've been looking for someone to spill my guts to, and he's been right here. We just had to give each other a chance. Dell and Bev and I talked for hours last night. Not just about The Fort, but about random things, too, like our favorite pizza toppings (Dell's is barbecue chicken, Bev's is banana peppers, and mine is cheese). And important things like words I shouldn't say. That came up when I asked Bev where she was from. "Georgia," she said.

"No, I mean where are you really from?"

"Georgia," she said again. "And FYI, that question is racist as hell."

"Why?" I asked.

She sighed. "Because it assumes I'm not American because of the way I look. My parents moved here from China, though, if that's what you're asking."

By the time I went to bed, my head spun with all the new information.

I touch Mom's picture, then pull on clean clothes and pad downstairs, skipping the squeaky steps. I'm craving the feel and smell of the woods. It's too stuffy inside to think. I need fresh air.

"Oh, you're up." Bev stands in front of the screen door. She sips from a steaming coffee mug. "There's a fresh pot if you want some."

I'm not much of a coffee drinker, but it does smell good and I didn't sleep all night. I pour myself a cup and stand bedside Bev.

"He was a mess when I met him, you know." She says it so low I'm not certain I heard her right. "That's why I was so against you living here. I was afraid you'd trigger him. He never told me what finally made him break. There's not much about those days he's willing to talk about. The shame just about killed him."

"I'm intimately aware," I whisper.

Bev cocks her head toward me. "I know."

We sip quietly, watching birds flit to and from the porch feeder. The coffee is as bitter as the past few months have been, but I'm already more alert. I choke down another swallow. The breeze kicks up through the screen and I shiver.

Bev wraps both hands around her mug. "He did tell me how they ended up there."

Now she really has my attention.

"Their good-for-nothing parents beat them constantly. Dell said they'd sometimes miss whole weeks of school because they couldn't walk. The other kids bullied them for their tattered clothes and bruised skin. Their teachers wrote them off as dumb and lazy. So one day, they left for school and never came back—hitched on the back of a hay truck."

My God, they weren't that different from Thomas Mayes. Other than the whole evil part—pretty certain he's still only a few steps shy of Satan. My poor mother, though. She never really stood a chance.

"They hitched all the way from West Virginia to West Kentucky. Dell said they were constantly worried their parents were right behind them. Turns out, they never cared enough. Dell looked them up later and found out they both died of drug overdoses in that same tiny town. Anyway, they met up with some guys from The Fort who took them in and offered them protection."

"Biggest mistake of my life." Dell's voice makes us both jump.

I slosh coffee on the floor, then mop it up with my sock before either of them notice.

Dell takes Bev's coffee cup and gulps down the rest. "I never should've judged you, Nate. I'm not any better. Hell,

I wish I'd had the strength to off my old man when I was a kid."

"No, you don't," I say quickly.

Dell's mouth flattens into a thin line.

I slump against the wall and swallow the golf ball in my throat. My ever-rebelling mouth struggles to form the words. "Living with yourself is hard . . . after. Going through every single day of your life knowing you're capable of . . . of murder. Knowing you really are the monster everyone thinks. It—"

"You're not a murderer," he says. "You're not. You hear me? You're *not*."

"But I—"

"If he was here right now. Would you shoot him?" Dell asks. "If he was unarmed, standing over there, would you do it?"

Would I? Would I kill *him* all over again? Or would I let *him* live and face the punishment *he* deserved?

"No. I'd want *him* to rot in jail. For the horrors *he* committed to haunt *him* every day of *his* life until they slowly drove *him* insane."

"Then you're not a murderer." Dell sounds like he did last night when he was crying. "I'm so sorry, Nate. I'm sorry it took so long for me to see that."

I look at him. He *is* crying. So is Bev.

So am I.

The tension rolls out of my body. I sag onto the couch, sobbing so hard my whole body shakes. I cry out all the anger and frustration and sadness and guilt—a torrent of it rains down around me and washes away through the spaces in the floorboards.

I've never cried like this. Not alone, and certainly not with people. Years of tears roll out. By the time I'm finished, I'm surprised my skin doesn't look like a raisin. I expect to feel hollow, like I did after writing the letter, scooped out and raw, but I'm strangely full. Less like a snake shedding old skin and more like a bird that's molted, its old feathers replaced by bright, new ones.

Dell bends down and looks me in the eye. His face is red and blotchy, but he doesn't seem ashamed. "I'm gonna tell it to you straight. You have his temper. You have his looks. You'll never escape the pieces of him that are in you, but you *can* overcome them."

It isn't new information—I've always known of the devils within my blood—but hearing Dell say it aloud cuts me deep.

"Is Jefferson the only one you killed?" he asks.

I nod.

"Did you ever come close?"

I nod again. He watches me, expecting me to say more. Doesn't he know the words are stuck inside? I chew on my bottom lip. He does know. He's been there, at The Fort.

The words wiggle like a loose tooth. "A few months before . . . before I killed *him*. *He* got pissed at me for leaving the fridge door open and beat me with a fire poker."

Something hot touches my hands. I look down and see a fresh cup of coffee. I didn't even notice Bev take the old one.

I sip and the hot liquid warms my body, melting the glue holding the words in place.

I never set out to hurt anyone. I always intended to hang back, to only do what was necessary to keep *him* satisfied. But sometimes the heat of the moment catches you in an updraft.

Sometimes, you're punching and punching and punching and you realize the person isn't awake anymore.

"I went to town to get away from *him*. I was so angry, so hurt, and there was nothing I could do about it. Nothing would ever make *him* stop. *He* was stronger and had more people on *his* side. So, I took it all out on this guy at the bar. I don't even remember what started it . . ."

One minute I was sitting on a bar stool, and the next a limp body was flopped over a trash can in the alley and my aching hands were sprayed with blood. I can't bear to see Dell and Bev's expressions, so I stare at the black coffee, rotating the mug, inhaling the steam.

The image of that guy stuck with me like my brain was one of those glue traps for catching mice. For months, every time I closed my eyes I saw the poor asshole who decided to cross me that night, an endless cycle of fractured pictures: the guy's face smashed in, blood pooling in puddles so deep red they were almost black, his head groggily trying to lift and clunking clumsily back onto the trash can.

Those images only got unstuck once they were replaced by even worse ones. Memories of blood and bone stuck to barren trees and splashed across fresh snow.

"He looked like a motorcycle wreck victim," I say. "I was only fourteen. If I could do that to a grown man, then . . ." Now I look up. They don't seem as horrified as I'd expected. "I don't know what would've happened if I'd stayed much longer."

Dell sits on the coffee table in front of me. "But you didn't. You got out. You know what that means?"

Only that I wasn't there long enough to go full-homicidal and require the body farm for myself.

"It means that while you got some of him in you, you got more of her. Jefferson wouldn't have stopped. Do you know how old he was when he killed for the first time?"

I shake my head.

"Barely thirteen. He beat a black kid with a tire iron. And he meant to do it. He told me before we went out that he was gonna earn his red laces and he was gonna do it up right. You stopped, Nate. He didn't. You planned to leave, he became The Fort's leader. You feel remorse, he felt nothing. You're not him, and you're not gonna be him. Not as long as I have anything to do with it."

He stands and gazes out the screen door. "Now, what are we going to do about The Fort being here?"

"They want me," I say. "They won't stop until they get me." The beast prowls in its flesh-and-bone cage, just thinking about The Fort being in Lewiston. "I have to leave."

"No," Dell says. "I'm not running."

"I'm not asking you to. I thought you were kicking me out, anyway."

"You know damn well I'm not," he says. "I'm your guardian. Where you go, I go."

"You know what they'll do to this town." I deepen my voice slightly. "Violence is meted out against the anti-Whites and antiracists who speak against the White message."

Dell shudders. "Don't do that again. You sound too much like Jefferson."

I cringe. "My point stands. They'll destroy this town and everyone in it who doesn't get on board with them. Just to get to me."

"We're not leaving," Dell says, again. "I've built too much here to walk away now. I'm sick of backing down, sick of tucking my tail and hiding. This is our home."

Our home? I've never felt at home anywhere before. Am I home here? Or am I risking everything Dell's worked so hard for?

"Where would you even go?" Bev asks.

My thoughts hadn't made it that far. Where would I feel safe? Where could The Fort not reach me? "Back to the Psych Center. I was better there anyway." There, I had four solid walls and strong locks keeping them out. And me in.

Dell's forehead wrinkles and his jaw sets. "You really believe that?"

Do I? I may have been safer there, but every day was a struggle to stay out of the darkness. I fought the meds—there was no reason to take them, then. If I had a flashback, they'd just strap me down and take care of me. Out here, the meds haven't been so bad. Once I got used to them.

And I think I may actually be growing. Making friends, starting to fit in. Not quite thriving, but I'm kind of like that tree in the hole by the woods. I'm making it.

"No," I say. "But what other choice do I have?"

Bev waves her cell phone. "We call the police."

"And tell them what?" I say. "That we brought a pack of neo-nazis here? At best, they'll write up a report on the flyers—they're not an immediate threat since we got them all. At worst, they'll have a ton of questions for us."

"I don't like it," Bev says.

Dell takes Bev's phone. "Me, neither. We tell the cops the truth and let them handle it."

I jump to my feet. "You said you've built too much to walk away. You think this town will let us stay when they find out our pasts? I say don't tell anyone. We keep this quiet and hope the Skynbyrds go away when they don't get a reaction out of us. Maybe they'll think they've got the wrong place."

"You honestly think that will happen?" Dell scoffs.

"Got a better idea? One that doesn't include everyone potentially learning they've been living among reformed white supremacists?"

Dell's grip tightens on the phone. "Fine. We do it your way for now. But if this happens again, we suck it up and call the cops. We'll get up early and canvas the town for more flyers. I can't let these bastards freak out my town. Other than that, we act normal."

668

Acting normal means dinner with Brandon's family. I'd forgotten all about it. If Brandon hadn't caught me in the hall before the last bell to tell me when to show up, I would've won the award for biggest jackass of the year.

Dell shakes his head when I tell him. "I don't think that's a good idea. It's not safe."

"Backing out now would be the opposite of normal. I'll be fine."

"I'm not thinking about you," Dell says. "I'm thinking of Brandon."

I pick at a hole in my T-shirt. "I know." It's way more dangerous for Brandon if he's seen with me. The Fort would lose their shit. "But we haven't seen flyers all week. I think we're okay. I think they're gone."

"I hope you're right."

Me, too. I don't want to think about what it means if I'm wrong.

"Fine," Dell says, "but you're sure as hell not wearing that."

"I don't have anything else."

Dell sighs. "Follow me."

Two hours later, I'm sitting in Brandon's driveway wearing a button-down that's two sizes too small. Dell said a T-shirt wasn't acceptable attire for a family dinner, especially with folks like the Kingsleys.

I tug at my sleeves self-consciously.

Dell shifts the truck into park. "Roll those things up and nobody will be able to tell."

The shirttail barely hits the top of my jeans. I don't think rolling the sleeves is going to do much good. "Oh, yeah, that'll do it," I say after I've pushed the cuffs to my elbows. "They'll never be able to tell now. Not until I bend, and a button flies into the gravy." He could've bought me a new shirt—I need some anyway, since it's getting colder—but no, Captain Cheap-Ass can't spare a few bucks on something as frivolous as me not freezing to death this winter.

"Keep your phone on," he says, ignoring me. "Don't spill nothin' on my shirt. And mind your manners. These are nice people. Don't be an ass."

You would know. I almost say it aloud out of habit. I'm still adjusting to the changes between Dell, Bev, and me, but the old feelings are folded in the corner of my mind like an origami scorpion.

"What are you waiting for," Dell asks, "a dinner bell?"

I glance at Brandon's house from the corner of my eye. I've been dying to see inside, but now that I'm here, I can't move. In my head, the house is as neat and put together as Brandon, but I know better than anyone how different my head can be from reality.

As curious as I am, I'm also terrified. Terrified that I'll screw up, but also that the inside will be like they claimed at The Fort. That The Fort will be right about something, and it will break the image I have of Brandon into tiny pieces.

"Nate," Dell says. "You're being rude. Get in there already."

I take a deep breath and pull the door handle. Dell's headlights sweep over me as he backs out of the driveway. My ever-present shadow stretches down the sidewalk in front of me, reaching greedily for the porch. I force myself to follow the shadow. Each step like walking through drying cement.

Because what I'm most afraid of is me.

What if everyone is right about me? What if I hurt Brandon's family?

My armpits are coated with sweat by the time I ring the doorbell, despite the crisp fall air.

Brandon opens the door before I've even taken my finger off the buzzer. "Thank God you're here." He grabs my arm and jerks me into a wide foyer. "The passive aggressiveness has already started and Henry's hardly been home an hour."

A family fight is the last thing I want to walk into right now. I can pretend I forgot to take my meds. Fake a flashback. Except Dell would be pissed if he had to turn right around and come get me.

And now that I've made it inside, curiosity pricks me with its porcupine quills. The house seems normal so far. Normal by sitcom standards, anyway. Dark wood floors span the length of the hall from the front entrance all the way to white French doors at the back. The whole place seems exposed, with open access between all the rooms. The arch to my left leads to a large living room filled with comfortable-looking furniture and a big-screen television. To the right, a staircase gently curves to a second-floor catwalk.

The walls are tan and are covered with family pictures. Everything is pristine and shiny. It's the nicest building I've ever been in, other than the white marble courthouse where my hearing was held. I'd normally be uncomfortable in a place like this, afraid to touch anything or relax. But I feel totally at ease. Relieved even.

The house matches Brandon. It's not some weird, alien thing. It's warm and comfortable. I want to curl up and take a nap on that couch.

"Brandon? Baby, is that Nate?" Brandon's mother steps into the hallway carrying a big blue platter piled high with spicy-smelling chicken. "Take this to the table." She hands the plate to Brandon and wraps her arms around me. My muscles constrict. If I were a turtle, I'd tuck myself into my shell right now and hide.

I stand, rigor mortis still. Mrs. Kingsley smells of herbs and spices and faint floral perfume. When was I hugged last? Mom?

Holy shit, would *he* flip if *he* saw me being in the arms of a black woman. In a black family's house. About to eat food they prepared, with their *hands*. I can almost see *him* in front of me, demanding I go outside and wash: *"Remove the stain of their filthy skin."*

Guilt works through me, warming my face. I'm worried the Kingsleys will be able to smell the ignorant racist on me as easily as I smell Mrs. Kingsley's cooking on her. I bury *his* voice deep, deep, deep. Below the beast. Stuff it all the way down where no one can catch a whiff.

"Come on, baby." Mrs. Kingsley takes my hand and leads me to the kitchen. "You're not going to break the tension by standing in the hall."

My eyes go wide.

"Of course I know why you're here." She pats my arm. "I am glad, though. James has to behave in front of company."

Brandon jogs up behind us as we enter the wide kitchen. Dell's entire ground floor could fit in this one room.

Two men stand by the granite island. The whole family looks like they stepped out of a magazine ad. My fingers work along the hem of my shirt, as though if I pull on it enough, it will magically grow a few inches.

The younger guy, who must be Henry, drags a small carrot through some ranch and takes a bite. "I'm just saying, Dad, let me make my own decisions for once. We can't all be the great professor—"

"Look who I found!" Brandon's mom pushes me forward. "This is my oldest, Henry, and the love of my life, Professor James Kingsley." She beams, obviously proud of Brandon's dad.

Dr. Kingsley looks slightly annoyed, but he forces a smile and extends his hand. "Nice to finally meet you, Nate."

The scent of cigar smoke follows him as he shakes my hand. Everything about this family is new and interesting, even the way they freaking smell. Is it because they're black? Do smells cling to them more than people with lighter skin? I feel like the biggest asshole ever for even wondering.

The lines beside the professor's eyes are more pronounced than Brandon's and his tuft of hair is mostly gray, but otherwise they're spitting images of each other. I shake his hand first, then Henry's. I can see more of Brandon's mother in Henry. His face and eyes are both rounder, like hers.

"Heard a lot about you," Henry says.

"Oh?" What does that mean? Does he know about me?

Henry skirts around me and grabs a bowl from his mother. "Glad you're here," he says under his breath.

"Yeah, thanks for coming, man," Brandon whispers as he comes from behind me and takes a bowl of shredded lettuce.

I have to calm down. They don't know my past. They never would've let me inside if they did. A guilty feeling bites at me. I push it down where I shoved *his* voice earlier.

Brandon's mom hands me a plate of squished corn bread things. "The dining room is right through there." She points at another wide doorway across the kitchen.

I walk into the dining room and set the plate on the oval table in the center. Black-and-white pictures of the family and old farmhouses and fruit in bowls cover the navy walls.

Brandon inclines his head at the chair beside him. Henry sits across from us and his parents take places at either end.

"I hope you like sweet tea," his mom says. "If not, we've got water. Or I can make you some unsweet?"

"Sweet's fine." I'm scared to look down and see the puddles of sweat that have seeped out of my body since I arrived. I angle my elbows away from my body to air my pits out. As I do, Brandon and his mom both reach for me. I jump back, almost tipping my chair over. *What the hell?* This must be it. The point when normal stops. Everything else was for show. They're about to perform some ritual on me.

Dr. Kingsley raises an eyebrow. "I'll say the blessing."

Brandon takes one hand and his mother takes my other, then they link hands with Henry and Dr. Kingsley, forming a circle. I'm stiff as an over-starched shirt. Everyone bows their heads and closes their eyes, so I do the same, but I crack one eye and watch them, in case shit gets weird.

"Father," Dr. Kingsley says. His voice sounds deeper in here, more rich. "Thank you for bringing us all together tonight, and for this food you have so graciously provided. Bless our meal and our conversation. Amen."

"Amen," everyone else echoes.

"Amen." My repetition lingers in the air. I don't think I've ever prayed before. Mom did a few times when we were hiding in those stuffy motel closets. At least that's what I think she was doing—muttering for someone to save her, help her, protect her.

Brandon scoops rice on his plate and covers it with soupy black gunk, then hands me the plate. "Put a couple johnny-cakes on there for me."

"Brandon," Dr. Kingsley says calmly, but with a warning note.

"Please," Brandon adds.

That's when I notice they're all handing one another plates, heaping on different sides.

"We eat family style," Mrs. Kingsley explains.

My expression must be as blank as my mind because she adds, "We serve one another."

Other than the disaster of a meal Dell and Bev tried to have, the closest I've ever come to a family dinner were the few barbecues they had at The Fort each summer. Those were different, though. They slapped the food on long tables and you served yourself. Everyone pushed and shoved in line, trying to get the best and biggest portions first. God forbid you helped someone else at The Fort.

I follow the Kingsleys' lead and pass plates around the table, watching in mild horror as they cram beans and rice and burned yellow things on my plate. The Professor adds several pieces of blackened chicken last and passes the plates back around. Only after everyone has theirs back do they begin eating.

No one speaks as they dig in. I stare at the lumps in front of me. The yellow things look okay, but I'd rather not risk it, so I start with the rice, picking at the part that doesn't have bean juice in it.

"Don't you like Caribbean?" Brandon's mom says. "Brandon, you didn't ask him first?"

Brandon's eyes go wide. "I forgot to. My bad."

Shit. Now I've made them feel bad. "I've never had it," I say, hoping that makes my snub better.

Henry grins. "Well, let me introduce you to the best food in the world."

"At least someone is learning something," the Professor says.

Henry bristles. I'm failing at everything tonight. This is exactly the sort of thing I'm here to prevent.

"Okay," I say. "What have we got?"

Henry uses his fork as a pointer. "You've got your jerk chicken, your black beans and rice, cabbage, kidney peas, sweet plantains—the best kind if you ask me—and johnny-cakes. Those are basically fried corn bread."

Brandon leans closer. "If you don't like it, there's sandwich stuff in the fridge."

"My grandmother is Jamaican," Mrs. Kingsley says. "She brought these recipes when she immigrated. They're not everyone's taste, though, so don't worry. I can whip you up something better than a sandwich."

Brandon grimaces.

"No, that's okay," I say.

Everyone watches me as I stab at a piece of chicken. Now I really feel like a zoo animal. I take a bite and flavors explode in my mouth. Sweet and herby at first. Then the fires of Hell unleash on my tongue.

I grab my glass and chug half my tea before I can come up for air.

"Oops," Henry says. "Forgot to warn you." He bursts out laughing. Mrs. Kingsley starts to scold him, but then she starts laughing, too. Laughing so hard she has to cover her face with her napkin.

"I'm sorry, Nate," she says. "We like it spicy."

Even Dr. Kingsley lets out a chuckle. "GramMa's spice blend can sneak up on you."

I'll say. I take another swig of tea. What I really need is a fire hose.

"Eat some plantains," Henry says. "The sweet will balance out the heat."

I tentatively poke at the mushy yellow things on my plate. How bad can it be? I take a bite. It's like a banana but so much better—sweet but tangy, and the crispy burnt ends are freaking amazing. I gobble up three in a row.

That sets everyone off again. "I'm glad you like them," Mrs. Kingsley says between giggles.

"This is the best thing I've ever eaten."

She smiles. "Then have as much as you want."

"So, Nate," Dr. Kingsley says, "tell us about yourself. Where are you from? What do you like to do?"

My mouth is suddenly Death Valley. Words evaporate from my head, leaving nothing but dusty doubt. What am I supposed to say? Everything I think of would completely spoil the mood.

"He's pretty good at basketball," Brandon says. "He might join the team."

I have to remember to thank Brandon later.

"Forward?" Henry asks, his mouth full of black beans.

Brandon twists cabbage around his fork. "Yeah, he's got a killer layup."

Dr. Kingsley clears his throat. "Brandon, why don't you let your guest speak for himself?"

I guzzle the rest of my tea. Now that I can taste it, it's more sugar water than anything.

Brandon's mom whisks away my glass as soon as I put it down. "I'll get you some more. For the chicken." She winks.

Dr. Kingsley sips from his own glass. "You enjoy basketball?"

"Um, yes. Yes, sir."

"You should come to the college sometime and watch a game."

Brandon's face lights up. "Yeah! Midnight Madness is coming soon, right, Pops?"

"A couple weeks I think." He wipes his mouth and spreads his napkin back over his lap. "You could bring your brother since that's the only way he'll step on campus now."

Henry rolls his eyes. "Dad—"

"Anyone else need more tea?" Brandon's mom plops my glass in front of me. "No? Okay. What did I miss?"

"We're going to Midnight Madness and Nate's joining the basketball team."

Henry shoots Brandon a grateful glance.

"Actually, I . . . my uncle won't let me play." I gulp down more tea. It's so sweet it hurts my stomach, but I'm thirstier than a flower in the desert.

"What?" Brandon asks. "Why not?"

Everyone's staring at me again. "He, um, needs my help, around the cabin and stuff. And I need to focus on school."

Dr. Kingsley smiles, looking more like Brandon than ever. "A perfectly legitimate reason. School should be everyone's focus."

Henry slumps in his chair. "Here we go."

Dr. Kingsley ignores him. "Did you know I was the first person in my family to attend college? And my father was the first black student admitted to Lewiston High when they desegregated. There's a statue of him downtown."

"I'm pretty sure no one in my family has gone to college," I reply.

"Well, then, you can be the first." Dr. Kingsley scoots his chair back and crosses one leg over the other. "Not a lot of kids from this area make it to college. It'd be a big honor."

Henry stands suddenly and begins stacking plates. "Anyone want dessert? Coffee?"

Dr. Kingsley scowls. "People are still eating, Henry."

Mrs. Kingsley shoots him a look. "Let me help you with that, baby." She takes the stack from Henry and herds him into the kitchen.

I wait until they disappear, thankful Mrs. Kingsley is picking up my slack. "I don't know if college is in my cards."

"Why not?"

I swallow hard. That's a good question. Because I'm not smart enough? Because guys from The Fort don't go to college? Because of my arrest record? Because they likely won't even let me in?

"Don't sell yourself short." The Professor balls up his napkin and flops it on the table. "I'm sure you're capable of much more than you believe."

I'd like to ask him how the hell he knows that. He doesn't know me or where I've been or the big, blank nothing that's ahead of me. But his tone and casual confidence are almost enough to make me believe him.

For a split second, I picture me dressed like a Kingsley, with my arm around a khaki-clad Kelsey, standing in front of a sweeping brick house. I'm a scientist—a geneticist maybe—so that I can figure out what makes us the way we are, and if anything really makes us all different, or if we're all the same at a base level. It's a good future.

Too bad it can never happen.

I blink and the picture vanishes again. The real future is as bleak as The Fort in winter.

Brandon and his mother manage to keep the conversation light over apple pie and ice cream. They talk about some incident with an overcooked Boston butt over the Fourth of July that has everyone laughing, but I can't focus.

I check my phone and am shocked to see it's almost ten. "I should probably get going."

"No rush," Dr. Kinglely says. "Stay as long as you like."

"My uncle will flip if I come home too late. I've got chores in the morning."

I help pick up the last of the dishes and Brandon runs off to get his keys. Dr. Kingsley stops me in the hall, laying a hand on my shoulder. "I mean it, son. You're welcome here anytime."

It's the most fatherly gesture anyone has ever given me. In the moment, the only difference I see is what a good person Brandon's dad is compared to every other man in my life.

"Definitely, Nate," Brandon's mom says, coming up behind her husband and slipping an arm around his waist. "You can stay the whole weekend if you like."

"I wish I could, but I really do have to go." I think I *could* stay here forever. I haven't felt this at ease since before Mom died. Maybe not even then.

"At least come to church and Sunday lunch with us sometime," she says. "Oh, and take these with you." She thrusts a plastic container in my hands. "Just don't let Henry know I'm giving you the rest of the plantains."

Brandon reappears, jacket and keys in hand. "Ready?"

"Thanks for dinner and everything. It was great."

Dr. Kingsley gives my shoulder another squeeze. "Any time."

"Hold up, I'm coming, too." Henry jogs down the stairs.

"Be careful," Mrs. Kingsley calls. "Remember—"

"Keep the music down, be polite, make sure my hands are visible, nothing shiny," Brandon says. "I got it, Mama."

It's the strangest set of rules I've ever heard. Now that's a custom even The Fort couldn't make up. "Night," I say and step out into the brisk air, then shiver. I'll have to talk Dell into another thrift store trip for winter clothes soon. There's no way around it. Maybe I'll offer to go to work with him again and earn the money myself. I may never be a scientist, but construction doesn't seem like such a bad gig.

I slip into the back seat of Brandon's Camry. "Sorry I wasn't much of a buffer."

Henry cocks his head to the side. "Are you kidding? You were great. If you weren't there, Dad would've griped about me all night. That's all we would have talked about."

Brandon twists in his seat to face me. "You sure you have to go home? We could ride around for a while. Fletch is supposed to be having a bonfire."

I know I've been about as social as I can for one night. "My uncle really will kill me if I'm not home soon."

Brandon meets my eyes. "All right. But you're coming out with us soon. Deal?"

"Deal."

I'm shocked to realize I mean it.

After the way I grew up, all I've been through, who would've thought I'd feel more comfortable—more at home—with this black family than anywhere else? If anything could make *him* rise from the dead, this would be it. I almost wish *he* and The Fort *could* see me now. I'm pretty sure this would kill them all.

679

"I wish you would just join the team." Brandon tosses me a water bottle. "I mean, you're already playing with us every day. You might as well get to play in real games."

I'd love to be on the team, but it's definitely not an option now. We haven't actually seen a skinhead yet, but they're somewhere, lurking. The flyers were back yesterday morning, blowing in the breeze, oozing sores scarring the town.

Once again, I talked Dell into holding off on calling the police—a second papering could still be a fluke. The Skynbyrds could be hitting multiple towns, waiting for me to pop up like one of the moles in that arcade game.

But I'm sure of one thing. I need to be more careful about hanging out with Brandon. Basketball's a way to spend time with him somewhere safe, away from The Fort's eyes.

Dell tried to get Bev to lay low, too, but she refused to stay locked in her house all day and said she absolutely won't stop coming over. Dell convinced her to leave work sites while it's still daylight and to take the back way through the woods to the cabin, at least.

I shoot a jet of lukewarm water in my mouth and throw the bottle back. "How's Henry?" I ask, changing the subject.

Brandon shrugs. "Mostly gone. College is all Pops talks about when he's around so Henry's been spending a lot of time by the river, working on his cast, I think."

I miss the river—the plop of the lure on the water, the click of the reel, even the damp, muddy smell—but this is good, too. While the musty gym and sweat-streaked dudes aren't as peaceful as standing quietly on the bank, the gym has its own rhythm. The steady *thunk* of basketballs and the squeak of rubber soles on polished wood and the swish of the net. It's calming in a weird way, and I feel better than I have in a long time.

Since I've been playing basketball, I've noticed the muscle building in my limbs. Weight lifting has made me strong and running's keeping me lean. I feel powerful again. Dangerous.

But I'm not worried about snapping. Dell hasn't wanted me to be alone in the woods anymore, but between running drills with the team and the adrenaline release from pushing myself with weights, the beast is more satisfied—and exhausted—than ever.

I'm actually okay with not being on the team. The thawed ice between me and Dell and Bev seemed to spread to everyone. People have been saying "hey" when they pass me in the halls, and the other day Caitlyn actually smiled at me.

Or maybe I'm thawing. Letting people in the way a kid eats a Tootsie Pop; little by little I'm allowing the folks here to get a taste of my true self.

"Hey, Bodyguard." Rainey jogs to the bleachers where Brandon and I are stretched out. He kicks Brandon's foot. "It's on, man."

Brandon fist bumps Rainey. "Seriously?"

"Yeah. Fletch and I have about a hundred water balloons in the cooler, Ellis has twenty cans of shaving cream, and Scott picked up like five dozen eggs."

Brandon slaps Rainey's hand. "Dude, that's awesome." He turns to me with a mischievous twinkle in his eye. "We're gonna nail the freshmen."

I raise an eyebrow.

"It's homecoming week," he says.

I squint my eyes and shake my head slightly.

Rainey drops to the bleachers beside us. "Geesh, Juvie, didn't you have homecoming at your old school?"

A buzz of panic rattles in my ribs. I don't know how to respond. What's homecoming? "They don't do that sort of thing in prison."

Brandon and Rainey laugh, so apparently that's a good enough answer.

"We do it up big, here," Rainey says. "Every day is a different spirit day. Didn't you wonder why everyone was wearing overalls today?"

"I figured you were all rednecks."

"No," Brandon says, "we're *over all* the rednecks at County High."

"That's completely ridiculous."

Rainey swipes Brandon's water bottle. "That's school spirit. Tomorrow is Decade Day."

Brandon jerks the bottle back. "Anyway, the big thing is the float. Each grade builds one for the parade Friday. If they can."

"What do you mean?"

Rainey grins. "Sabotage. It's usually sophomores versus freshmen, and seniors versus juniors, but sometimes the sophomores and juniors prank each other."

"We're heading over to the freshmen build site tonight and declaring war," Brandon explains. "You in?"

It sounds like a terrible idea. Exactly the sort of thing that could trigger me, especially with the Skynbyrds waiting. But I'm just getting in with these guys, and I still haven't hung out with Brandon like I said I would.

Besides, it's water and shaving cream, not bricks and lead pipes.

"Sure," I say.

"Awesome!" Brandon claps me on the shoulder. "I'll pick you up at eight. Wear something black."

✧

The only black clothing I own is the T-shirt Dell bought me that first day. I finally talked him into another thrift store trip for winter clothes, but the store didn't have much. The cashier said to come back in a couple weeks after people cleaned out their closets for the town's fall yard sale.

"I don't think this is a good idea," Dell says when I come downstairs. "What if they're following you?"

"If the Skynbyrds were following me, we'd know by now. The rest of The Fort would've already been here."

"I still don't like it."

"The guys and I are just working on the float."

Dell's mouth turns down in his trademark scowl. "Then why are you wearin' black?"

"That's what they said to wear. It's a spirit week thing." The lie rolls off my tongue. Guess all that training at The Fort gave me a useful skill after all.

Dell folds his arms and looks me up and down. "Fine, but you spot one pair of combat boots and you call me *immediately*."

I hold up my hands like I'm surrendering. "I swear."

"And you'll be at the Stevenses', right?"

"Yes."

Tires crunch outside and Brandon honks.

"Keep your phone on you," Dell says as I walk out the door. "Anything's off and your ass better be dialing."

A shiver works down my spine. I push thoughts of neo-nazis out of my mind and jog to the idling Camry. Brandon tosses a plastic bag over the seat as I climb in the passenger side. "Extra provisions. This is going to be so badass."

"So, what's the plan?"

"We work on the float for a while, so if anyone asks we can say we were there. Then we'll leave some guys behind to protect our stuff while the rest of us drive to Annie Williams's house to wreak havoc."

Good. I'm positive Dell is going to ask about the float. This way I can give him details.

We turn off the main road soon as a giant weathered barn with SEE ROCK CITY painted on the roof comes into view.

Kelsey always wanted to go to Rock City. She ate up all that tourist shit. Every time we stopped at a new gas station, she'd beeline for the rack with brochures and pamphlets. She hid them under her shirt. Not that they cost anything, but she didn't want anyone at The Fort to catch her with one.

Kelsey used them as bookmarks for our hidden books. She'd lie beside the holly bush, planning our escape route so we could hit as many tourist traps as possible. The Rock City pamphlet was her favorite. She looked at it so often, it wasn't so much brochure as it was four individual battered pages. "We're going here first," she'd say.

"Why, so you can see the 'Enchanted Trail' and 'Fairyland Caverns'?" I'd tease.

She'd pout, sticking out her bottom lip farther than I thought possible. "No, so we can see seven states at once. Seven! I've only ever seen this one, and it sucks."

I never caught anything she said after that point. I was too busy thinking about kissing her bottom pouty lip. I almost did once. Went so far as to lean in, but stopped myself at the last second and pretended to swat a bug on her shoulder. If I'd made a move and she'd kissed me back, I wouldn't have been able to keep my hands off her, and I couldn't risk that. I might've made *him* notice her more. One of *his* favorite speeches was about how women were nothing but distractions from the cause. *He* definitely didn't want me distracted. One of *his* lackeys teased *him* once about losing *his* moves after Mom, but *he*'d shut that down with a sudden punch to the dude's throat. The guy didn't say anything else about it after that. Didn't say anything at all for a few weeks.

I've always wondered if some tiny piece of *him* really did love her or if Mom stole the only part of *him* capable of love when she ran.

I should've kissed Kelsey when I had the chance. Now it's too late.

Brandon jerks the car off the road and bumps through the field, jarring me back to the present. He parks in front of the barn, in full view of the road. "We build here because it's wide open. Harder for a sneak attack." He grabs the bag from his back seat. "Last year, we couldn't drive, so we camped here and waited on folks to come to us. We bombarded them from the hayloft."

I laugh and follow him inside. Pretty much everyone from our class is here, clustered around a flatbed trailer wrapped in chicken wire. Caitlyn and Fletch stand by a bale of wire and a pile of wood, arguing.

"We are *not* building a giant hot dog with EAT ME, COUNTY on the side," she shrieks.

Fletch shakes his head. "Obviously not. 'Eat me' goes on top in mustard and ketchup."

"Argh!" She throws down a can of spray paint and stomps over to her boyfriend.

"You forgot your paint." Fletch shakes the can and pretends to spray it on a group of girls. They squeal and run away.

Rainey spots us and jogs over. "Hey, man, did you get the stuff?"

Brandon pats the bag. "Right here." He opens it slightly to reveal white feathers.

Rainey frowns. "That's it?"

"Be glad you got this much. I had to rip apart two guest pillows."

"Better than nothing," Griff says, from behind us. "We've got everything else loaded in the truck. Miranda spread the word that we don't even know what we're building, so the freshmen think we're caught up with that tonight." He and Rainey fist bump.

"What *are* we building?" I ask.

The guys all look at me funny.

"Doesn't matter. The freshmen always win. The grades that can actually drive spend more time sabotaging than building."

"Although Fletch's hot dog idea is gold." Ellis pops up from behind a stack of wood. He jams his iPhone on a portable speaker and cranks the volume. A few people around the bonfire out back start dancing, but most just sing along while they wrap chicken wire around a flatbed trailer. I turn to help and almost smack into Caitlyn.

She narrows her eyes. "What are *you* doing here?"

I shrug. "Helping."

"Hmph." She eyes me almost exactly the same way as Dell. "You're dressed like you're going to pick on the freshmen."

Shit. She's going to rat us out to the principal or someone.

"Let me know before you leave," she says. "I have some cans of Silly String in my car."

I stare at her, stunned. She doesn't seem to notice.

"Grab that chicken wire behind you and follow me. Help us build the nurse before y'all go."

"Nurse?"

"Yeah, like half of County has come down with some flu, so our theme is 'Quarantine the Crows.'" She picks up four packs of multicolored tissue paper.

We spend the next hour constructing a giant tissue paper nurse in a hazmat helmet. Caitlyn and her boyfriend have actually been nice to me. Or I've just chosen to see them that way instead of making assumptions. Now that I know Caitlyn has problems she's dealing with, too, it's easier to think of her as a human being.

I'm tucking white tissue paper into the nurse when Brandon taps my shoulder. "You ready?"

"Yeah." I push my last bit of paper into the nurse's stomach and follow him to Griff's truck, picking up Caitlyn's Silly String on the way. Fellow sophomores climb into two trucks. Some of the guys from the basketball team are already in Griff's, plus there are a few others I've never talked to, including a couple girls. Brandon and I climb in and he bangs on the truck's side.

"What about Scott?" I ask.

Brandon inclines his head toward the bonfire. "He's busy."

Scott has Maddie pressed against his tailgate, where they're practically licking each other's throats.

I'm not entirely sure what to say to a guy whose crush is making out with his friend. "Well, at least you don't have to worry about all that interracial dating stuff." I almost smack my forehead. Of all the things I could say, that's what pops out?

To my surprise, Brandon laughs before I can apologize. "True, man, true." He slaps the side of the truck again and Griff peels out of the field. Cold night air whips through the truck bed, freezing my ears. Anticipation has us all quiet. Not that we could hear one another over the rushing wind anyway. I shiver and fold my arms against my chest.

Goose bumps prickle my bare skin. This is the coldest I've been since *that* night when it all went down at The Fort. I breathe deeply and can almost feel sharp snowflakes stinging my nostrils. A metallic scent rides the wind. It's probably just rust from the truck, but it smells like blood.

My hand goes to my cheek where Thomas Mayes hit me by the holly bush. His knuckles had split the thin skin over my cheekbone. Blood poured down my cheek, leaving a trail in the snow that I'd followed when I ran later that night. God, I want to pay him back one of these days, to—

"Nate, you okay?" Brandon yells.

My eyes snap to his. Brandon's brows are furrowed. A prickle of panic tingles in my stomach as I realize how dangerously close to a flashback I just was. "Yeah," I say, but my fingers find my button through my shirt.

Before long, Griff cuts his lights and pulls to the side of the road. Fletch and Mateo are the first on the ground.

"Load up," Mateo whispers.

I arm myself with as many water balloons as I can carry and stick a can of shaving cream in my pocket. Brandon takes the feathers and a dozen eggs. Griff motions for us to follow him into the woods.

Of course it's the woods. It couldn't be a nice house-lined street. I'm tempted to put some balloons back so I can hang onto my button, but it's too late. Everyone is already jogging ahead of me, and I don't know where I'm going.

So stay here, a small voice whispers in my head.

I can't. I've already come this far. I take off after the shadows cutting through the trees.

After a couple hundred yards, lights wink into view.

That's good. There was no light that night. Nothing but darkness.

I zero in on the light, watching it get closer.

Feral screams whip through the air as we burst into the yard where the freshmen are hard at work. Water balloons fly. Several kids are drenched before they realize what's happening.

Their mouths hang open, their eyes wide with fear. I've seen that look too many times. I stop mid-throw and a balloon breaks by my feet, splashing my shoes.

Shrieks pierce my ears. The freshmen run for cover. All I see is terror. And blood. Cracking eggs sound too much like breaking bones. Everything is in slow motion and hyperspeed at once. The world is a blur of light and dark, color and cold.

Damn cold.

Freezing water seeps into my sock.

Someone nails me with a stream of shaving cream, but I barely notice. The *pfft pfft pfft* of a low-caliber gun fires to my left. I hit the dirt. Water soaks into my shirt. A blossom of red spreads near my arm.

I've been shot. Oh my God oh my God oh my God. The Fort is here. They found me.

He's coming.

There's nothing I can do. Except give in. Let *him* finish the job and kill me. Be free.

"Nate!"

The cry is so close, practically on top of me.

No. *He* doesn't get to win. I push myself upright. Someone grabs my arm. I twist, breaking the grip. My body tenses to fight. The figure in front of me laughs. Freaking *laughs*.

Wait, that's not right.

I blink and the night comes back into focus. Brandon turns to face me, but his smile shrivels like a slug under salt. "You okay?"

I scan the yard. The sounds around me aren't the panicked screams of fear, but happy cries, like kids on roller coasters. People race past, whooping and hollering. Almost everyone is splattered with blue, yellow, green, and red splotches. Red. My fingers tentatively graze my arm. Paint. The freshmen have paintball guns.

"Dude." Brandon's at my side. "What's wrong? Are you having some kind of episode?"

I shiver and the scraps of flashback fall to the damp earth. "No. No. I just—" I just what? Was bombarded with memories I thought I'd put behind me? Reminders of all the damage I've done? "That was fun." I manage. "I'm just afraid my uncle will be pissed that I ruined my clothes."

I mentally pat myself on the back for coming up with that one. Brandon doesn't look like he buys it, though.

Feet thunder on the ground, and then Mateo darts in between us. "They're reloading," he yells. "Go, go, go!"

"Better run," I say before Brandon can speak. He trots alongside me back to the truck, where our paint-covered classmates have all congregated. They look like they've been fighting a unicorn. A handful are even coated with silver glitter. They're all laughing and throwing their remaining balloons at each other.

Their happiness zooms past me, leaving a jet stream of jealousy behind. I'd give anything to be normal. To be able to have a water balloon fight without being thrust back to the night I murdered my father. I'm overwhelmed by sudden hate for them and their silly, simple lives.

Brandon climbs into the truck bed. I intentionally hang back and squeeze in the corner by the tailgate. I don't want to talk. I don't even want my woods right now. I want to curl up someplace warm and quiet and soft and sleep away this flashback hangover. Too bad that place doesn't exist.

The ride back is livelier. I turn my back on everyone and train my eyes on the asphalt zipping away behind us, wishing it could carry me to another place, another world. One without racism and hate and evil fathers.

Too bad that doesn't exist either.

690

Dell and I are up before dawn, like every day since the flyers first appeared. He hands me a thick jacket to block out the cold that dropped over North Alabama like a winter bomb. A thin layer of frost covers the grass. Fog dances off our shoulders as we cross the yard to the truck and my breath hangs in the air like dust motes in a slant of sun, shimmering in the sliver of light parting the sky.

We drive to town in tense silence, but the tension draws us together now instead of pushing us apart like it used to.

Surprisingly, he's been on my side lately. He hasn't mentioned calling the police again. At first, I thought he was holding off for me, but maybe he doesn't exactly trust cops either.

I've never had a good experience with police. All the ones in Farmer were lying, racist bastards. They threw me in that hellhole of a jail and turned their backs while the other inmates ganged up on me. From what Dell's told me, the cops where he and Mom grew up weren't great either. Dell said their neighbors called the police a few times when their parents' drunken drugfests got out of hand. The cops would drive by, tell them to keep it down, but not one of them ever noticed the frightened kids curled in the corner. Not one ever took Mom and Dell away.

Besides, we're handling the situation well enough on our own. Thanks to her recent downtime, Bev even figured out how The Fort found us—they must've used the picture that ran with the article. In the upper left corner, WISTON TOWN GROCERY is visible. Bev did a search and came up with four Lewistons: Idaho, Maine, New York, and Alabama. An image search of those towns and *bam*, there's Lewiston Town Grocery for anyone to see.

I could kill that damn reporter. Circle my hands around her thick throat and—

The truck rocks to a stop. I shiver and pretend it's from the cold.

I've been pent up inside too much. I've avoided Brandon since homecoming so that he won't try to make me talk. That means no running, no weight lifting, no breaking branches. The beast needs a release. Soon.

We're parked at one end of Main Street, same as every morning for the past week.

But something feels different today. I can't put my finger on it: the weather, the predawn light, something. I ease out of the truck and close the door as quietly as possible, keeping a look out as I approach the street. The hairs on the back of my neck are standing at attention.

Dell shoves his hands in his jacket pockets and starts down the street. We walk slowly, keeping close to the empty buildings. The rubber soles of our shoes whisper across the cracking sidewalk.

"I think we're good today," Dell says. "The flyers would be up by now if—"

"Shh." I hold up my hand and stop. There's something ahead. A hint of red in the fog. I take a step and stop again. Another pop of red appears down the street, closer. Flyers. Going up now.

We're not alone.

I press against the dirty glass store window behind me, grateful for once that my clothes are old and faded. I blend with the grungy buildings like we were painted together. Dell squishes beside me.

"They're—" I begin.

He nods. The fog is thinning; the sun is rising. The truck's a couple blocks away. We can leave now and reach it before the Skynbyrds notice us, but we'd have to leave the flyers, too, and our efforts to protect the town—my efforts to keep the cops out of it—will have been for nothing.

We could duck in the abandoned diner where I met the reporter and wait them out, but I only know how to get in the back door and the Skynbyrds will see us before we get to the corner. I can already make out their white and red laces against their black combat boots.

"We'll have to come back," Dell whispers. He turns toward the truck and stops.

Flyers hang on the poles between us and the truck.

They're on both sides of us.

Every store is closed.

"We'll jimmy a lock," Dell says.

"What?"

"Follow my lead." He turns up his collar and walks quickly to the closest business. He stops in front of a door and jangles his keys.

"What are you doing?" I hiss.

"I hate this damn lock," he says louder. He scrapes a key against the door. "It always sticks. I'm breaking down and buying a new one this afternoon."

Boots stomp on the street.

Look down, look down, look down.

I look up.

My stomach drops to my feet.

Two girls walk toward me with armfuls of flyers, but I'm only staring at one of them. Her brown ponytail swishes from side to side as she walks. Her green flight jacket is zipped up to her chin. She smiles at the other girl and, all of a sudden, my skin feels hot. I'm flooded by the desire to rush to her and sweep her into my arms, to hold her, protect her, love her the way I should've years ago. But she looks so . . . happy.

That's not the girl I knew. The one who was bitter as unsweetened chocolate every time she had to put up flyers. The one who would only smile at another Skynbyrd if she was punching her in the face. The girl walking down the street is a stranger to me.

Then she looks up, too.

Her smile droops, like a time-lapse video of a wilting flower. Her friend hasn't seen me yet. I tense. Is she going to alert everyone else? Call for help?

She shakes her head so slightly I almost think I imagined it, almost as though she can read my mind. She probably can. Her eyes go cold and flat for an instant, then she drops her gaze. Her friend finishes taping her flyer and says something. I whirl toward Dell and dip my head. The girls pass us, talking in cheery voices. They could be two regular teens chatting about their classes, if it weren't for the propaganda in their hands and the *weiss & stolz* patches on their backs.

As soon as they've passed, Dell takes off down the street, but I hang back. I glance over my shoulder, willing her to look at me, wanting to see her face once more. Her unbruised, unbloodied, beautiful face.

Kelsey.

As I watch her back, I try to convince myself that she didn't finally drink the Kool-Aid. That she's just pretending, passing the time until she can get out. But I know better. They got to her. I knew it a little over a year ago when she strode into the courtroom at my trial.

I remember her testimony too clearly. Her words that stung like a thousand angry bees.

"Nathaniel hated his father," she'd said. "His *father.* Nathaniel couldn't wait until he didn't have to deal with him anymore. It's all he talked about."

"Tell me about your personal relationship with Mr. Fuller," the prosecutor had asked.

It was the only time Kelsey looked at me that whole day. Her brown eyes flashed. "I hate him." Her stare had burned through me.

The prosecutor's flustered reaction told me Kelsey had gone off script. He floundered for something to say, but Kelsey simply leveled her gaze at the jury and shrugged.

"He murdered an amazing leader. Why wouldn't I hate him for that?"

She never technically lied, but she didn't tell the truth, either. Not that I blame her. I left her at The Fort. I ran away and left her behind with them.

I watch her brown hair swish away now—not a trace of the blue she always wanted. They may not have killed her body, but they certainly killed her spirit, same as *he* killed Mom's. And it's all my fault.

I'd hate me, too.

✧

Dell and I circle around until the Skynbyrds are gone. I don't say anything about Kelsey. He'll freak if he knows I've been spotted. I don't know why she let me go. Maybe she doesn't hate me as much as I thought. Or maybe she was as shocked to see me as I was to see her. Either way, Dell will find out soon enough if she tells. No sense in worrying about it now.

Once we're certain the coast is clear, we jump out of the truck and race back and forth, tearing down flyers. By the time we've gotten them all, I'm regretting wearing my jacket, sweating despite the cold. We shove the flyers into a plastic bag to burn later tonight and then Dell drops me off at school.

I'd started tricking myself into thinking I was turning into the guy everyone at school sees. But that's still a lie. This past week has shown that to me. My outer shell is still as fake as ever.

I can't let myself forget that again.

I pause outside the school's front doors, pushing thoughts of Kelsey and the flyers to the back of my mind.

They don't stay there long, though.

When I open the door, red flyers assault me from every angle, taped to the walls, covering the floor, in students' hands.

Hot bile surges up my throat. I choke it down before it spews across the gray tile. It burns like Kelsey's stare, leaving an acidic taste in my mouth.

This is why the Skynbyrds were late getting to Main Street. Where else did they hit? Who else has seen them? Doesn't matter. The entire town will know now. Everyone. My classmates, the police, Brandon. My bones turn molten and I start to sink into a puddle on the floor.

A hand claps me on the back and I bolt upright. "What is this shit?" Brandon shoves a flyer in my face.

Oh God, he knows. The flyers have my name and picture and a list of what I've done. He's going to hate me now, too. I should've come clean to him a long time ago.

"Who would do this?" he asks.

I train my eyes on the flyer and relax a little. It's the standard crap. Nothing personal. Not yet.

Brandon crumples the paper and slams it into the closest trash can. "Disgusting."

I help Brandon throw away as many flyers as we can before the bell rings.

"Attention, students," a voice crackles over the intercom, "proceed immediately to the gym for an assembly. I repeat, proceed immediately to the gym."

Everyone's whispering about the flyer as we file into the gym. Several people have their phones out, and are looking up the white extinction website. I want to knock the phones out of their hands and scream, but it's too late. They've already given the site hits. They've seen The Fort's message, which is what the Skynbyrds were after. The Fort won this round.

I find a seat with Brandon and Fletch. Brandon's still seething. So is the principal. Her cheeks are the same color as the flyer in her hand. She clips a small microphone to her blazer lapel and scowls at the crowd.

"I'm sure you have all seen the disturbing messages plastered across the school this morning. This is unacceptable. It isn't funny. It isn't a game. It's hate speech and it's a criminal offense. Come forward and your punishment will be less severe. If you know who is responsible, speak up now." She scans the student body. I slump lower in my seat. I'm certain her gaze stops on me a beat too long. "You will not be in trouble for holding the perpetrator accountable."

Everyone exchanges glances. Daggers of speculation fly around the room. I want a flashback to whisk me away. Reliving past horror has to be better than this present one.

"I wish I knew who did it," Brandon says, "but I wouldn't turn them in." There's a menacing look on his face that I've never seen before.

I can't imagine Brandon so much as yelling out of anger. He didn't even raise his voice when he ranted about his friends the day he came clean about Henry. But he looks like he wants to straight up murder someone right now.

I have to tell the principal about the Skynbyrds. I'll start with seeing them downtown today. Except that will invite too many questions. She'll ask how I know about the Skynbyrds, how I know they're behind the flyers, why I didn't call the cops as soon as I saw them. She'll have to inform the police, or at least the town council, that there's a hate group in Lewiston.

They'll definitely connect me to the article then. I'll be shunned. Or arrested. I'll lose Brandon. Dell will lose everything.

I should speak up.

I shouldn't keep quiet again.

Except, last time I said anything about my past it backfired. That's the only reason the Skynbyrds are here right now.

It all comes back to me. That damn snake is still eating its tail.

So I keep quiet.

Dell and I will figure this out. We have to.

✧

The flyers are all anyone can talk about the rest of the day. My history teacher even cancels her planned lesson, launching into a discussion on racism and the ugly pasts of Alabama and Lewiston—including Brandon's grandfather and his work in the Civil Rights Movement.

She pulls up the white extinction website and projects it onto the board. "I want to have a dialogue about this and make sure you know why it's wrong and why it's not funny," she says.

I focus on my notebook writing 690 over and over and over to keep from yelling at her.

We should be ignoring this monster, not feeding it. The main page is a list of anti-immigration articles. The Latina girl beside me shifts uncomfortably in her seat. The teacher clicks on the ABOUT US tab.

"'What is White Extinction?'" she reads. "'The systematic dilution of White People by forced assimilation of anti-whites through immigration and encouraged intermingling of the races.'"

I taste stomach acid again. Classmates glance around the room, their eyes resting on the girl beside me, before flitting to the other minorities in the room.

This isn't just wrong, it's dangerous. The news lately has already been covered with deportation stories. People waking up to immigration officials beating down their doors, tourists getting detained at airports. Then there are all the shootings and other attacks on Muslims and black people. We don't need more of this kind of talk.

The teacher drones on about how racism is wrong and all people are the same and the benefits of immigration, but no one is listening. They're too busy reading and whispering about the rest of the page, especially the comparison of the looming extinction of white tigers to that of white humans.

My pencil snaps. I slam the two stumps on my desk.

This is exactly what they want! Can't everyone see that? All the teacher has to do is read the last paragraph: the one that states, "How Can You Help? By spreading our message through word of mouth, flyers, or posters. If you're afraid to actively speak out, fake alarm and anger and give the flyers to the media. Anything that spreads the word helps!"

They *want* us to talk about it, draw attention to their words, think about their message. They want people to turn on their neighbors. They want to get in our heads— exactly what they're doing—and none of these zombies even realize it.

Nothing on the website names The Fort or the Nazi Socialist Party. There's no reference to skinheads or violence against the "anti-whites," and not a single thing that can tie the white extinction mission back to the neo-nazis. The connections are still plain, if these people will only *see*.

The bell rings and I storm out of the classroom. The hallway is packed, louder than it's been since my first day. I get trapped behind two guys in heavy camouflage jackets—I think they're juniors.

"You know Uncle Jake lost his job at the lumberyard last fall to a Mexican," one says.

"They're like roaches," the other responds.

"Yeah," says the first guy. "Sneakin' in and stealin' what's rightfully ours. We need to protect our borders. Keep 'em outta our country."

"They're just gonna ruin America like they ruined Mexico."

The Latina girl from class pushes past us. She had to have heard everything those guys said. I want to run after her and see if she's all right, but the hall is too clogged. People are standing in clumps, talking instead of moving to their next classes like normal.

My head spins. I left all this behind.

I left it behind.

I left it behind!

"Nate Clemons," a voice says behind me.

I take a deep breath and turn to face the principal. She's flanked by two of Lewiston's eight police officers—if you count the two part-timers who also run the post office. These guys are both shorter than me and both white. One is bald and has a slight potbelly. The other seems like he was in the military at one point. Thin but muscular, with close-clipped hair. Unlike the police in Farmer, they don't look mean, but they still make my blood pump harder.

"I'd like to see you in my office," the principal says. "Now, please."

My heart thunders like a pack of scared deer. Wide-eyed stares and curious whispers follow us to the office. Oh my

God, do they think I did this? Maybe Kelsey ratted me out after all.

The principal gestures at the same chair I sat in on my first day. I sit slowly. The cops stand beside the desk, arms folded. They both frown down at me, like they're trying to act tough.

You're way out of your element here, boys. I may hate cops, but I'm sure as shit not intimidated by them.

The principal pushes a flyer across her desk. "Do you know anything about this?"

I can do this. I've been interrogated before. I can keep my cool.

"No," I say, with zero inflection.

She narrows her eyes. "You realize this is a hate crime."

"Yes."

"And you know that Lewiston High has a zero-tolerance policy."

"Yes."

Simple, one-word answers. The kind they can't twist or misstate. That's what my attorney trained me to give when we practiced my cross-examination last year.

The principal drops into the big leather chair on the other side of desk and folds her hands on the desktop. "Look, Nate." She sighs. "You've been doing well so far. I'd hate for this to sidetrack you. If you did this, or know anything about it, just tell me. Come clean now and we can help you, but if you lie to us, I won't be able to intervene."

She's wrong. I already came clean, and all it did was make things worse.

"We'll find out if you're lying," the bald cop says. "We're already looking for evidence, and we'll find it." He drops his fists to the desk and leans on them like a gorilla. "We know where you live."

The other one flips open a notebook. "Nathaniel Clemons. Resides with his uncle, Dell Clemons, at 724 Cedar Drive. Moved here from the West Kentucky Psychiatric Center at the beginning of August. History of mental disturbances." He snaps the notebook shut. "This seems right up your alley, son."

He has no idea. If they knew more they'd have already arrested me.

The first cop smiles. "You know we can trace paper back to specific printer? Like a fingerprint."

Somebody may be able to, but I doubt they have that technology in this shithole town.

"I told you I won't tolerate trouble," the principal says. "This is your last chance."

"We don't own a printer, there's no print shop in Lewiston, and I can't drive." I tuck my history book under my arm and stand. "Can I go now? I'm going to miss lunch."

They exchange tired glances, then the principal shoos me away. "We're still watching you," she calls as I leave the office.

I'm supposed to be intimidated, but I'm oddly comforted.

The Fort will have a harder time reaching me if I'm being watched.

701

The flyers stopped.

Like *his* heart. One minute, it pumped hate, and the next, nothing.

Dell and I had decided not to take them down again. The risk of being seen and having to answer questions is too great, and the entire town knows anyway.

But they stopped.

It's been over a week and other than a few crinkled pages some jackass put on the bulletin board at school, there's been nothing.

The cops are still searching, though. They've been hauling people to the principal's office for questioning all week—all the known troublemakers and pranksters. Even Fletcher. He tried to make a joke of it, but I could tell it shook him up pretty bad. He's been more serious since then, especially around Brandon.

I have, too. Brandon hasn't been his normal self lately. He looks at almost everyone with distrust.

"You think it was the senior stunt?" Rainey asks at lunch.

Brandon drops his burger and glares across the table. "You think this was some *prank*? This is some next-level shit, man. Way beyond letting cows loose in the halls and filling the radiators with chicken poop."

"Geez, man, calm down." Rainey drags his fork through the puddle of ketchup on his tray. "I'm just sayin'. Remember when we were freshmen and the seniors broke the finger off your granddad's statue?"

"That was an accident." Brandon says. "This is different."

They stare at each other. Tension hangs over the group, heavy as the Alabama air.

Ellis glances around, then scoots forward. "I've been thinking." His voice is so low we all have to lean in to hear him. "What if it wasn't a student? What if it was someone else?"

I almost choke on my bite of sandwich. I gulp down half my bottle of water trying to force the chunk of bread and bologna down.

"Like who?" Brandon asks.

Ellis bends closer. "I overheard Ma talkin' to Auntie Georgina, up in Tennessee, she said the same thing happened near them at Easter. Except someone covered the town in plastic Easter eggs with the website written on papers inside. Same site and everything."

I'm burning up. The room is stifling. Did someone crank the heat?

"What happened after that?" Brandon asks.

Ellis shrugs. "Nothin'. It was on the news, but that's as far as it went."

Brandon sits back. He chews his bottom lip for a minute, then grabs his burger. "Yeah. Thanks, Ellis. That makes me feel better." He takes a bite, swallows, and grins. "Pops had me worried it was about to turn all 1965 up in here, but it sounds like some ignorant assholes trying to get on TV."

When Brandon relaxes, everyone else does, too. Everyone except me. The guys start talking about the upcoming basketball game against County. I shove the rest of my sandwich and chips in my paper sack and ball it up.

"Nate, you okay?" Brandon asks.

"Just not hungry." I start to stand, but he catches my arm.

"Hold up, I'll walk with you." He shoves the last bit of burger in his mouth.

I throw away my lunch and wait for him by the door.

"You're not bothered by this anymore?" I ask, accusation in my voice.

He starts for his locker "Of course I am. But what good is it doing?" When I don't follow, he stops and turns back to me. "You heard Rainey. He thinks this was a prank. It doesn't do any good for them to see me sweat. I'm in a lose-lose here, Nate. If I get too angry, then I'm seen as the 'angry black man,' but if I laugh it off I'm not acknowledging how screwed up this is. You saw how everything shifted when I said I believed Ellis."

"*Do* you believe Ellis?"

He tilts his head back and studies the ceiling tiles. "I believe that happened in his auntie's town, and I hope that's what will happen here." He levels his head and meets my eyes. "But I'm terrified. All the time. I wish I could explain what it's like. Lewiston has always been a safe area, thanks to my grandfather and everyone else who fought racist shit like this back in the sixties. The folks here know me, but outside this town . . ."

He shakes his head. All the light is gone from his face and it's like the sun supernovaed and all that's left is a black hole.

"I was accused of stealing once because I wore a hoodie in a gas station. Henry got pulled over last semester because the university cop thought he'd stolen his Lexus. I never carry anything that might resemble a gun or even walk with my hands in my pockets or wear baggy clothes or run outside the gym. I have this whole list of rules just to live my life. Stuff white people don't even have to think about twice. It's exhausting."

I'm such an asshole. The list of rules he rattled off to his mom that night after dinner . . . they weren't a strange family thing; they were because that's how he has to live to stay safe. He's right. They're things I've never thought about, and it's never occurred to me that other people—especially

Brandon—did. With all the horrors I've committed in my life, I've never worried someone would believe I'm a criminal based on nothing more than the color of my skin.

Would I have gotten away with half the things I've done if I'd been black? Is that why I was never caught? Did people automatically assume I was okay because I'm white?

Oh my God. Does being white make it easier to hurt people?

My chest constricts. Even the beast is still. Every part of me is disappointed—in myself, my race, this Godforsaken world where every day is a struggle for some people. Where they can't go to school without the fear of being deported, or to the grocery store without being profiled.

"Then something like this happens," Brandon says, interrupting my thoughts, "and the fear that's always hiding under my skin is exposed. It surfaces every time another black body winds up on the news. Every time a name becomes a hashtag, a movement. But this is different. This is *here*. I thought Lewiston was different. None of the racist shit I've experienced has been anything like what Granddad faced. But it's still here, all these years later. There are still people who hate me because of how I look. Whether they're local or outsiders like Ellis thinks, they exist. And being confronted with that out of nowhere *in my town* terrifies me. But I realized in that lunchroom that I can't show my fear, because then they win."

I wish I could melt into the floor. Slither between the tiles, away from Brandon's words. Away from his rules, his fear.

It breaks my heart. Brandon's not Inside-Out Boy after all. He puts on a separate skin every day, too. A mask to hide his real feelings.

And it's because of people like me.

I may not have shared *his* hate in my heart, but I haven't done anything to stop it, either. I've been a coward this whole time. Protecting myself instead of the people who need protecting.

I have to come clean. For real this time.

Brandon has to be the first to know. He deserves to hear it straight from me—that I'm the cause of his fear. I'm the reason he has to live according to so many rules, the reason racism still exists, the reason he's face-to-face with it right now.

Then I'll tell the principal and the police. Regardless of what might have happened where Ellis's aunt lives, this isn't going away on its own. There's another shoe waiting to drop, and the cops need to know what they're dealing with.

If I was scared of telling Brandon before, I'm petrified now. With his family's history, there's no way he won't hate me.

"I need to tell you something." My voice is barely loud enough for even me to hear.

"What?" His brow furrows. "I didn't hear you."

"I—"

Feet slap the tile behind us. Maddie races by, her face white as the tigers on the white extinction website.

"Maddie," Brandon yells.

She skids to stop and turns to us.

"What's wrong?"

She shakes her head. "I . . . I need the police."

Brandon's at her side in a flash. "Are you hurt? What happened? What is—"

"I can't. Especially not to *you*." Maddie bursts into tears.

He wraps his arms around her. "You can tell me anything."

She clings to him, burying her face in his shirt so I can't hear what she says next.

"What word?" Brandon asks. He looks back at me.

I whip around and sprint the direction Maddie came from. A crowd has started to form in front of the exit closest to the lunchroom. I push through until I'm outside, then I vomit on my shoes.

Crude black spray paint covers the sand-colored sidewalk. A giant swastika surrounded by every racial slur in the book, and the words *"Repent now. Repent or BURN."*

✧

Police have taken over the school. We're stuck in the gym again. This time it isn't a plea from the principal to come clean. It's a threat. The officers—all eight of them—each set up shop in a separate classroom so they can hold multiple interviews at the same time.

They started with Maddie, once they got her calmed down. Then Brandon, because she wouldn't leave his side. I caught a glimpse of them walking down the hall afterward, their arms around each other. I'm dying to know what she said, what she saw. Was it Kelsey? Did she do this? Has she mentioned me? I texted Brandon but he hasn't responded yet.

I don't know what that means, if he's busy taking care of Maddie, or if he knows something. I'm sweating all over. And dizzy. Every time I blink, the graffiti is tattooed on the backs of my eyelids.

Graffiti I've seen before.

Graffiti I've *sprayed* before.

I never stuck around long enough to see the aftermath. It seemed harmless at the time. Painting a word was better than hitting a person. There was no real damage. Words could be washed off or painted over.

I was wrong.

Words are powerful.

One look around the gym tells me that. The counselor has set up shop in the far corner, trying to get a group to open up about how they feel. People cling to one another—in tears, in shock, in anger. Each group surveys those around them with mistrust and fear.

Words did that.

Words that are Molotov cocktails primed to explode and scorch the town with fear and hate.

All my friends have already been called in for their interviews, so I'm sitting alone at the top of the bleachers.

Three Asian guys huddle together down toward the bottom. They keep glancing nervously over the rail, into the tunnel made up of gym wall on one side and bleachers on the other. I scoot to the end of my row to see what they're looking at. A group of guys clusters below me. I can only see the tops of their heads and a couple of hunting camo jackets. I crawl down a couple rows to hear what they're saying.

"You think the Wilson boys did it?" one asks. "Their granddaddy was part of those KKK lynchin's back in the sixties."

I suck in a breath at the word *lynching*.

How long have those assholes been talking like that. What else have they said?

I never took part in a lynching, but I had to take care of a victim of one once. Trying to keep his swollen, purple face covered while I dragged his body into the woods was impossible. Looking at what The Fort had done to him made me burn with disgust, but having to be the one disposing of him made me cold with shame.

One of the camo jackets shakes his head. "I don't think the KKK uses swastikas."

"Well, who painted it then?" the first boy asks.

A thick-necked guy in Carhartt overalls pushes back his ball cap. "Does it matter? I don't want nothin' to do with that shit."

"Zeke's got a point," Camo Jacket says. I recognize his voice. He's one of the guys I got stuck behind in the hall the other day. "It don't matter who did it. Long as we're on the right side of things, we're good."

"That ain't what I mean," Carhartt—Zeke—says.

The first guy holds up his hands. "Man, I ain't puttin' no swastika nowhere."

"We shouldn't be talking about this, y'all." Zeke glances around. "Especially not here."

"Settle down, Zeke. We ain't nazis." Camo pulls a can of Skoal from his back pocket and pops his finger against it. "All I'm sayin' is whoever painted that will leave us alone. You don't see us runnin' around with no blacks or Mexicans. 'Cept for John, here."

"I can't exactly avoid them," another guy says. I know that voice. I slide closer. "A few of them are on the team."

Holy shit. It's Rainey.

My heart drops to the bottom of the bleachers, bounces all the way to the gym floor, and splatters on the waxed boards. The same boards we've played on together. Where's he's played with Brandon and Ellis and Mateo. What the hell is he doing with these guys? How are those words coming out of his mouth?

"Whatever." Camo tucks a clump of tobacco between his lip and gums. "We saw you at homecoming. Looked like you and that Kingsley was havin' a good time."

"Guys," Zeke says. "Seriously."

Rainey shrugs. "I gotta do all that team-building shit. Besides, some of them are all right, but it's not like I'd have them at my house."

"'Course not." Camo spits into a drink can. "I ain't breakin' bread with 'em, but ain't tryin' to do somethin' crazy like run off to join the Klan neither."

Zeke swipes his ball cap off and settles it back on his head. "I can't with this shit. Y'all are talking like they ain't even people."

Rainey laughs. "Didn't realize you were so fragile, Z. Sorry we're not sensitive enough for you."

Zeke throws up his hands. "Screw you, Rainey. I'm out." He bumps Camo's shoulder as he walks off.

"Nate Clemons." I jump and almost fall into the assholes below. A police officer stands in the gym door, impatiently tapping a pen against a clipboard. He's not one of the ones from the other day, but he has the same military bearing.

I swallow hard and walk toward him, trying to collect myself before I reach his side. Hearing Rainey say that shit shook me up. I'd expect it from the others guys in that group, but not him. He and Brandon are friends. The guys with Rainey glance at me briefly, then turn back to their conversation and their chewing tobacco. They think they're different from neo-nazis, that they're not as bad because they're not riding around in bedsheets and burning crosses. It almost makes me sad for them. They don't get it.

I guess racists come in as many colors as people.

The officer leads me to my homeroom classroom and closes the door. He places a recorder on the teacher's desk and mashes a button.

"Nate Clemons?"

I nod.

The officer sighs and gestures at the recorder. "I'm gonna need you to speak out loud, son."

"Yes, sir. I'm Nate. Clemons." My hand goes to Mom's button. I pause with my hand in midair, then drop it to my side.

"I'm Officer Davis. Have a seat." He points at the closest desk.

I force myself to breathe slowly, normally. This is a standard interview. I've done nothing wrong.

Except I have. This is all my fault.

I need to spill everything right now. This is my chance. Before things get worse.

"Where were you between the hours of ten and eleven thirty this morning?"

"I was in history until ten fifty, then lunch."

He scribbles on the clipboard. "What time did you arrive at lunch?"

Hell, I don't know. "I put my books in my locker, then went straight to the lunchroom."

"Did you go outside?"

"No."

He doesn't even look up. "Not at any point?"

"Not until Maddie told us—"

"Maddie Lyons?" He sounds robotic, bored even. How can he be bored when something this major is happening? What's wrong with him?

"Yes. She—"

"And 'us' is . . ."

"Me and Brandon Kingsley."

The cop flips back a couple pages and makes a note. "So you lied to me. You did go outside."

I wipe my sweaty palms on my jeans. He's twisting my words. "No, I didn't go out this morning. Not until after lunch."

"But you did go out." It's a statement, not a question.

"Yes, and saw the graffiti."

"Saw it or sprayed it?"

I narrow my eyes. "*Saw* it."

"And had you *seen* that message before?"

Say yes, a voice in my head pleads. Rip the duct tape off your mouth and talk. I watch the cop. He checks the time on his watch and sighs again.

He couldn't care less about the hate speech. He just wants to catch someone and go home. If I told him the truth, I doubt he'd actually listen to me. He's more likely to put words in my mouth like he's already done. He won't understand the danger. And thanks to my doctored school record he'll think I'm some delinquent playing a sick joke.

"No." The lie rolls off my tongue like a well-greased ball bearing.

"Have you ever used those words?" he asks.

"No."

"Have you ever heard anyone use those words?"

"No."

"Have you been in contact with any spray paint recently?"

"No. Wait, yes. While working on the homecoming float." This is what I get for being social.

He perks up. "When was that?"

I shrug. "A couple weeks ago?"

"What happened to the paint?"

"No idea."

He looks irritated. "Show me your hands."

I extend my arms, palms up. The officer examines my fingertips.

His eyes shift to my face. He flings my hands away in disgust. "Do you have any other information regarding this incident that you would like to disclose?" His voice is as robotic as it was with his initial questions.

Speak now or forever hold your peace.

"No," I say evenly.

He tears a page from the back of his stack and hands it to me. "Thank you for your cooperation. You will be contacted if we require anything further. If you think of anything else that will assist this investigation please contact me."

The paper lists two different phone numbers and an email address for the officer.

"That's it?"

"You're free to go. The remainder of classes have been cancelled for the afternoon."

The cop shows me out. He flops his head back with a heavy sigh. "All this shit over a little graffiti," he mutters as he walks back to the gym.

When he's out of sight, I slump against the bank of lockers. My hands shake so hard I'm afraid I'll tear the page. I don't care who's watching anymore. I grip my button and close my eyes and force myself to see my mother's face instead of those ugly words on the concrete.

A little graffiti. That's how he sees the hate speech stamped on the sidewalk.

One thing is clear. I've crossed a line. It's too late to fess up. I lied to the police. Why would they believe anything I say now?

I have to figure out how to stop The Fort on my own. Before Step Three begins. If I don't, that asshole cop will have more than just a little graffiti to deal with.

702

There's only one way to keep Brandon and Lewiston safe: give The Fort what they want.

Me.

I wait until that point where I can no longer tell if it's late night or early morning, when even the night creatures have gone to sleep and the world is at its most still and quiet. I wait so long I'm afraid I'll back out. Then, before I can change my mind, I shove my clothes in a dirt-crusted black duffle bag I found in the back of my closet, not because I'll need them, but so Dell won't have to take care of them once I'm gone.

God, I hope they don't know about Dell yet. If I leave now, there's a chance they won't find out he's here. If I leave now, there's a chance I can stop Step Three from happening.

I may not be able to prevent The Fort from hurting another Dell or another Brandon or another town, but I can make damn sure they don't hurt this one.

After I earned my red laces, *he* decided I was ready to move up to the "real work." *"You're a man now, son. Time to truly commit to the cause and save the White species."*

He dragged me to this small town in West Virginia where tensions had been rising. The cops there sucked almost as badly as the ones in Farmer. Someone had called 911 about a robbery. The cops saw a black man who allegedly fit the caller's description on the dark front porch of a house. They told him to stop. The man raised his hands. The cops saw something shiny and opened fire.

Nineteen bullet holes later, the police felt safe enough to approach the man and remove his "weapon": a freaking house key.

The cops got additional training. The man got a closed casket.

The black community in that town was outraged. They protested with peaceful sit-ins. They rioted with violence—rocks and looting. The police were too self-righteous to admit they'd been wrong, and too chickenshit to face the protestors themselves.

So they called *him*.

The Skynbyrds went first, taking Kelsey with them. She wasn't smiling or giggling then. She said the whole thing made her stomach turn. When the flyers didn't scare anyone off, the men started on Step Two.

I painted my first swastika on a beauty supply store window. On the other side of the glass, a display of wigs rested on mannequins, a line of decapitated heads on spikes watching me spray hate. The swastika's shadow fell over their mouths like a censorship bar, but the symbols did nothing to quiet the people. Our graffiti only made them angrier.

The peaceful protests ramped up, with protesters marching around the clock. The people in that town tried to avoid violence. The Fort made sure that didn't happen. They hurled the town into Step Three, attacking with bats and pipes. They goaded the people into fighting back to protect themselves, and then twisted it so that the protesters looked like the violent ones. Every punch and grunt and scream shot me back to that Middle Eastern kid who'd earned me my red laces. They were his screams, his grunts, his blood, his face twisted in agony.

I hated myself more than any supremacist ever hated another person. I couldn't participate and I couldn't flee, so I did what any coward would. I hid. I ducked behind the shell of a smoldering car and waited.

I smeared blood from the street across my face and hands and clothes and blended in with the group as they returned to the trucks. No one knew I hadn't done a thing.

We broke the people, killed the riots, and the town went back to its normal, oppressed existence. That's when Kelsey and I decided to run, so that we wouldn't be on the wrong side of history again.

And now, look at us. It's happening again and we're both in the middle of it all over again. Lewiston could easily turn into that West Virginian town. Those guys in the gym proved that racism here is a hive of hibernating hornets. Whack the nest enough and all those feelings will wake up and attack.

Kelsey and I are stuck in the same cycle. No matter what we do, or how far we go, we just circle around and around and around.

Well, I'm jumping off the merry-go-round. It's going to hurt like hell, but I'd rather be bruised and broken than let that happen to Brandon.

I'm tiptoeing to the stairs when my phone vibrates. *Incoming call: Brandon,* flashes on the screen. There's no reason for him to call this early, or to call at all. We have a strictly texting relationship.

I'm back in my room in flash. "Brandon?"

"They . . . someone . . ." He sounds hoarse, strained.

Tentacles of fear snake around my chest and squeeze. "Are you hurt? Did they attack you?"

"No, no."

The tentacles loosen and I sigh into the phone. "Good. Then why the hell—"

"Not me," Brandon says.

The duffle bag slips from my shoulder. The buckles rattle softly as they hit the wooden floor. An image of Mrs. Kingsley leaps in my head, her body on the ground, hair haloed with blood. I will kill them if they went after Brandon's family. This time it *will* be straight murder.

"It's my granddad. Well not *him,* but his statue. I'm scared, man." He starts speaking fast, his words tumbling over one another. "My whole family's freaking out. The cops have been in and out since Henry saw it on his way home from night fishing. They want to put surveillance on us. Pop said no, but I kind of want it. I want the police watching me. What if—what if they try to do it for real?"

"Whoa, slow down. Do what for real?"

His voice drops to a whisper. "Lynch me."

The phone slips from my hand. I bobble it, barely stopping it from clattering to the floor. "What?" I ask, pressing the phone to my ear again. "Why? Why would someone l-lynch you?"

"Because of the noose," he says. "They hung a noose on Granddad's statue."

✧

There are so many police cruisers downtown we can't even get close.

Dell parks down the block and cuts the engine. "They must've called every guy in four counties."

"They're finally realizing this is more than a school prank." I crane my neck. The officer who interviewed me dashes along the outside edge of the crowd. He doesn't look bored now. He looks pissed, but I'm betting it has more to do with the early time than the noose.

Dell massages his temples with one hand. "I knew we should've told them since the start." He slams his palm against the steering wheel. "This is what I get for panicking and listening to some kid."

I hunker down in my coat. "Well, we sure as hell can't tell them now."

Dell glares at me. "That's exactly what we're gonna do." He reaches for the door handle."

"They'll think we did it," I say. "We march up there and tell them a pack of neo-nazis from Kentucky is responsible and they'll think we're covering our asses. And if they actually believe us and check our story, then what?" I drop my tone. "Why would we be all the way down in Alabama? We're just a like-minded gathering of peaceable folks tucked off in the Kentucky hills where nobody can bother us."

Dell grimaces. "I told you not to imitate that man again. It's unsettling how much you sound like your father."

Tell me about it. I pull my own jacket tighter. "It'll be our word against theirs. Who do you think the cops will believe? Especially once they uncover our real pasts."

A flash goes off down the street and the officers yell. Shit. The media. A skinny guy scurries between two cops and hops into a van with CHANNEL 9 NEWS painted on the side. A noose hanging from the statue of the first black man to integrate the West Alabama public school system is bound to earn national attention, which means reporters will be swarming like sharks on chum.

More exposure means more of a chance for Lewiston to discover the wolf hiding in their flock.

"Are they setting me up?" I ask. My mind goes to Kelsey again. To the look that flashed in her eyes on the street. Did she let me go because she's still on my side, or because The Fort already had a plan in motion?

Dell shakes his head. "Your name would've come up by now."

My breath fogs the window. I swipe the cuff of my sleeve over it and watch the cops. One of them stands on a ladder, gingerly lifting a coil of rope from the statue's neck. He drops it in a large evidence bag.

"Then it doesn't make sense," I say. "The Fort is here because of me. Why haven't they come after me yet? Why target Lewiston like it's any other town?"

Dell rubs his hands together and blows into them. "They came all the way down here. It would be a waste if they didn't have some fun while they were at it."

"Then why not make the town turn on me?"

He considers for a minute. "You ever see a cat catch a mouse?"

I roll my eyes. "Cliché much?"

"Hear me out. It's not about the kill. Cats don't just pounce on their prey and bite their heads off. They injure the mouse first, so it can't get away, then play with it for a while. Only when they get bored or the mouse starts to die on its own do they kill it."

"Yeah, but The Fort is playing with the town, not me."

Dell scrubs his hand over his graying whiskers. "It's no fun if they out you from the get-go. Lewiston would turn on you all right. They'd throw you in jail and The Fort would lose their toy. They're not ready to kill you yet."

A shiver works through me.

Dell's eyes widen. "Not literally kill you. I didn't mean—"

"No, you're right. They will." I meet Dell's eyes. "I can't give them that chance."

The beginnings of a plan start to take shape, the way fuzzy gray mountains on the horizon become clearer the closer you get. Handing myself over to The Fort would keep Brandon and Lewiston safe, but it's only cutting one head off a hydra. I think I know how to kill the whole damn creature.

705

"Thanks for coming." Brandon tugs on his tie. He looks as nervous as I feel.

"No problem," I say, scanning the never-ending stream of people filing into the Lewiston A.M.E. Church for the community togetherness service. I'm not sure what I'm looking for—fatigues among the suit pants, combat boots in step with high heels, Kelsey? I'm being ridiculous. Jumpy. Not myself. Not even the fake me.

"Sorry I didn't come earlier," I say. Dell has barely let me out of his sight since the noose incident.

"You couldn't have gotten to the house anyway," Brandon says. "In fact, you probably won't be able to come over for a while." He fiddles with his tie again. His mother sweeps his hand aside and gives the next man in line a piece of paper that has the order of the service printed on it.

"Leave it alone, baby," she says. A lady I've never met stands beside her, handing out white candles with white paper circles around the bottoms. A parade of people in dresses and suits marches past me, taking papers and candles. I self-consciously smooth the wrinkles in my thrift store button-down.

Brandon motions to me, then ducks through the crowd and into a nook just inside the front doors. He loosens the tie knot and leans against the wall. "The police have barricaded my street. They're only letting residents through."

"What does your dad think of that?"

"He hates it. But I'm relieved. I sleep better knowing the police are watching. Now, if I only knew why this was all happening in the first place. This is way scarier than Ellis's auntie finding some racist Easter eggs."

I run a fingernail down my candle, peeling off a curl of wax. If only it were as easy to peel back the layers of myself. If only I were wax underneath my skin—no feelings, no pain.

"I know," I say. But my voice is hardly loud enough for even me to hear.

Brandon's forehead wrinkles. "Huh?"

I swallow hard and try again. "I know why," I say more forcefully. "I know why this—"

"Boys." Brandon's mother appears at the edge of our nook. "We're about to start. And quit it with the tie!" She tightens the knot around Brandon's neck again, lifting it up to adjust his collar underneath.

The coil around his neck, the strip of fabric held over his head, it looks . . .

Oh God.

It looks like a noose. A black-and-gray paisley noose.

I blink and see that body I dragged into the woods. Except it's Brandon's face that's swollen and purple.

I stumble back into an empty umbrella stand. Metal clatters against the wall. Mrs. Kingsley's head jerks toward me. "Nate, baby, you okay? You're white as a fish belly."

Brandon meets my eyes. His face is a mask of confusion and something else . . . Hurt? Curiosity? His mother takes my arm on one side and Brandon's on the other. He shoots me a look over the top of her head.

"Later," I mouth. "After."

His forehead wrinkles more. We shuffle to a middle row where Dr. Kingsley and Henry saved us seats. Dell and Bev are squished against the bench rail along the inside aisle. Brandon tries to maneuver around his mom to sit beside me, but she plops down first, stranding me on the outside edge, alone.

The entire church is packed—standing room only. Most of the faces are shades of black and brown and tan. Every minority in town must be here. There are plenty of white folks, too, though. We're all mixed together on the benches, in the balcony, along the walls. With all these bodies crammed against one another, I'm surprised the place doesn't spontaneously combust.

A black man in a black suit mounts the plush, red carpeted steps at the front of the room. He places one hand on the walnut podium and raises the other high above his head. The thrum of the crowd fades as though someone is twisting a volume knob.

"Ga-wd," he says in a deep voice.

Every head drops as if the man has put them all in a trance. I shrink against the bench and dip my head, too, watching Brandon's mother out of the corner of my eye for cues.

"Our precious, precious Ga-wd. Our Lord!" he shouts.

Oh, he said *God*. We're praying.

"Bless this place!" the man yells. The concept of an indoor voice seems to have escaped him. "Hold each person here in the palm of your hand. Take care of us, Jesus. And take care of these *aggressors!*" Each word is drawn out, elongated.

"Amen!" someone calls. I start to look up, but the Kingsleys' heads are still bowed. I don't think I'll ever get the hang of this praying thing.

"Show them the error of their ways. *Lead* them to peace. *FILL* them with your spirit!"

More people shout, "Amen!" Around me, hands raise, palms up like the man by the podium.

"And guide us," he says, softer. "Help us show these aggressors your love. Teach *us* how to treat them with the same grace and mercy you exhibit every day. And all Ga-wd's people say . . ."

"Amen!" everyone calls out so loud I jump in my seat.

A stick of a woman moves into the light near the preacher and starts singing about getting your house in order. Her voice is full and thick and can't possibly be coming out of that tiny person.

After the first line, the crowd sings back in unison. I've stumbled into one of those movie musicals where everyone suddenly breaks out in song. Is this a black church thing, or just a church thing in general?

The woman's voice lifts over the people, surrounding us like a fuzzy blanket. After a couple lines, the congregation responds again. Mrs. Kingsley removes a book from the seat in front of her and flips to a page. I mumble the words on the line she points to, stumbling along until the song ends and the building goes so silent that it feels like God pressed mute on an all-powerful universal remote. Then there's the flutter of pages as Mrs. Kingsley puts the songbook away. The woman sits to the right of the stage and the preacher moves back to the podium again.

"Congregation," he says, not as yell-y this time. "There's a plague in our house. A scourge of *evil*! Now, we don't know who's behind it or why."

Brandon inclines his head to me ever so slightly. I stare at the lines of wax under my nails, choking down the urge to stand up and shout that it's all my fault.

"But we do know this." The preacher scans the crowd slowly, his gaze pausing on different people. "It's a test. You see it's been quiet in Lewiston for too long and the enemy don't like that. So he's testin' us. Tryin' to see if we're really *Ga-wd's*. Or if we're his. So you know what we're gonna do?"

Several people mumble answers.

"We're gonna make sure our houses are in order," the preacher says. He strides from one side of the stage to the other. "We're gonna make sure our hearts stay in the right place. Gonna come together as a town. Black, white, purple, yellow, green, and *everything* in between."

"Amen!" choruses around me.

"We're gonna show that Devil he ain't gonna divide Lewiston! Not this time!"

"Yes, Lord!"

"Gonna show these aggressors that we're united!"

"Yes, Lord!"

"That noooooobody's gonna tear down *this house*!" He jumps up and down. People around me start clapping, sporadically at first, then the woman is singing again and the claps hit the beat. Someone lights their candle and passes the flame down the aisle.

When it's my turn, my hands are so sweaty the candle slides through my fingers and rolls across the floor. Brandon picks it up and passes it back to me, his face a giant question mark. I light my candle off Mrs. Kingsley's, and let the white guy against the wall light his off mine.

When all the candles are lit, the overhead lights go out. Hundreds of tiny, yellow flames dance, illuminating the darkness. I focus on the dot of light in front of me.

I wish it could always be this easy to find light in the darkness. Just look down, and there it is. I used to think it was for some people—people like Ms. Erica and Brandon—but I don't think so anymore. I think all of us have a little bit of darkness inside in some form or other.

The preacher is right, though. We can't let our darkness win.

I can't let it win.

The song shifts into a new one, slow and soft. Candles rise in the air and wave in time with the tune. The tiny singer's voice swells. She lets out a long, warbling note then falls back down to a whisper, taking the entire congregation along on the ride. No one hollers out this time. We're all quiet. Transfixed. The notes weave an invisible cord between us, drawing us all close, threading a sense of peace through me that I've never felt before. The pianist hits a final note and there's only the singer's voice. The candles grow still. I hardly dare to breathe. I raise my candle with all the others, watch the small flickering dots of hope. The singer's last word hangs in the air for a moment, then the entire church falls silent. Motionless. No one wanting to be the first to break the spell.

CRASH!

Sharp points graze my face. Cold air rushes in from my left. A glittering shower of glass rains down around me.

CRASH!

CRASH!

Bloodcurdling screams as piercing as the glass sweep in with the air. I turn, trying to locate the source of each sound, but something heavy falls on top of me. My candle slips out of my hand to the carpet. Flames nibble at the red cloth.

I can't move. I'm wedged against the pew by the hot mass on top of me.

A body.

There's a body on me and the fire is eating the carpet now. I wrench my foot free and stamp out the candle. The man slumped over me—the one I'd passed my tiny drop of light to—is slick. There's water on his back.

Not water. Blood.

Glass sparkles on his shirt like deadly fairy dust. He's not awake. I'm not sure he's even breathing. I have to get help.

I wriggle free, bumping into Mrs. Kingsley still sitting in her spot on the pew. She turns to me, dazed. Blood pours from a cut on her forehead. Her candle has fallen to the floor, too. I stomp on the wick

"Mrs. Kingsley? Are you okay?"

Her head wobbles on her shoulders, like one of those dashboard figurines. "I'm okay," she mutters.

"Mama!" Brandon cries.

"Something hit me." Her hand falls into her lap and she lifts a rectangular object.

My body immediately goes cold.

"A brick?" she asks.

Brandon tears it from her hands. It's covered with blood, but I don't think it's Mrs. Kingsley's.

I think it's from the man beside me. I think he might be dead.

Bodies jostle around us. The fallen man blocks the side aisle, but that doesn't stop people from trying to climb over him in the dark. Someone trips in the next pew up. Another candle tumbles to the floor. I can't reach this one, but from the amount of smoke curling to the ceiling, I don't think it's the only fire to worry about.

Brandon tears something away from the brick. A rubber band. A sheet of paper. He holds his own candle to the page. "'We said you'd burn.'"—the blood-smeared paper shakes in his hands—"'Courtesy of Nathaniel *Clemons*.'" He stares at me hard. "You—"

"Nate!" Dell pushes through the crowd, appearing in the next pew. "Are you okay?"

"I am, but they aren't." I point at Mrs. Kingsley and the man. Another window breaks and fresh shrieks erupt.

People are screaming. Shouting names. Crying for help. Just plain crying. We have to get out of here. I try to pull Mrs. Kingsley to her feet.

"We have to go. Now!" Dell says, echoing my thoughts. "Help Mrs. Kingsley." He and Dr. Kingsley climb over the pews to the shattered window. They each take a side of the possibly dead man and lift.

Brandon loops his arm under his mom's, the bloody page crumpled in his fist. I take her other arm and we haul her down the row. People push and shove and scream. We're propelled forward and back in a living, breathing current as everyone surges for the door.

Glass crunches under our feet. Freezing air rushes through the room. Candlelight flickers. No one has thought to turn the lights back on. No one seems to know what's going on, only that there are dozens of broken windows.

That means dozens of bricks.

Dozens of notes.

Sirens wail. Police? Paramedics? Does Lewiston even have paramedics? Whatever they are, they sound forever away.

I have no concept of time, of how long ago the bricks flew, or how long we stand in the aisle trying to get out. The only thing I'm aware of is how hot the room has gotten with all the terrified bodies pressed together and how difficult breathing has become and how the door is miles away.

Brandon and his mother and I cling to one another. Behind us, Dell and Dr. Kingsley drag the maybe-dead man. Bev and Henry have disappeared, faceless bodies in the current.

The crowd surges forward. Someone falls. A woman. The singing woman, maybe? People scramble to help her up before she's trampled under all those dress shoes and high heels.

Fresh, cold air tickles my nostrils, but it's tinged with something familiar and woody.

Suddenly, we're outside.

But outside is no better than in. In fact, it may be worse. Fire rages around us, licking the night sky with its hateful tongues.

"What are those?" Brandon asks, his voice clogged with smoke and fear. "Are they . . ."

"Crosses," I answer. "They're burning crosses."

✧

In every direction, fire laps at sky, spewing from the eight giant crosses forming a semicircle in front of the church. The skinheads have to be close, but where? Between the screams and the sirens and the crackle of burning wood, I can't hear myself think.

Someone tears Brandon's mother away from us. I try to object, but Brandon holds me back. "Fire medic," he says. He levels his gaze at me and I turn back to the crosses. Their fire is nothing compared to the one blazing in Brandon's eyes. I know that look. I've felt it. It's the thorn that shoots out of fear and anger, that leads to impulsive decisions and bad choices. I have to do something before the spines sting him too deep, before he steps on my path and gets trapped in the muck.

I tug on Brandon's arm. "Come on. I need to—"

A hand falls on my back and I flinch. "Thank God." Bev squeezes my shoulder. Her voice sounds higher than normal. "I thought I'd lost you. Have you seen Dell?"

"He was behind us," I say, "helping someone who was hit by a brick."

A megaphone buzzes nearby. "Across the street. Away from the fire. Go across the street."

The crowd heaves again. People scramble around us, their nicest clothes torn and bloody. A man shuffles past, a stunned expression on his face. He's missing one shoe, but he doesn't seem to notice.

Police and firemen and nurses scurry every which way, directing people away from the burning crosses and shattered building. Brandon, Bev, and I cling to one another as we weave through the crowd. Nurses have set up folding tables and are unloading bandages and gauze. Fire medics wheel out oxygen tanks and carry out blankets.

The sweat-tinged odor of terror mingles with the smoke pouring off of the crosses. It smells like that town in West Virginia. My hands shake and my throat closes up. I can't swallow. I can't breathe. I can't think. Frightened faces stream past me. Tear-streaked cheeks and wailing mouths. I close my eyes and see swastikas on shop windows and blood in gutters. All I want to do is run away. Hide in a closet. Cover myself with Mom's clothes. But I know I can't run anymore.

We scan the emergency nurses' stations until we spot Mrs. Kingsley with Dell, Henry, and Dr. Kingsley.

She holds up a hand. "Before you ask, I'm fine. Just a couple stitches. The other gentleman took the brunt of the hit. How is he?"

Dr. Kingsley shakes his head. "We don't know. They loaded him in an ambulance as soon as we got him outside. He was breathing, so there's that."

"Oh, Lord," Mrs. Kingsley says. "It's at least forty-five minutes to the closest hospital."

Dr. Kingsley pats her arm. "Once we're squared away here, I'll go up and wait for him. I didn't even get his name, but at least he won't be alone when he wakes up."

I hear loud hissing behind us, like a giant, angry cat. The smoke gets thicker, stinging my eyes. I turn, blinking away the smoky tears. The firemen have put out the fire and darkness creeps into the spaces between the flames, slithering across the street and down my nostrils, snuffing out all the light inside. I clench my fists tighter.

I hate them, The godforsaken Fort and everyone in it. Everyone who did this.

They're going to regret ever stepping into Lewiston.

I close my eyes and breathe in smoke-tinged air. It's easy to read articles or watch reports on TV and think "oh how sad" for the victims without really feeling anything, but when it's people you know—people you could've shopped behind or passed on the street—it throws the whole picture into clear focus.

They're not characters in a book or movie. They're real people feeling real pain. Real fear. Bleeding real blood. I grew up with it all, but this town . . . it's experiencing it for the first time in fifty years. Some of the people, for the first time ever.

This can't happen again.

My eyes flutter open. Dell and Bev are beside an ambulance gathering armfuls of bottled water and blankets. Dr. Kingsley and Henry are huddled by Mrs. Kingsley, but I don't see Brandon.

I whirl around, looking up and down the street. He can't have gone far. Too much could happen on this packed street where faces blend into a featureless mass. Every time I blink, I swear I see that tie-noose around his neck. I weave through the crowd, trying not to panic. Red and blue lights flash, washing the street with eerie light. An ambulance blips its siren and the crowd parts so it can pull onto the street. Its headlights highlight a familiar shape: Brandon.

He's besides a police cruiser, talking to a cop.

Why would he be—

He hands the officer a blocky object: the brick. I'm close enough to see the cop pull a latex glove from his pocket. Close enough to see that it's the bald guy from the principal's office. Brandon gave him the note, the one that points the finger at me.

My body screams at me to run, but my feet aren't listening. Is Brandon turning me in?

I'm not sure. That look he shot me earlier . . .

He stalks toward me. I still don't run. I have nowhere to go. Brandon doesn't stop. He doesn't even look my way as he passes.

"Brandon," I call.

"I don't even want to hear it."

Mom's button is clamped in my fist. I probably look like a weirdo, but I don't care. I cling to the button, holding myself in place. I trail behind him. "Are you okay?"

Brandon whirls. "Am I okay? Of course not! Bricks flew through my church's windows. People are hurt. My mama is hurt. *Crosses* are burning, Nate! What do you mean 'am I okay?'"

I'm not sure what to say. My cheeks flush with guilt. This is all my fault. "What can I do?" That was the wrong thing to ask. There's nothing I can do now. Except maybe tell the truth.

"Oh, now you want to help? Then start by telling me what the hell is going on! What do you know?"

I hesitate. Cling to my button. This is my chance.

"Don't even think about lying to me, man," Brandon says.

People flow past, many I don't recognize from the church. Could they be from The Fort? Weaving through the crowd, waiting to lash out from the inside? Even though the cops are here, they'd still be outnumbered if The Fort showed up in force. We aren't safe.

Brandon especially isn't safe.

"Not here," I say.

Brandon glowers. "No bullshit, Nate. Or is it Nathaniel?"

A few people look up. My hands start shaking. This is so much worse than finding the flyers. I can't keep my cool this time. There's too much to lose. The Fort probably knows what I look like now—assuming Kelsey told them. If they see Brandon with me, what will they do to him?

"Can we go somewhere more private?"

Brandon chews his bottom lip. He looks like he's going to say no.

"Somewhere safer."

He rolls his eyes. "Hold up."

I follow him back to the nurses' station and hang back as he pulls Henry aside. Henry shakes his head, waving wildly, but Brandon grabs his arms and says something else. Henry steals a glance at me, relaxes, and nods.

Brandon marches back. My muscles are so tight my right calf is cramping.

"You get five minutes."

We slip between two nearby houses where it's quieter, but still in view of the church. An engine rumbles somewhere behind us. The flashing emergency vehicle lights fade away, giving way to moonlight. The air smells like smoke and the threat of rain.

Brandon crosses his arms. He looks angrier than I've ever seen him. More than when he saw the flyers at school. But there's a hint of fear there, too.

My throat feels knotted, trapping the words behind my tongue. How do you tell someone you've been lying for months? That those lies injured his mother? Terrorized his town? I cough, and the words come up like phlegm. "This is all my fault."

I can make out Brandon's glare in the dim moonlight filtering through the clouds. "You did this?"

"No. Not exactly, I mean—" Thunder rumbles behind us.

"I don't have time for this shit. Spit it out." His voice is all sharp corners.

My mouth works like that damn ventriloquist dummy from the Psych Center. I can't say the words out loud. I *can't*.

Thunder growls again, closer. If only the rain could wash everything away. This entire day. Hell, my entire life. "They're neo-nazis," I blurt. "Skinheads. And they're here because of me. For me. They're from back home."

"I know you're not about to tell me you're a Klansman or some shit. After all we've been through this year. What the f—"

"I'm not! Not anymore."

"Uh-uh." Brandon holds up his hands and starts to back away. "I can't hear this."

"I was born there," I say quickly. "Grew up there. I ran away after I . . ." I take a deep breath. "After I killed my father. Their leader."

Brandon's eyes widen. His hand flies to his throat, fingers clawing at his shirt buttons. He doubles over, heaving.

"Brandon—"

He pukes in the gutter. My eyes sting. Thunder roars again.

Headlights wink down the street. Brandon wipes his mouth with his sleeve and straightens. "You're him," he gasps.

Now I feel sick. He knows.

"You lied to me. I knew I recognized you. You asshole." He yanks off his tie and shoves it in his pocket. "I trusted you, and you're *that* guy?"

I nod and try swallow away that knot in my throat. Rain sprinkles around us. The headlights get brighter as the oncoming vehicle closes in. It needs to turn, to go away before the light shines on Brandon's face. I'm terrified to see his expression. He turns away.

"Brandon, wait. Hear me out."

"No. You had weeks, months, to tell me this, and you wait until we're attacked? I don't owe you shit."

"I know. But I owe you."

The thunder sounds closer. The rain picks up. Brandon waits.

I take a deep breath. I can do this. I have to do this. "I wanted to tell you, but I've been hiding. The people who did this, they want me dead."

He glares at me over his shoulder. "Oh, so they attacked us to flush you out."

"I didn't mean for that to happen."

"It's not about what you meant, Nate. It's about what happened." Brandon looks at me dead-on. "Could you have stopped this?"

Rain falls heavier. Cold drops spread across my shoulders, stinging my skin. Smoke billows from the church. Back on the street, people scatter, crowding under the emergency tents.

"I'm getting soaked," Brandon says. "I can't deal with this shit right now."

"Can we go somewhere else and talk?" I plead. "You deserve the truth." And you need to get out of sight. Just in case. I can't decide if it would be more dangerous to squeeze under one of those tents, where a blade could slip out of a pocket and into Brandon's flesh without so much as a glint of steel, or for him to be separated from the group, alone. I just want us both to get behind closed doors somewhere.

"You put me, my family, in danger to save your own ass. So, no. I'm going home." He starts between the houses, away from the church, toward the next street over.

"Brandon."

"Keep my name out of your mouth," he snaps. "I'm done, Nate. You and me? We're done." He has to raise his voice to speak over the thunder.

Except it's not thunder. It's the truck that just passed. A giant black truck. One I've seen. One I've ridden in.

It skids to stop, then starts to turn around.

Oh my God.

"Brandon!" I yell it this time.

"I don't care, Nate."

The truck faces us, idling. High beams flash, petrifying me, like a deer.

"What the hell?" Brandon asks.

Tires squeal. The truck accelerates, snarling like a hungry bear.

"RUN!" I grab Brandon's arm and take off, dragging him behind me.

It's going to run us down.

I bodycheck Brandon onto the sidewalk. He stumbles, but manages to stay upright. We sprint into a yard as the truck smashes through a mailbox. We cut between two houses, a gap too narrow for the truck to follow.

The engine grumbles as it reverses. Voices shout after us, but the rain and the waterfall pulse rushing in my ears drowns the noise out. Headlights sweep the yard as the truck swerves back to the street.

Brandon and I take off again, weaving through yards. We emerge on a side street and I recognize where we are—near the path to the river, and so close to Brandon's house that I swear I see his back porch light up ahead.

Our feet slap the pavement, each step drawing us closer and closer to that light.

The truck roars onto the road in front of us, blocking our path to the house. We turn back the way we came, but three figures emerge from the darkness.

Behind us is only woods and river. The truck squeals to a stop, inches away.

"Nate." Brandon manages between gasps. "What do we do?"

We break for the woods, trying to lose them.

"Looky here, boys," says a voice from my nightmares.

Too late.

Thomas Mayes jumps to the dirt. He balances a metal rod or bat across his shoulders, draping his arms over it. "If it ain't Nathaniel Fuller and his little darkie friend?"

Boots crunch on the other side of the truck. Jeremy Connor and his brother circle around, stopping in front of the headlights beside Thomas Mayes. I can't see their faces, but their ugly sneers are imprinted on my brain. The three guys behind us spread out. Brandon and I are surrounded, outnumbered, and there's no telling how many more assholes are crammed in that truck bed.

"You been a bad boy, Nathaniel," says Thomas Mayes. "We're gonna have to teach you a lesson."

The beast stirs in my gut. I straighten up and puff out my chest. "Is that right?"

Out of the corner of my eye I see Brandon stand taller. He clenches his fists.

Aside from Dell, my last fight was back in jail. And I lost.

But I'm stronger than ever now, thanks to Brandon making me play basketball. I've never seen Brandon fight, but he's about my size, and he's strong. If one of us can wrangle that weapon away from Thomas Mayes, maybe we stand a chance. "Too afraid to take me alone? Or can you still feel the knife I slid in your stomach, Tommy?"

He stiffens. He hates that name almost as much as he hates anyone who isn't white.

"Don't you sound just like your daddy?" Thomas Mayes hawks a wad of chewing tobacco in the dirt at my feet. "It ain't right to hear Jefferson's voice comin' outta his murderer's mouth. I think we're just gonna have to make it so you cain't talk no more." He strides forward and the headlights glint off his dented silver bat. God he's gotten big. Huge. A low hum comes from beside me, almost like a cat's purr.

Brandon closes the space between us. "I'm calling the police," he whispers. Faint light glows through the fabric of his pants pocket. Hopefully too faint for the skinheads to notice.

Thomas Mayes is quickly closing the distance. He'll be on us before the dispatcher even answers Brandon's call. Green flight jackets, black combat boots, bald heads, and baseball bats were scary enough when I was part of their group. But being on this side, staring down the barrel of a bloodstained bat, is more horrifying than I ever could've imagined. The Connor brothers are scrawny little shits, and so is one of the new guys, but the other two are as big as Thomas Mayes.

"Look," Brandon says, his voice steady. "We can work this out."

Thomas Mayes laughs. "Ain't that cute?" He points the bat at Brandon. "You know what I wanna hear? I wanna hear you beg, black boy."

A tinny voice speaks from Brandon's pocket, but the skinheads don't seem to have heard.

The guy closest to Brandon grins, making the swastika tattoo on his neck ripple. He hocks up a loogie and spits it at Brandon's feet. "You gonna die tonight, boy."

Brandon's hand twitches for his phone. Does he have time to pull it out? Can the police track us with just the call?

Thomas Mayes circles me, stopping inches from my face. "Tell you what, Nathaniel. We'll do your friend here first. Give you a nice blood shower before we send you to Hell."

"HELP!" Brandon yells. *"I'M ON ELM STREET AND I NEED HELP!"*

"God cain't help you now, boy," Thomas Mayes says.

I lunge for Mayes. Strong arms grab mine, pinning them behind my back.

A jagged bolt of lightning breaks the sky. Thunder crashes. Brandon raises his fists. Jeremy Connor takes a swing at Brandon's head. Brandon ducks and buries a punch in his stomach. Connor stumbles back. Brandon swings at his head, but its wild and misses.

Come on, Brandon. You can take this asshole.

I flail against the guy holding me. He jerks me sideways, off balance, but I see Brandon's fist connect with Jeremy's nose. He hollers and dives at Brandon, knocking him to the mud.

Thomas Mayes laughs. "This has been fun to watch and all, but I think it's time to end it." He and the other big guy approach Brandon. The other guy yanks Brandon to his feet.

Oh God no. No, no, no! It's the woods and Kelsey and everything all over again. I kick at the dude holding me but he's damn strong.

Mayes raises the bat.

"NO!" I scream. "Take me! Leave him alone and take me!"

Brandon kicks at the guy holding him. Lightning whips across the sky. I can see Brandon's determined, pissed off expression.

Then the bat zooms through the air and I swear I feel the wind from it on my face. There's a sickening *crack,* followed by the most haunting scream I've ever heard.

Brandon falls. The guy raises the bat again.

"NO!" I thrash, breaking the grip holding me down, leaping for Thomas Mayes, tackling him. His face makes a

satisfying crunch under my fist as I punch again and again and again. Someone pulls on my shirt collar, jerking me back. A steel-toed boot smashes into my ribs.

Metal pings and Brandon howls again.

I roll toward the person kicking me and knock him into the dust. *"Brandon! Run!"* I scream, even though I know good and well he won't be running anywhere for a long time. We only have one shot to make it out of this alive.

The beast.

"Shut him up!" Thomas Mayes yells.

The guy on the ground scrabbles for me. I stomp on his fingers and dart between the Connor brothers. Brandon lies on the ground at their feet, clutching his leg. He's covered with blood and dirt.

I move between the skinheads and Brandon. The guy who kicked me first sits a few feet away clutching his face, dark, thick blood gushing between his fingers. The bat lays between us.

I lunge for it, but Thomas Mayes gets there first. I duck and bury my shoulder in his gut. I dig my fingers into his stomach, into the scar I gave him when I was eight. He grunts and stumbles back, falling hard.

The bat rolls away and I dive for it.

The Connor brothers and their asshole friends have descended on Brandon again. Kicking and jeering. The beast is full-on awake now. More than awake. It's all I am.

I grip the bat and level a swing at the closest head. Jason Connor. It connects with the back of his skull and he crumples to the ground. The bat whirs through the air again before anyone can process what just happened.

I catch one of the new guys in the back. Something hard hits me in the side. I pivot and swing again. The bat strikes flesh and something snaps. Everything is a blur. Lightning cracks and the sky breaks open. Blood mixes with mud.

A fist smashes into my jaw. I shove the bat handle toward the fist and end up smacking into a face. I can't even tell who's who anymore. I whirl and find Thomas Mayes crouching over Brandon.

With a roar of rage, I propel myself at the son of a bitch. We hit the ground again, rolling, fists flying. I punch and punch until I can't feel my hand or my arm or anything at all. Nothing exists anymore. I'm on autopilot, doing what I was trained to do—what I was born to do.

I'm vaguely aware of a rumble to my right, then whoever I'm on top of—I'm not even sure it's Thomas Mayes anymore—is being pulled out from under me. I rocket to my feet, ready to attack.

But no one's there.

I hear the peel of tires and then I'm looking at taillights.

Panic lurches in my stomach. They took Brandon.

But, no. Brandon's still here. On the ground.

Not moving.

Water puddles around him.

I drop to my knees, cradling his head. "Brandon." He doesn't make a sound. "Brandon, please. Oh God. Oh please. Brandon, oh please!" Tears roll off my nose and splash onto his face, making little splotches where his dark skin peeks through the dirt covering him.

And that's how the police find me. Bloody and broken and crying over my best friend's body with a bat beside me and the rain washing all the evidence away.

The Lewiston Learner

Town Faces First Racist Attack in Decades

By Darlene Sampson
Staff Writer

Police are labeling an attack on Lewiston A.M.E. Church last night as a hate crime. The attack occurred during a community togetherness service.

Church leaders held the service after a string of incidents of racism around town, the most recent being a noose hung around the neck of Herschel Kingsley's statue downtown.

The service, intended to unite the town against these acts, ended in terror when bricks smashed through the church's windows.

"We'd just lit our candles and started to sing when we heard glass breaking," said Nakia Reid, who led the singing. "It didn't register at first, then people started screaming and running. It was chaos."

Outside the church, eight crosses had been set on fire. No one witnessed the crosses being placed or lit. The volunteer fire department got the blaze under control within minutes. This marks the first cross burning in Ridge County in two decades.

While the crosses did not cause any injuries, the bricks did. Several people sustained injuries fleeing the scene. Only two individuals, Clark Green, 45, and Brett Hawkins, 51, were struck with the bricks. Green suffered head trauma and Hawkins was hit in the back. Both were taken to Baptist Memorial Hospital for treatment.

Eight bricks were found at the church. All had notes attached to them with the message, "We said you'd burn. Courtesy of Nathaniel *Clemons*."

The message is similar to the one graffitied at Lewiston High School. Lewiston Police have traced the notes back to 16-year-old Nate Clemons, a Lewiston High student who started attending the school in the fall.

Clemons was found near the

woods several miles from the scene beside the injured body of classmate Brandon Kingsley, grandson of Herschel Kingsley.

Kingsley was unconscious, and had a broken leg and fractured arm. He was taken to Baptist Memorial Hospital where he remains in a coma. Witnesses overheard Clemons and Kingsley arguing just after the attack on the church, and Clemons was found with a baseball bat, a weapon that doctors say matches Kingsley's injuries.

Clemons was detained and interrogated but no formal charges have been filed at this time. Police say they are still investigating.

718

It's happening again. Misinformation, jail, blood on my hands. Everyone blames me, hates me. Even my own conscience is against me. I can't think about Brandon too long without feeling like I'm about to shatter into more pieces than the church windows.

Only one thing holds me together: revenge.

It's hiding under that damn shell I've grown so accustomed to wearing, biding its time, waiting until I can slip away from the cops' watchful eyes and get out of this hellhole.

It's been two weeks.

Thanksgiving came and went, but I couldn't think of much to be thankful for. Every morning I wake up expecting to end the day in cuffs, and every night I'm haunted by nightmares. By Brandon's bloody face. Christmas is around the corner. So is my birthday. I don't care as much about spending those in jail as I do the anniversary of that night. I'll lose it if I'm stuck in there then. Two weeks.

And Brandon still hasn't woken up.

They're all convinced I did it. They don't want to hear anything else. They have the notes from the church blaming me, the blood, Brandon's injuries, which are consistent with being clubbed with a bat, and my fingerprints on the only bat at the scene. And, of course, the way they found us.

The police detained me that night, but I refused to speak. Not without a lawyer. They've brought me in twice since I lawyered up. Interviewing me. Grilling me. Trying to trip me up by switching facts. Having to repeat the gory details again and again and again hurts my soul. Having to make sure my lawyer is there each time hurts Dell's bank account. Turns out the State only pays for an attorney if you've been formally charged.

Which hasn't happened. Yet. They don't have enough evidence to charge me with anything, but they did give the whole "don't leave town" speech. Hell, I don't even leave the house. A cop car sits at the end of our driveway. Watching. Always watching.

Then there's the rumors. Things tend to spread quick in a small town. If only they spread correct.

Of course, the incident with Maddie's broken nose on the first day of school bubbled back up, and apparently the store owner who saw me with the flyers that day on Main Street called in a tip. Even my freaking social worker felt she had a "moral obligation" to tell police that I talked—joked—about a plot to burn down the town. That one really bit me in the ass.

No one believes that Brandon and I were fighting racist skinheads. They think *I'm* a racist skinhead, and that I was working with others to commit all the hate crimes in Lewiston. Sad thing is, I can't say I blame them.

The 911 recording is too garbled because of Brandon's pocket. The only clear words are Brandon pleading for help. Words that play on a loop in my mind, slicing me deeper and deeper each time.

My lawyer insisted that the police send samples of the blood found at the scene for DNA testing, but there was so much there, in so many places. It will be at least four weeks to receive results, and the samples could be tainted. Even then, it doesn't prove I was a victim. Only that other people were there. People who have probably fled the state by now.

At least Dell and Bev believe me. They keep demanding that the police listen to me, but they also refused to hand over my arrest and hospitalization records, so they're not exactly high on the cops' trustworthy list.

Doesn't matter. The police applied for a warrant to access all my records, anyway. My lawyer is trying to stop it, but we all know he won't win. And once the cops uncover my past, it'll all be over. They already know enough, thanks to the Internet.

Everything I was afraid of has happened. My past caught up to me, the town turned against me, and my best friend is in a coma he may never wake up from.

Because of me.

I'm scratching 718 into the soft wood of my desk with my fingernail when a knock rattles the door.

"Nate?" Bev pokes her head in. "You have visitors."

I can't think of a single person who would visit me. No one who knows me well enough. Not except . . .

My lungs forget how to work. The iron in my blood hardens, pricking me from the inside.

The Kingsleys.

Do they have news about Brandon? Did he wake up? Would they really come here?

"I . . . I think you should talk to them," Bev says. "Dell doesn't agree, but it can't hurt."

I stand, surprised my legs can bear my weight. I'm already out the door when I realize I'm not wearing shoes. Splinters from the rough boards catch my socks, like the house is trying to hold me back. Or hurt me, itself.

I like the feeling, though. Mom's button disappeared in the fight. Gone forever. At least the scratchy boards ground me in the here and now.

Bev catches my arm before we reach the stairs and I remember the first time I saw her on this landing. In some ways, we've come so far, but in others we're still right back there.

"It's okay to be nervous," she says. "Try to be open-minded, though. Okay?"

I'm confused, but I mumble "okay" anyway. I'm grateful when she leads me downstairs. I don't think I can make it on my own. The living room is empty. Why aren't they inside? What's going on?

Bev opens the front door and I suck in a breath.

Two strangers stand on the porch. A tall black man with a shiny bald head pushes back his brown blazer to reveal an even shiner badge. Beside him stands an almost equally tall Latina woman. Her long black hair is slicked back in a high ponytail. She's also in a blazer. A blue one.

No Kingsleys.

Dell stands between us, looking as happy as a cotton-mouth that's been stepped on.

"Nate?" the woman asks.

I nod.

"I'm Agent Michelle Torres. This is Agent Andre Peters. We're with the FBI. We'd like to ask you some questions."

My stomach lurches. I stumble back a step, certain I'm about to puke on Agent Torres's cowboy boots. This is it. No screwing around now. I don't stand a chance if the freaking FBI is after me.

Dell's nostrils flare. "I already told them you got nothing to say. And I called your attorney."

Agent Torres smiles without showing her teeth. "Nate, we're not here about you. We're here about The Fort. We have reason to believe you might have information that could help our investigation."

My head spins. Her words circle like a buzzard. Information. Investigation. Nate. That's what she keeps calling me. Not Nathaniel. Nate.

"Investigation?" For the first time in years I sound like a little kid.

Agent Peters crosses his arms. "You were affiliated with the Nazi Socialist Party, correct?"

"Don't answer," Dell spits.

"We're looking into allegations of domestic terrorism." Agent Torres puts her hands on her hips. "We were told you had inside knowledge of The Fort's operation."

"Who told you that?" Bev asks. Even she sounds guarded.

The agents exchange a glance.

"Your name has come up several times," Agent Peters says.

My heart thuds against my sternum. My palms sweat. What does a stroke feel like? Because I'm afraid I'm having one.

Agent Torres adjusts her blazer. "Look, Nate. I'll level with you. The incident a couple weeks ago piqued our interest in you, but if you agree to help us, we can make sure you're taken care of."

Tires crunch on gravel. My attorney's SUV eases down our drive.

"We want to take them down." Agent Torres holds out a card. "Think about it."

They start down the porch steps. Agent Peters turns back when he reaches the bottom. "You should do it, Nate. Not for us, or for you. Do it for the victims."

They get in their black sedan and crank the engine as my lawyer is cutting hers.

"What do you think?" Bev asks.

"I don't know," Dell says. "I hope they mean it, but can we trust them?"

Agent Peters's voice rings in my ears. *Not for us, or for you. Do it for the victims.*

Brandon grins in my mind.

Do it for the victims.

I'd do anything to help Brandon, but Dell's right. Neither of us have much faith in the cops. Is the FBI any different? You'd think they wouldn't be as corrupt, but I just don't know.

The Feds are already planning to take down The Fort.

So am I.

But what if it's a trick to arrest me along with The Fort? Trusting that damn reporter already got me burned once. Is it worth the risk again?

Dell and Bev show the attorney inside. Dell drops Agent Torres's card on the counter and puts on a fresh pot of coffee to settle in for long discussions, but I'm too exhausted to think about it anymore tonight. I pocket the card and tell myself I'll decide later.

721

"This is a terrible idea." I gaze out the truck window at Main Street. New flyers flutter in the wind, but these aren't anti-minority. They're anti-me.

PUT NATE BEHIND BARS

RID LEWISTON OF HATEFUL NATE

JUSTICE FOR BRANDON

Each fluttering page slices into me. A million paper cuts, leaching blood from my heart, freezing my muscles, reminding me how I failed Brandon.

"I can't go out there."

Dell reaches over me and thrusts my door open. "You can, and you will. I won't let you hide. You did nothing wrong."

"According to them I did." I don't add that I agree with them. Doing the right thing at the wrong time is as bad as not even trying. I want to hit something and break down crying at the same time.

Dell scowls. "They ain't your jury."

"Yet."

"Not ever." He punches the button on my seat belt and it goes slack across my chest. "We're gonna prove your story. Now get your ass in that drugstore and buy some medicine for your face."

My face and hands are festering wounds that have drilled into my soul. I probably should've gone to the hospital the night of the attack, but I was too tired. I've just been taking care of the cuts by myself, and I've run through every bandage and cream in the cabin.

Dell shoves me out of the truck. "Get the stuff on the list and meet me at Bud's Hardware. The quicker we knock this out, the quicker we can get home." He leans over the console. "Keep your head high. You hear me?"

I manage a nod. The street is mostly empty this time of morning, too early for even the media vultures who have been chewing on the carcass of all my old stories. I keep expecting to run into my new nemesis, Shaw Holt, but I guess she got what she was after and moved on. Lucky her. I wish it were that easy for me.

The few people who are out this early glare as I pass them. I drop my eyes to my shoes and duck into Lewiston Value Drug. Bev's handwriting is tiny and cramped. I grab everything I can decipher and carry my armload of antibiotic creams and gauze to the counter.

Brandon grins up at me. I startle and almost drop a box of bandages. A giant picture of his face is taped to the counter beneath a jar with DONATE HERE! HELP THE KINGSLEYS COVER BRANDON'S HOSPITAL FEES taped to it.

Brandon may never smile like that again. With the Santa Claus crinkles and piano key teeth. And it's because of me.

I'll make this right, I swear.

An old woman shuffles in front of me and adds a bottle of fiber powder to her pile of prescriptions by the register. "That should do it," she says.

The clerk scans the bottle and starts bagging the woman's items. "That'll be twenty-four nineteen."

The old woman counts out cash. She drops her change in Brandon's jar and makes a *tut-tut* noise. "That poor boy," she says, nodding at the jar. "Shame it happened to one of the good black kids and not one of those thugs. You know how *they* are." She inches closer to the clerk. "I hear it was a racist who did it. That Clemons boy. I saw him once, and I'll tell you what, he looks like the kind of person who'd do this. I just hope they put him away for a long time. We can't be havin' that 'round here."

She has to be freaking kidding. Even I know that was racist. If Brandon wore baggy jeans and let his hair grow, would she think he was a "thug," too? It doesn't matter who the victim was or what they might've done in the past. No one deserves that. I bite down on the inside of my cheeks to keep from exploding. Judging me while not realizing the racist shit pouring out of her own mouth. Or maybe she thinks degrees of racism are okay. As long as she only turns the knob one or two clicks, and doesn't bump it up all the way.

The woman takes her bags and hobbles by. I raise the crap in my arms to block my face. When she's gone past, I drop everything on the counter and study a magazine so the clerk won't recognize me.

My eyes keep going to Brandon's picture, though. To his warm, open face, which makes me want to believe everything will be all right, even when I know it won't. Not until he's awake and laughing and smiling that sunshine smile again. Maybe not even then.

"Sir? Sir? It's twenty-six eighty. Sir!"

My head snaps up. Big mistake. The clerk's eyes go wide. I snatch up my bags, throw thirty bucks at her, and hightail it out of there. She can keep the change. Or put it in the donation jar.

I run all the way to the hardware store, afraid to look up, afraid to see more shocked, angry gazes aimed at me. I narrowly avoid smacking into Dell as he's coming out of the store. I expect him to yell at me to watch where I'm going.

He hardly even notices me, instead storming to his truck and flinging open the toolbox across the back of the bed. "Bunch of assholes."

I trail behind him. "What happened?"

"They didn't want to sell to me. *Me.* After all the business I've given them. Hell, I patched Bud's damn roof after that hailstorm last summer and only took store credit. That was before I 'harbored a criminal.'"

I should be pissed, ready to fight, but the beast got swept away with the storm that night. Now I'm costing Dell his connections to his town. "I'm sorry."

He waves me off. "They can eat a bag of dicks for all I care." He shoves the bags in the toolbox and slams it shut. "Let's get this last stop over with."

This is the one I'm dreading most. Ghost-memories haunt the entire Lewiston High School campus: Brandon running off the reporter in the entryway, waiting for me in the parking lot, the hallway, the lunchroom, the gym. He's everywhere. And not just in my mind

Shrines to Brandon are spread all over the school grounds. Candles and pictures and teddy bears holding freaking basketballs. Everyone's acting like he's dead.

Guilt sucker punches me as we pull up to the red awning, almost doubling me over. If Brandon doesn't wake up soon, he might as well be.

Dead.

Another notch on my gruesome belt.

The principal and counselor wait for us on the sidewalk. This could be the last time I ever enter this building. I'm just as pissed off and scared as I was the first time. My feet are stuck to a treadmill. No matter how far I think I'm going, I'm always stuck in the same place. Dell parks and hops out first.

"Mr. Clemons," the principal says with all the warmth of a snowball encased in ice and dropped in liquid nitrogen.

"Collect Nate's belongings and leave the premises as quickly as possible."

I climb out of the truck and start up the walk. The principal holds up her hand. "You," she sneers, "are not allowed here. Your uncle will retrieve your things."

"But—"

She recoils like I'm about to attack her. "One more step, and I'm calling the authorities and having you removed."

My body wants to wilt, but I stay rod stiff. I will not let this woman break me. Especially not in front of all the faces peeking out of classroom windows. I lean against the truck and cross my arms. "My locker combination is thirty-one, seventeen, four."

Ice slithers through my veins. The first conversation I had with Brandon was reciting those numbers. I can almost hear *him* laughing; *his* voice practically shouts in my head.

Atta boy, son. Knew you'd come around. Knew you'd hurt that n—

I pinch the sensitive skin under my upper arms until my eyes water. Without my button, pain is all I have.

Dell grits his teeth. "I'm gonna need help carrying everything."

The principal shrugs. "I'm sure you'll figure it out." She turns on her heel and marches inside without giving me another glance.

The counselor sighs. "I had such high hopes for you, Nate. Such hopes." He turns his back on me, too, and I'm left alone outside. I don't even get a goodbye. No final turn of the lock that started my friendship with Brandon, no last glance at the basketball court where I found more friends. Nothing.

The front doors open and I resist the urge to jog to Dell—the principal would probably freak out if I made a sudden move. Only, it isn't Dell storming out. It's Fletch.

"You son of a bitch," he yells. He tears off his jacket and flings it to the ground, then runs at me. "How could you?"

At first, I'm too stunned to move, then instinct kicks in. I cover my face just in time. Fletch's fists thump against my arms.

"I don't want to fight you, Fletch." I'd kill him. The boy can't punch for shit.

"Why'd you do it?" he screams. "Why?" He pummels me with his weak hits. I stand there and take it.

Then Rainey and Ellis and Mateo are there, pulling Fletch off. "It's not worth it, man," Rainey says. "Let the courts handle it. He's not worth it."

The irony of that statement coming out of Rainey's mouth after the shit I heard him say in the gym almost makes me laugh. Then I lower my arms and see the whole crowd that has formed in a semicircle around the truck and any thought of laughter disappears.

"Why?" Fletch is still screaming. "Just tell me why. Why Brandon? What did he ever do to you?" He's crying now, thrashing against the guys, but it's half-hearted.

"All right, break it up!" the principal shouts. "Back to class. All of you!"

Rainey and Ellis wrap their arms around Fletch and help him inside. The others flow back inside behind them like geese in a flying *V.* Two stragglers arc close to me on their way into the building: Maddie and Caitlyn. Maddie sniffles. Her face is red and splotchy.

Caitlyn fixes her death-ray stare on me. "I knew we shouldn't have trusted you. I hope you burn in Hell."

I slump against the truck, unable to pretend I'm okay. There's officially nothing for me here anymore. No school, no friends, no future, no Brandon.

Nothing.

When we get back to the cabin, I hole up in my room and call the number Agent Torres gave me. I still don't trust the FBI, but what have I got to lose?

722

There's this pocket of space where the earth meets the pre-dawn sky, a whitish line on the horizon where the world splits open in a gap-toothed smile, that I always thought I could catch. As a kid, riding all night in a stolen car with Mom at the wheel, I used to think we could get there. That if we could only go fast enough, far enough, we could catch the gap and tumble into it, and disappear forever. No more neo-nazis with ugly tattoos, no more fear, no more running. Just eternally falling into a perfect nothing.

As I walk away from the cabin, away from Dell and Bev and Brandon and Lewiston and all the problems I've caused, I find myself once again facing that gap, and once again wishing I could somehow dive through it and fall off the earth.

The longer I walk, the more my cheap tennis shoes rub blisters on my heels, and the more the reality of my decision rubs a blister on my soul.

I could steal a car and reach The Fort faster, but I'm afraid I'll flub it and get caught. Enough cops are already after me and I should have plenty of time before the Feds are ready to take it down. Instead, I walk as fast as I can, and focus on the physical pain to distract me from the carnage inside.

I'm six again, watching that slip of sky, hoping I can eventually tip into it and vanish.

728

The blare from of a speeding car narrowly escaping an accident jolts me awake. I sit up against a tree, rub the sleep from my eyes, and yawn so hard the muscles under my chin cramp. Overhead, traffic whooshes by, close enough that diesel exhaust and burning rubber have replaced the oxygen in my body, but far enough away that I can't be seen. My back is stiff from another night of sleeping on the ground. The rocks are as unforgiving as the people of Lewiston.

I stretch and twist to work the kinks out, then roll up my stolen sleeping bag and strap it to my duffle before eating a stale, stolen gas station cinnamon roll. I've stolen plenty of things in the past—books, alcohol, candy, all the stuff The Fort didn't let me have—but I felt a strange sense of guilt this time. Compared to all the other shit I've done, it's surprising

I can still feel bad over something so trivial. The first time I stole water, I almost left a note with Dell's address.

Then I thought better of it.

I'm hoping what I'm about to do will start fixing the things I broke a long time ago. I don't know if I'll ever be able to live with myself, but this is the beginning. And really, it's not about me. All this time, I just wanted to be able to escape my past. But it doesn't work that way. I don't get to forget the damage I've done. I don't get to move on or "start fresh." I *do* have a duty. To do what I can to make people like The Fort stop. To make the world a little bit better.

Once I'm packed and ready, I pull out my phone and stick the battery back in. I don't know how tracking works, but I figure the police need power to find a phone signal. I turn it on just long enough to check my messages. The voice mail box is full of the usual. Dell and Bev: *Where the hell are you? Are you safe? Get your ass home*. The police: *Mr. Clemons, we warned you not to leave. There's a warrant out for your arrest.* And reporters who somehow got my number: *We'll pay for your first televised interview. Let us subsidize your tell-all book. Give us an exclusive.*

Same old, same old.

Except for the last one.

This message is for Nate Fuller. This is Agent Michelle Torres. Return my call at 555-655-3446 extension 979.

Her words are short and clipped, all business, just like last time I spoke with her. She answers on the first ring. "Agent Torres."

The knots in my back swing around to my stomach. For a second, I'm afraid I'm going to vomit old cinnamon roll on the phone.

"This is Nate. You left a message."

"Yes, Nate. Our investigation coupled with your statement has given us sufficient probable cause to apply for a warrant. I just need some additional information first."

I brace myself against the tree. It's actually going down. I knew that was the goal when I called the FBI, but it was distant, then—at an unknown point in the future that may or may not have ever arrived. Now, it's here. Quicker than I'd expected.

"I need you to describe the places containing evidence of the crimes: the exact location of the mass grave site, murder weapons, hate speech, and any other means of domestic terrorism. Be specific and give me as much as possible. The warrant has to state exactly what we're after if we're going to nail these bastards."

My head spins. There's so much information stuffed in my brain that I don't know where to start. "The meeting hall is the prep site. That's where you'll find the flyers, signs, posters, bats, guns—everything. It's the large building on the left edge of the big field. Every house there will be chock-full of stuff, too. So will all the vehicles."

"And the graves?"

"In the woods. The place is hard to find. Best way is to go to the second row of houses and take a right into the woods. There isn't a real path, but the brush should be cleared enough to follow. The bodies start about five miles in and keep going up. I don't know how far they're up to by now. At least another couple miles. They tried to space them out so they wouldn't . . . so they wouldn't smell."

Computer keys *clack* on the other end of the line. "Is this information based on your personal knowledge?"

Intimately personal. "Yes."

"Can we use your name in the affidavit?"

The hairs on my neck bristle. "I'd rather keep my name out of it." It doesn't matter now that everything is out in the open, but I've been burned too much.

"We can seal the affidavit. It will carry more weight with the judge than if I said 'confidential informant.'"

Bark digs into my palm. "If it means you'll get the warrant . . ."

"It will."

"Then fine."

I feel like I just signed my life away. This better not come back and bite me in the ass.

"Thank you for your cooperation. The federal prosecutor will apply for the warrant today. Our team is assembled and ready to go as soon as we receive it."

"And when will that be?"

More typing echoes through the phone. "Should have the warrant by tomorrow afternoon, and be ready to serve it by tomorrow evening."

"To-tomorrow evening?"

"Yes. We'll be in touch."

Bark scrapes my back as I slide down the trunk. This is real. The tree is real. The pain is real. The call was real. Soon, the warrant will be real, too. I hang onto the phone for several more minutes after she hangs up. Then I remember the Lewiston police are after me and pop the battery out.

Tomorrow night. Less than thirty-six hours before I can close the coffin on The Fort.

It's time to stop messing around.

729

It takes all of my willpower not to speed down the highway in the car I stole. "Car" isn't quite accurate. Minivan. I walked for another solid day before I found it, and that was only a happy accident. I stopped at a Walmart this morning to use the facilities and spotted an unattended purse in a shopping cart. I snatched the keys and hightailed it out of there.

I felt bad about leaving the baby seats and diaper bag in the parking lot, but I didn't have much choice. I have to reach The Fort before the Feds. I have to make sure they find everything. The bodies. All those people who deserve real graves.

After I've put enough distance between me and the Walmart, I pull over into another shopping center parking lot and, using a tool kit I found in the van, switch plates with the car beside me. Then I scrape off the bumper stickers and hit the highway again.

My heart threatens to jump ship every time blue lights appear in my rearview. I stay under the speed limit, obey all the traffic laws, and make it to Kentucky without incident.

The winter sun has given up and died by the time I reach the Farmer city limits. I ease the van past the jail where they almost killed me, past the courthouse where I hid from the cameras, past the dumpster where the police found me, and the bookstore—Kelsey's and my safe place. It's now out of business.

Every building, every stoplight, every inch of pavement wakes the beast up more and more. I grip the steering wheel and force myself to drive slowly, to drink in every miserable inch of this shithole.

Then I'm on the other side, fifteen minutes from Hell. The closer I get, the angrier the beast grows. This is the place that broke me. That broke Dell, and Mom, and Kelsey. And Brandon. That robbed me of my innocence, my freedom, possibly my soul. And it's finally time for this place to pay.

When I spot the dirt road, I pull over and kill the engine. Kelsey and I had planned to run from this very spot. I slip on my jacket, pocket my knife, and start through the woods.

Cold stings my cheeks. I pull my jacket tighter and zip it up to my chin. My tennis shoes crunch on the thin layer of frost that now covers the ground. Slivers of ice slip through the mesh toes, tiny daggers that stab my ice-cube-cold feet before melting into my socks. Boots would be nice. Not combat boots, but the farm kind like Dell wears.

I walk faster to keep warm. The cold is more penetrating in Kentucky than in Alabama. The intertwined tree branches overhead let the moon slink through, but I don't need its light to navigate these woods. I don't need light for anything right now. I need the darkness that's coursed through me for so long, begging to be set free. If I'm spotted here, the beast is the only thing that will keep me alive.

Dr. Sterling's voice echoes in my ears: *Don't let it overtake you, Nate. Close your eyes and find the light.* I see Ms. Erica's face, bright as the sun, nodding as the doctor says it.

Shaking my head, the memories vanish with the breath puffing out of me. I reach the tall fence and fumble with the freezing metal. There's an opening here somewhere if they didn't mend it after I ran. I work down the fence, shaking it in different places. My fingers are so numb, I'm afraid a wayward barb will rip open my flesh before I notice it.

A section of the fence is looser than the others. I give it a kick and it pops free of its pole. I drop to my knees and squeeze through the hole. I'm definitely wider than I was the last time I did this. My foot hits something hard.

No. It can't still be here.

I kick up the dead, frozen leaves. Sure enough, a mound of canned food hides under the earth.

She left it. Does that mean she's been keeping it here, just in case, or that she hasn't thought about leaving again? I re-cover the stash and keep moving.

The blisters covering my feet still hurt, but the cold is at least numbing them. I take a deep breath, hoping it numbs the rest of me. These woods smell different. Familiar, but off. They aren't my woods anymore. They're *his*. I swear I taste gunpowder and blood mixed with the evergreens.

I close my eyes and feel the weight of the gun again. It wasn't far from here. Does *his* blood still stain the trees? Did they scrape the bits of *his* brain off the roots? Are pieces of *him* still here, tangled with the new trees that have sprung up in the last two years, born from *his* flesh and blood?

If I could burn the whole thing down, I would. Cleanse the earth with fire.

A strong breeze shrieks around me. *Nathaniel.*

"You're not real." I open my eyes and give my leg hair a sharp tug through my jeans. "Not real."

I forgot my meds on the battered dresser at home. Just as well. If I'm going to do this, I want my mind sharp. I want to feel everything, even if it hurts. Especially then.

Nathaniel, the wind cries.

I trudge onward. Through the skeletal trees, over the ridge where the root trapped me, past the holly bush. A shadow slides over the frost. I freeze, my hand on the knife in my pocket. It could be a deer or some other animal.

The shadow shifts so slightly I almost miss it. I flick the blade out.

A head pokes out from behind a tree. Long brown hair blows in the wind.

"Nate?"

"Kelsey?"

She steps into a shaft of moonlight. Her flight jacket has been replaced with a black leather one, black fatigues, black boots, black laces. She crosses her arms over her chest, a gesture as cold as the ground beneath us. Despite everything, my first impulse is to wrap my arms around her. But I still don't know where she stands. With The Fort, or against it.

"What are you doing here?" I ask.

"Me?" she laughs. "You show up out of nowhere in the middle of the night and you ask *me* what I'm doing here? I'm always here. Every freaking night *I'm* here."

I'm not sure what to say to that. We're off. Stiff as wet clothes in the snow.

Kelsey shifts, jutting her hip to the side. "Did you come to kill them?" She asks it matter-of-factly, like we're discussing stops for the road trip we'll never take.

"No." The thought of taking another life makes me want to throw up.

"They deserve it."

They deserve worse than death. I can't give them the easy out the gun gave *him*. Regardless of how much as I'd love to see them in the same agony they caused Brandon.

Kelsey tucks her hair behind one ear. "If you're not here to kill them, then what *are* you here for? Why come back now?"

"Justice."

She laughs again. "'Justice.' What does that even mean?"

"It means they have to pay."

"And what about us?"

I meet her eyes. "We have to pay, too."

She steps back into the shadows. "I've been paying, Nate. Being trapped here, pretending for all these years. Isn't that enough?"

"No."

She backs up farther. "What are you going to do?"

What side is she on? Do I believe her? Has she really been pretending this whole time? I want to start seeing the best in people first, but damn it's hard. Only one thing is clear: things have shifted between us. We've become different people, for better or worse.

I step toward her. "I should've taken you with me, then."

"I know."

"I'm sorry."

She reaches in her pockets and tugs on a pair of fingerless gloves. "I don't need saving, Nate. Not anymore."

That's when I notice the backpack strapped to her. "You're finally running."

"Finally?" she scoffs. "What do you think I've been doing this whole time, quilting? I come here every night planning to leave. I stand by our holly bush and try to make my body keep moving, try not to let myself remember what happened the last time I didn't stop." She straightens her spine. "Tonight is it. I'm doing it. I'm out, Nate."

I drop my gaze to my frozen feet. "But . . . you looked so happy. On the street, with the Skynbyrds."

"I was *surviving*. After you abandoned me, I tried to run. I made it to the fence before they caught me, dragged me back,

Indoctrinated me, watched every move, forced me to testify against you. Testify or die."

My chest swells. "You didn't want to testify?"

"Honestly?" She digs her toe into the frost, carving out a divot. "Sort of. You deserted me. I was angry. I hated you and I loved you and—"

I notice the past tense there. Lov*ed*. Hat*ed*.

I loved her, too.

What are we now?

I think we're also past. I think it's time we both let go and let ourselves grow into the people we need to be. For me, that's making amends for all the horrible things I've done—as much as those things can be amended for anyway. For Kelsey, I don't know. I think she has to figure that out. I do know this: I didn't help her get out before. I won't stop her now. I choose to believe she's not like them. That she'll be better once she's gone.

"Here." I toss her the van key. She catches it in her gloved hand. "It's stolen, but it'll be good for a little while."

"Thanks." She starts toward the fence. "Don't die," she says over her shoulder. "If anyone gets to kill you, it should be me."

She melds with the shadows, heading for our stash of food and the gap in the fence and the freedom we both should've grabbed years ago.

✧

The wind taunts me with the sounds of The Fort before see it.

". . . conscious of its blood can never be enslaved by the antiracists. In this world, we must fortify the future of the White people and the White people alone."

I only catch pieces, but I know the mantra well enough.

I crest the hill and there it is, spread out before me. Not much has changed in the last two years. The big field is lit up like the Lewiston High football field on a Friday night. A couple stragglers dart under the lights and into the meeting hall. Must be newcomers. Everyone else knows better than to be late to a gathering. The Feds should make it before the members throw a boot party on those two miserable beings.

The voices swell for an instant as the door opens wide enough for them to dart inside.

"White Power! White Power! White Power!"

A couple hundred men, women, and children, united in their ignorance and hatred. It's terrifying and depressing at the same time. Every one of them would rip me apart if they got their hands on me. No more cat-and-mouse games—just death.

I pick my way down the hill, sticking to the long shadows cast by the trees. The FBI should be here by now. I press against a wide tree and snap the battery back into my phone. Maybe the Feds called to say there was a problem with the warrant, some administrative delay.

There's no messages from them.

I dial Agent Torres's number, but it goes straight to voice mail. Maybe they're assembling outside the gates right now.

Now is the perfect time, before the gathering ends, so they can catch all the skinheads in one place. I make sure my phone is on vibrate and slide it back into my pocket. Let the Lewiston police find me here. Maybe then they'll believe my story.

Steeling myself, I creep all the way to the edge of the field. All the houses at The Fort have motion sensor floodlights except the ones on the edge of the field. Those are constantly on to light night marches.

Only one house is dark. The one in the center, with a giant red *X* painted on the door. I know that house all too well, but the *X* is new.

The smart thing to do would be stay put. Wait for the FBI, watch the arrests, make sure they find the bodies, then leave.

But the house calls to me. The *X* reaches off the battered wood, summoning me.

Everyone's in the meeting hall. There were plenty of nights I made it from the house to here without being seen. I can do it again. One last time.

I skirt the field as quickly as possible. The smell of cold threatens to attack me with memories of the last time I ran in these woods. I dig my nails into my palms and zero in on the *X* that doesn't exist in my flashbacks, only slowing when I'm at the porch.

A quick glance around confirms that I'm still alone. No one has seen me yet. Standing here in plain view is reckless, but I can't bring myself to go in. My hand rests on the screen handle. I shouldn't be here. I should stay hidden until the FBI shows up.

With a deep breath, I ease the screen open, lifting up slightly as I pull to keep it from squeaking, then my hand is on the knob. It's probably locked. Someone else—the current leader—could've moved in, even though the *X* seems to indicate otherwise.

The knob turns easily.

I cross the threshold for the first time since I left for the woods to meet Kelsey that night.

It's exactly the same. Eerily the same. Like a giant mausoleum, a memorial to the great leader who once lived here. The swastika flag still hangs over the fireplace, lording its hate over everyone who enters.

Large framed pictures rest on the mantle on either side of the flag. On one side is Hitler, hand raised in the Bellamy salute, and on the other is *him*. Someone laid fake white edelweiss—Hitler's favorite flower—in tribute before the photos. Plastic pearls of dew cling to the tiny white petals.

Someone has been here recently. The room is strangely dust-free, but still unlived in. The multicolored afghan still lies across the back of the black leather couch, looking even more out of place now than it did then. A bright red SS armband lies in the straight-backed chair across the room. The brass fire poker *he* once used to beat me gleams in its stand.

Holy shit, it really is a museum. Do they parade children through here, telling stories about their fearless leader and *his* disrespectful child who stripped the world of *his* glory?

Unable to stomach it any longer, I cross the living room to the hall, my feet automatically avoiding the noisiest floorboards. Boards still darkened with bloodstains, splotchy reminders of all the horrors that occurred under this roof. That's my blood. And Mom's. And who knows how many others have dripped their lives out here. I pause in my bedroom doorway for an instant before pushing on—there's nothing I want from there.

His room is the one I need.

Just standing outside it makes me nervous. Even though I know *he*'s not here.

He yells in my head, *What the hell do you want, Nathaniel? You spyin', boy?*

"Yes," I say aloud. I step into his room and immediately leave.

It still smells like *him*. After all these years. Stale cigarettes and gunpowder and cinnamon gum. I start to fall back and catch myself on the wall. Pictures of Joseph Goebbels and Hermann Göring rattle on their nails.

The last time I was in *his* room, I was thirteen. *He* was drunk, coming off a celebration of one of *his* buddies slipping an assault charge.

"Nathaniel! Get your ass in here," *he*'d yelled. "Gotta show you somethin'."

I'd paused outside the door, same as tonight. *He* grabbed me by the scruff of the neck and pulled me to *him*, even though I was almost as tall as *he* was by then. Cigarette ash rained down on my arms. *He* waved a pistol under my nose.

"See this, boy?" *he* slurred. "This here is my new best friend, GG. Every good leader's gotta have good sidekicks." *He* twisted me around and pointed at the pictures of Hitler's right-hand men. "Them was his." *He* shook the gun again, inches from my temple, the same place *he*'d point it directly in a year. "GG is mine. A little present to myself. Yessir, everything's goin' my way tonight!"

The memory echoes through the empty house. GG is in an evidence locker somewhere—the one friend who turned on *him*. Goebbels and Göring sneer at me from their positions of honor on the wall outside *his* room. There's not one single picture of me hanging anywhere. None of Mom.

I rip down Hitler's right-hand men and smash their faces on the floor, shattering the glass and the memories of *his* voice.

The shards crunch as I barrel into the room again. This time I'm prepared for *his* scent. I start with the closet. It's full of fatigue pants and blue jeans and combat boots and not much else. I drag it all down, tearing at the patches with my fingers before grabbing my knife. I slash and rip until the floor is littered with swastikas and "White Power" and *weiss & stolz*.

His bathroom is next. I sweep everything off the counter. Shaving cream and razors and magazines fall into the toilet. The shower curtain rips free, leaving tatters of white fabric clinging to the plastic hooks.

I've wanted to do this since I was eleven. Since I first cowered in this bathtub, scrubbing my boots clean of an innocent Muslim kid's blood.

I storm back into the bedroom, about to tackle the nightstand, when unnatural light sweeps over me. I drop to my stomach, breathing heavily. *Shit!* I lost myself, made too much noise destroying the skinheads' little gallery. I crawl to the window and peek out.

A black-clad, helmeted swarm crosses the field, their flashlights glowing at the end of their drawn guns. Three beautiful white letters—FBI—stand out on their chests. They're here. Finally. I slump against the wall and swallow my heart back into my chest.

Time to get out of here. I'm about to stand when I notice a weird board under the bed. One end is slightly elevated, like someone had pried it up and didn't quite replace it. I inch under the bed and use my knife to wrench the board up enough to grab it. Instead of subfloor beneath, there's a hole. I can't see, so I plunge my hand in blind, crossing my fingers a rat doesn't bite off one of my fingers.

My fingertip hits something hard. I drag it out from under the bed with me. It's a metal box, not much bigger than *his* beloved GG. Unlike the living room, thick dust covers the lid. I examine it in the moonlight pouring through the window, then flick up the simple latch and open the lid.

Mom smiles up at me. I almost drop the box. Can it really be her? Am I imaging it? I flip through the stack of pictures. There are dozens of her. Smiling, laughing, pouting. Some are only of half her face, others are of the two of them together. They both look happy. There are even a couple of her holding me.

I found her. Finally.

She was here at The Fort with me all along.

At the bottom of the box is a simple gold band. Nothing fancy, no stone. I shuffle back to a picture of me and Mom. She's wearing the ring in them. Third finger of her left hand. Her wedding band. She left it behind.

And *he* kept it.

He kept all this stuff, buried under his bed. As cold and hard and evil as *he* was, *he* couldn't completely throw her away. It doesn't destroy my image of *him*, but it twists it a little. All these years, I've seen *him* from a certain angle—me on the ground and *him* above me. Now, I feel like I'm finally above *him*, looking down and seeing the full puzzle spread out before me, seeing all the pieces clicked into place. The whole picture is more complex than I ever thought.

I'll never understand *him*, or know what Mom saw in *him*, but I can learn from *him*. At one point, *he* was capable of love and something broke that part of *him*. And whatever it was, *he* let it shape *him* into something distorted and ugly.

I refuse to do that. I choose to be shaped, polished by my past. I choose to be like that tree in the hole at Dell's. I choose to grow in spite of where I started.

I tuck most of the pictures and the wedding band into my inner jacket pocket and drop the box back under the bed. Screams erupt from the meeting hall. I peek out the window again. The FBI has broken up the gathering. A few people try to make a run for it and agents take off after them.

A squad of FBI vests advances toward the houses. I have to go before they start checking them. Without ID, would they believe me if I told them who I am? I press against the wall as they pass by, then watch again, expecting them to start their search.

They hit the second row, then turn right.

They're looking for the bodies. I wade through the mess of shredded clothing and tiptoe down the hall to the back door. My instinct urges me to run, run, run.

But I'm tired of running.

I slip between the houses and enter the woods parallel to the agents. I'll just keep an eye on them and make sure they head in the right direction. Their flashlights sweep over the brush. One starts toward me and I freeze behind a tree.

"Paul, this look like a path to you?" he calls.

"I think it's here," another responds.

The light moves away and I risk a glance. They've found the path. I move with them, staying a hundred feet or so away, stopping when they stop, pressing on when they find the trail again.

I don't know how long we go like that. Long enough for my feet and my brain to stop interacting, for the moon to rise high overhead. Then they lose the path for good. The brush is thick. Even though most of the land out here is barren, the leaves left a wall of thorns and branches behind. The Feds have entered an impassable nook. They veered too far left and got turned around.

How do I help them? Appear out of nowhere and say, *Hey, guys. I'm your friendly former skinhead sent to guide the way?* That would never work. I can get ahead of them, though. They'll eventually get through the brush. I can make the trail clear enough for them to follow.

Quiet as possible, I dash up the hill, arcing out of the way before circling back to the path. I break sticks and stomp my feet in the frost to make a clean trail. They're so close, if they can just push through this—

A boulder slams into my side, pinning me to the ground. Fists pummel my face. I fling a knee up and nail the massive human in the groin. He groans and doubles over. I push him to the hard ground. The moonlight bounces off his face.

Thomas-freaking-Mayes.

He looks like an extra in horror movie. His face is yellow and green from almost-healed bruises, still recovering from our last fight. I did a better job on him than I thought. He lunges for me. I slam the heel of my hand into his nose, pulling back just before the point the bone could pierce his brain. He flops back into the snow, blood spurting out of his face.

"This way!" an agent shouts. They found the trail again.

"I don't have time for this shit," I hiss.

Thomas Mayes claws at me. "You did this. You brought them here, you spineless asswipe. Too scared to come alone?"

I scramble out of his reach.

"I'm gonna finish you. Shoulda done it years ago," he says. "Woulda done us all a favor." He springs. His shoulder catches me in the ribs and it's all I can do to keep from yowling. Sharp pain stings my side.

Thomas Mayes draws his hand back. A knife glints in the faint light. Son of a bitch stabbed me. I punch him across the jaw with my right fist and grab at his knife hand with my left. The punch knocks him off balance. We roll down the hill a few feet, grappling for the knife.

The Feds are almost on top of us. If they catch us here, they'll arrest us both. I hit Thomas Mayes in the gut three times, knocking the wind out of him. It's enough to pry the knife away.

He snatches for it. I duck under his arm and grasp him from behind, pressing the knife against his throat.

One deep slash, and this will be over. This feud that has raged between us for nine years will end. What's another death on my conscience, another body for the mass grave we're so close to? It would be fitting to leave him here with all the corpses he contributed to. One swipe and I save the world from another neo-nazi.

The knife shakes in my hand. It would be so easy and I'd probably save so many innocent people.

"Stop," I whisper. "Just stop."

I shove him to the ground and run uphill. Sharp pain shoots through my side. I'm losing blood from the stab wound. How much? Did the knife hit anything critical or—

Stop.

If I keep thinking about this it will overwhelm me.

The Feds are ahead of me now, looking for the trail. I stumble forward, actually grateful for the cold that wraps its ice pack arms around me, numbing my aching body. My side is sticky and wet. I touch it and my hand comes away red.

Thomas Mayes got me deeper than I thought. My jacket is soaked through. I'm freezing. I don't think I've ever been this cold in my life. I can't die here. Anywhere but here. I have to keep going.

Footsteps thunder behind me. Someone is coming.

They can't catch me. I can't go back.

I run. Frost crunches underfoot. Or is it snow?

It's snow. It grazes my lashes, hangs in my arm hair for an instant before melting way. My arms are bare. When did I lose my jacket? Or did I not grab a jacket? Why didn't I think to get one before I ran?

Too late now. Have to keep running.

"Nathaniel!" someone yells. It shakes the trees. There's so much anger in that voice. Panic, almost.

I have to get away from it.

If *he* catches me, *he*'ll kill me. Actually murder me.

I stagger forward. My foot catches on a root and I crash to the ground. My boot is stuck, the red laces stand out on the white snow like streaks of blood.

"Nathaniel!" *He*'s closer. Too close.

I don't want to die. I have to live. *Need* to live.

I fight the root, but its greedy hands won't release me. My numb fingers tear at the laces. The knot won't loosen. I pull with all my might.

"Nathaniel!"

My foot slips out of the combat boot. I drag myself up the hill. Icy water seeps into my sock from the slushy snow. I can't stop can't stop can't stop.

My face is pressed into the snow again. *He*'s on top of me. *He* manhandles me onto my back and pins my arms with *his* knees. Then *he*'s punching me again and again and again.

"I'll teach you to disobey me," *he* says.

I stare at *his* face, into *his* dead brown eyes. *His* expression doesn't change as *he* draws *his* gun out of his waistband.

"I don't wanna kill you, boy," *he* says. "But sometimes, we gotta do things we don't want to do."

Air whooshes as the gun butt flies at my head. Time seems to slow until it's one of those flip-books I used to draw as a kid. Frame by frame, I see the gun about to smash into my face, my arm coming up to block it, hitting *his* arm, knocking the gun to the snow.

We both leap for it. I throw an elbow and catch *him* in the eye. *He* counters with a backhand so hard fireworks erupt behind my eyes. I claw at the snow for the gun. My fingertips graze the freezing steel.

His hand wraps around it first. This time, it's not the butt *he* has pointed at me, but the muzzle. *His* finger slides to the trigger.

I push *him* back and dive to the side. *He* fires and it's so freaking loud. All I hear is white noise. The Fort is hundreds of miles away and I'm floating in space. My arm burns like I've just been branded.

I don't have time to process the fact I've just been shot by my own father, because *he*'s lifting the gun again and this time *he* won't just graze my arm. The beast in my gut takes over my body and there's no stopping it.

I lower my shoulder and plow into my father's stomach. *He* clings to the gun, trying to hit me with it. I grab *his* arm and twist, and the gun falls into my hand. It's heavier than I thought it would be—the weight of the world.

He comes at me, *his* pocketknife out now, swiping the air.

I raise the gun.

Point it at *his* head.

And fire.

Red blood and gray brain matter and white bone explode from *his* skull, splattering the snow in a disgusting tie-dye. *His* body slumps to the ground. The tang of gunpowder and blood taint the air. The gun drops to the snow, still smoking. There's a little hiss as it hits.

Voices shout behind me.

Holy shit.

I have to get out of here.

I take off, but I don't make it far. Strong arms hold me. I struggle against them. I can't go back. "This can't be for nothing," I mutter. "It can't be for nothing."

"Shh," a familiar voice says in my ear. "It won't be, Nate. You got 'em. You did good."

That's not right. No one from The Fort would tell me killing *him* was a good thing. "I killed *him*. Let me go, I have to go."

"Hush," the voice says. "I'm here. Come back to me. Back to the now. Open your eyes and look at me."

Against my better judgment, I do as the voice says. I open my eyes. My mother stands over me. She's hazy, glowing in the white light behind her like an angel. My body relaxes. I'm dead, but it's okay, because I'm with Mom. I'm home. I blink and her features sharpen. It's not my mother, it's Dell. For a moment, I'm overwhelmed with disappointment, then it oozes away with the blood from my side.

"Hey," Dell says. "Good. Can you walk?"

"Dell? How?"

He scowls. "The FBI knocking on the door in the middle of the night was a pretty good clue. They needed me to sign the affidavit since you're still a minor."

"And you signed?"

"If you'd stuck around you would've learned that I came around to their thinking. Now, can you walk?"

I move my legs. They seem to work. "I think so."

"Good. 'Cause you need to get that seen to." He holds something out. "Put your jacket back on. And next time you decide to run away, take your damn medicine with you. Your little flashbacks aren't good for either of us."

He turns toward the light and I notice the fresh scratch marks on his cheeks. He helps me into my jacket and to my feet.

We stand side by side and look down the mountain. A wide smile breaks out across his face. I've never seen him smile like that before. He looks like Mom, and I don't exactly mind it. Almost as suddenly as it appeared, the smile slips back into his infamous scowl. "Oh, and you're grounded for pretty much forever."

I hobble down the slope with my uncle, leaning on him for support. Agent Torres calls a medic and we wait in the field until someone can patch me up. The first rays of early morning sunlight show up as we're finally leaving, breaking through the darkness shrouding The Fort, and bringing the start of a new day.

730.

Exactly two years to the day I shot my father.

The Washington Times

Over 100 Bodies Found in Kentucky Woods

By Paula Alvarez
Contributor

Last night, the FBI raided a Neo-Nazi compound in West Kentucky.

The raid was a result of an anonymous tip claiming that several assaults, missing persons cases, and unsolved murders could be tied to the compound, known by those in the area as "The Fort."

Federal authorities arrived at the compound around 9:30 p.m. and found a large crowd gathered in a central hall. As they attempted to detain the individuals present, Agent Andre Peters led a squad into the woods, where the informant stated they would find a mass grave.

Agent Peters and agents Michelle Torres, Paul Tipton, Jon Carroll, and Special Agent Eric Dayton investigated the woods behind The Fort for several hours before locating the first victim.

"I've never seen so many bodies in one place," said Special Agent Dayton. "It'll take a while to process them all, but a lot of families will finally have closure."

While the FBI has been silent on the details, *The Times* managed to gain brief access to the burial ground and can confirm that most, if not all, of the bodies are those of minorities, indicating a string of hate crimes. Local authorities were contacted but refused to comment.

The FBI has apprehended at least forty individuals connected with The Fort, including their alleged leader, Joseph "Tire Iron" Stanton, of the famous Connecticut Stanton family.

Stanton has been arrested five

times for assault and battery in various states, and twice for larceny. He currently has three warrants out for his arrest in Indiana, Ohio, and Michigan.

Agent Tipton said they were still excavating the area to ensure they located all the bodies. He expects DNA to identify the majority of them and that names will be released in the coming months.

Continued C27

SIX MONTHS LATER

The phone rings four times before he picks up.

"Hello?"

"Hey." I can't keep the nerves out of my voice. I'm shaking more than I did when the Feds showed up at the cabin. "How's it going?"

"Hanging in there," Brandon says.

It's good to hear his voice. I wasn't sure I'd ever hear it again. Even after he came out of his coma, things were touch and go.

"How's the leg?"

"Better. Almost back to a hundred percent. I should be able to play next season."

"That's awesome." This is our third conversation since he woke up, but it's not any less awkward than the first. "How's the family?" I ask.

"Good. Henry got all As this semester, so of course Pops is happy."

I laugh. I miss them. I'm not sure if it hurts more or less to keep in touch. "Brandon, I know it doesn't change anything, but I really am sorry." I can't undo anything, but I can do better going forward.

"I know, man," Brandon says.

"I'm glad we're talking."

Brandon sucks in a breath. "I am, too."

He didn't take my calls for two months. I eventually stopped trying. Mrs. Kingsley is the one who reached out. Shocked the hell out of me. She said they were slowly piecing things back together, but she wanted me to know that they didn't hate me. She also wanted to make sure Dell and Bev and I were okay in North Dakota. I told her that we're making it. Best we can in this place.

I swear, Dell picked the only town smaller than Lewiston in the entire country.

With good reason. Hawaii and Alaska are the only states without a hate group, but Hawaii's way too expensive, and Bev straight-out refused to move all the way to Alaska, so we settled for the state with the fewest. I don't see how North Dakota is much better than Alaska, though. Maine was another option—apparently extreme racists hate extreme cold—but there were too many in the surrounding area. Forty-seven known groups in New York State, fifteen in New Jersey, forty in Pennsylvania.

There are ten in both Montana and Minnesota, and seven in South Dakota, so we're about isolated from them as we're going to get. Other than Alaska.

"I hope . . ." I hesitate, afraid to say the words. Afraid of what the answer will be. "I hope we can be friends again."

Brandon pauses and my stomach drops. "I hope so, too. One day. I'm just not there yet."

"I know." I'll take "one day." It's better than never. I push my desk chair in front of the laptop Bev bought me for a belated seventeenth birthday present. "I know it doesn't fix anything, but I'm ready to go public and stop hiding."

"Brandon!" a girl yells in the background.

"Hey, man, I've got to go. Maddie and I have a hot date in an open field."

I smile. "Have fun."

"Good luck, Nate," Brandon says. "I mean that."

I hang up and lay the cell phone on the corner of the desk. I don't think we'll ever be the same, but I won't stop trying. Not unless he tells me to. I owe my freedom to him. The first thing he did when he woke up was tell the Lewiston cops, and the whole town, that I was innocent in the attack.

That was right after the bust at The Fort, so it didn't take much for the police to corroborate Brandon's story. They decided not to press charges, and dropped the fresh charges for skipping town, but Dell and Bev and I didn't exactly feel safe going back there, all the same. Better if we moved somewhere new. Started over fresh. Fresh as we can, anyway.

The FBI offered to put us in witness protection, but none of us wanted that. I'm tired of hiding. We took down the biggest hate group in the country. The others are pissed, but disorganized. Thanks to Thomas Mayes, I suffered two broken ribs, a stabbed kidney, and a bruised spleen. The Fort, itself, caused me more mental scarring than anyone should be allowed to live with, but there are people who think I got away with no consequences. I've decided those people will always exist. I can't be afraid of them forever.

It sucks that we had to start all over, but it's actually not so bad the second time around. Dell had a nice pot of money stowed away in case he had to move again—turns out he was a cheap-ass for a reason. He and Bev have their own construction business and I've actually made some new friends. Friends I've been honest with about my past. They were surprisingly understanding. I guess the whole "taking down The Fort" thing helped.

And that's why I have to do what I'm about to do. I have to tell the world my side of the story, once and for all. I have to admit to the things I've done. That shadow is still there. The beast still stirs—and probably always will—but I can at least cast full light on the shadow. Even if that means going to jail for what I've done. After all, I always had the chance to say no, I was just too big a coward to do it.

I'm tired of living in the darkness.

Martin, the big bloodhound we rescued after I got out of the hospital, noses my bedroom door open. "Not now, buddy." I pat his head and try to push him out of the room.

He winds around my legs and jumps on my bed, laying his head between his paws. "Okay, you can stay, but keep quiet."

He sighs and stretches out. It took a few months for Martin to adjust to us—we're pretty sure his previous owner abused him—but once he realized we weren't going to hurt him, he thawed. He's still nervous around strangers, but we're getting there.

I sit at the desk and adjust my shirt. I can do this. I have to do this. I've relied on other people to tell my story for far too long. It's high time I find my own voice. I touch the photo of Mom on my desk. I don't have her button anymore, but I have her. Within me. "Love you, Mom."

Beside her photo sits a postcard with no note. The picture on the front says, "See Rock City."

I take a deep breath and face my laptop camera. I can do this.

I turn on the camera, run a hand through my shaggy hair, and hit RECORD.

"I have a lot to say, and this will probably take a while. But let me start here: my name is Nathaniel Fuller, and I'm sorry."

AUTHOR'S NOTE

In 2013, I read an article about a ten-year-old who shot his father in the head while he slept on the couch. His father led a white supremacist group in California. That story stuck with me. I'd seen documentaries that showed "baby's first cross burning" and the like, but until that moment, it never occurred to me to wonder what these kids went through growing up in that kind of environment, surrounded by hate from birth. A character started to form in my head, but I didn't find the courage to tell his story for another year.

I grew up in Alabama, "The Heart of Dixie," and the cradle of the Civil Rights Movement. I'm no stranger to what racism is and how it can look, but this was a different level. I had to learn what the main white supremacist groups are, where they're located, how they recruit and operate. Things

I never wanted to know. But the more I learned, the more I had to tell this story.

The Fort and the neo-nazi group that lives there are fictional, but they're rooted in fact. They're amalgamations of several different groups that currently operate in the United States and abroad. A real compound like The Fort exists in Alabama, and in other parts of the country, and the methods The Fort uses to spread its hate—the white extinction website, racist notes in Easter eggs, flyers, media training, boot parties, red laces—are all real.

The hate incidents in this book are also real. I relied heavily on data and research collected by the Southern Poverty Law Center (SPLC), whose website is full of informative resources—like their hate map, which shows the number and location of every hate group in the United States. All the statistics in this book are accurate as of the date of publication, but this is not a static number. These groups move, shrink, grow, and change. If you want to know the most recent numbers, and be aware of hate groups in your area, visit: www.splcenter.org/hate-map.

The SPLC also keeps a running list of hate crimes. I used this list when writing about the hate crimes that appear in this story. I had some trepidation in doing this, but the one piece of writing advice that has stuck with me the most was Stephen King's admonition to "write honestly." So here it is. These things are real. They've happened, and are happening, to real people, in real places. A noose was actually hung around the statue of James Meredith, the first African

American to enroll at the University of Mississippi, a year before I started writing this book. Racist graffiti, cross burnings, and physical attacks on people of color occur across the United States every day, in almost every state. These aren't isolated incidents or holdovers from bygone days. They are, sadly, current events. The SPLC's list of hate incidents can be found at: www.splcenter.org/fighting-hate/hate-incidents.

I was in the middle of writing this book when Eric Garner was killed in Staten Island, New York, followed by Michael Brown in Ferguson, Missouri. I had just finished writing when the Emanuel African Methodist Episcopal church in Charleston, South Carolina, was attacked. I saw the way the media biased public opinions of the individuals involved. The way they cherry-picked which pictures of Michael Brown to use. The way they called him, at age eighteen, a "man" but the Emanuel AME shooter, at age twenty-one, a "boy." I tried to weave this media bias into the book because it's important to look at the lens through which news is being told.

It's also important for me to say this: no part of this book was easy to write, but the story needed to be told. I don't know if I'm the right person to tell this story. I've questioned my ability to write this book from day one. However, it's not the job of people of color to educate white folks on how they deserve to be treated and on what is and isn't racist. This is a burden we've been putting on their backs for far too long. And here's the thing: there have been too many times in my life when I've sat silent while people around me made racist and derogatory comments. Too many times when I should've stood up, but didn't. So, I'm standing up now.

Additional research, resources, and information can be found on my website, www.sfhenson.com/

I hope you'll continue to read, learn, and talk about these issues. Education and discussion are the first steps to opening hearts and changing minds.

ACKNOWLEDGMENTS

I've always considered writing to be a solitary endeavor, with the majority of my writing time being spent alone with a computer or notebook while the images in my head slowly make their way onto the page. But when I look back, I realize that I haven't been alone at all. I've dreamed of being a published author since I was four years old. That's thirty years of people guiding me to this place, which means it's impossible to list every single person who helped make this dream a reality, but here's my feeble attempt—and if I leave anyone out (which I'm sure I have), then my sincerest apologies.

First and foremost, I have to thank God. Everything I do is through and for Him.

Mandy Hubbard, my agent, ledge-talker-offer, and gif queen, you are extraordinary. You've been listening to my weird ideas and reading my wordy drafts for five years now.

You've believed in me when I haven't believed in myself, and you've made me a better writer. This book absolutely would not have happened without you. Thank you for reading and editing, and building killer bonfires to have strange late-night discussions over.

To my editor, Alison Weiss, and the entire team at Sky Pony Press and Skyhorse Publishing, I can never say thank you enough. You took on a risky book with an eyebrow-raising premise and you never balked. Alison, your vision made this book so much better than I ever could have on my own. Thank you for your support, your encouragement, your countless hours spent hunched over my manuscript, and your incredible ability to shape my words into something I'm proud to put my name on.

To Alison Kemper, my first critique partner and the first person to ever read Nate's story, thank you for your time, your patience, and your feedback on so many very rough pages. Because of you I found my agent, I grew more confident in my abilities, and I gained my first author friend.

I also have to thank all of my other readers, critique partners, and writers who have helped me over the years: Nic Stone, Ronni Davis, Leah Henderson, Misa Sigiura, Rachel Simon, Courtney Gilfillian, Mary Dunbar, and everyone at Absolute Write who ever critiqued my pages or queries. Huge thanks to my local writing group, WYSIUR, and to the Word Girls. If I left your name off of this list, please know that it absolutely wasn't intentional and I'm grateful for all your help. I seriously wouldn't have had any success as a writer without all of you.

To the Southern Poverty Law Center and Tyler Roe, thank you for the research and information you provided that made this book more honest and realistic. Any errors or inaccuracies are mine alone.

To J.F. Sargent, Frank Meeink, John Haltiwanger, Lawrence Otis Graham, and Susie Rodarme, thank you for the articles you wrote, which opened my eyes to experiences and stories that I wouldn't have had otherwise and that helped me shape this book.

I also have to thank all of the Civil Rights leaders who fought, and who continue to fight, for equality. Your work, and your resources, influenced this book immensely. Special thanks to the "Big Six": Roy Wilkins, A. Philip Randolph, Martin Luther King Jr., Whitney Young, John Lewis, and John Farmer, and to Dorothy Height. There are references to all of you sprinkled throughout this book. I also want to thank James Meredith, who was the inspiration for Brandon's grandfather.

To all of my teachers, especially Janet Wallace—who slaughtered my papers until their pages were bloody with corrections (sorry for reviving some of the words in your word graveyard!)—thank you for all your time, your guidance, and your wisdom.

Thanks to my family for all of their support. That list would be almost as long as the book itself, so just know that you are all loved and valued and I appreciate you more than you'll ever know.

Emily, Sister Sledge, thank you for reading my first novel and for supporting me, even though you don't particularly enjoy reading. I promise if any of my books ever become movies, I'll push for a Beyoncé song on the soundtrack, just for you.

Coleman, a legend in your own mind (and mine if I'm being honest), you have no idea how much I appreciate your help critiquing my pages and working through plot snags. Your journalistic eye made the articles in this book read like actual news. I'm lucky that my little brother is such an excellent writer.

Momma, thank you for pushing me to be not only the best student and writer I could be, but also the best person. Thank you for teaching me (sometimes, literally), for encouraging me to be civic-minded, and for forcing me to think critically about the world. You taught me how to form my own opinions and how to lead. The person and writer I am today is because of you.

To my grandmother, Karma, my earliest memories of reading are all with you. You are the reason I ever dreamed of being a writer. You fed my imagination, made up stories with me, and held my hand through so many steps in life. Thank you for all that you've given me, for all that you are, and for all that you do.

This is the hardest one. Thank you, Daddy, even though you'll never read these words. You put my first favorite book in my hands (and most of my favorites to follow). You gave me the idea for the first book I tried to write, and you helped me plot the first book I ever finished writing. You'll never get to read the first book I publish, but I want the world to know that I achieved it because of you. You supported my dreams and taught me how to fight for them. You raised me to be the independent, strong-willed person I am. You were my best friend and I miss you every single day.

Finally, to Phillip, my biggest fan, sturdiest support, and partner in life. Thank you for all that you do, but especially for the hours and hours and *hours* you spend across from me at coffee shops while I write, and for perusing bookstore shelves with me, discussing book ideas, and listening to me talk about books, and writing in general. You hold me up when I forget how to stand and you let me fly when I remember I have wings. I am incredibly lucky to have you by my side in all of my journeys. I love you to infinity (times two).